Michael

by

E F Benson

The Echo Library 2005

Published by

The Echo Library

Paperbackshop Ltd
Cockrup Farm House
Coln St Aldwyns
Cirencester GL7 5AZ

www.echo-library.com

ISBN 1-84637-692-0

MICHAEL

by E. F. Benson

CHAPTER I

Though there was nothing visibly graceful about Michael Comber, he apparently had the art of giving gracefully. He had already told his cousin Francis, who sat on the arm of the sofa by his table, that there was no earthly excuse for his having run into debt; but now when the moment came for giving, he wrote the cheque quickly and eagerly, as if thoroughly enjoying it, and passed it over to him with a smile that was extraordinarily pleasant.

"There you are, then, Francis," he said; "and I take it from you that that will put you perfectly square again. You've got to write to me, remember, in two days' time, saying that you have paid those bills. And for the rest, I'm delighted that you told me about it. In fact, I should have been rather hurt if you hadn't."

Francis apparently had the art of accepting gracefully, which is more difficult than the feat which Michael had so successfully accomplished.

"Mike, you're a brick," he said. "But then you always are a brick. Thanks awfully."

Michael got up, and shuffled rather than walked across the room to the bell by the fireplace. As long as he was sitting down his big arms and broad shoulders gave the impression of strength, and you would have expected to find when he got up that he was tall and largely made. But when he rose the extreme shortness of his legs manifested itself, and he appeared almost deformed. His hands hung nearly to his knees; he was heavy, short, lumpish.

"But it's more blessed to give than to receive, Francis," he said. "I have the best of you there."

"Well, it's pretty blessed to receive when you are in a tight place, as I was," he said, laughing. "And I am so grateful."

"Yes, I know you are. And it's that which makes me feel rather cheap, because I don't miss what I've given you. But that's distinctly not a reason for your doing it again. You'll have tea, won't you?"

"Why, yes," said Francis, getting up, also, and leaning his elbow on the chimney-piece, which was nearly on a level with the top of Michael's head. And if Michael had gracefulness only in the art of giving, Francis's gracefulness in receiving was clearly of a piece with the rest of him. He was tall, slim and alert, with the quick, soft movements of some wild animal. His face, brown with sunburn and pink with brisk-going blood, was exceedingly handsome in a boyish and almost effeminate manner, and though he was only eighteen months younger than his cousin, he looked as if nine or ten years might have divided their ages.

"But you are a brick, Mike," he said again, laying his long, brown hand on his cousin's shoulder. "I can't help saying it twice."

"Twice more than was necessary," said Michael, finally dismissing the subject.

The room where they sat was in Michael's flat in Half Moon Street, and high up in one of those tall, discreet-looking houses. The windows were wide open on this hot July afternoon, and the bourdon hum of London, where Piccadilly poured by at the street end, came in blended and blunted by distance, but with the suggestion of heat, of movement, of hurrying affairs. The room was very empty of furniture; there was a rug or two on the parquet floor, a long, low bookcase taking up the end near the door, a table, a sofa, three or four chairs, and a piano. Everything was plain, but equally obviously everything was expensive, and the general impression given was that the owner had no desire to be surrounded by things he did not want, but insisted on the superlative quality of the things he did. The rugs, for instance, happened to be of silk, the bookcase happened to be Hepplewhite, the piano bore the most eminent of makers' names. There were three mezzotints on the walls, a dragon's-blood vase on the high, carved chimney-piece; the whole bore the unmistakable stamp of a fine, individual taste.

"But there's something else I want to talk to you about, Francis," said Michael, as presently afterwards they sat over their tea. "I can't say that I exactly want your advice, but I should like your opinion. I've done something, in fact, without asking anybody, but now that it's done I should like to know what you think about it."

Francis laughed.

"That's you all over, Michael," he said. "You always do a thing first, if you really mean to do it—which I suppose is moral courage—and then you go anxiously round afterwards to see if other people approve, which I am afraid looks like moral cowardice. I go on a different plan altogether. I ascertain the opinion of so many people before I do anything that I end by forgetting what I wanted to do. At least, that seems a reasonable explanation for the fact that I so seldom do anything."

Michael looked affectionately at the handsome boy who lounged long- legged in the chair opposite him. Like many very shy persons, he had one friend with whom he was completely unreserved, and that was this cousin of his, for whose charm and insouciant brilliance he had so adoring an admiration.

He pointed a broad, big finger at him.

"Yes, but when you are like that," he said, "you can just float along. Other people float you. But I should sink heavily if I did nothing. I've got to swim all the time."

"Well, you are in the army," said Francis. "That's as much swimming as anyone expects of a fellow who has expectations. In fact, it's I who have to swim all the time, if you come to think of it. You are somebody; I'm not!"

Michael sat up and took a cigarette.

"But I'm not in the army any longer," he said. "That's just what I am wanting to tell you."

Francis laughed.

"What do you mean?" he asked. "Have you been cashiered or shot or something?"

"I mean that I wrote and resigned my commission yesterday," said Michael. "If you had dined with me last night—as, by the way, you promised to do—I should have told you then."

Francis got up and leaned against the chimney-piece. He was conscious of not thinking this abrupt news as important as he felt he ought to think it. That was characteristic of him; he floated, as Michael had lately told him, finding the world an extremely pleasant place, full of warm currents that took you gently forward without entailing the slightest exertion. But Michael's grave and expectant face—that Michael who had been so eagerly kind about meeting his debts for him—warned him that, however gossamer-like his own emotions were, he must attempt to ballast himself over this.

"Are you speaking seriously?" he asked.

"Quite seriously. I never did anything that was so serious."

"And that is what you want my opinion about?" he asked. "If so, you must tell me more, Mike. I can't have an opinion unless you give me the reasons why you did it. The thing itself—well, the thing itself doesn't seem to matter so immensely. The significance of it is why you did it."

Michael's big, heavy-browed face lightened a moment. "For a fellow who never thinks," he said, "you think uncommonly well. But the reasons are obvious enough. You can guess sufficient reasons to account for it."

"Let's hear them anyhow," said Francis.

Michael clouded again.

"Surely they are obvious," he said. "No one knows better than me, unless it is you, that I'm not like the rest of you. My mind isn't the build of a guardsman's mind, any more than my unfortunate body is. Half our work, as you know quite well, consists in being pleasant and in liking it. Well, I'm not pleasant. I'm not breezy and cordial. I can't do it. I make a task of what is a pastime to all of you, and I only shuffle through my task. I'm not popular, I'm not liked. It's no earthly use saying I am. I don't like the life; it seems to me senseless. And those who live it don't like me. They think me heavy—just heavy. And I have enough sensitiveness to know it."

Michael need not have stated his reasons, for his cousin could certainly have guessed them; he could, too, have confessed to the truth of them. Michael had not the light hand, which is so necessary when young men work together in a companionship of which the cordiality is an essential part of the work; neither had he in the social side of life that particular and inimitable sort of easy self-confidence which, as he had said just now, enables its owner to float. Except in years he was not young; he could not manage to be "clubable"; he was serious and awkward at a supper party; he was altogether without the effervescence which is necessary in order to avoid flatness. He did his work also in the same conscientious but leaden way; officers and men alike felt it. All this Francis knew perfectly well; but instead of acknowledging it, he tried quite fruitlessly to smooth it over.

"Aren't you exaggerating?" he asked.

Michael shook his head.

"Oh, don't tone it down, Francis!" he said. "Even if I was exaggerating—which I don't for a moment admit—the effect on my general efficiency would be the same. I think what I say is true."

Francis became more practical.

"But you've only been in the regiment three years," he said. "It won't be very popular resigning after only three years."

"I have nothing much to lose on the score of popularity," remarked Michael.

There was nothing pertinent that could be consoling here.

"And have you told your father?" asked Francis. "Does Uncle Robert know?"

"Yes; I wrote to father this morning, and I'm going down to Ashbridge to-morrow. I shall be very sorry if he disapproves."

"Then you'll be sorry," said Francis.

"I know, but it won't make any difference to my action. After all, I'm twenty-five; if I can't begin to manage my life now, you may be sure I never shall. But I know I'm right. I would bet on my infallibility. At present I've only told you half my reasons for resigning, and already you agree with me."

Francis did not contradict this.

"Let's hear the rest, then," he said.

"You shall. The rest is far more important, and rather resembles a sermon."

Francis appropriately sat down again.

"Well, it's this," said Michael. "I'm twenty-five, and it is time that I began trying to be what perhaps I may be able to be, instead of not trying very much—because it's hopeless—to be what I can't be. I'm going to study music. I believe that I could perhaps do something there, and in any case I love it more than anything else. And if you love a thing, you have certainly a better chance of succeeding in it than in something that you don't love at all. I was stuck into the army for no reason except that soldiering is among the few employments which it is considered proper for fellows in my position—good Lord! how awful it sounds!—proper for me to adopt. The other things that were open were that I should be a sailor or a member of Parliament. But the soldier was what father chose. I looked round the picture gallery at home the other day; there are twelve Lord Ashbridges in uniform. So, as I shall be Lord Ashbridge when father dies, I was stuck into uniform too, to be the ill-starred thirteenth. But what has it all come to? If you think of it, when did the majority of them wear their smart uniforms? Chiefly when they went on peaceful parades or to court balls, or to the Sir Joshua Reynolds of the period to be painted. They've been tin soldiers, Francis! You're a tin soldier, and I've just ceased to be a tin soldier. If there was the smallest chance of being useful in the army, by which I mean standing up and being shot at because I am English, I would not dream of throwing it up. But there's no such chance."

Michael paused a moment in his sermon, and beat out the ashes from his pipe against the grate.

"Anyhow the chance is too remote," he said. "All the nations with armies and navies are too much afraid of each other to do more than growl. Also I happen to want to do something different with my life, and you can't do anything unless you believe in what you are doing. I want to leave behind me something more than the portrait of a tin soldier in the dining-room at Ashbridge. After all, isn't an artistic profession the greatest there is? For what counts, what is of value in the world to-day? Greek statues, the Italian pictures, the symphonies of Beethoven, the plays of Shakespeare. The people who have made beautiful things are they who are the benefactors of mankind. At least, so the people who love beautiful things think."

Francis glanced at his cousin. He knew this interesting vital side of Michael; he was aware, too, that had anybody except himself been in the room, Michael could not have shown it. Perhaps there might be people to whom he could show it but certainly they were not those among whom Michael's life was passed.

"Go on," he said encouragingly. "You're ripping, Mike."

"Well, the nuisance of it is that the things I am ripping about appear to father to be a sort of indoor game. It's all right to play the piano, if it's too wet to play golf. You can amuse yourself with painting if there aren't any pheasants to shoot. In fact, he will think that my wanting to become a musician is much the same thing as if I wanted to become a billiard-marker. And if he and I talked about it till we were a hundred years old, he could never possibly appreciate my point of view."

Michael got up and began walking up and down the room with his slow, ponderous movement.

"Francis, it's a thousand pities that you and I can't change places," he said. "You are exactly the son father would like to have, and I should so much prefer being his nephew. However, you come next; that's one comfort."

He paused a moment.

"You see, the fact is that he doesn't like me," he said. "He has no sympathy whatever with my tastes, nor with what I am. I'm an awful trial to him, and I don't see how to help it. It's pure waste of time, my going on in the Guards. I do it badly, and I hate it. Now, you're made for it; you're that sort, and that sort is my father's sort. But I'm not; no one knows that better than myself. Then there's the question of marriage, too."

Michael gave a mirthless laugh.

"I'm twenty-five, you see," he said, "and it's the family custom for the eldest son to marry at twenty-five, just as he's baptised when he's a certain number of weeks old, and confirmed when he is fifteen. It's part of the family plan, and the Medes and Persians aren't in it when the family plan is in question. Then, again, the lucky young woman has to be suitable; that is to say, she must be what my father calls 'one of us.' How I loathe that phrase! So my mother has a list of the suitable, and they come down to Ashbridge in gloomy succession, and she and I are sent out to play golf together or go on the river. And when, to our unutterable relief, that is over, we hurry back to the house, and I escape to my piano, and she goes and flirts with you, if you are there. Don't deny it. And then another one comes, and she is drearier than the last—at least, I am."

Francis lay back and laughed at this dismal picture of the rejection of the fittest.

"But you're so confoundedly hard to please, Mike," he said. "There was an awfully nice girl down at Ashbridge at Easter when I was there, who was simply pining to take you. I've forgotten her name."

Michael clicked his fingers in a summary manner.

"There you are!" he said. "You and she flirted all the time, and three months afterwards you don't even remember her name. If you had only been me, you would have married her. As it was, she and I bored each other stiff. There's an irony for you! But as for pining, I ask you whether any girl in her senses could pine for me. Look at me, and tell me! Or rather, don't look at me; I can't bear to be looked at."

Here was one of Michael's morbid sensitivenesses. He seldom forgot his own physical appearance, the fact of which was to him appalling. His stumpy figure with its big body, his broad, blunt- featured face, his long arms, his large hands and feet, his clumsiness in movement were to him of the nature of a constant nightmare, and it was only with Francis and the ease that his solitary presence gave, or when he was occupied with music that he wholly lost his self-consciousness in this respect. It seemed to him that he must be as repulsive to others as he was to himself, which was a distorted view of the case. Plain without doubt he was, and of heavy and ungainly build; but his belief in the finality of his uncouthness was morbid and imaginary, and half his inability to get on with his fellows, no less than with the maidens who were brought down in single file to Ashbridge, was due to this. He knew very well how light-heartedly they escaped to the geniality and attractiveness of Francis, and in the clutch of his own introspective temperament he could not free himself from the handicap of his own sensitiveness, and, like others, take himself for granted. He crushed his own power to please by the weight of his judgments on himself.

"So there's another reason to complain of the irony of fate," he said. "I don't want to marry anybody, and God knows nobody wants to marry me. But, then, it's my duty to become the father of another Lord Ashbridge, as if there had not been enough of them already, and his mother must be a certain kind of girl, with whom I have nothing in common. So I say that if only we could have changed places, you would have filled my niche so perfectly, and I should have been free to bury myself in Leipzig or Munich, and lived like the grub I certainly am, and have drowned myself in a sea of music. As it is, goodness knows what my father will say to the letter I wrote him yesterday, which he will have received this morning. However, that will soon be patent, for I go down there to-morrow. I wish you were coming with me. Can't you manage to for a day or two, and help things along? Aunt Barbara will be there."

Francis consulted a small, green morocco pocket-book.

"Can't to-morrow," he said, "nor yet the day after. But perhaps I could get a few days' leave next week."

"Next week's no use. I go to Baireuth next week."

"Baireuth? Who's Baireuth?" asked Francis.

"Oh, a man I know. His other name was Wagner, and he wrote some tunes."

Francis nodded.

"Oh, but I've heard of him," he said. "They're rather long tunes, aren't they? At least I found them so when I went to the opera the other night. Go on with your plans, Mike. What do you mean to do after that?"

"Go on to Munich and hear the same tunes over, again. After that I shall come back and settle down in town and study."

"Play the piano?" asked Francis, amiably trying to enter into his cousin's schemes.

Michael laughed.

"No doubt that will come into it," he said. "But it's rather as if you told somebody you were a soldier, and he said: 'Oh, is that quick march?'"

"So it is. Soldiering largely consists of quick march, especially when it's more than usually hot."

"Well, I shall learn to play the piano," said Michael.

"But you play so rippingly already," said Francis cordially. "You played all those songs the other night which you had never seen before. If you can do that, there is nothing more you want to learn with the piano, is there?"

"You are talking rather as father will talk," observed Michael.

"Am I? Well, I seem to be talking sense."

"You weren't doing what you seemed, then. I've got absolutely everything to learn about the piano."

Francis rose.

"Then it is clear I don't understand anything about it," he said. "Nor, I suppose, does Uncle Robert. But, really, I rather envy you, Mike. Anyhow, you want to do and be something so much that you are gaily going to face unpleasantnesses with Uncle Robert about it. Now, I wouldn't face unpleasantnesses with anybody about anything I wanted to do, and I suppose the reason must be that I don't want to do anything enough."

"The malady of not wanting," quoted Michael.

"Yes, I've got that malady. The ordinary things that one naturally does are all so pleasant, and take all the time there is, that I don't want anything particular, especially now that you've been such a brick——"

"Stop it," said Michael.

"Right; I got it in rather cleverly. I was saying that it must be rather nice to want a thing so much that you'll go through a lot to get it. Most fellows aren't like that."

"A good many fellows are jelly-fish," observed Michael.

"I suppose so. I'm one, you know. I drift and float. But I don't think I sting. What are you doing to-night, by the way?"

"Playing the piano, I hope. Why?"

"Only that two fellows are dining with me, and I thought perhaps you would come. Aunt Barbara sent me the ticket for a box at the Gaiety, too, and we might look in there. Then there's a dance somewhere."

"Thanks very much, but I think I won't," said Michael. "I'm rather looking forward to an evening alone."

"And that's an odd thing to look forward to," remarked Francis.

"Not when you want to play the piano. I shall have a chop here at eight, and probably thump away till midnight."

Francis looked round for his hat and stick.

"I must go," he said. "I ought to have gone long ago, but I didn't want to. The malady came in again. Most of the world have got it, you know, Michael."

Michael rose and stood by his tall cousin.

"I think we English have got it," he said. "At least, the English you and I know have got it. But I don't believe the Germans, for instance, have. They're in deadly earnest about all sorts of things—music among them, which is the point that concerns me. The music of the world is German, you know!"

Francis demurred to this.

"Oh, I don't think so," he said. "This thing at the Gaiety is ripping, I believe. Do come and see."

Michael resisted this chance of revising his opinion about the German origin of music, and Francis drifted out into Piccadilly. It was already getting on for seven o'clock, and the roadway and pavements were full of people who seemed rather to contradict Michael's theory that the nation generally suffered from the malady of not wanting, so eagerly and numerously were they on the quest for amusement. Already the street was a mass of taxicabs and private motors containing, each one of them, men and women in evening dress, hurrying out to dine before the theatre or the opera. Bright, eager faces peered out, with sheen of silk and glitter of gems; they all seemed alert and prosperous and keen for the daily hours of evening entertainment. A crowd similar in spirit pervaded the pavements, white-shirted men with coat on arm stepped in and out of swinging club doors and the example set by the leisured class seemed copiously copied by those whom desks and shops had made prisoners all day. The air of the whole town, swarming with the nation that is supposed to make so grave an affair of its amusements, was indescribably gay and lighthearted; the whole city seemed set on enjoying itself. The buses that boomed along were packed inside and out, and each was placarded with advertisement of some popular piece at theatre or music-hall. Inside the Green Park the grass was populous with lounging figures, who, unable to pay for indoor entertainment, were making the most of what the coolness of sunset and grass supplied them with gratis; the newsboards of itinerant sellers contained nothing of more serious import than the result of cricket matches; and, as the dusk began to fall, street lamps and signs were lit, like early rising stars, so that no hint of the gathering night should be permitted to intrude on the perpetually illuminated city. All that was sordid and sad, all that was busy (except on these gay errands of pleasure) was shuffled away out of sight, so that the pleasure seekers might be excused for believing that there was nothing in the world that could demand their attention except the need of amusing themselves successfully. The workers toiled in order that when the working day was over the fruits of their labour might yield a harvest of a few hours' enjoyment; silkworms had spun so that from carriage windows might glimmer the wrappings made from their cocoons; divers had been imperilled in deep seas so that the pearls they had won might embellish the necks of these fair wearers.

To Francis this all seemed very natural and proper, part of the recognised order of things that made up the series of sensations known to him as life. He did not, as he had said, very particularly care about anything, and it was undoubtedly true that there was no motive or conscious purpose in his life for which he would voluntarily have undergone any important stress of discomfort or annoyance. It was true that in pursuance of his profession there was a certain amount of "quick marching" and drill to be done in the heat, but that was incidental to the fact that he was in the Guards, and more than compensated for by the pleasures that were also naturally incidental to it. He would have been quite unable to think of anything that he would sooner do than what he did; and he had sufficient of the ingrained human tendency to do something of the sort, which was a matter of routine rather than effort, than have nothing whatever, except the gratification of momentary whims, to fill his day. Besides, it was one of the conventions or even conditions of life that every boy on leaving school "did" something for a certain number of years. Some went into business in order to acquire the wealth that should procure them leisure; some, like himself, became soldiers or sailors, not because they liked guns and ships, but because to boys of a certain class these professions supplied honourable employment and a pleasant time. Without being in any way slack in his regimental duties, he performed them as many others did, without the smallest grain of passion, and without any imaginative forecast as to what fruit, if any, there might be to these hours spent in drill and discipline. He was but one of a very large number who do their work without seriously bothering their heads about its possible meaning or application. His particular job gave a young man a pleasant position and an easy path to general popularity, given that he was willing to be sociable and amused. He was extremely ready to be both the one and the other, and there his philosophy of life stopped.

And, indeed, it seemed on this hot July evening that the streets were populated by philosophers like unto himself. Never had England generally been more prosperous, more secure, more comfortable. The heavens of international politics were as serene as the evening sky; not yet was the storm-cloud that hung over Ireland bigger than a man's hand; east, west, north and south there brooded the peace of the close of a halcyon day, and the amazing doings of the Suffragettes but added a slight incentive to the perusal of the morning paper. The arts flourished, harvests prospered; the world like a newly-wound clock seemed to be in for a spell of serene and orderly ticking, with an occasional chime just to show how the hours were passing.

London was an extraordinarily pleasant place, people were friendly, amusements beckoned on all sides; and for Francis, as for so many others, but a very moderate amount of work was necessary to win him an approved place in the scheme of things, a seat in the slow- wheeling sunshine. It really was not necessary to want, above all to undergo annoyances for the sake of what you wanted, since so many pleasurable distractions, enough to fill day and night twice over, were so richly spread around.

Some day he supposed he would marry, settle down and become in time one of those men who presented a bald head in a club window to the gaze of passers-by. It was difficult, perhaps, to see how you could enjoy yourself or lead a life that paid its own way in pleasure at the age of forty, but that he trusted that he would learn in time. At present it was sufficient to know that in half an hour two excellent friends would come to dinner, and that they would proceed in a spirit of amiable content to the Gaiety. After that there was a ball somewhere (he had forgotten where, but one of the others would be sure to know), and to-morrow and to-morrow would be like unto to-day. It was idle to ask questions of oneself when all went so well; the time for asking questions was when there was matter for complaint, and with him assuredly there was none. The advantages of being twenty-three years old, gay and good- looking, without a care in the world, now that he had Michael's cheque in his pocket, needed no comment, still less complaint. He, like the crowd who had sufficient to pay for a six-penny seat at a music-hall, was perfectly content with life in general; to-morrow would be time enough to do a little more work and glean a little more pleasure.

It was indeed an admirable England, where it was not necessary even to desire, for there were so many things, bright, cheerful things to distract the mind from desire. It was a day of dozing in the sun, like the submerged, scattered units or duets on the grass of the Green Park, of behaving like the lilies of the field. . . . Francis found he was rather late, and proceeded hastily to his mother's house in Savile Row to array himself, if not "like one of these," like an exceedingly well-dressed young man, who demanded of his tailor the utmost of his art; with the prospect, owing to Michael's generosity, of being paid to-morrow.

Michael, when his cousin had left him, did not at once proceed to his evening by himself with his piano, though an hour before he had longed to be alone with it and a pianoforte arrangement of the Meistersingers, of which he had promised himself a complete perusal that evening. But Francis's visit had already distracted him, and he found now that Francis's departure took him even farther away from his designed evening. Francis, with his good looks and his gay spirits, his easy friendships and perfect content (except when a small matter of deficit and dunning letters obscured the sunlight for a moment), was exactly all that he would have wished to be himself. But the moment he formulated that wish in his mind, he knew that he would not voluntarily have parted with one atom of his own individuality in order to be Francis or anybody else. He was aware how easy and pleasant life would become if he could look on it with Francis's eyes, and if the world would look on him as it looked on his cousin. There would be no more bother. . . . In a moment, he would, by this exchange, have parted with his own unhappy temperament, his own deplorable body, and have stepped into an amiable and prosperous little neutral kingdom that had no desires and no regrets. He would have been free from all wants, except such as could be gratified so easily by a little work and a great capacity for being amused; he would have found himself excellently fitting the niche into which the rulers of birth and death had placed him: an eldest son of a great territorial magnate, who had what was called a stake in the country, and desired nothing better.

Willingly, as he had said, would he have changed circumstances with Francis, but he knew that he would not, for any bait the world could draw in front of him, have changed natures with him, even when, to all appearance, the gain would so vastly have been on his side. It was better to want and to miss than to be content. Even at this moment, when Francis had taken the sunshine out of the room with his departure, Michael clung to his own gloom and his own uncouthness, if by getting rid of them he would also have been obliged to get rid of his own temperament, unhappy as it was, but yet capable of strong desire. He did not want to be content; he wanted to see always ahead of him a golden mist, through which the shadows of unconjecturable shapes appeared. He was willing and eager to get lost, if only he might go wandering on, groping with his big hands, stumbling with his clumsy feet, desiring . . .

There are the indications of a path visible to all who desire. Michael knew that his path, the way that seemed to lead in the direction of the ultimate goal, was music. There, somehow, in that direction lay his destiny; that was the route. He was not like the majority of his sex and years, who weave their physical and mental dreams in the loom of a girl's face, in her glance, in the curves of her mouth. Deliberately, owing chiefly to his morbid consciousness of his own physical defects, he had long been accustomed to check the instincts natural to a young man in this regard. He had seen too often the facility with which others, more fortunate than he, get delightedly lost in that golden haze; he had experienced too often the absence of attractiveness in himself. How could any girl of the London ballroom, he had so frequently asked himself, tolerate dancing or sitting out with him when there was Francis, and a hundred others like him, so pleased to take his place? Nor, so he told himself, was his mind one whit more apt than his body. It did not move lightly and agreeably with unconscious smiles and easy laughter. By nature he was monkish, he was celibate. He could but cease to burn incense at such ineffectual altars, and help, as he had helped this afternoon, to replenish the censers of more fortunate acolytes.

This was all familiar to him; it passed through his head unbidden, when Francis had left him, like the refrain of some well-known song, occurring spontaneously without need of an effort of memory. It was a possession of his, known by heart, and it no longer, except for momentary twinges, had any bitterness for him. This afternoon, it is true, there had been one such, when Francis, gleeful with his cheque, had gone out to his dinner and his theatre and his dance, inviting him cheerfully to all of them. In just that had been the bitterness—namely, that Francis had so overflowing a well-spring of content that he could be cordial in bidding him cast a certain gloom over these entertainments. Michael knew, quite unerringly, that Francis and his friends would not enjoy themselves quite so much if he was with them; there would be the restraint of polite conversation at dinner instead of completely idle babble, there would be less outspoken normality at the Gaiety, a little more decorum about the whole of the boyish proceedings. He knew all that so well, so terribly well. . . .

His servant had come in with the evening paper, and the implied suggestion of the propriety of going to dress before he roused himself. He decided not to dress, as he was going to spend the evening alone, and, instead, he seated himself at the piano with his copy of the Meistersingers and, mechanically at first, with the ragged cloud-fleeces of his reverie hanging about his brain, banged away at the overture. He had extraordinary dexterity of finger for one who had had so little training, and his hands, with their great stretch, made light work of octaves and even tenths. His knowledge of the music enabled him to wake the singing bird of memory in his head, and before long flute and horn and string and woodwind began to make themselves heard in his inner ear. Twice his servant came in to tell him that his dinner was ready, but Michael had no heed for anything but the sounds which his flying fingers suggested to him. Francis, his father, his own failure in the life that had been thrust on him were all gone; he was with the singers of Nuremberg.

CHAPTER II

The River Ashe, after a drowsy and meandering childhood, passed peacefully among the sedges and marigolds of its water meadows, suddenly and somewhat disconcertingly grows up and, without any period of transition and adolescence, becomes, from being a mere girl of a rivulet, a male and full-blooded estuary of the sea. At Coton, for instance, the tips of the sculls of a sauntering pleasure-boat will almost span its entire width, while, but a mile farther down, you will see stone-laden barges and tall, red-winged sailing craft coming up with the tide, and making fast to the grey wooden quay wall of Ashbridge, rough with barnacles. For the reeds and meadow-sweet of its margin are exchanged the brown and green growths of the sea, with their sharp, acrid odour instead of the damp, fresh smell of meadow flowers, and at low tide the podded bladders of brown weed and long strings of marine macaroni, among which peevish crabs scuttle sideways, take the place of the grass and spires of loosestrife; and over the water, instead of singing larks, hang white companies of chiding seagulls. Here at high tide extends a sheet of water large enough, when the wind blows up the estuary, to breed waves that break in foam and spray against the barges, while at the ebb acres of mud flats are disclosed on which the boats lean slanting till the flood lifts them again and makes them strain at the wheezing ropes that tie them to the quay.

A year before the flame of war went roaring through Europe in unquenchable conflagration it would have seemed that nothing could possibly rouse Ashbridge from its red-brick Georgian repose. There was never a town so inimitably drowsy or so sternly uncompetitive. A hundred years ago it must have presented almost precisely the same appearance as it did in the summer of 1913, if we leave out of reckoning a few dozen of modern upstart villas that line its outskirts, and the very inconspicuous railway station that hides itself behind the warehouses near the river's bank. Most of the trains, too, quite ignore its existence, and pass through it on their way to more rewarding stopping-places, hardly recognising it even by a spurt of steam from their whistles, and it is only if you travel by those that require the most frequent pauses in their progress that you will be enabled to alight at its thin and depopulated platform.

Just outside the station there perennially waits a low-roofed and sanguine omnibus that under daily discouragement continues to hope that in the long-delayed fulness of time somebody will want to be driven somewhere. (This nobody ever does, since the distance to any house is so small, and a porter follows with luggage on a barrow.) It carries on its floor a quantity of fresh straw, in the manner of the stage coaches, in which the problematic passenger, should he ever appear, will no doubt bury his feet. On its side, just below the window that is not made to open, it carries the legend that shows that it belongs to the Comber Arms, a hostelry so self-effacing that it is discoverable only by the sharpest-eyed of pilgrims. Narrow roadways, flanked by proportionately narrower pavements, lie ribbon-like between huddled shops and squarely- spacious Georgian houses; and an air of leisure and content, amounting almost to stupefaction, is the moral atmosphere of the place.

On the outskirts of the town, crowning the gentle hills that lie to the north and west, villas in acre plots, belonging to business men in the county town some ten miles distant, "prick their Cockney ears" and are strangely at variance with the sober gravity of the indigenous houses. So, too, are the manners and customs of their owners, who go to Stoneborough every morning to their work, and return by the train that brings them home in time for dinner. They do other exotic and unsuitable things also, like driving swiftly about in motors, in playing golf on the other side of the river at Coton, and in having parties at each other's houses. But apart from them nobody ever seems to leave Ashbridge (though a stroll to the station about the time that the evening train arrives is a recognised diversion) or, in consequence, ever to come back. Ashbridge, in fact, is self-contained, and desires neither to meddle with others nor to be meddled with.

The estuary opposite the town is some quarter of a mile broad at high tide, and in order to cross to the other side, where lie the woods and park of Ashbridge House, it is necessary to shout and make staccato prancings in order to attract the attention of the antique ferryman, who is invariably at the other side of the river and generally asleep at the bottom of his boat. If you are strong- lunged and can prance and shout for a long time, he may eventually stagger to his feet, come across for you and row you over. Otherwise you will stand but little chance of arousing him from his slumbers, and you will stop where you are, unless you choose to walk round by the bridge at Coton, a mile above.

Periodical attempts are made by the brisker inhabitants of Ashbridge, who do not understand its spirit, to substitute for this aged and ineffectual Charon someone who is occasionally awake, but nothing ever results from these revolutionary moves, and the requests addressed to the town council on the subject are never heard of again. "Old George" was ferryman there before any members of the town council were born, and he seems to have established a right to go to sleep on the other side of the river which is now inalienable from him. Besides, asleep or awake, he is always perfectly sober, which, after all, is really one of the first requirements for a suitable ferryman. Even the representations of Lord Ashbridge himself who, when in residence, frequently has occasion to use the ferry when crossing from his house to the town, failed to produce the smallest effect, and he was compelled to build a boathouse of his own on the farther bank, and be paddled across by himself or one of the servants. Often he rowed himself, for he used to be a fine oarsman, and it was good for the lounger on the quay to see the foaming prow of his vigorous progress and the dignity of physical toil.

In all other respects, except in this case of "Old George," Lord Ashbridge's wishes were law to the local authorities, for in this tranquil East-coast district the spirit of the feudal system with a beneficent lord and contented tenants strongly survived. It had triumphed even over such modern innovations as railroads, for Lord Ashbridge had the undoubted right to stop any train he pleased by signal at Ashbridge station. This he certainly enjoyed doing; it fed his sense of the fitness of things to progress along the platform with his genial, important tiptoe walk, and elbows squarely stuck out, to the carriage that was at once reserved for him, to touch the brim of his grey top-hat (if travelling up to town) to the obsequious guard, and to observe the heads of passengers who wondered why their express was arrested, thrust out of carriage windows to look at him. A livened footman, as well as a valet, followed him, bearing a coat and a rug and a morning or evening paper and a dispatch-box with a large gilt coronet on it, and bestowed these solaces to a railway journey on the empty seats near him. And not only his sense of fitness was hereby fed, but that also of the station-master and the solitary porter and the newsboy, and such inhabitants of Ashbridge as happened to have strolled on to the platform. For he was THEIR Earl of Ashbridge, kind, courteous and dominant, a local king; it was all very pleasant.

But this arrest of express trains was a strictly personal privilege; when Lady Ashbridge or Michael travelled they always went in the slow train to Stoneborough, changed there and abided their time on the platform like ordinary mortals. Though he could undoubtedly have extended his rights to the stopping of a train for his wife or son, he wisely reserved this for himself, lest it should lose prestige. There was sufficient glory already (to probe his mind to the bottom) for Lady Ashbridge in being his wife; it was sufficient also for Michael that he was his son.

It may be inferred that there was a touch of pomposity about this admirable gentleman, who was so excellent a landlord and so hard working a member of the British aristocracy. But pomposity would be far too superficial a word to apply to him; it would not adequately connote his deep-abiding and essential conviction that on one of the days of Creation (that, probably, on which the decree was made that there should be Light) there leaped into being the great landowners of England.

But Lord Ashbridge, though himself a peer, by no means accepted the peerage en bloc as representing the English aristocracy; to be, in his phrase, "one of us" implied that you belonged to certain well- ascertained families where brewers and distinguished soldiers had no place, unless it was theirs already. He was ready to pay all reasonable homage to those who were distinguished by their abilities, their riches, their exalted positions in Church and State, but his homage to such was transfused with a courteous condescension, and he only treated as his equals and really revered those who belonged to the families that were "one of us."

His wife, of course, was "one of us," since he would never have permitted himself to be allied to a woman who was not, though for beauty and wisdom she might have been Aphrodite and Athene rolled compactly into one peerless identity. As a matter of fact, Lady Ashbridge had not the faintest resemblance to either of these effulgent goddesses. In person she resembled a camel, long and lean, with a drooping mouth and tired, patient eyes, while in mind she was stunned. No idea other than an obvious one ever had birth behind her high, smooth forehead, and she habitually brought conversation to a close by the dry enunciation of something indubitably true, which had no direct relation to the point under discussion. But she had faint, ineradicable prejudices, and instincts not quite dormant. There was a large quantity of mild affection in her nature, the quality of which may be illustrated by the fact that when her father died she cried a little every day after breakfast for about six weeks. Then she did not cry any more. It was impossible not to like what there was of her, but there was really very little to like, for she belonged heart and soul to the generation and the breeding among which it is enough for a woman to be a lady, and visit the keeper's wife when she has a baby.

But though there was so little of her, the balance was made up for by the fact that there was so much of her husband. His large, rather flamboyant person, his big white face and curling brown beard, his loud voice and his falsetto laugh, his absolutely certain opinions, above all the fervency of his consciousness of being Lord Ashbridge and all which that implied, completely filled any place he happened to be in, so that a room empty except for him gave the impression of being almost uncomfortably crowded. This keen consciousness of his identity was naturally sufficient to make him very good humoured, since he was himself a fine example of the type that he admired most. Probably only two persons in the world had the power of causing him annoyance, but both of these, by an irony of fate that it seemed scarcely possible to consider accidental, were closely connected with him, for one was his sister, the other his only son.

The grounds of their potentiality in this respect can be easily stated. Barbara Comber, his sister (and so "one of us"), had married an extremely wealthy American, who, in Lord Ashbridge's view, could not be considered one of anybody at all; in other words, his imagination failed to picture a whole class of people who resembled Anthony Jerome. He had hoped when his sister announced her intention of taking this deplorable step that his future brother-in-law would at any rate prove to be a snob—he had a vague notion that all Americans were snobs—and that thus Mr. Jerome would have the saving grace to admire and toady him. But Mr. Jerome showed no signs of doing anything of the sort; he treated him with an austere and distant politeness that Lord Ashbridge could not construe as being founded on admiration and a sense of his own inferiority, for it was so clearly founded on dislike. That, however, did not annoy Lord Ashbridge, for it was easy to suppose that poor Mr. Jerome knew no better. But Barbara annoyed him, for not only had she shown herself a renegade in marrying a man who was not "one of us," but with all the advantages she had enjoyed since birth of knowing what "we" were, she gloried in her new relations, saying, without any proper reticence about the matter, that they were Real People, whose character and wits vastly transcended anything that Combers had to show.

Michael was an even more vexatious case, and in moments of depression his father thought that he would really turn in his grave at the dismal idea of Michael having stepped into his honourable shoes. Physically he was utterly unlike a Comber, and his mind, his general attitude towards life seemed to have diverged even farther from that healthy and unreflective pattern. Only this morning his father had received a letter from him that summed Michael up, that fulfilled all the doubts and fears that had hung about him; for after three years in the Guards he had, without consultation with anybody, resigned his commission on the inexplicable grounds that he wanted to do something with his life. To begin with that was rankly heretical; if you were a Comber there was no need to do anything with your life; life did everything for you. . . . And what this un-Comberish young man wanted to do with his life was to be a musician. That musicians, artists, actors, had a right to exist Lord Ashbridge did not question. They were no doubt (or might be) very excellent people in their way, and as a matter of fact he often recognised their existence by going to the opera, to the private view of the Academy, or to the play, and he took a very considerable pride of proprietorship in his own admirable collection of family portraits. But then those were pictures of Combers; Reynolds and Romney and the rest of them had enjoyed the privilege of perpetuating on their canvases these big, fine men and charming women. But that a Comber—and that one positively the next Lord Ashbridge— should intend to devote his energies to an artistic calling, and allude to that scheme as doing something with his life, was a thing as unthinkable as if the butler had developed a fixed idea that he was "one of us."

The blow was a recent one; Michael's letter had only reached his father this morning, and at the present moment Lord Ashbridge was attempting over a cup of tea on the long south terrace overlooking the estuary to convey—not very successfully—to his wife something of his feelings on the subject. She, according to her custom, was drinking a little hot water herself, and providing her Chinese pug with a mixture of cream and crumbled rusks. Though the dog was of undoubtedly high lineage, Lord Ashbridge rather detested her.

"A musical career!" he exclaimed, referring to Michael's letter. "What sort of a career for a Comber is a musical career? I shall tell Michael pretty roundly when he arrives this evening what I think of it all. We shall have Francis next saying that he wants to resign, too, and become a dentist."

Lady Ashbridge considered this for a moment in her stunned mind.

"Dear me, Robert, I hope not," she said. "I do not think it the least likely that Francis would do anything of the kind. Look, Petsy is better; she has drunk her cream and rusks quite up. I think it was only the heat."

He gave a little good-humoured giggle of falsetto laughter.

"I wish, Marion," he said, "that you could manage to take your mind off your dog for a moment and attend to me. And I must really ask you not to give your Petsy any more cream, or she will certainly be sick."

Lady Ashbridge gave a little sigh.

"All gone, Petsy," she said.

"I am glad it has all gone," said he, "and we will hope it won't return. But about Michael now!"

Lady Ashbridge pulled herself together.

"Yes, poor Michael!" she said. "He is coming to-night, is he not? But just now you were speaking of Francis, and the fear of his wanting to be a dentist!"

"Well, I am now speaking of Michael's wanting to be a musician. Of course that is utterly out of the question. If, as he says, he has sent in his resignation, he will just have to beg them to cancel it. Michael seems not to have the slightest idea of the duties which his birth and position entail on him. Unfitted for the life he now leads . . . waste of time. . . . Instead he proposes to go to Baireuth in August, and then to settle down in London to study!"

Lady Ashbridge recollected the almanac.

"That will be in September, then," she said. "I do not think I was ever in London in September. I did not know that anybody was."

"The point, my dear, is not how or where you have been accustomed to spend your Septembers," said her husband. "What we are talking about is—"

"Yes, dear, I know quite well what we are talking about," said she. "We are talking about Michael not studying music all September."

Lord Ashbridge got up and began walking across the terrace opposite the tea-table with his elbows stuck out and his feet lifted rather high.

"Michael doesn't seem to realise that he is not Tom or Dick or Harry," said he. "Music, indeed! I'm musical myself; all we Combers are musical. But Michael is my only son, and it really distresses me to see how little sense he has of his responsibilities. Amusements are all very well; it is not that I want to cut him off his amusements, but when it comes to a career—"

Lady Ashbridge was surreptitiously engaged in pouring out a little more cream for Petsy, and her husband, turning rather sooner than she had expected, caught her in the act.

"Do not give Petsy any more cream," he said, with some asperity; "I absolutely forbid it."

Lady Ashbridge quite composedly replaced the cream-jug.

"Poor Petsy!" she observed.

"I ask you to attend to me, Marion," he said.

"But I am attending to you very well, Robert," said she, "and I understand you perfectly. You do not want Michael to be a musician in September and wear long hair and perhaps play at concerts. I am sure I quite agree with you, for such a thing would be as unheard of in my family as in yours. But how do you propose to stop it?"

"I shall use my authority," he said, stepping a little higher.

"Yes, dear, I am sure you will. But what will happen if Michael doesn't pay any attention to your authority? You will be worse off than ever. Poor Michael is very obedient when he is told to do anything he intends to do, but when he doesn't agree it is difficult to do anything with him. And, you see, he is quite independent of you with my mother having left him so much money. Poor mamma!"

Lord Ashbridge felt strongly about this.

"It was a most extraordinary disposition of her property for your mother to make," he observed. "It has given Michael an independence which I much deplore. And she did it in direct opposition to my wishes."

This touched on one of the questions about which Lady Ashbridge had her convictions. She had a mild but unalterable opinion that when anybody died, all that they had previously done became absolutely flawless and laudable.

"Mamma did as she thought right with her property," she said, "and it is not for us to question it. She was conscientiousness itself. You will have to excuse my listening to any criticism you may feel inclined to make about her, Robert."

"Certainly, my dear. I only want you to listen to me about Michael. You agree with me on the impossibility of his adopting a musical career. I cannot, at present, think so ill of Michael as to suppose that he will defy our joint authority."

"Michael has a great will of his own," she remarked. "He gets that from you, Robert, though he gets his money from his grandmother."

The futility of further discussion with his wife began to dawn on Lord Ashbridge, as it dawned on everybody who had the privilege of conversing with her. Her mind was a blind alley that led nowhere; it was clear that she had no idea to contribute to the subject except slightly pessimistic forebodings with which, unfortunately, he found himself secretly disposed to agree. He had always felt that Michael was an uncomfortable sort of boy; in other words, that he had the inconvenient habit of thinking things out for himself, instead of blindly accepting the conclusions of other people.

Much as Lord Ashbridge valued the sturdy independence of character which he himself enjoyed displaying, he appreciated it rather less highly when it was manifested by people who were not sensible enough to agree with him. He looked forward to Michael's arrival that evening with the feeling that there was a rebellious standard hoisted against the calm blue of the evening sky, and remembering the advent of his sister he wondered whether she would not join the insurgent. Barbara Jerome, as has been remarked, often annoyed her brother; she also genially laughed at him; but Lord Ashbridge, partly from affection, partly from a loyal family sense of clanship, always expected his sister to spend a fortnight with him in August, and would have been much hurt had she refused to do so. Her husband, however, so far from spending a fortnight with his brother-in-law, never spent a minute in his presence if it could possibly be avoided, an arrangement which everybody concerned considered to be wise, and in the interests of cordiality.

"And Barbara comes this evening as well as Michael, does she not?" he said. "I hope she will not take Michael's part in his absurd scheme."

"I have given Barbara the blue room," said Lady Ashbridge, after a little thought. "I am afraid she may bring her great dog with her. I hope he will not quarrel with Petsy. Petsy does not like other dogs."

The day had been very hot, and Lord Ashbridge, not having taken any exercise, went off to have a round of golf with the professional of the links that lay not half a mile from the house. He considered exercise an essential part of the true Englishman's daily curriculum, and as necessary a contribution to the traditional mode of life which made them all what they were—or should be—as a bath in the morning or attendance at church on Sunday. He did not care so much about playing golf with a casual friend, because the casual friend, as a rule, casually beat him—thus putting him in an un- English position—and preferred a game with this first-class professional whose duty it was—in complete violation of his capacities—to play just badly enough to be beaten towards the end of the round after an exciting match. It required a good deal of cleverness and self-control to accomplish this, for Lord Ashbridge was a notably puerile performer, but he generally managed it with tact and success, by dint of missing absurdly easy putts, and (here his skill came in) by pulling and slicing his ball into far-distant bunkers. Throughout the game it was his business to keep up a running fire of admiring ejaculations such as "Well driven, my lord," or "A fine putt, my lord. Ah! dear me, I wish I could putt like that," though occasionally his chorus of praise betrayed him into error, and from habit he found himself saying: "Good shot, my lord," when my lord had just made an egregious mess of things. But on the whole he devised so pleasantly sycophantic an atmosphere as to procure a substantial tip for himself, and to make Lord Ashbridge conscious of being a very superior performer. Whether at the bottom of his heart he knew he could not play at all, he probably did not inquire; the result of his matches and his opponent's skilfully-showered praise was sufficient for him. So now he left the discouraging companionship of his wife and Petsy and walked swingingly across the garden and the park to the links, there to seek in Macpherson's applause the self-confidence that would enable him to encounter his republican sister and his musical son with an unyielding front.

His spirits mounted rapidly as he went. It pleased him to go jauntily across the lawn and reflect that all this smooth turf was his, to look at the wealth of well-tended flowers in his garden and know that all this polychromatic loveliness was bred in Lord Ashbridge's borders (and was graciously thrown open to the gaze of the admiring public on Sunday afternoon, when they were begged to keep off the grass), and that Lord Ashbridge was himself. He liked reminding himself that the towering elms drew their leafy verdure from Lord Ashbridge's soil; that the rows of hen-coops in the park, populous and cheeping with infant pheasants, belonged to the same fortunate gentleman who in November would so unerringly shoot them down as they rocketted swiftly over the highest of his tree-tops; that to him also appertained the long-fronted Jacobean house which stood so commandingly upon the hill-top, and glowed with all the mellowness of its three-hundred-years-old bricks. And his satisfaction was not wholly fatuous nor entirely personal; all these spacious dignities were insignia (temporarily conferred on him, like some order, and permanently conferred on his family) of the splendid political constitution under which England had made herself mistress of an empire and the seas that guarded it. Probably he would have been proud of belonging to that even if he had not been "one of us"; as it was, the high position which he occupied in it caused that pride to be slightly mixed with the pride that was concerned with the notion of the Empire belonging to him and his peers.

But though he was the most profound of Tories, he would truthfully have professed (as indeed he practised in the management of his estates) the most Liberal opinions as to schemes for the amelioration of the lower classes. Only, just as the music he was good enough to listen to had to be played for him, so the tenants and farmers had to be his dependents. He looked after them very well indeed, conceiving this to be the prime duty of a great landlord, but his interest in them was really proprietary. It was of his bounty, and of his complete knowledge of what his duties as "one of us" were, that he did so, and any legislation which compelled him to part with one pennyworth of his property for the sake of others less fortunate he resisted to the best of his ability as a theft of what was his. The country, in fact, if it went to the dogs (and certain recent legislation distinctly seemed to point kennelwards), would go to the dogs because ignorant politicians, who were most emphatically not "of us," forced him and others like him to recognise the rights of dependents instead of trusting to their instinctive fitness to dispense benefits not as rights but as acts of grace. If England trusted to her aristocracy (to put the matter in a nutshell) all would be well with her in the future even as it had been in the past, but any attempt to curtail their splendours must inevitably detract from the prestige and magnificence of the Empire. . . . And he responded suitably to the obsequious salute of the professional, and remembered that the entire golf links were his property, and that the Club paid a merely nominal rental to him, just the tribute money of a penny which was due to Caesar.

For the next hour or two after her husband had left her, Lady Ashbridge occupied herself in the thoroughly lady-like pursuit of doing nothing whatever; she just existed in her comfortable chair, since Barbara might come any moment, and she would have to entertain her, which she frequently did unawares. But as Barbara continued not to come, she took up her perennial piece of needlework, feeling rather busy and pressed, and had hardly done so when her sister-in-law arrived.

She was preceded by an enormous stag-hound, who, having been shut up in her motor all the way from London, bounded delightedly, with the sense of young limbs released, on to the terrace, and made wild leaps in a circle round the horrified Petsy, who had just received a second saucerful of cream. Once he dashed in close, and with a single lick of his tongue swept the saucer dry of nutriment, and with hoarse barkings proceeded again to dance corybantically about, while Lady Ashbridge with faint cries of dismay waved her embroidery at him. Then, seeing his mistress coming out of the French window from the drawing-room, he bounded calf-like towards her, and Petsy, nearly sick with cream and horror, was gathered to Lady Ashbridge's bosom.

"My dear Barbara," she said, "how upsetting your dog is! Poor Petsy's heart is beating terribly; she does not like dogs. But I am very pleased to see you, and I have given you the blue room."

It was clearly suitable that Barbara Jerome should have a large dog, for both in mind and body she was on the large scale herself. She had a pleasant, high-coloured face, was very tall, enormously stout, and moved with great briskness and vigour. She had something to say on any subject that came on the board; and, what was less usual in these days of universal knowledge, there was invariably some point in what she said. She had, in the ordinary sense of the word, no manners at all, but essentially made up for this lack by her sincere and humourous kindliness. She saw with acute vividness the ludicrous side of everybody, herself included, and to her mind the arch-humourist of all was her brother, whom she was quite unable to take seriously. She dressed as if she had looted a milliner's shop and had put on in a great hurry anything that came to hand. She towered over her sister-in-law as she kissed her, and Petsy, safe in her citadel, barked shrilly.

"My dear, which is the blue room?" she said. "I hope it is big enough for Og and me. Yes, that is Og, which is short for dog. He takes two mutton-chops for dinner, and a little something during the night if he feels disposed, because he is still growing. Tony drove down with me, and is in the car now. He would not come in for fear of seeing Robert, so I ventured to tell them to take him a cup of tea there, which he will drink with the blinds down, and then drive back to town again. He has been made American ambassador, by the way, and will go in to dinner before Robert. My dear, I can think of few things which Robert is less fitted to bear than that. However, we all have our crosses, even those of us who have our coronets also."

Lady Ashbridge's hospitable instincts asserted themselves. "But your husband must come in," she said. "I will go and tell him. And Robert has gone to play golf."

Barbara laughed.

"I am quite sure Tony won't come in," she said. "I promised him he shouldn't, and he only drove down with me on the express stipulation that no risks were to be run about his seeing Robert. We must take no chances, so let him have his tea quietly in the motor and then drive away again. And who else is there? Anybody? Michael?"

"Michael comes this evening."

"I am glad; I am particularly fond of Michael. Also he will play to us after dinner, and though I don't know one note from another, it will relieve me of sitting in a stately circle watching Robert cheat at patience. I always find the evenings here rather trying; they remind me of being in church. I feel as if I were part of a corporate body, which leads to misplaced decorum. Ah! there is the sound of Tony's retreating motor; his strategic movement has come off. And now give me some news, if you can get in a word. Dear me, there is Robert coming back across the lawn. What a mercy that Tony did not leave the motor. Robert always walks as if he was dancing a minuet. Look, there is Og imitating him! Or is he stalking him, thinking he is an enemy. Og, come here!"

She whistled shrilly on her fingers, and rose to greet her brother, whom Og was still menacing, as he advanced towards her with staccato steps. Barbara, however, got between Og and his prey, and threw her parasol at him.

"My dear, how are you?" she said. "And how did the golf go? And did you beat the professional?"

He suspected flippancy here, and became markedly dignified.

"An excellent match," he said, "and Macpherson tells me I played a very sound game. I am delighted to see you, Barbara. And did Michael come down with you?"

"No. I drove from town. It saves time, but not expense, with your awful trains."

"And you are well, and Mr. Jerome?" he asked. He always called his brother-in-law Mr. Jerome, to indicate the gulf between them. Barbara gave a little spurt of laughter.

"Yes, his excellency is quite well," she said. "You must call him excellency now, my dear."

"Indeed! That is a great step."

"Considering that Tony began as an office-boy. How richly rewarding you are, my dear. And shan't I make an odd ambassadress! I haven't been to a Court since the dark ages, when I went to those beloved States. We will practise after dinner, dear, and you and Marion shall be the King and Queen, and I will try to walk backwards without tumbling on my head. You will like being the King, Robert. And then we will be ourselves again, all except Og, who shall be Tony and shall go out of the room before you."

He gave his treble little giggle, for on the whole it answered better not to be dignified with Barbara, whenever he could remember not to be; and Lady Ashbridge, still nursing Petsy, threw a bombshell of the obvious to explode the conversation.

"Og has two mutton-chops for his dinner," she said, "and he is growing still. Fancy!"

Lord Ashbridge took a refreshing glance at the broad stretch of country that all belonged to him.

"I am rather glad to have this opportunity of talking to you, my dear Barbara," he said, "before Michael comes."

"His train gets in half an hour before dinner" said Lady Ashbridge. "He has to change at Stoneborough."

"Quite so. I heard from Michael this morning, saying that he has resigned his commission in the Guards, and is going to take up music seriously."

Barbara gave a delighted exclamation.

"But how perfectly splendid!" she said. "Fancy a Comber doing anything original! Michael and I are the only Combers who ever have, since Combers 'arose from out the azure main' in the year one. I married an American; that's something, though it's not up to Michael!"

"That is not quite my view of it," said he. "As for its being original, it would be original enough if Marion eloped with a Patagonian."

Lady Ashbridge let fall her embroidery at this monstrous suggestion.

"You are talking very wildly, Robert," she said, in a pained voice.

"My dear, get on with your sacred carpet," said he. "I am talking to Barbara. I have already ascertained your—your lack of views on the subject. I was saying, Barbara, that mere originality is not a merit."

"No, you never said that," remarked Lady Ashbridge.

"I should have if you had allowed me to. And as for your saying that he has done it, Barbara, that is very wide of the mark, and I intend shall continue to be so."

"Dear great Bashaw, that is just what you said to me when I told you I was going to marry his Excellency. But I did. And I think it is a glorious move on Michael's part. It requires brain to find out what you like, and character to go and do it. Combers haven't got brains as a rule, you see. If they ever had any, they have degenerated into conservative instincts."

He again refreshed himself with the landscape. The roofs of Ashbridge were visible in the clear sunset. . . . Ashbridge paid its rents with remarkable regularity.

"That may or may not be so," he said, forgetting for a moment the danger of being dignified. "But Combers have position."

Barbara controlled herself admirably. A slight tremor shook her, which he did not notice.

"Yes, dear," she said. "I allow that Combers have had for many generations a sort of acquisitive cunning, for all we possess has come to us by exceedingly prudent marriages. They have also—I am an exception here—the gift of not saying very much, which certainly has an impressive effect, even when it arises from not having very much to say. They are sticky; they attract wealth, and they have the force called vis inertiae, which means that they invest their money prudently. You should hear Tony—well, perhaps you had better not hear Tony. But now here is Michael showing that he has got tastes. Can you wonder that I'm delighted? And not only has he got tastes, but he has the strength of character to back them. Michael, in the Guards too! It was a perfect farce, and he's had the sense to see it. He hated his duties, and he hated his diversions. Now Francis—"

"I am afraid Michael has always been a little jealous of Francis," remarked his father.

This roused Barbara; she spoke quite seriously:

"If you really think that, my dear," she said, "you have the distinction of being the worst possible judge of character that the world has ever known. Michael might be jealous of anybody else, for the poor boy feels his physical awkwardness most sensitively, but Francis is just the one person he really worships. He would do anything in the world for him."

The discussion with Barbara was being even more fruitless than that with his wife, and Lord Ashbridge rose.

"All I can do, then, is to ask you not to back Michael up," he said.

"My dear, he won't need backing up. He's a match for you by himself. But if Michael, after thoroughly worsting you, asks me my opinion, I shall certainly give it him. But he won't ask my opinion first. He will strew your limbs, Robert, over this delightful terrace."

"Michael's train is late," said Lady Ashbridge, hearing the stable clock strike. "He should have been here before this."

Barbara had still a word to say, and disregarded this quencher.

"But don't think, Robert," she said, "that because Michael resists your wishes and authority, he will be enjoying himself. He will hate doing it, but that will not stop him."

Lord Ashbridge was not a bully; he had merely a profound sense of his own importance.

"We will see about resistance," he said.

Barbara was not so successful on this occasion, and exploded loudly:

"You will, dear, indeed," she said.

Michael meantime had been travelling down from London without perturbing himself over the scene with his father which he knew lay before him. This was quite characteristic of him; he had a singular command over his imagination when he had made up his mind to anything, and never indulged in the gratuitous pain of anticipation. Today he had an additional bulwark against such self-inflicted worries, for he had spent his last two hours in town at the vocal recital of a singer who a month before had stirred the critics into rhapsody over her gift of lyric song. Up till now he had had no opportunity of hearing her; and, with the panegyrics that had been showered on her in his mind, he had gone with the expectation of disappointment. But now, an hour afterwards, the wheels of the train sang her songs, and in the inward ear he could recapture, with the vividness of an hallucination, the timbre of that wonderful voice and also the sweet harmonies of the pianist who accompanied her.

The hall had been packed from end to end, and he had barely got to his seat, the only one vacant in the whole room, when Miss Sylvia Falbe appeared, followed at once by her accompanist, whose name occurred nowhere on the programme. Two neighbours, however, who chatted shrilly during the applause that greeted them, informed him that this was Hermann, "dear Hermann; there is no one like him!" But it occurred to Michael that the singer was like him, though she was fair and he dark. But his perception of either of them visually was but vague; he had come to hear and not to see. Neither she nor Hermann had any music with them, and Hermann just glanced at the programme, which he put down on the top of the piano, which, again unusually, was open. Then without pause they began the set of German songs—Brahms, Schubert, Schumann—with which the recital opened. And for one moment, before he lost himself in the ecstasy of hearing, Michael found himself registering the fact that Sylvia Falbe had one of the most charming faces he had ever seen. The next he was swallowed up in melody.

She had the ease of the consummate artist, and each note, like the gates of the New Jerusalem, was a pearl, round and smooth and luminous almost, so that it was as if many-coloured light came from her lips. Nor was that all; it seemed as if the accompaniment was made by the song itself, coming into life with the freshness of the dawn of its creation; it was impossible to believe that one mind directed the singer and another the pianist, and if the voice was an example of art in excelsis, not less exalted was the perfection of the player. Not for a moment through the song did he take his eyes off her; he looked at her with an intensity of gaze that seemed to be reading the emotion with which the lovely melody filled her. For herself, she looked straight out over the hall, with grey eyes half-closed, and mouth that in the pauses of her song was large and full-lipped, generously curving, and face that seemed lit with the light of the morning she sang of. She was the song; Michael thought of her as just that, and the pianist who watched and understood her so unerringly was the song, too. They had for him no identity of their own; they were as remote from everyday life as the mind of Schumann which they made so vivid. It was then that they existed.

The last song of the group she sang in English, for it was "Who is Sylvia?" There was a buzz of smiles and whispers among the front row in the pause before it, and regaining her own identity for a moment, she smiled at a group of her friends among whom clearly it was a cliche species of joke that she should ask who Sylvia was, and enumerate her merits, when all the time she was Sylvia. Michael felt rather impatient at this; she was not anybody just now but a singer. And then came the divine inevitable simplicity of perfect words and the melody preordained for them. The singer, as he knew, was German, but she had no trace of foreign accent. It seemed to him that this was just one miracle the more; she had become English because she was singing what Shakespeare wrote.

The next group, consisting of modern French songs, appeared to Michael utterly unworthy of the singer and the echoing piano. If you had it in you to give reality to great and simple things, it was surely a waste to concern yourself with these little morbid, melancholy manikins, these marionettes. But his emotions being unoccupied he attended more to the manner of the performance, and in especial to the marvellous technique, not so much of the singer, but of the pianist who caused the rain to fall and the waters reflect the toneless grey skies. He had never, even when listening to the great masters, heard so flawless a comprehension as this anonymous player, incidentally known as Hermann, exhibited. As far as mere manipulation went, it was, as might perhaps be expected, entirely effortless, but effortless no less was the understanding of the music. It happened. . . . It was like that.

All of this so filled Michael's mind as he travelled down that evening to Ashbridge, that he scarcely remembered the errand on which he went, and when it occurred to him it instantly sank out of sight again, lost in the recollection of the music which he had heard to-day and which belonged to the art that claimed the allegiance of his soul. The rattle of the wheels was alchemised into song, and as with half-closed eyes he listened to it, there swam across it now the full face of the singer, now the profile of the pianist, that had stood out white and intent against the dark panelling behind his head. He had gleaned one fact at the box-office as he hurried out to catch his train: this Hermann was the singer's brother, a teacher of the piano in London, and apparently highly thought of.

CHAPTER III

Michael's train, as his mother had so infallibly pronounced, was late, and he had arrived only just in time to hurry to his room and dress quickly, in order not to add to his crimes the additional one of unpunctuality, for unpunctuality, so

Lord Ashbridge held, was the politeness not only of kings, but of all who had any pretence to decent breeding. His father gave him a carefully-iced welcome, his mother the tip of her long, camel-like lips, and they waited solemnly for the appearance of Aunt Barbara, who, it would seem, had forfeited her claims to family by her marriage. A man-servant and a half looked after each of them at dinner, and the twelve Lord Ashbridges in uniform looked down from their illuminated frames on their degenerate descendant.

The only bright spot in this portentous banquet was Aunt Barbara, who had chosen that evening, with what intention may possibly be guessed, to put on an immense diamond tiara and a breastplate of rubies, while Og, after one futile attempt to play with the footmen, yielded himself up to the chilling atmosphere of good breeding, and ate his mutton-chops with great composure. But Aunt Barbara, fortified by her gems, ate an excellent dinner, and talked all the time with occasional bursts of unexplained laughter.

Afterwards, when Michael was left alone with his father, he found that his best efforts at conversation elicited only monosyllabic replies, and at last, in the despairing desire to bring things to a head, he asked him if he had received his letter. An affirmative monosyllable, followed by the hissing of Lord Ashbridge's cigarette end as he dropped it into his coffee cup, answered him, and he perceived that the approaching storm was to be rendered duly impressive by the thundery stillness that preceded it. Then his father rose, and as he passed Michael, who held the door open for him, said:

"If you can spare the time, Michael, I would like to have a talk with you when your mother and aunt have gone to bed."

That was not very long delayed; Michael imagined that Aunt Barbara must have had a hint, for before half-past ten she announced with a skilfully suppressed laugh that she was about to retire, and kissed Michael affectionately. Both her laugh and her salute were encouraging; he felt that he was being backed up. Then a procession of footmen came into the room bearing lemonade and soda water and whiskey and a plate of plain biscuits, and the moment after he was alone with his father.

Lord Ashbridge rose and walked, very tall and majestic, to the fireplace, where he stood for a moment with his back to his son. Then he turned round.

"Now about this nonsense of your resigning your commission, Michael," he said. "I don't propose to argue about it, and I am just going to tell you. If, as you have informed me, you have actually sent it in, you will write to-morrow with due apologies and ask that it may be withdrawn. I will see your letter before you send it."

Michael had intended to be as quiet and respectful as possible, consistent with firmness, but a sentence here gave him a spasm of anger.

"I don't know what you mean, sir," he said, "by saying 'if I have sent it in.' You have received my letter in which I tell you that I have done so."

Already, even at the first words, there was bad blood between them. Michael's face had clouded with that gloom which his father would certainly call sulky, and for himself he resented the tone of Michael's reply. To make matters worse he gave his little falsetto cackle, which no doubt was intended to convey the impression of confident good humour. But there was, it must be confessed, very little good humour about it, though he still felt no serious doubt about the result of this interview.

"I'm afraid, perhaps, then, that I did not take your letter quite seriously, my dear Michael," he said, in the bantering tone that froze Michael's cordiality completely up. "I glanced through it; I saw a lot of nonsense—or so it struck me—about your resigning your commission and studying music; I think you mentioned Baireuth, and settling down in London afterwards."

"Yes. I said all that," said Michael. "But you make a mistake if you do not see that it was written seriously."

His father glanced across at him, where he sat with his heavy, plain face, his long arms and short legs, and the sight merely irritated him. With his passion for convention (and one of the most important conventions was that Combers should be fine, strapping, normal people) he hated the thought that it was his son who presented that appearance. And his son's mind seemed to him at this moment as ungainly as his person. Again, very unwisely, he laughed, still thinking to carry this off by the high hand.

"Yes, but I can't take that rubbish seriously," he said. "I am asking your permission now to inquire, without any nonsense, into what you mean."

Michael frowned. He felt the insincerity of his father's laugh, and rebelled against the unfairness of it. The question, he knew well, was sarcastically asked, the flavour of irony in the "permission to inquire" was not there by accident. To speak like that implied contempt of his opposition; he felt that he was being treated like a child over some nursery rebellion, in which, subsequently, there is no real possibility of disobedience. He felt his anger rising in spite of himself.

"If you refer to it as rubbish, sir, there is the end of the matter."

"Ah! I thought we should soon agree," said Lord Ashbridge, chuckling.

"You mistake me," said Michael. "There is the end of the matter, because I won't discuss it any more, if you treat me like this. I will say good night, if you intend to persist in the idea that you can just brush my resolves away like that."

This clearly took his father aback; it was a perfectly dignified and proper attitude to take in the face of ridicule, and Lord Ashbridge, though somewhat an adept at the art of self-deception— as, for instance, when he habitually beat the golf professional— could not disguise from himself that his policy had been to laugh and blow away Michael's absurd ideas. But it was abundantly clear at this moment that this apparently easy operation was out of his reach.

He got up with more amenity in his manner than he had yet shown, and laid his hand on Michael's shoulder as he stood in front of him, evidently quite prepared to go away.

"Come, my dear Michael. This won't do," he said. "I thought it best to treat your absurd schemes with a certain lightness, and I have only succeeded in irritating you."

Michael was perfectly aware that he had scored. And as his object was to score he made another criticism.

"When you say 'absurd schemes,' sir," he said, with quiet respect, "are you not still laughing at them?"

Lord Ashbridge again retreated strategically.

"Very well; I withdraw absurd," he said. "Now sit down again, and we will talk. Tell me what is in your mind."

Michael made a great effort with himself. He desired, in the secret, real Michael, to be reasonable and cordial, to behave filially, while all the time his nerves were on edge with his father's ridicule, and with his instinctive knowledge of his father's distaste for him.

"Well, it's like this, father," he said. "I'm doing no good as I am. I went into the Guards, as you know, because it was the right thing to do. A business man's son is put into business for the same reason. And I'm not good at it."

Michael paused a moment.

"My heart isn't in it," he said, "and I dislike it. It seems to me useless. We're for show. And my heart is quite entirely in music. It's the thing I care for more than anything else."

Again he paused; all that came so easily to his tongue when he was speaking to Francis was congealed now when he felt the contempt with which, though unexpressed, he knew he inspired his father.

Lord Ashbridge waited with careful politeness, his eyes fixed on the ceiling, his large person completely filling his chair, just as his atmosphere filled the room. He said nothing at all until the silence rang in Michael's ears.

"That is all I can tell you," he said at length.

Lord Ashbridge carefully conveyed the ash from his cigarette to the fireplace before he spoke. He felt that the time had come for his most impressive effort.

"Very well, then, listen to me," he said. "What you suffer from, Michael, is a mere want of self-confidence and from modesty. You don't seem to grasp—I have often noticed this—who you are and what your importance is—an importance which everybody is willing to recognise if you will only assume it. You have the privileges of your position, which you don't sufficiently value, but you have, also, the responsibilities of it, which I am afraid you are inclined to shirk. You haven't got the large view; you haven't the sense of patriotism. There are a great many things in my position— the position into which you will step—which I would much sooner be without. But we have received a tradition, and we are bound to hand it on intact. You may think that this has nothing to do with your being in the Guards, but it has. We"—and he seemed to swell a little—"we are bound in honour to take the lead in the service of our country, and we must do it whether we like it or not. We have to till, with our own efforts, 'our goodly heritage.' You have to learn the meaning of such words as patriotism, and caste, and duty."

Lord Ashbridge thought that he was really putting this very well indeed, and he had the sustaining consciousness of sincerity. He entirely believed what he said, and felt that it must carry conviction to anyone who listened to it with anything like an open mind. The only thing that he did not allow for was that he personally immensely enjoyed his social and dominant position, thinking it indeed the only position which was really worth having. This naturally gave an aid to comprehension, and he did not take into account that Michael was not so blessed as he, and indeed lacked this very superior individual enlightenment. But his own words kindled the flame of this illumination, and without noticing the blank stolidity of Michael's face he went on with gathering confidence:

"I am sure you are high-minded, my dear Michael," he said. "And it is to your high-mindedness that I—yes, I don't mind saying it— that I appeal. In a moment of unreflectiveness you have thrown overboard what I am sure is real to you, the sense, broadly speaking, that you are English and of the highest English class, and have intended to devote yourself to more selfish and pleasure- loving aims, and to dwell in a tinkle of pleasant sounds that please your ear; and I'm sure I don't wonder, because, as your mother and I both know, you play charmingly. But I feel confident that your better mind does not really confuse the mere diversions of life with its serious issues."

Michael suddenly rose to his feet.

"Father, I'm afraid this is no use at all," he said. "All that I feel, and all that I can't say, I know is unintelligible to you. You have called it rubbish once, and you think it is rubbish still."

Lord Ashbridge's eloquence was suddenly arrested. He had been cantering gleefully along, and had the very distinct impression of having run up against a stone wall. He dismounted, hurt, but in no way broken.

"I am anxious to understand you, Michael," he said.

"Yes, father, but you don't," said he. "You have been explaining me all wrong. For instance, I don't regard music as a diversion. That is the only explanation there is of me."

"And as regards my wishes and my authority?" asked his father.

Michael squared his shoulders and his mind.

"I am exceedingly sorry to disappoint you in the matter of your wishes," he said; "but in the matter of your authority I can't recognise it when the question of my whole life is at stake. I know that I am your son, and I want to be dutiful, but I have my own individuality as well. That only recognises the authority of my own conscience."

That seemed to Lord Ashbridge both tragic and ludicrous. Completely subservient himself to the conventions which he so much enjoyed, it was like the defiance of a child to say such things. He only just checked himself from laughing again.

"I refuse to take that answer from you," he said.

"I have no other to give you," said Michael. "But I should like to say once more that I am sorry to disobey your wishes."

The repetition took away his desire to laugh. In fact, he could not have laughed.

"I don't want to threaten you, Michael," he said. "But you may know that I have a very free hand in the disposal of my property."

"Is that a threat?" asked Michael.

"It is a hint."

"Then, father, I can only say that I should be perfectly satisfied with anything you may do," said Michael. "I wish you could leave everything you have to Francis. I tell you in all sincerity that I wish he had been my elder brother. You would have been far better pleased with him."

Lord Ashbridge's anger rose. He was naturally so self-complacent as to be seldom disposed to anger, but its rarity was not due to kindliness of nature.

"I have before now noticed your jealousy of your cousin," he observed.

Michael's face went white.

"That is infamous and untrue, father," he said.

Lord Ashbridge turned on him.

"Apologise for that," he said.

Michael looked up at his high towering without a tremor.

"I wait for the withdrawal of your accusation that I am jealous of Francis," he replied.

There was a dead silence. Lord Ashbridge stood there in swollen and speechless indignation, and Michael faced him undismayed. . . . And then suddenly to the boy there came an impulse of pure pity for his father's disappointment in having a son like himself. He saw with the candour which was so real a part of him how hopeless it must be, to a man of his father's mind, to have a millstone like himself unalterably bound round his neck, fit to choke and drown him.

"Indeed, I am not jealous of Francis, father," he said, "and I speak quite truthfully when I say how I sympathise with you in having a son like me. I don't want to vex you. I want to make the best of myself."

Lord Ashbridge stood looking exactly like his statue in the market- place at Ashbridge.

"If that is the case, Michael," he said, "it is within your power. You will write the letter I spoke about."

Michael paused a moment as if waiting for more. It did not seem to him possible that his appeal should bear no further fruit than that. But it was soon clear that there was no more to come.

"I will wish you good night, father," he said.

Sunday was a day on which Lord Ashbridge was almost more himself than during the week, so shining and public an example did he become of the British nobleman. Instead of having breakfast, according to the middle-class custom, rather later than usual, that solid sausagy meal was half an hour earlier, so that all the servants, except those whose presence in the house was imperatively necessary for purposes of lunch, should go to church. Thus "Old George" and Lord Ashbridge's private boat were exceedingly busy for the half-hour preceding church time, the last boat-load holding the family, whose arrival was the signal for service to begin. Lady Ashbridge, however, always went on earlier, for she presided at the organ with the long, camel-like back turned towards the congregation, and started playing a slow, melancholy voluntary when the boy who blew the bellows said to her in an ecclesiastical whisper: "His lordship has arrived, my lady." Those of the household who could sing (singing being construed in the sense of making a loud and cheerful noise in the throat) clustered in the choir-pews near the organ, while the family sat in a large, square box, with a stove in the centre, amply supplied with prayer-books of the time when even Protestants might pray for Queen Caroline. Behind them, separated from the rest of the church by an ornamental ironwork grille, was the Comber chapel, in which antiquarians took nearly as much pleasure as Lord Ashbridge himself. Here reclined a glorious company of sixteenth century knights, with their honourable ladies at their sides, unyielding marble bolsters at their heads, and grotesque dogs at their feet. Later, when their peerage was conferred, they lost a little of their yeoman simplicity, and became peruked and robed and breeched; one, indeed, in the age of George III., who was blessed with poetical aspirations, appeared in bare feet and a Roman toga with a scroll of manuscript in his hand; while later again, mere tablets on the walls commemorated their almost uncanny virtues.

And just on the other side of the grille, but a step away, sat the present-day representatives of the line, while Lady Ashbridge finished the last bars of her voluntary, Lord Ashbridge himself and his sister, large and smart and comely, and Michael beside them, short and heavy, with his soul full of the aspirations his father neither could nor cared to understand. According to his invariable custom, Lord Ashbridge read the lessons in a loud, sonorous voice, his large, white hands grasping the wing-feathers of the brass eagle, and a great carnation in his buttonhole; and when the time came for the offertory he put a sovereign in the open plate himself, and proceeded with his minuet-like step to go round the church and collect the gifts of the encouraged congregation. He followed all the prayers in his book, he made the responses in a voice nearly as loud as that in which he read the lessons; he sang the hymns with a curious buzzing sound, and never for a moment did he lose sight of the fact that he was the head of the Comber family, doing his duty as the custom of the Combers was, and setting an example of godly piety. Afterwards, as usual, he would change his black coat, eat a good lunch, stroll round the gardens (for he had nothing to say to golf on Sunday), and in the evening the clergyman would dine with him, and would be requested to say grace both before and after the meal. He knew exactly the proper mode of passing the Sunday for the landlord on his country estate, and when Lord Ashbridge knew that a thing was proper he did it with invariable precision.

Michael, of course, was in disgrace; his father, pending some further course of action, neither spoke to him nor looked at him; indeed, it seemed doubtful whether he would hand him the offertory plate, and it was perhaps a pity that he unbent even to this extent, for Michael happened to have none of the symbols of thankfulness about his person, and he saw a slight quiver pass through Aunt Barbara's hymn-book. After a rather portentous lunch, however, there came some relief, for his father did not ask his company on the usual Sunday afternoon stroll, and Aunt Barbara never walked at all unless she was obliged. In consequence, when the thunderstorm had stepped airily away across the park, Michael joined her on the terrace, with the intention of talking the situation over with her.

Aunt Barbara was perfectly willing to do this, and she opened the discussion very pleasantly with peals of laughter.

"My dear, I delight in you," she said; "and altogether this is the most entertaining day I have ever spent here. Combers are supposed to be very serious, solid people, but for unconscious humour there isn't a family in England or even in the States to compare with them. Our lunch just now; if you could put it into a satirical comedy called The Aristocracy it would make the fortune of any theatre."

A dawning smile began to break through Michael's tragedy face.

"I suppose it was rather funny," he said. "But really I'm wretched about it, Aunt Barbara."

"My dear, what is there to be wretched about? You might have been wretched if you had found you couldn't stand up to your father, but I gather, though I know nothing directly, that you did. At least, your mother has said to me three times, twice on the way to church and once coming back: 'Michael has vexed his father very much.' And the offertory plate, my dear, and, as I was saying, lunch! I am in disgrace too, because I said perfectly plainly yesterday that I was on your side; and there we were at lunch, with your father apparently unable to see either you or me, and unconscious of our presence. Fancy pretending not to see me! You can't help seeing me, a large, bright object like me! And what will happen next? That's what tickles me to death, as they say on my side of the Atlantic. Will he gradually begin to perceive us again, like objects looming through a fog, or shall we come into view suddenly, as if going round a corner? And you are just as funny, my dear, with your long face, and air of depressed determination. Why be heavy, Michael? So many people are heavy, and none of them can tell you why."

It was impossible not to feel the unfreezing effect of this. Michael thawed to it, as he would have thawed to Francis.

"Perhaps they can't help it, Aunt Barbara," he said. "At least, I know I can't. I really wish I could learn how to. I—I don't see the funny side of things till it is pointed out. I thought lunch a sort of hell, you know. Of course, it was funny, his appearing not to see either of us. But it stands for more than that; it stands for his complete misunderstanding of me."

Aunt Barbara had the sense to see that the real Michael was speaking. When people were being unreal, when they were pompous or adopting attitudes, she could attend to nothing but their absurdity, which engrossed her altogether. But she never laughed at real things; real things were not funny, but were facts.

"He quite misunderstands," went on Michael, with the eagerness with which the shy welcome comprehension. "He thinks I can make my mind like his if I choose; and if I don't choose, or rather can't choose, he thinks that his wishes, his authority, should be sufficient to make me act as if it was. Well, I won't do that. He may go on,"—and that pleasant smile lit up Michael's plain face— "he may go on being unaware of my presence as long as he pleases. I am very sorry it should be so, but I can't help it. And the worst of it is, that opposition of that sort—his sort—makes me more determined than ever."

Aunt Barbara nodded.

"And your friends?" she asked. "What will they think?"

Michael looked at her quite simply and directly.

"Friends?" he said. "I haven't got any."

"Ah, my dear, that's nonsense!" she said.

"I wish it was. Oh, Francis is a friend, I know. He thinks me an odd old thing, but he likes me. Other people don't. And I can't see why they should. I'm sure it's my fault. It's because I'm heavy. You said I was, yourself."

"Then I was a great ass," remarked Aunt Barbara. "You wouldn't be heavy with people who understood you. You aren't heavy with me, for instance; but, my dear, lead isn't in it when you are with your father."

"But what am I to do, if I'm like that?" asked the boy.

She held up her large, fat hand, and marked the points off on her fingers.

"Three things," she said. "Firstly, get away from people who don't understand you, and whom, incidentally, you don't understand. Secondly, try to see how ridiculous you and everybody else always are; and, thirdly, which is much the most important, don't think about yourself. If I thought about myself I should consider how old and fat and ugly I am. I'm not ugly, really; you needn't be foolish and tell me so. I should spoil my life by trying to be young, and only eating devilled codfish and drinking hot plum- juice, or whatever is the accepted remedy for what we call obesity. We're all odd old things, as you say. We can only get away from that depressing fact by doing something, and not thinking about ourselves. We can all try not to be egoists. Egoism is the really heavy quality in the world."

She paused a moment in this inspired discourse and whistled to Og, who had stretched his weary limbs across a bed of particularly fine geraniums.

"There!" she said, pointing, "if your dog had done that, you would be submerged in depression at the thought of how vexed your father would be. That would be because you are thinking of the effect on yourself. As it's my dog that has done it—dear me, they do look squashed now he has got up—you don't really mind about your father's vexation, because you won't have to think about yourself. That is wise of you; if you were a little wiser still, you would picture to yourself how ridiculous I shall look apologising for Og. Kindly kick him, Michael; he will understand. Naughty! And as for your not having any friends, that would be exceedingly sad, if you had gone the right way to get them and failed. But you haven't. You haven't even gone among the people who could be your friends. Your friends, broadly speaking, must like the same sort of things as you. There must be a common basis. You can't even argue with somebody, or disagree with somebody unless you have a common ground to start from. If I say that black is white, and you think it is blue, we can't get on. It leads nowhere. And, finally—"

She turned round and faced him directly.

"Finally, don't be so cross, my dear," she said.

"But am I?" asked he.

"Yes. You don't know it, or else probably, since you are a very decent fellow, you wouldn't be. You expect not to be liked, and that is cross of you. A good-humoured person expects to be liked, and almost always is. You expect not to be understood, and that's dreadfully cross. You think your father doesn't understand you; no more he does, but don't go on thinking about it. You think it is a great bore to be your father's only son, and wish Francis was instead. That's cross; you may think it's fine, but it isn't, and it is also ungrateful. You can have great fun if you will only be good-tempered!"

"How did you know that—about Francis, I mean?" asked Michael.

"Does it happen to be true? Of course it does. Every cross young man wishes he was somebody else."

"No, not quite that," began Michael.

"Don't interrupt. It is sufficiently accurate. And you think about your appearance, my dear. It will do quite well. You might have had two noses, or only one eye, whereas you have two rather jolly ones. And do try to see the joke in other people, Michael. You didn't see the joke in your interview last night with your father. It must have been excruciatingly funny. I don't say it wasn't sad and serious as well. But it was funny too; there were points."

Michael shook his head.

"I didn't see them," he said.

"But I should have, and I should have been right. All dignity is funny, simply because it is sham. When dignity is real, you don't know it's dignity. But your father knew he was being dignified, and you knew you were being dignified. My dear, what a pair of you!"

Michael frowned.

"But is nothing serious, then?" he asked. "Surely it was serious enough last night. There was I in rank rebellion to my father, and it vexed him horribly; it did more, it grieved him."

She laid her hand on Michael's knee.

"As if I didn't know that!" she said. "We're all sorry for that, though I should have been much sorrier if you had given in and ceased to vex him. But there it is! Accept that, and then, my dear, swiftly apply yourself to perceive the humour of it. And now, about your plans!"

"I shall go to Baireuth on Wednesday, and then on to Munich," began Michael.

"That, of course. Perhaps you may find the humour of a Channel crossing. I look for it in vain. Yet I don't know. . . . The man who puts on a yachting-cap, and asks if there's a bit of a sea on. It proves to be the case, and he is excessively unwell. I must look out for him next time I cross. And then?"

"Then I shall settle in town and study. Oh, here's my father coming home."

Lord Ashbridge approached down the terrace. He stopped for a moment at the desecrated geranium bed, saw the two sitting together, and turned at right angles and went into the house. Almost immediately a footman came out with a long dog-lead and advanced hesitatingly to Og. Og was convinced that he had come to play with him, and crouched and growled and retreated and advanced with engaging affability. Out of the windows of the library looked Lord Ashbridge's baleful face. . . . Aunt Barbara swayed out of her chair, and laid a trembling hand on Michael's shoulder.

"I shall go and apologise for Og," she said. "I shall do it quite sincerely, my dear. But there are points."

CHAPTER IV

Michael practised a certain mature and rather elderly precision in the ordinary affairs of daily life. His habits were almost unduly tidy and punctual; he answered letters by return of post, he never mislaid things nor tore up documents which he particularly desired should be preserved; he kept his gold in a purse and his change in a trousers-pocket, and in matters of travelling he always arrived at stations with plenty of time to spare, and had such creature comforts as he desired for his journey in a neat Gladstone bag above his head. He never travelled first-class, for the very simple and adequate reason that, though very well off, he preferred to spend his money in ways that were more productive of usefulness or pleasure; and thus, when he took his place in the corner of a second-class compartment of the Dover-Ostend express on the Wednesday morning following, he was the only occupant of it.

Probably he had never felt so fully at liberty, nor enjoyed a keener zest for life and the future. For the first time he had asserted his own indisputable right to stand on his own feet, and though he was genuinely sorry for his father's chagrin at not being able to tuck him up in the family coach, his own sense of independence could not but wave its banners. There had been a second interview, no less fruitless than the first, and Lord Ashbridge had told him that when next his presence was desired at home, he would be informed of the fact. His mother had cried in a mild, trickling fashion, but it was quite obvious that in her heart of hearts she was more concerned with a bilious attack of peculiar intensity that had assailed Petsy. She wished Michael would not be so disobedient and vex his father, but she was quite sure that before long some formula, in diplomatic phrase, would be found on which reconciliation could be based; whereas it was highly uncertain whether any formula could be found that would produce the desired effect on Petsy, whose illness she attributed to the shock of Og's sudden and disconcerting appearance on Saturday, when all Petsy's nervous force was required to digest the copious cream. Consequently, though she threw reproachful glances at Michael, those directed at Barbara, who was the cause of the acuter tragedy, were pointed with more penetrating blame. Indeed, it is questionable whether Lady Ashbridge would have cried at all over Michael's affairs had not Petsy's also been in so lamentable and critical a state.

Just as the train began to move out of the station a young man rushed across the platform, eluded the embrace of the guard who attempted to stop him with amazing agility, and jumped into Michael's compartment. He slammed the door after him, and leaned out, apparently looking for someone, whom he soon saw.

"Just caught it, Sylvia," he shouted. "Send on my luggage, will you? It's in the taxi still, I think, and I haven't paid the man. Good-bye, darling."

He waved to her till the curving line took the platform out of sight, and then sat down with a laugh, and eyes of friendly interest for Michael.

"Narrow squeak, wasn't it?" he said gleefully. "I thought the guard had collared me. And I should have missed Parsifal."

Michael had recognised him at once as he rushed across the platform; his shouting to Sylvia had but confirmed the recognition; and here on the day of his entering into his new kingdom of liberty was one of its citizens almost thrown into his arms. But for the moment his old invincible habit of shyness and sensitiveness forbade any responsive lightness of welcome, and he was merely formal, merely courteous.

"And all your luggage left behind," he said. "Won't you be dreadfully uncomfortable?"

"Uncomfortable? Why?" asked Falbe. "I shall buy a handkerchief and a collar every day, and a shirt and a pair of socks every other day till it arrives."

Michael felt a sudden, daring impulse. He remembered Aunt Barbara's salutary remarks about crossness being the equivalent of thinking about oneself. And the effort that it cost him may be taken as the measure of his solitary disposition.

"But you needn't do that," he said, "if—if you will be good enough to borrow of me till your things come."

He blurted it out awkwardly, almost brusquely, and Falbe looked slightly amused at this wholly surprising offer of hospitality.

"But that's awfully good of you," he said, laughing and saying nothing direct about his acceptance. "It implies, too, that you are going to Baireuth. We travel together, then, I hope, for it is dismal work travelling alone, isn't it? My sister tells me that half my friends were picked up in railway carriages. Been there before?"

Michael felt himself lured from the ordinary aloofness of attitude and demeanour, which had been somewhat accustomed to view all strangers with suspicion. And yet, though till this moment he had never spoken to him, he could hardly regard Falbe as a stranger, for he had heard him say on the piano what his sister understood by the songs of Brahms and Schubert. He could not help glancing at Falbe's hands, as they busied themselves with the filling and lighting of a pipe, and felt that he knew something of those long, broad-tipped fingers, smooth and white and strong. The man himself he found to be quite different to what he had expected; he had seen him before, eager and intent and anxious-faced, absorbed in the task of following another mind; now he looked much younger, much more boyish.

"No, it's my first visit to Baireuth," he said, "and I can't tell you how excited I am about it. I've been looking forward to it so much that I almost expect to be disappointed."

Falbe blew out a cloud of smoke and laughter.

"Oh, you're safe enough," he said. "Baireuth never disappoints. It's one of the facts—a reliable fact. And Munich? Do you go to Munich afterwards?"

"Yes. I hope so."

Falbe clicked with his tongue

"Lucky fellow," he said. "How I wish I was. But I've got to get back again after my week. You'll spend the mornings in the galleries, and the afternoons and evenings at the opera. O Lord, Munich!"

He came across from the other side of the carriage and sat next Michael, putting his feet up on the seat opposite.

"Talk of Munich," he said. "I was born in Munich, and I happen to know that it's the heavenly Jerusalem, neither more nor less."

"Well, the heavenly Jerusalem is practically next door to Baireuth," said Michael.

"I know; but it can't be managed. However, there's a week of unalloyed bliss between me now and the desolation of London in August. What is so maddening is to think of all the people who could go to Munich and don't."

Michael held debate within himself. He felt that he ought to tell his new acquaintance that he knew who he was, that, however trivial their conversation might be, it somehow resembled eavesdropping to talk to a chance fellow-passenger as if he were a complete stranger. But it required again a certain effort to make the announcement.

"I think I had better tell you," he said at length, "that I know you, that I've listened to you at least, at your sister's recital a few days ago."

Falbe turned to him with the friendliest pleasure.

"Ah! were you there?" he asked. "I hope you listened to her, then, not to me. She sang well, didn't she?"

"But divinely. At the same time I did listen to you, especially in the French songs. There was less song, you know."

Falbe laughed.

"And more accompaniment!" he said. "Perhaps you play?"

Michael was seized with a fit of shyness at the idea of talking to Falbe about himself.

"Oh, I just strum," he said.

Throughout the journey their acquaintanceship ripened; and casually, in dropped remarks, the two began to learn something about each other. Falbe's command of English, as well as his sister's, which was so complete that it was impossible to believe that a foreigner was speaking, was explained, for it came out that his mother was English, and that from infancy they had spoken German and English indiscriminately. His father, who had died some dozen years before, had been a singer of some note in his native land, but was distinguished more for his teaching than his practice, and it was he who had taught his daughter. Hermann Falbe himself had always intended to be a pianist, but the poverty in which they were left at his father's death had obliged him to give lessons rather than devote himself to his own career; but now at the age of thirty he found himself within sight of the competence that would allow him to cut down his pupils, and begin to be a pupil again himself.

His sister, moreover, for whom he had slaved for years in order that she might continue her own singing education unchecked, was now more than able, especially after these last three months in London, where she had suddenly leaped into eminence, to support herself and contributed to the expenses of their common home. But there was still, so Michael gathered, no great superabundance of money, and he guessed that Falbe's inability to go to Munich was due to the question of expense.

All this came out by inference and allusion rather than by direct information, while Michael, naturally reticent and feeling that his own uneventful affairs could have no interest for anybody, was less communicative. And, indeed, while shunning the appearance of inquisitiveness, he was far too eager to get hold of his new acquaintance to think of volunteering much himself. Here to him was this citizen of the new country who all his life had lived in the palace of art, and that in no dilettante fashion, but with set aim and serious purpose. And Falbe abounded in such topics; he knew the singers and the musicians of the world, and, which was much more than that, he was himself of them; humble, no doubt, in circumstances and achievement as yet, but clearly to Michael of the blood royal of artistry. That was the essential thing about him as regards his relations with his fellow-traveller, though, when next morning the spires of Cologne and the swift river of his Fatherland came into sight, he burst out into a sort of rhapsody of patriotism that mockingly covered a great sincerity.

"Ah! beloved land!" he cried. "Soil of heaven and of divine harmony! Hail to thee! Hail to thee! Rhine, Rhine deep and true and steadfast. . . ." And he waved his hat and sang the greeting of Brunnhilde. Then he turned laughingly to Michael.

"I am sufficiently English to know how ridiculous that must seem to you," he said, "for I love England also, and the passengers on the boat would merely think me mad if I apostrophised the cliffs of Dover and the mud of the English roads. But here I am a German again, and I would willingly kiss the soil. You English— we English, I may say, for I am as much English as German—I believe have got the same feeling somewhere in our hearts, but we lock it up and hide it away. Pray God I shall never have to choose to which nation I belong, though for that matter there in no choice in it at all, for I am certainly a German subject. Guten Tag, Koln; let us instantly have our coffee. There is no coffee like German coffee, though the French coffee is undeniably pleasanter to the mere superficial palate. But it doesn't touch the heart, as everything German touches my heart when I come back to the Fatherland."

He chattered on in tremendous high spirits.

"And to think that to-night we shall sleep in true German beds," he said. "I allow that the duvet is not so convenient as blankets, and that there is a watershed always up the middle of your bed, so that during the night your person descends to one side while the duvet rolls down the other; but it is German, which makes up for any trifling inconvenience. Baireuth, too; perhaps it will strike you as a dull and stinking little town, and so I dare say it is. But after lunch we shall go up the hillside to where the theatre stands, at the edge of the pine-woods, and from the porch the trumpets will give out the motif of the Grail, and we shall pass out of the heat into the cool darkness of the theatre. Aren't you thrilled, Comber? Doesn't a holy awe pervade you! Are you worthy, do you think?"

All this youthful, unrestrained enthusiasm was a revelation to Michael. Intentionally absurd as Falbe's rhapsody on the Fatherland had been, Michael knew that it sprang from a solid sincerity which was not ashamed of expressing itself. Living, as he had always done, in the rather formal and reticent atmosphere of his class and environment, he would have thought this fervour of patriotism in an English mouth ridiculous, or, if persevered in, merely bad form. Yet when Falbe hailed the Rhine and the spires of Cologne, it was clear that there was no bad form about it at all. He felt like that; and, indeed, as Michael was beginning to perceive, he felt with a similar intensity on all subjects about which he felt at all. There was something of the same vivid quality about Aunt Barbara, but Aunt Barbara's vividness was chiefly devoted to the hunt of the absurdities of her friends, and it was always the concretely ridiculous that she pursued. But this handsome, vital young man, with his eagerness and his welcome for the world, who had fallen with so delightful a cordiality into Michael's company, had already an attraction for him of a sort he had never felt before.

Dimly, as the days went by, he began to conjecture that he who had never had a friend was being hailed and hallooed to, was being ordered, if not by precept, at any rate by example, to come out of the shell of his reserve, and let himself feel and let himself express. He could see how utterly different was Falbe's general conception and practice of life from his own; to Michael it had always been a congregation of strangers—Francis excepted—who moved about, busy with each other and with affairs that had no allure for him, and were, though not uncivil, wholly alien to him. He was willing to grant that this alienation, this absence of comradeship which he had missed all his life, was of his own making, in so far as his shyness and sensitiveness were the cause of it; but in effect he had never yet had a friend, because he had never yet taken his shutters down, so to speak, or thrown his front door open. He had peeped out through chinks, and felt how lonely he was, but he had not given anyone a chance to get in.

Falbe, on the other hand, lived at his window, ready to hail the passer-by, even as he had hailed Michael, with cheerful words. There he lounged in his shirt-sleeves, you might say, with elbows on the window-sill; and not from politeness, but from good fellowship, from the fact that he liked people, was at home to everybody. He liked people; there was the key to it. And Michael, however much he might be capable of liking people, had up till now given them no sign of it. It really was not their fault if they had not guessed it.

Two days passed, on the first of which Parsifal was given, and on the second Meistersinger. On the third there was no performance, and the two young men had agreed to meet in the morning and drive out of the town to a neighbouring village among the hills, and spend the day there in the woods. Michael had looked forward to this day with extraordinary pleasure, but there was mingled with it a sort of agony of apprehension that Falbe would find him a very boring companion. But the precepts of Aunt Barbara came to his mind, and he reflected that the certain and sure way of proving a bore was to be taken up with the idea that he might be. And anyhow, Falbe had proposed the plan himself.

They lunched in a little restaurant near a forest-enclosed lake, and since the day was very hot, did no more than stroll up the hill for a hundred yards, where they would get some hint of breeze, and disposed themselves at length on the carpet of pine-needles. Through the thick boughs overhead the sunlight reached them only in specks and flakes, the wind was but as a distant sea in the branches, and Falbe rolled over on to his face, and sniffed at the aromatic leaves with the gusto with which he enjoyed all that was to him enjoyable.

"Ah; that's good, that's good!" he said. "How I love smells— clean, sharp smells like this. But they've got to be wild; you can't tame a smell and put it on your handkerchief; it takes the life out of it. Do you like smells, Comber?"

"I—I really never thought about it," said Michael.

"Think now, then, and tell me," said Falbe. "If you consider, you know such a lot about me, and, as a matter of fact, I know nothing whatever about you. I know you like music—I know you like blue trout, because you ate so many of them at lunch to-day. But what else do I know about you ? I don't even know what you thought of Parsifal. No, perhaps I'm wrong there, because the fact that you've never mentioned it probably shows that you couldn't. The symptom of not understanding anything about Parsifal is to talk about it, and say what a tremendous impression it has made on you."

"Ah! you've guessed right there," said Michael. "I couldn't talk about it; there's nothing to say about it, except that it is Parsifal."

"That's true. It becomes part of you, and you can't talk of it any more than you can talk about your elbows and your knees. It's one of the things that makes you. . . ."

He turned over on to his back, and laid his hands palm uppermost over his eyes.

"That's part of the glory of it all," he said; "that art and its emotions become part of you like the food you eat and the wine you drink. Art is always making us; it enters into our character and destiny. As long as you go on growing you assimilate, and thank God one's mind or soul, or whatever you like to call it, goes on growing for a long time. I suppose the moment comes to most people when they cease to grow, when they become fixed and hard; and that is what we mean by being old. But till then you weave your destiny, or, rather, people and beauty weave it for you, as you'll see the Norns weaving, and yet you never know what you are making. You make what you are, and you never are because you are always becoming. You must excuse me; but Germans are always metaphysicians, and they can't help it."

"Go on; be German," said Michael.

"Lieber Gott! As if I could be anything else," said Falbe, laughing. "We are the only nation which makes a science of experimentalism; we try everything, just as a puppy tries everything. It tries mutton bones, and match-boxes, and soap and boots; it tries to find out what its tail is for, and bites it till it hurts, on which it draws the conclusion that it is not meant to eat. Like all metaphysicians, too, and dealers in the abstract, we are intensely practical. Our passion for experimentalism is dictated by the firm object of using the knowledge we acquire. We are tremendously thorough; we waste nothing, not even time, whereas the English have an absolute genius for wasting time. Look at all your games, your sports, your athletics—I am being quite German now, and forgetting my mother, bless her!—they are merely devices for getting rid of the hours, and so not having to think. You hate thought as a nation, and we live for it. Music is thought; all art is thought; commercial prosperity is thought; soldiering is thought."

"And we are a nation of idiots?" asked Michael.

"No; I didn't say that. I should say you are a nation of sensualists. You value sensation above everything; you pursue the enjoyable. You are a nation of children who are always having a perpetual holiday. You go straying all over the world for fun, and annex it generally, so that you can have tiger-shooting in India, and lots of gold to pay for your tiger-shooting in Africa, and fur from Canada for your coats. But it's all a game; not one man in a thousand in England has any idea of Empire."

"Oh, I think you are wrong there," said Michael. "You believe that only because we don't talk about it. It's—it's like what we agreed about Parsifal. We don't talk about it because it is so much part of us."

Falbe sat up.

"I deny it; I deny it flatly," he said. "I know where I get my power of foolish, unthinking enjoyment from, and it's from my English blood. I rejoice in my English blood, because you are the happiest people on the face of the earth. But you are happy because you don't think, whereas the joy of being German is that you do think. England is lying in the shade, like us, with a cigarette and a drink—I wish I had one—and a golf ball or the world with which she has been playing her game. But Germany is sitting up all night thinking, and every morning she gives an order or two."

Michael supplied the cigarette.

"Do you mean she is thinking about England's golf ball?" asked Michael.

"Why, of course she is! What else is there to think about?"

"Oh, it's impossible that there should be a European war," said Michael, "for that is what it will mean!"

"And why is a European war impossible?" demanded Falbe, lighting his cigarette.

"It's simply unthinkable!"

"Because you don't think," he interrupted. "I can tell you that the thought of war is never absent for a single day from the average German mind. We are all soldiers, you see. We start with that. You start by being golfers and cricketers. But 'der Tag' is never quite absent from the German mind. I don't say that all you golfers and cricketers wouldn't make good soldiers, but you've got to be made. You can't be a golfer one day and a soldier the next."

Michael laughed.

"As for that," he said, "I made an uncommonly bad soldier. But I am an even worse golfer. As for cricket—"

Falbe again interrupted.

"Ah, then at last I know two things about you," he said. "You were a soldier and you can't play golf. I have never known so little about anybody after three—four days. However, what is our proverb? 'Live and learn.' But it takes longer to learn than to live. Eh, what nonsense I talk."

He spoke with a sudden irritation, and the laugh at the end of his speech was not one of amusement, but rather of mockery. To Michael this mood was quite inexplicable, but, characteristically, he looked about in himself for the possible explanation of it.

"But what's the matter?" he asked. "Have I annoyed you somehow? I'm awfully sorry."

Falbe did not reply for a moment.

"No, you've not annoyed me," he said. "I've annoyed myself. But that's the worst of living on one's nerves, which is the penalty of Baireuth. There is no charge, so to speak, except for your ticket, but a collection is made, as happens at meetings, and you pay with your nerves. You must cancel my annoyance, please. If I showed it I did not mean to."

Michael pondered over this.

"But I can't leave it like that," he said at length. "Was it about the possibility of war, which I said was unthinkable?"

Falbe laughed and turned on his elbow towards Michael.

"No, my dear chap," he said. "You may believe it to be unthinkable, and I may believe it to be inevitable; but what does it matter what either of us believes? Che sara sara. It was quite another thing that caused me to annoy myself. It does not matter."

Michael lay back on the soft slope.

"Yet I insist on knowing," he said. "That is, I mean, if it is not private."

Falbe lay quietly with his long fingers in the sediment of pine- needles.

"Well, then, as it is not private, and as you insist," he said, "I will certainly tell you. Does it not strike you that you are behaving like an absolute stranger to me? We have talked of me and my home and my plans all the time since we met at Victoria Station, and you have kept complete silence about yourself. I know nothing of you, not who you are, or what you are, or what your flag is. You fly no flag, you proclaim no identity. You may be a crossing- sweeper, or a grocer, or a marquis for all I know. Of course, that matters very little; but what does matter is that never for a moment have you shown me not what you happen to be, but what you are. I've got the impression that you are something, that there's a real 'you' in your inside. But you don't let me see it. You send a polite servant to the door when I knock. Probably this sounds very weird and un-English to you. But to my mind it is much more weird to behave as you are behaving. Come out, can't you. Let's look at you."

It was exactly that—that brusque, unsentimental appeal—that Michael needed. He saw himself at that moment, as Falbe saw him, a shelled and muffled figure, intangible and withdrawn, but observing, as it were, through eye-holes, and giving nothing in exchange for what he saw.

"I'm sorry," he said. "It's quite true what you tell me. I'm like that. But it really has never struck me that anybody cared to know."

Falbe ceased digging his excavation in the pine-needles and looked up on Michael.

"Good Lord, man!" he said; "people care if you'll only allow them to. The indifference of other people is a false term for the secretiveness of oneself. How can they care, unless you let them know what there is to care for?"

"But I'm completely uninteresting," said Michael.

"Yes; I'll judge of that," said Falbe.

Slowly, and with diffident pauses, Michael began to speak of himself, feeling at first as if he was undressing in public. But as he went on he became conscious of the welcome that his story received, though that welcome only expressed itself in perfectly unemotional monosyllables. He might be undressing, but he was undressing in front of a fire. He knew that he uncovered himself to no icy blast or contemptuous rain, as he had felt when, so few days before, he had spoken of himself and what he was to his father. There was here the common land of music to build upon, whereas to Lord Ashbridge that same soil had been, so to speak, the territory of the enemy. And even more than that, there was the instinct, the certain conviction that he was telling his tale to sympathetic ears, to which the mere fact that he was speaking of himself presupposed a friendly hearing. Falbe, he felt, wanted to know about him, regardless of the nature of his confessions. Had he said that he was an undetected kleptomaniac, Falbe would have liked to know, have been pleased at any tidings, provided only they were authentic. This seemed to reveal itself to him even as he spoke; it had been there waiting for him to claim it, lying there as in a poste restante, only ready for its owner.

At the end Falbe gave a long sigh.

"And why the devil didn't you give me any hint of it before?" he asked.

"I didn't think it mattered," said Michael.

"Well, then, you are amazingly wrong. Good Lord, it's about the most interesting thing I've ever heard. I didn't know anybody could escape from that awful sort of prison-house in which our—I'm English now—in which our upper class immures itself. Yet you've done it. I take it that the thing is done now?"

"I'm not going back into the prison-house again, if you mean that," said Michael.

"And will your father cut you off?" asked he.

"Oh, I haven't the least idea," said Michael.

"Aren't you going to inquire?"

Michael hesitated.

"No, I'm sure I'm not," he said. "I can't do that. It's his business. I couldn't ask about what he had done, or meant to do. It's a sort of pride, I suppose. He will do as he thinks proper, and when he has thought, perhaps he will tell me what he intends."

"But, then, how will you live?" asked Falbe.

"Oh, I forgot to tell you that. I've got some money, quite a lot, I mean, from my grandmother. In some ways I rather wish I hadn't. It would have been a proof of sincerity to have become poor. That wouldn't have made the smallest difference to my resolution."

Falbe laughed.

"And so you are rich, and yet go second-class," he said. "If I were rich I would make myself exceedingly comfortable. I like things that are good to eat and soft to touch. But I'm bound to say that I get on quite excellently without them. Being poor does not make the smallest difference to one's happiness, but only to the number of one's pleasures."

Michael paused a moment, and then found courage to say what for the last two days he had been longing to give utterance to.

"I know; but pleasures are very nice things," he said. "And doesn't it seem obvious now that you are coming to Munich with me? It's a purely selfish suggestion on my part. After being with you it will be very stupid to be alone there. But it would be so delightful if you would come."

Falbe looked at him a moment without speaking, but Michael saw the light in his eyes.

"And what if I have my pride too?" he said. "Then I shall apologise for having made the proposal," said Michael simply.

For just a second more Falbe hesitated. Then he held out his hand.

"I thank you most awfully," he said. "I accept with the greatest pleasure."

Michael drew a long breath of relief.

"I am glad," he said. "So that's settled. It's really nice of you."

The heat of the day was passing off, and over the sun-bleached plain the coolness of evening was beginning to steal. Overhead the wind stirred more resonantly in the pines, and in the bushes birds called to each other. Presently after, they rose from where they had lain all the afternoon and strolled along the needled slope to where, through a vista in the trees, they looked down on the lake and the hamlet that clustered near it. Down the road that wound through the trees towards it passed labourers going homeward from their work, with cheerful guttural cries to each other and a herd of cows sauntered by with bells melodiously chiming, taking leisurely mouthfuls from the herbage of the wayside. In the village, lying low in the clear dusk, scattered lights began to appear, the smoke of evening fires to ascend, and the aromatic odour of the burning wood strayed towards them up the wind.

Falbe, whose hand lay in the crook of Michael's arm, pointed downwards to the village that lay there sequestered and rural.

"That's Germany," he said; "it's that which lies at the back of every German heart. There lie the springs of the Rhine. It's out of that originally that there came all that Germany stands for, its music, its poetry, its philosophy, its kultur. All flowed from these quiet uplands. It was here that the nation began to think and to dream. To dreamt! It's out of dreams that all has sprung."

He laughed.

"And then next week when we go to Munich, you will find me saying that this, this Athens of a town, with its museums and its galleries and its music, is Germany. I shall be right, too. Out of much dreaming comes the need to make. It is when the artist's head and heart are full of his dreams that his hands itch for the palette or the piano. Nuremberg! Cannot we stop a few hours, at least, in Nuremberg, and see the meadow by the Pegnitz where the Meistersingers held their contest of song and the wooden, gabled house where Albrecht Durer lived? That will teach you Germany, too. The bud of their dream was opening then; and what flower, even in the magnificence of its full-blowing, is so lovely? Albrecht Durer, with his deep, patient eyes, and his patient hands with their unerring stroke; or Bach, with the fugue flowing from his brain through his quick fingers, making stars—stars fixed forever in the heaven of harmony! Don't tell me that there is anything in the world more wonderful! We may have invented a few more instruments, we may have experimented with a few more combinations of notes, but in the B minor Mass, or in the music of the Passion, all is said. And all that came from the woods and the country and the quiet life in little towns, when the artist did his work because he loved it, and cared not one jot about what anybody else thought about it. We are a nation of thinkers and dreamers."

Michael hesitated a moment.

"But you said not long ago that you were also the most practical nation," he said. "You are a nation of soldiers, also."

"And who would not willingly give himself for such a Fatherland?" said Falbe. "If need be, we will lay our lives down for that, and die more willingly than we have lived. God grant that the need comes not. But should it come we are ready. We are bound to be ready; it would be a crime not to be ready—a crime against the Fatherland. We love peace, but the peace-lovers are just those who in war are most terrible. For who are the backbone of war when war comes? The women of the country, my friend, not the ministers, not the generals and the admirals. I don't say they make war, but when war is made they are the spirit of it, because, more than men, they love their homes. There is not a woman in Germany who will not send forth brother and husband and father and child, should the day come. But it will not come from our seeking."

He turned to Michael, his face illuminated by the red glow of the sinking sun.

"Germany will rise as one man if she's told to," he said, "for that is what her unity and her discipline mean. She is patient and peaceful, but she is obedient."

He pointed northwards.

"It is from there, from Prussia, from Berlin," he said, "that the word will come, if they who rule and govern us, and in whose hands are all organisation and equipment, tell us that our national existence compels us to fight. They rule. The Prussians rule; there is no doubt of that. From Germany have come the arts, the sciences, the philosophies of the world, and not from there. But they guard our national life. It is they who watch by the Rhine for us, patient and awake. Should they beckon us one night, on some peaceful August night like this, when all seems so tranquil, so secure, we shall go. The silent beckoning finger will be obeyed from one end of the land to the other, from Poland on the east to France on the west."

He turned away quickly.

"It does not bear thinking of," he said; "and yet there are many, oh, so many, who night and day concern themselves with nothing else. Let us be English again, and not think of anything serious or unpleasant. Already, as you know, I am half English; there is something to build upon. Ah, and this is the sentimental hour, just when the sun begins to touch the horizon line of the stale, weary old earth and turns it into rosy gold and heals its troubles and its weariness. Schon, Schon!"

He stood for a moment bareheaded to the breeze, and made a great florid salutation to the sun, now only half-disk above the horizon.

"There! I have said my evensong," he remarked, "like a good German, who always and always is ridiculous to the whole world, except those who are German also. Oh, I can see how we look to the rest of the world so well. Beer mug in one hand, and mouth full of sausage and song, and with the other hand, perhaps, fingering a revolver. How unreal it must seem to you, how affected, and yet how, in truth, you miss it all. Scratch a Russian, they say, and you find a Tartar; but scratch a German and you find two things—a sentimentalist and a soldier. Lieber Gott! No, I will say, Good God! I am English again, and if you scratch me you will find a golf ball."

He took Michael's arm again.

"Well, we've spent one day together," he said, "and now we know something of who we are. I put this day in the bank; it's mine or yours or both of ours. I won't tell you how I've enjoyed it, or you will say that I have enjoyed it because I have talked almost all the time. But since it's the sentimental hour I will tell you that you mistake. I have enjoyed it because I believe I have found a friend."

CHAPTER V

Hermann Falbe had just gone back to his lodgings at the end of the Richard Wagner Strasse late on the night of their last day at Baireuth, and Michael, who had leaned out of his window to remind him of the hour of their train's departure the next morning, turned back into the room to begin his packing. That was not an affair that would take much time, but since, on this sweltering August night, it would certainly be a process that involved the production of much heat, he made ready for bed first, and went about his preparations in pyjamas. The work of dropping things into a bag was soon over, and finding it impossible to entertain the idea of sleep, he drew one of the stiff, plush-covered arm-chairs to the window and slipped the rein from his thoughts, letting them gallop where they pleased.

In all his life he had never experienced so much sheer emotion as the last week had held for him. He had enjoyed his first taste of liberty; he had stripped himself naked to music; he had found a friend. Any one of these would have been sufficient to saturate him, and they had all, in the decrees of Fate, come together. His life hitherto had been like some dry sponge, dusty and crackling; now it was plunged in the waters of three seas, all incomparably sweet.

He had gained his liberty, and in that process he had forgotten about himself, the self which up till now had been so intolerable a burden. At school, and even before, when first the age of self- consciousness dawned upon him, he had seen himself as he believed others saw him—a queer, awkward, ill-made boy, slow at his work, shy with his fellows, incapable at games. Walled up in this fortress of himself, this gloomy and forbidding fastness, he had altogether failed to find the means of access to others, both to the normal English boys among whom his path lay, and also to his teachers, who, not unnaturally, found him sullen and unresponsive. There was no key among the rather limited bunches at their command which unlocked him, nor at home had anything been found which could fit his wards. It had been the business of school to turn out boys of certain received types. There was the clever boy, the athletic boy, the merely pleasant boy; these and the combinations arrived at from these types were the output. There was no use for others.

Then had succeeded those three nightmare years in the Guards, where, with his more mature power of observation, he had become more actively conscious of his inability to take his place on any of the recognised platforms. And all the time, like an owl on his solitary perch, he had gazed out lonelily, while the other birds of day, too polite to mock him, had merely passed him by. One such, it is true—his cousin—had sat by him, and the poor owl's heart had gone out to him. But even Francis, so he saw now, had not understood. He had but accepted the fact of him without repugnance, had been fond of him as a queer sort of kind elder cousin.

Then there was Aunt Barbara. Aunt Barbara, Michael allowed, had understood a good deal; she had pointed out with her unerringly humourous finger the obstacles he had made for himself.

But could Aunt Barbara understand the rapture of living which this one week of liberty had given him? That Michael doubted. She had only pointed out the disabilities he made for himself. She did not know what he was capable of in the way of happiness. But he thought, though without self-consciousness, how delightful it would be to show himself, the new, unshelled self, to Aunt Barbara again.

A laughing couple went tapping down the street below his window, boy and girl, with arms and waists interlaced. They were laughing at nothing at all, except that they were boy and girl together and it was all glorious fun. But the sight of them gave Michael a sudden spasm of envy. With all this enlightenment that had come to him during this last week, there had come no gleam of what that simplest and commonest aspect of human nature meant. He had never felt towards a girl what that round-faced German boy felt. He was not sure, but he thought he disliked girls; they meant nothing to him, anyhow, and the mere thought of his arm round a girl's waist only suggested a very embarrassing attitude. He had nothing to say to them, and the knowledge of his inability filled him with an uncomfortable sense of his want of normality, just as did the consciousness of his long arms and stumpy legs.

There was a night he remembered when Francis had insisted that he should go with him to a discreet little supper party after an evening at the music-hall. There were just four of them—he, Francis, and two companions—and he played the role of sour gooseberry to his cousin, who, with the utmost gaiety, had proved himself completely equal to the inauspicious occasion, and had drank indiscriminately out of both the girls' glasses, and lit cigarettes for them; and, after seeing them both home, had looked in on Michael, and gone into fits of laughter at his general incompatibility.

The steps and conversation passed round the corner, and Michael, stretching his bare toes on to the cool balcony, resumed his researches—those joyful, unegoistic researches into himself. His liberty was bound up with his music; the first gave the key to the second. Often as he had rested, so to speak, in oases of music in London, they were but a pause from the desert of his uncongenial life into the desert again. But now the desert was vanished, and the oasis stretched illimitable to the horizon in front of him. That was where, for the future, his life was to be passed, not idly, sitting under trees, but in the eager pursuit of its unnumbered paths. It was that aspect of it which, as he knew so well, his father, for instance, would never be able to understand. To Lord Ashbridge's mind, music was vaguely connected with white waistcoats and opera glasses and large pink carnations; he was congenitally incapable of viewing it in any other light than a diversion, something that took place between nine and eleven o'clock in the evening, and in smaller quantities at church on Sunday morning. He would undoubtedly have said that Handel's Messiah was the noblest example of music in the world, because of its subject; music did not exist for him as a separate, definite and infinite factor of life; and since it did not so exist for himself, he could not imagine it existing for anybody else. That Michael correctly knew to be his father's general demeanour towards life; he wanted everybody in their respective spheres to be like what he was in his. They must take their part, as he undoubtedly did, in the Creation-scheme when the British aristocracy came into being.

A fresh factor had come into Michael's conception of music during these last seven days. He had become aware that Germany was music. He had naturally known before that the vast proportion of music came from Germany, that almost all of that which meant "music" to him was of German origin; but that was a very different affair from the conviction now borne in on his mind that there was not only no music apart from Germany, but that there was no Germany apart from music.

But every moment he spent in this wayside puddle of a town (for so Baireuth seemed to an unbiased view), he became more and more aware that music beat in the German blood even as sport beat in the blood of his own people. During this festival week Baireuth existed only because of that; at other times Baireuth was probably as non- existent as any dull and minor town in the English Midlands. But, owing to the fact of music being for these weeks resident in Baireuth, the sordid little townlet became the capital of the huge, patient Empire. It existed just now simply for that reason; to- night, with the curtain of the last act of Parsifal, it had ceased to exist again. It was not that a patriotic desire to honour one of the national heroes in the home where he had been established by the mad genius of a Bavarian king that moved them; it was because for the moment that Baireuth to Germans meant Germany. From Berlin, from Dresden, from Frankfurt, from Luxemburg, from a hundred towns those who were most typically German, whether high or low, rich or poor, made their joyous pilgrimage. Joy and solemnity, exultation and the yearning that could never be satisfied drew them here. And even as music was in Michael's heart, so Germany was there also. They were the people who understood; they did not go to the opera as a be-diamonded interlude between a dinner and a dance; they came to this dreadful little town, the discomforts of which, the utter provinciality of which was transformed into the air of the heavenly Jerusalem, as Hermann Falbe had said, because their souls were fed here with wine and manna. He would find the same thing at Munich, so Falbe had told him, the next week.

The loves and the tragedies of the great titanic forces that saw the making of the world; the dreams and the deeds of the masters of Nuremberg; above all, sacrifice and enlightenment and redemption of the soul; how, except by music, could these be made manifest? It was the first and only and final alchemy that could by its magic transformation give an answer to the tremendous riddles of consciousness; that could lift you, though tearing and making mincemeat of you, to the serenity of the Pisgah-top, whence was seen the promised land. It, in itself, was reality; and the door- keeper who admitted you into that enchanted realm was the spirit of Germany. Not France, with its little, morbid shiverings, and its meat-market called love; not Italy, with its melodious declamations and tawdry tunes; not Russia even, with the wind of its impenetrable winters, its sense of joys snatched from its eternal frosts gave admittance there; but Germany, "deep, patient Germany," that sprang from upland hamlets, and flowed down with ever-broadening stream into the illimitable ocean.

Here, then, were two of the initiations that had come, with the swiftness of the spate in Alpine valleys at the melting of the snow, upon Michael; his own liberty, namely, and this new sense of music. He had groped, he felt now, like a blind man in that direction, guided only by his instinct, and on a sudden the scales had fallen from his eyes, and he knew that his instinct had guided him right. But not less epoch-making had been the dawn of friendship. Throughout the week his intimacy with Hermann Falbe had developed, shooting up like an aloe flower, and rising into sunlight above the mists of his own self-occupied shyness, which had so darkly beset him all life long. He had given the best that he knew of himself to his cousin, but all the time there had never quite been absent from his mind his sense of inferiority, a sort of aching wonder why he could not be more like Francis, more careless, more capable of enjoyment, more of a normal type. But with Falbe he was able for the first time to forget himself altogether; he had met a man who did not recall him to himself, but took him clean out of that tedious dwelling which he knew so well and, indeed, disliked so much. He was rid for the first time of his morbid self-consciousness; his anchor had been taken up from its dragging in the sand, and he rode free, buoyed on waters and taken by tides. It did not occur to him to wonder whether Falbe thought him uncouth and awkward; it did not occur to him to try to be pleasant, a job over which poor Michael had so often found himself dishearteningly incapable; he let himself be himself in the consciousness that this was sufficient.

They had spent the morning together before this second performance of Parsifal that closed their series, in the woods above the theatre, and Michael, no longer blurting out his speeches, but speaking in the quiet, orderly manner in which he thought, discussed his plans.

"I shall come back to London with you after Munich," he said, "and settle down to study. I do know a certain amount about harmony already; I have been mugging it up for the last three years. But I must do something as well as learn something, and, as I told you, I'm going to take up the piano seriously."

Falbe was not attending particularly.

"A fine instrument, the piano," he remarked. "There is certainly something to be done with a piano, if you know how to do it. I can strum a bit myself. Some keys are harder than others—the black notes."

"Yes; what of the black notes?" asked Michael.

"Oh! they're black. The rest are white. I beg your pardon!"

Michael laughed.

"When you have finished drivelling," he said, "you might let me know."

"I have finished drivelling, Michael. I was thinking about something else."

"Not really?"

"Really."

"Then it was impolite of you, but you haven't any manners. I was talking about my career. I want to do something, and these large hands are really rather nimble. But I must be taught. The question is whether you will teach me."

Falbe hesitated.

"I can't tell you," he said, "till I have heard you play. It's like this: I can't teach you to play unless you know how, and I can't tell if you know how until I have heard you. If you have got that particular sort of temperament that can put itself into the notes out of the ends of your fingers, I can teach you, and I will. But if you haven't, I shall feel bound to advise you to try the Jew's harp, and see if you can get it out of your teeth. I'm not mocking you; I fancy you know that. But some people, however keenly and rightly they feel, cannot bring their feelings out through their fingers. Others can; it is a special gift. If you haven't got it, I can't teach you anything, and there is no use in wasting your time and mine. You can teach yourself to be frightfully nimble with your fingers, and all the people who don't know will say: 'How divinely Lord Comber plays! That sweet thing; is it Brahms or Mendelssohn?' But I can't really help you towards that; you can do that for yourself. But if you've got the other, I can and will teach you all that you really know already."

"Go on!" said Michael.

"That's just the devil with the piano," said Falbe. "It's the easiest instrument of all to make a show on, and it is the rarest sort of person who can play on it. That's why, all those years, I have hated giving lessons. If one has to, as I have had to, one must take any awful miss with a pigtail, and make a sham pianist of her. One can always do that. But it would be waste of time for you and me; you wouldn't want to be made a sham pianist, and simply I wouldn't make you one."

Michael turned round.

"Good Lord!" he said, "the suspense is worse than I can bear. Isn't there a piano in your room? Can't we go down there, and have it over?"

"Yes, if you wish. I can tell at once if you are capable of playing—at least, whether I think you are capable of playing— whether I can teach you."

"But I haven't touched a piano for a week," said Michael.

"It doesn't matter whether you've touched a piano for a year."

Michael had not been prevented by the economy that made him travel second-class from engaging a carriage by the day at Baireuth, since that clearly was worth while, and they found it waiting for them by the theatre. There was still time to drive to Falbe's lodging and get through this crucial ordeal before the opera, and they went straight there. A very venerable instrument, which Falbe had not yet opened, stood against the wall, and he struck a few notes on it.

"Completely out of tune," he said; "but that doesn't matter. Now then!"

"But what am I to play?" asked Michael.

"Anything you like."

He sat down at the far end of the room, put his long legs up on to another chair and waited. Michael sent a despairing glance at that gay face, suddenly grown grim, and took his seat. He felt a paralysing conviction that Falbe's judgment, whatever that might turn out to be, would be right, and the knowledge turned his fingers stiff. From the few notes that Falbe had struck he guessed on what sort of instrument his ordeal was to take place, and yet he knew that Falbe himself would have been able to convey to him the sense that he could play, though the piano was all out of tune, and there might be dumb, disconcerting notes in it. There was justice in Falbe's dictum about the temperament that lay behind the player, which would assert itself through any faultiness of instrument, and through, so he suspected, any faultiness of execution.

He struck a chord, and heard it jangle dissonantly.

"Oh, it's not fair," he said.

"Get on!" said Falbe.

In spite of Germany there occurred to Michael a Chopin prelude, at which he had worked a little during the last two months in London. The notes he knew perfectly; he had believed also that he had found a certain conception of it as a whole, so that he could make something coherent out of it, not merely adding bar to correct bar. And he began the soft repetition of chord-quavers with which it opened.

Then after stumbling wretchedly through two lines of it, he suddenly forgot himself and Falbe, and the squealing unresponsive notes. He heard them no more, absorbed in the knowledge of what he meant by them, of the mood which they produced in him. His great, ungainly hands had all the gentleness and self-control that strength gives, and the finger-filling chords were as light and as fine as the settling of some poised bird on a bough. In the last few lines of the prelude a deep bass note had to be struck at the beginning of each bar; this Michael found was completely dumb, but so clear and vivid was the effect of it in his mind that he scarcely noticed that it returned no answer to his finger. . . . At the end he sat without moving, his hands dropped on to his knees.

Falbe got up and, coming over to the piano, struck the bass note himself.

"Yes, I knew it was dumb," he said, "but you made me think it wasn't. . . . You got quite a good tone out of it."

He paused a moment, again striking the dumb note, as if to make sure that it was soundless.

"Yes; I'll teach you," he said. "All the technique you have got, you know, is wrong from beginning to end, and you mustn't mind unlearning all that. But you've got the thing that matters."

All this stewed and seethed in Michael's mind as he sat that night by the window looking out on to the silent and empty street. His thoughts flowed without check or guide from his will, wandering wherever their course happened to take them, now lingering, like the water of a river in some deep, still pool, when he thought of the friendship that had come into his life, now excitedly plunging down the foam of swift-flowing rapids in the exhilaration of his newly-found liberty, now proceeding with steady current at the thought of the weeks of unremitting industry at a beloved task that lay in front of him. He could form no definite image out of these which should represent his ordinary day; it was all lost in a bright haze through which its shape was but faintly discernible; but life lay in front of him with promise, a thing to be embraced and greeted with welcome and eager hands, instead of being a mere marsh through which he had to plod with labouring steps, a business to be gone about without joy and without conviction in its being worth while.

He wondered for a moment, as he rose to go to bed, what his feelings would have been if, at the end of his performance on the sore-throated and voiceless piano, Falbe had said: "I'm sorry, but I can't do anything with you." As he knew, Falbe intended for the future only to take a few pupils, and chiefly devote himself to his own practice with a view to emerging as a concert-giver the next winter; and as Michael had sat down, he remembered telling himself that there was really not the slightest chance of his friend accepting him as a pupil. He did not intend that this rejection should make the smallest difference to his aim, but he knew that he would start his work under the tremendous handicap of Falbe not believing that he had it in him to play, and under the disappointment of not enjoying the added intimacy which work with and for Falbe would give him. Then he had engaged in this tussle with refractory notes till he quite lost himself in what he was playing, and thought no more either of Falbe or the piano, but only of what the melody meant to him. But at the end, when he came to himself again, and sat with dropped hands waiting for Falbe's verdict, he remembered how his heart seemed to hang poised until it came. He had rehearsed again to himself his fixed determination that he would play and could play, whatever his friend might think about it; but there was no doubt that he waited with a greater suspense than he had ever known in his life before for that verdict to be made known to him.

Next day came their journey to Munich, and the installation in the best hotel in Europe. Here Michael was host, and the economy which he practised when he had only himself to provide for, and which made him go second-class when travelling, was, as usual, completely abandoned now that the pleasure of hospitality was his. He engaged at once the best double suite of rooms that the hotel contained, two bedrooms with bathrooms, and an admirable sitting-room, looking spaciously out on to the square, and with brusque decision silenced Falbe's attempted remonstrance. "Don't interfere with my show, please," he had said, and proceeded to inquire about a piano to be sent in for the week. Then he turned to his friend again. "Oh, we are going to enjoy ourselves," he said, with an irresistible sincerity.

Tristan und Isolde was given on the third day of their stay there, and Falbe, reading the morning German paper, found news.

"The Kaiser has arrived," he said. "There's a truce in the army manoeuvres for a couple of days, and he has come to be present at Tristan this evening. He's travelled three hundred miles to get here, and will go back to-morrow. The Reise-Kaiser, you know."

Michael looked up with some slight anxiety.

"Ought I to write my name or anything?" he asked. "He has stayed several times with my father."

"Has he? But I don't suppose it matters. The visit is a widely- advertised incognito. That's his way. God be with the All- highest," he added.

"Well, I shan't" said Michael. "But it would shock my father dreadfully if he knew. The Kaiser looks on him as the type and model of the English nobleman."

Michael crunched one of the inimitable breakfast rusks in his teeth.

"Lord, what a day we had when he was at Ashbridge last year," he said. "We began at eight with a review of the Suffolk Yeomanry; then we had a pheasant shoot from eleven till three; then the Emperor had out a steam launch and careered up and down the river till six, asking a thousand questions about the tides and the currents and the navigable channels. Then he lectured us on the family portraits till dinner; after dinner there was a concert, at which he conducted the 'Song to Aegir,' and then there was a torch- light fandango by the tenants on the lawn. He was on his holiday, you must remember."

"I heard the 'Song to Aegir' once," remarked Falbe, with a perfectly level intonation.

"I was—er—luckier," said Michael politely, "because on that occasion I heard it twice. It was encored."

"And what did it sound like the second time?" asked Falbe.

"Much as before," said Michael.

The advent of the Emperor had put the whole town in a ferment. Though the visit was quite incognito, an enormous military staff which had been poured into the town might have led the thoughtful to suspect the Kaiser's presence, even if it had not been announced in the largest type in the papers, and marchings and counter- marchings of troops and sudden bursts of national airs proclaimed the august presence. He held an informal review of certain Bavarian troops not out for manoeuvres in the morning, visited the sculpture gallery and pinacothek in the afternoon, and when Hermann and Michael went up to the theatre they found rows of soldiers drawn up, and inside unusual decorations over a section of stalls which had been removed and was converted into an enormous box. This was in the centre of the first tier, nearly at right angles to where they sat, in the front row of the same tier; and when, with military punctuality, the procession of uniforms, headed by the Emperor, filed in, the whole of the crowded house stood up and broke into a roar of recognition and loyalty.

For a minute, or perhaps more, the Emperor stood facing the house with his hand raised in salute, a figure the uprightness of which made him look tall. His brilliant uniform was ablaze with decorations; he seemed every inch a soldier and a leader of men. For that minute he stood looking neither to the right nor left, stern and almost frowning, with no shadow of a smile playing on the tightly-drawn lips, above which his moustache was brushed upwards in two stiff protuberances towards his eyes. He was there just then not to see, but to be seen, his incognito was momentarily in abeyance, and he stood forth the supreme head of his people, the All-highest War Lord, who had come that day from the field, to which he would return across half Germany tomorrow. It was an impressive and dignified moment, and Michael heard Falbe say to himself: "Kaiserlich! Kaiserlich!"

Then it was over. The Emperor sat down, beckoned to two of his officers, who had stood in a group far at the back of the box, to join him, and with one on each side he looked about the house and chatted to them. He had taken out his opera-glass, which he adjusted, using his right hand only, and looked this way and that, as if, incognito again, he was looking for friends in the house. Once Michael thought that he looked rather long and fixedly in his direction, and then, putting down his glass, he said something to one of the officers, this time clearly pointing towards Michael. Then he gave some signal, just raising his hand towards the orchestra, and immediately the lights were put down, the whole house plunged in darkness, except where the lamps in the sunk orchestra faintly illuminated the base of the curtain, and the first longing, unsatisfied notes of the prelude began.

The next hour passed for Michael in one unbroken mood of absorption. The supreme moment of knowing the music intimately and of never having seen the opera before was his, and all that he had dreamed of or imagined as to the possibilities of music was flooded and drowned in the thing itself. You could not say that it was more gigantic than The Ring, more human than the Meistersingers, more emotional than Parsifal, but it was utterly and wholly different to anything else he had ever seen or conjectured. Falbe, he himself, the thronged and silent theatre, the Emperor, Munich, Germany, were all blotted out of his consciousness. He just watched, as if discarnate, the unrolling of the decrees of Fate which were to bring so simple and overpowering a tragedy on the two who drained the love-potion together. And at the end he fell back in his seat, feeling thrilled and tired, exhilarated and exhausted.

"Oh, Hermann," he said, "what years I've wasted!"

Falbe laughed.

"You've wasted more than you know yet," he said. "Hallo!"

A very resplendent officer had come clanking down the gangway next them. He put his heels together and bowed.

"Lord Comber, I think?" he said in excellent English.

Michael roused himself.

"Yes?" he said.

"His Imperial Majesty has done me the honour to desire you to come and speak to him," he said.

"Now?" said Michael.

"If you will be so good," and he stood aside for Michael to pass up the stairs in front of him.

In the wide corridor behind he joined him again.

"Allow me to introduce myself as Count von Bergmann," he said, "and one of His Majesty's aides-de-camp. The Kaiser always speaks with great pleasure of the visits he has paid to your father, and he saw you immediately he came into the theatre. If you will permit me, I would advise you to bow, but not very low, respecting His Majesty's incognito, to seat yourself as soon as he desires it, and to remain till he gives you some speech of dismissal. Forgive me for going in front of you here. I have to introduce you to His Majesty's presence."

Michael followed him down the steps to the front of the box.

"Lord Comber, All-highest," he said, and instantly stood back.

The Emperor rose and held out his hand, and Michael, bowing over it as he took it, felt himself seized in the famous grip of steel, of which its owner as well as its recipient was so conscious.

"I am much pleased to see you, Lord Comber," said he. "I could not resist the pleasure of a little chat with you about our beloved England. And your excellent father, how is he?"

He indicated a chair to Michael, who, as advised, instantly took it, though the Emperor remained a moment longer standing.

"I left him in very good health, Your Majesty," said Michael.

"Ah! I am glad to hear it. I desire you to convey to him my friendliest greetings, and to your mother also. I well remember my last visit to his house above the tidal estuary at Ashbridge, and I hope it may not be very long before I have the opportunity to be in England again."

He spoke in a voice that seemed rather hoarse and tired, but his manner expressed the most courteous cordiality. His face, which had been as still as a statue's when he showed himself to the house, was now never in repose for a moment. He kept turning his head, which he carried very upright, this way and that as he spoke; now he would catch sight of someone in the audience to whom he directed his glance, now he would peer over the edge of the low balustrade, now look at the group of officers who stood apart at the back of the box.

His whole demeanour suggested a nervous, highly-strung condition; the restlessness of it was that of a man overstrained, who had lost the capability of being tranquil. Now he frowned, now he smiled, but never for a moment was he quiet. Then he launched a perfect hailstorm of questions at Michael, to the answers to which (there was scarcely time for more than a monosyllable in reply) he listened with an eager and a suspicious attention. They were concerned at first with all sorts of subjects: inquired if Michael had been at Baireuth, what he was going to do after the Munich festival was over, if he had English friends here. He inquired Falbe's name, looked at him for a moment through his glasses, and desired to know more about him. Then, learning he was a teacher of the piano in England, and had a sister who sang, he expressed great satisfaction.

"I like to see my subjects, when there is no need for their services at home," he said, "learning about other lands, and bringing also to other lands the culture of the Fatherland, even as it always gives me pleasure to see the English here, strengthening by the study of the arts the bonds that bind our two great nations together. You English must learn to understand us and our great mission, just as we must learn to understand you."

Then the questions became more specialised, and concerned the state of things in England. He laughed over the disturbances created by the Suffragettes, was eager to hear what politicians thought about the state of things in Ireland, made specific inquiries about the Territorial Force, asked about the Navy, the state of the drama in London, the coal strike which was threatened in Yorkshire. Then suddenly he put a series of personal questions.

"And you, you are in the Guards, I think?" he said.

"No, sir; I have just resigned my commission," said Michael.

"Why? Why is that? Have many of your officers been resigning?"

"I am studying music, Your Majesty," said Michael.

"I am glad to see you came to Germany to do it. Berlin? You ought to spend a couple of months in Berlin. Perhaps you are thinking of doing so."

He turned round quickly to one of his staff who had approached him.

"Well, what is it?" he said.

Count von Bergmann bowed low.

"The Herr-Director," he said, "humbly craves to know whether it is Your Majesty's pleasure that the opera shall proceed."

The Kaiser laughed.

"There, Lord Comber," he said, "you see how I am ordered about. They wish to cut short my conversation with you. Yes, Bergmann, we will go on. You will remain with me, Lord Comber, for this act."

Immediately after the lights were lowered again, the curtain rose, and a most distracting hour began for Michael. His neighbour was never still for a single moment. Now he would shift in his chair, now with his hand he would beat time on the red velvet balustrade in front of him, and a stream of whispered appreciation and criticism flowed from him.

"They are taking the opening scene a little too slow," he said. "I shall call the director's attention to that. But that crescendo is well done; yes, that is most effective. The shawl—observe the beautiful lines into which the shawl falls as she waves it. That is wonderful—a very impressive entry. Ah, but they should not cross the stage yet; it is more effective if they remain longer there. Brangane sings finely; she warns them that the doom is near."

He gave a little giggle, which reminded Michael of his father.

"Brangane is playing gooseberry, as you say in England," he said. "A big gooseberry, is she not? Ah, bravo! bravo! Wunderschon! Yes, enter King Mark from his hunting. Very fine. Say I was particularly pleased with the entry of King Mark, Bergmann. A wonderful act! Wagner never touched greater heights."

At the end the Emperor rose and again held out his hand.

"I am pleased to have seen you, Lord Comber," he said. "Do not forget my message to your father; and take my advice and come to Berlin in the winter. We are always pleased to see the English in Germany."

As Michael left the box he ran into the Herr-Director, who had been summoned to get a few hints.

He went back to join Falbe in a state of republican irritation, which the honour that had been done him did not at all assuage. There was an hour's interval before the third act, and the two drove back to their hotel to dine there. But Michael found his friend wholly unsympathetic with his chagrin. To him, it was quite clear, the disappointment of not having been able to attend very closely to the second act of Tristan was negligible compared to the cause that had occasioned it. It was possible for the ordinary mortal to see Tristan over and over again, but to converse with the Kaiser was a thing outside the range of the average man. And again in this interval, as during the act itself, Michael was bombarded with questions. What did the Kaiser say? Did he remember Ashbridge? Did Michael twice receive the iron grip? Did the All-highest say anything about the manoeuvres? Did he look tired, or was it only the light above his head that made him appear so haggard? Even his opinion about the opera was of interest. Did he express approval?

This was too much for Michael.

"My dear Hermann," he said, "we alluded very cautiously to the 'Song to Aegir' this morning, and delicately remarked that you had heard it once and I twice. How can you care what his opinion of this opera is?"

Falbe shook his handsome head, and gesticulated with his fine hands.

"You don't understand," he said. "You have just been talking to him himself. I long to hear his every word and intonation. There is the personality, which to us means so much, in which is summed up all Germany. It is as if I had spoken to Rule Britannia herself. Would you not be interested? There is no one in the world who is to his country what the Kaiser is to us. When you told me he had stayed at Ashbridge I was thrilled, but I was ashamed lest you should think me snobbish, which indeed I am not. But now I am past being ashamed."

He poured out a glass of wine and drank it with a "Hoch!"

"In his hand lies peace and war," he said. "It is as he pleases. The Emperor and his Chancellor can make Germany do exactly what they choose, and if the Chancellor does not agree with the Emperor, the Emperor can appoint one who does. That is what it comes to; that is why he is as vast as Germany itself. The Reichstag but advises where he is concerned. Have you no imagination, Michael? Europe lies in the hand that shook yours."

Michael laughed.

"I suppose I must have no imagination," he said. "I don't picture it even now when you point it out."

Falbe pointed an impressive forefinger.

"But for him," he said, "England and Germany would have been at each other's throats over the business at Agadir. He held the warhounds in leash—he, their master, who made them."

"Oh, he made them, anyhow," said Michael.

"Naturally. It is his business to be ready for any attack on the part of those who are jealous at our power. The whole Fatherland is a sword in his hand, which he sheathes. It would long ago have leaped from the scabbard but for him."

"Against whom?" asked Michael. "Who is the enemy?"

Falbe hesitated.

"There is no enemy at present," he said, "but the enemy potentially is any who tries to thwart our peaceful expansion."

Suddenly the whole subject tasted bitter to Michael. He recalled, instinctively, the Emperor's great curiosity to be informed on English topics by the ordinary Englishman with whom he had acquaintance.

"Oh, let's drop it," he said. "I really didn't come to Munich to talk politics, of which I know nothing whatever."

Falbe nodded.

"That is what I have said to you before," he remarked. "You are the most happy-go-lucky of the nations. Did he speak of England?"

"Yes, of his beloved England," said Michael. "He was extremely cordial about our relations."

"Good. I like that," said Falbe briskly.

"And he recommended me to spend two months in Berlin in the winter," added Michael, sliding off on to other topics.

Falbe smiled.

"I like that less," he said, "since that will mean you will not be in London."

"But I didn't commit myself," said Michael, smiling back; "though I can say 'beloved Germany' with equal sincerity."

Falbe got up.

"I would wish that—that you were Kaiser of England," he said.

"God forbid!" said Michael. "I should not have time to play the piano."

During the next day or two Michael often found himself chipping at the bed-rock, so to speak, of this conversation, and Falbe's revealed attitude towards his country and, in particular, towards its supreme head. It seemed to him a wonderful and an enviable thing that anyone could be so thoroughly English as Falbe certainly was in his ordinary, everyday life, and that yet, at the back of this there should lie so profound a patriotism towards another country, and so profound a reverence to its ruler. In his general outlook on life, his friend appeared to be entirely of one blood with himself, yet now on two or three occasions a chance spark had lit up this Teutonic beacon. To Michael this mixture of nationalities seemed to be a wonderful gift; it implied a widening of one's sympathies and outlook, a larger comprehension of life than was possible to any of undiluted blood.

For himself, like most young Englishmen of his day, he was not conscious of any tremendous sense of patriotism like this. Somewhere, deep down in him, he supposed there might be a source, a well of English waters, which some explosion in his nature might cause to flood him entirely, but such an idea was purely hypothetical; he did not, in fact, look forward to such a bouleversement as being a possible contingency. But with Falbe it was different; quite a small cause, like the sight of the Rhine at Cologne, or a Bavarian village at sunset, or the fact of a friend having talked with the Emperor, was sufficient to make his innate patriotism find outlet in impassioned speech. He wondered vaguely whether Falbe's explanation of this—namely, that nationally the English were prosperous, comfortable and insouciant—was perhaps sound. It seemed that the notion was not wholly foundationless.

CHAPTER VI

Michael had been practising all the morning of a dark November day, had eaten a couple of sandwiches standing in front of his fire, and observed with some secret satisfaction that the fog which had lifted for an hour had come down on the town again in earnest, and that it was only reasonable to dismiss the possibility of going out, and spend the afternoon as he had spent the morning. But he permitted himself a few minutes' relaxation as he smoked his cigarette, and sat down by the window, looking out, in Lucretian mood, on to the very dispiriting conditions that prevailed in the street.

Though it was still only between one and two in the afternoon, the densest gloom prevailed, so that it was impossible to see the outlines even of the houses across the street, and the only evidence that he was not in some desert spot lay in the fact of a few twinkling lights, looking incredibly remote, from the windows opposite and the gas-lamps below. Traffic seemed to be at a standstill; the accustomed roar from Piccadilly was dumb, and he looked out on to a silent and vapour-swathed world. This isolation from all his fellows and from the chances of being disturbed, it may be added, gave him a sense of extreme satisfaction. He wanted his piano, but no intrusive presence. He liked the sensation of being shut up in his own industrious citadel, secure from interruption.

During the last two months and a half since his return from Munich he had experienced greater happiness, had burned with a stronger zest for life than during the whole of his previous existence. Not only had he been working at that which he believed he was fitted for, and which gave him the stimulus which, one way or another, is essential to all good work, but he had been thrown among people who were similarly employed, with whom he had this great common ground of kinship in ambition and aim. No more were the days too long from being but half-filled with work with which he had no sympathy, and diversions that gave him no pleasure; none held sufficient hours for all that he wanted to put into it. And in this busy atmosphere, where his own studies took so much of his time and energy, and where everybody else was in some way similarly employed, that dismal self-consciousness which so drearily looked on himself shuffling along through fruitless, uncongenial days was cracking off him as the chestnut husk cracks when the kernel within swells and ripens.

Apart from his work, the centre of his life was certainly the household of the Falbes, where the brother and sister lived with their mother. She turned out to be in a rather remote manner "one of us," and had about her, very faint and dim, like an antique lavender bag, the odour of Ashbridge. She lived like the lilies of the field, without toiling or spinning, either literally or with the more figurative work of the mind; indeed, she can scarcely be said to have had any mind at all, for, as with drugs, she had sapped it away by a practically unremitting perusal of all the fiction that makes the average reader wonder why it was written. In fact, she supplied the answer to that perplexing question, since it was clearly written for her. She was not in the least excited by these tales, any more than the human race are excited by the oxygen in the air, but she could not live without them. She subscribed to three lending libraries, which, by this time had probably learned her tastes, for if she ever by ill-chance embarked on a volume which ever so faintly adumbrated the realities of life, she instantly returned it, as she found it painful; and, naturally, she did not wish to be pained. This did not, however, prevent her reading those that dealt with amiable young men who fell in love with amiable young women, and were for the moment sundered by red- haired adventuresses or black-haired moneylenders, for those she found not painful but powerful, and could often remember where she had got to in them, which otherwise was not usually the case. She wore a good deal of lace, spoke in a tired voice, and must certainly have been of the type called "sweetly pretty" some quarter of a century ago. She drank hot water with her meals, and continually reminded Michael of his own mother.

Sylvia and Hermann certainly did all that could be done for her; in other words, they invariably saw that her water was hot, and her stock of novels replenished. But when that was accomplished, there really appeared to be little more that could be done for her. Her presence in a room counted for about as much as a rather powerful shadow on the wall, unexplained by any solid object which could have made it appear there. But most of the day she spent in her own room, which was furnished exactly in accordance with her twilight existence. There was a writing-table there, which she never used, several low arm-chairs (one of which she was always using), by each of which was a small table, on to which she could put the book that she was at the moment engaged on. Lace hangings, of the sort that prevent anybody either seeing in or out, obscured the windows; and for decoration there were china figures on the chimney-piece, plush-rimmed plates on the walls, and a couple of easels, draped with chiffon, on which stood enlarged photographs of her husband and her children.

There was, it may be added, nothing in the least pathetic about her, for, as far as could be ascertained, she had everything she wanted. In fact, from the standpoint of commonsense, hers was the most successful existence; for, knowing what she liked, she passed her entire life in its accomplishment. The only thing that caused her emotion was the energy and vitality of her two children, and even then that emotion was but a mild surprise when she recollected how tremendous a worker and boisterous a gourmand of life was her late husband, on the anniversary of whose death she always sat all day without reading any novels at all, but devoted what was left of her mind to the contemplation of nothing at all. She had married him because, for some inscrutable reason, he insisted on it; and she had been resigned to his death, as to everything else that had ever happened to her.

All her life, in fact, she had been of that unchangeable, drab quality in emotional affairs which is characteristic of advanced middle-age, when there are no great joys or sorrows to look back on, and no expectation for the future. She had always had something of the indestructible quality of frail things like thistledown or cottonwool; violence and explosion that would blow strong and distinct organisms to atoms only puffed her a yard or two away where she alighted again without shock, instead of injuring or annihilating her. . . . Yet, in the inexplicable ways of love, Sylvia and her brother not only did what could be done for her, but regarded her with the tenderest affection. What that love lived on, what was its daily food would be hard to guess, were it not that love lives on itself.

The rest of the house, apart from the vacuum of Mrs. Falbe's rooms, conducted itself, so it seemed to Michael, at the highest possible pressure. Sylvia and her brother were both far too busy to be restless, and if, on the one hand, Mrs. Falbe's remote, impenetrable life was inexplicable, not less inexplicable was the rage for living that possessed the other two. From morning till night, and on Sundays from night till morning, life proceeded at top speed.

As regards household arrangements, which were all in Sylvia's hands, there were three fixed points in the day. That is to say, that there was lunch for Mrs. Falbe and anybody else who happened to be there at half-past one; tea in Mrs. Falbe's well-liked sitting-room at five, and dinner at eight. These meals—Mrs. Falbe always breakfasted in her bedroom—were served with quiet decorum. Apart from them, anybody who required anything consulted the cook personally. Hermann, for instance, would have spent the morning at his piano in the vast studio at the back of their house in Maidstone Crescent, and not arrived at the fact that it was lunch time till perhaps three in the afternoon. Unless then he settled to do without lunch altogether, he must forage for himself; or Sylvia, having to sing at a concert at eight, would return famished and exultant about ten; she would then proceed to provide herself, unless she supped elsewhere, with a plate of eggs and bacon, or anything else that was easily accessible. It was not from preference that these haphazard methods were adopted; but since they only kept two servants, it was clear that a couple of women, however willing, could not possibly cope with so irregular a commissariat in addition to the series of fixed hours and the rest of the household work. As it was, two splendidly efficient persons, one German, the other English, had filled the posts of parlourmaid and cook for the last eight years, and regarded themselves, and were regarded, as members of the family. Lucas, the parlourmaid, indeed, from the intense interest she took in the conversation at table, could not always resist joining in it, and was apt to correct Hermann or his sister if she detected an inaccuracy in their statements. "No, Miss Sylvia," she would say, "it was on Thursday, not Wednesday," and then recollecting herself, would add, "Beg your pardon, miss."

In this milieu, as new to Michael as some suddenly discovered country, he found himself at once plunged and treated with instant friendly intimacy. Hermann, so he supposed, must have given him a good character, for he was made welcome before he could have had time to make any impression for himself, as Hermann's friend. On the first occasion of his visiting the house, for the purpose of his music lesson, he had stopped to lunch afterwards, where he met Sylvia, and was in the presence of (you could hardly call it more than that) their mother.

Mrs. Falbe had faded away in some mist-like fashion soon after, but it was evident that he was intended to do no such thing, and they had gone into the studio, already comrades, and Michael had chiefly listened while the other two had violent and friendly discussions on every subject under the sun. Then Hermann happened to sit down at the piano, and played a Chopin etude pianissimo prestissimo with finger-tips that just made the notes to sound and no more, and Sylvia told him that he was getting it better; and then Sylvia sang "Who is Sylvia?" and Hermann told her that she shouldn't have eaten so much lunch, or shouldn't have sung; and then, by transitions that Michael could not recollect, they played the Hailstone Chorus out of Israel in Egypt (or, at any rate, reproduced the spirit of it), and both sang at the top of their voices. Then, as usually happened in the afternoon, two or three friends dropped in, and though these were all intimate with their hosts, Michael had no impression of being out in the cold or among strangers. And when he left he felt as if he had been stretching out chilly hands to the fire, and that the fire was always burning there, ready for him to heat himself at, with its welcoming flames and core of sincere warmth, whenever he felt so disposed.

At first he had let himself do this much less often than he would have liked, for the shyness of years, his over-sensitive modesty at his own want of charm and lightness, was a self-erected barrier in his way. He was, in spite of his intimacy with Hermann, desperately afraid of being tiresome, of checking by his presence, as he had so often felt himself do before, the ease and high spirits of others. But by degrees this broke down; he realised that he was now among those with whom he had that kinship of the mind and of tastes which makes the foundation on which friendship, and whatever friendship may ripen into, is securely built. Never did the simplicity and sincerity of their welcome fail; the cordiality which greeted him was always his; he felt that it was intended that he should be at home there just as much as he cared to be.

The six working days of the week, however, were as a rule too full both for the Falbes and for Michael to do more than have, apart from the music lessons, flying glimpses of each other; for the day was taken up with work, concerts and opera occurred often in the evening, and the shuttles of London took their threads in divergent directions. But on Sunday the house at Maidstone Crescent ceased, as Hermann said, to be a junction, and became a temporary terminus.

"We burst from our chrysalis, in fact," he said. "If you find it clearer to understand this way, we burst from our chrysalis and become a caterpillar. Do chrysalides become caterpillars! We do, anyhow. If you come about eight you will find food; if you come later you will also find food of a sketchier kind. People have a habit of dropping in on Sunday evening. There's music if anyone feels inclined to make any, and if they don't they are made to. Some people come early, others late, and they stop to breakfast if they wish. It's a gaudeamus, you know, a jolly, a jamboree. One has to relax sometimes."

Michael felt all his old unfitness for dreadful crowds return to him.

"Oh, I'm so bad at that sort of thing," he said. "I am a frightful kill-joy, Hermann."

Hermann sat down on the treble part of his piano.

"That's the most conceited thing I've heard you say yet," he remarked. "Nobody will pay any attention to you; you won't kill anybody's joy. Also it's rather rude of you."

"I didn't mean to be rude," said Michael.

"Then we must suppose you were rude by accident. That is the worst sort of rudeness."

"I'm sorry; I'll come," said Michael.

"That's right. You might even find yourself enjoying it by accident, you know. If you don't, you can go away. There's music; Sylvia sings quite seriously sometimes, and other people sing or bring violins, and those who don't like it, talk—and then we get less serious. Have a try, Michael. See if you can't be less serious, too."

Michael slipped despairingly from his seat.

"If only I knew how!" he said. "I believe my nurse never taught me to play, only to remember that I was a little gentleman. All the same, when I am with you, or with my cousin Francis, I can manage it to a certain extent."

Falbe looked at him encouragingly.

"Oh, you're getting on," he said. "You take yourself more for granted than you used to. I remember you when you used to be polite on purpose. It's doing things on purpose that makes one serious. If you ever play the fool on purpose, you instantly cease playing the fool."

"Is that it?" said Michael.

"Yes, of course. So come on Sunday, and forget all about it, except coming. And now, do you mind going away? I want to put in a couple of hours before lunch. You know what to practise till Tuesday, don't you?"

That was the first Sunday evening that Michael had spent with his friends; after that, up till this present date in November, he had not missed a single one of those gatherings. They consisted almost entirely of men, and of the men there were many types, and many ages. Actors and artists, musicians and authors were indiscriminately mingled; it was the strangest conglomeration of diverse interests. But one interest, so it seemed to Michael, bound them all together; they were all doing in their different lives the things they most delighted in doing. There was the key that unlocked all the locks—namely, the enjoyment that inspired their work. The freemasonry of art and the freemasonry of the eager mind that looks out without verdict, but with only expectation and delight in experiment, passed like an open secret among them, secret because none spoke of it, open because it was so transparently obvious. And since this was so, every member of that heterogeneous community had a respect for his companions; the fact that they were there together showed that they had all passed this initiation, and knew what for them life meant.

Very soon after dinner all sitting accommodation, other than the floor, was occupied; but then the floor held the later comers, and the smoke from many cigarettes and the babble of many voices made a constantly-ascending incense before the altar dedicated to the gods that inspire all enjoyable endeavour. Then Sylvia sang, and both those who cared to hear exquisite singing and those who did not were alike silent, for this was a prayer to the gods they all worshipped; and Falbe played, and there was a quartet of strings.

After that less serious affairs held the rooms; an eminent actor was pleased to parody another eminent actor who was also present. This led to a scene in which each caricatured the other, and a French poet did gymnastic feats on the floor and upset a tray of soda-water, and a German conductor fluffed out his hair and died like Marguerite. And when in the earlier hours of the morning part of the guests had gone away, and part were broiling ham in the kitchen, Sylvia sang again, quite seriously, and Michael, in Hermann's absence, volunteered to play her accompaniment for her. She stood behind him, and by a finger on his shoulder directed him in the way she would have him go. Michael found himself suddenly and inexplicably understanding this; her finger, by its pressure or its light tapping, seemed to him to speak in a language that he found himself familiar with, and he slowed down stroking the notes, or quickened with staccato touch, as she wordlessly directed him.

Out of all these things, which were but trivialities, pleasant, unthinking hours for all else concerned, several points stood out for Michael, points new and illuminating. The first was the simplicity of it all, the spontaneousness with which pleasure was born if only you took off your clothes, so to speak, and left them on the bank while you jumped in. All his life he had buttoned his jacket and crammed his hat on to his head. The second was the sense, indefinable but certain, that Hermann and Sylvia between them were the high priests of this memorable orgie.

He himself had met, at dreadful, solemn evenings when Lady Ashbridge and his father stood at the head of the stairs, the two eminent actors who had romped to-night, and found them exceedingly stately personages, just as no doubt they had found him an icy and awkward young man. But they, like him, had taken their note on those different occasions from their environment. Perhaps if his father and mother came here . . . but Michael's imagination quailed before such a supposition.

The third point, which gradually through these weeks began to haunt him more and more, was the personality of Sylvia. He had never come across a girl who in the least resembled her, probably because he had not attempted even to find in a girl, or to display in himself, the signals, winked across from one to the other, of human companionship. Always he had found a difficulty in talking to a girl, because he had, in his self-consciousness, thought about what he should say.

There had been the cabalistic question of sex ever in front of him, a thing that troubled and deterred him. But Sylvia, with her hand on his shoulder, absorbed in her singing, and directing him only as she would have pressed the pedal of the piano if she had been playing to herself, was no more agitating than if she had been a man; she was just singing, just using him to help her singing. And even while Michael registered to himself this charming annihilation of sex, which allowed her to be to him no more than her brother was—less, in fact, but on the same plane— she had come to the end of her song, patted him on the back, as she would have patted anybody else, with a word of thanks, and, for him, suddenly leaped into significance. It was not only a singer who had sung, but an individual one called Sylvia Falbe. She took her place, at present a most inconspicuous one, on the back-cloth before which Michael's life was acted, towards which, when no action, so to speak, was taking place, his eyes naturally turned themselves. His father and mother were there, Francis also and Aunt Barbara, and of course, larger than the rest, Hermann. Now Sylvia was discernible, and, as the days went by and their meetings multiplied, she became bigger, walked into a nearer perspective. It did not occur to Michael, rightly, to imagine himself at all in love with her, for he was not. Only she had asserted herself on his consciousness.

Not yet had she begun to trouble him, and there was no sign, either external or intimate, in his mind that he was sickening with the splendid malady. Indeed, the significance she held for him was rather that, though she was a girl, she presented none of the embarrassments which that sex had always held for him. She grew in comradeship; he found himself as much at ease with her as with her brother, and her charm was just that which had so quickly and strongly attracted Michael to Hermann. She was vivid in the same way as he was; she had the same warm, welcoming kindliness—the same complete absence of pose. You knew where you were with her, and hitherto, when Michael was with one of the young ladies brought down to Ashbridge to be looked at, he only wished that wherever he was he was somewhere else. But with Sylvia he had none of this self-consciousness; she was bonne camarade for him in exactly the same way as she was bonne camarade to the rest of the multitude which thronged the Sunday evenings, perfectly at ease with them, as they with her, in relationship entirely unsentimental.

But through these weeks, up to this foggy November afternoon, Michael's most conscious preoccupation was his music. Falbe's principles in teaching were entirely heretical according to the traditional school; he gave Michael no scale to play, no dismal finger-exercise to fill the hours.

"What is the good of them?" he asked. "They can only give you nimbleness and strength. Well, you shall acquire your nimbleness and strength by playing what is worth playing. Take good music, take Chopin or Bach or Beethoven, and practise one particular etude or fugue or sonata; you may choose anything you like, and learn your nimbleness and strength that way. Read, too; read for a couple of hours every day. The written language of music must become so familiar to you that it is to you precisely what a book or a newspaper is, so that whether you read it aloud—which is playing—or sit in your arm-chair with your feet on the fender, reading it not aloud on the piano, but to yourself, it conveys its definite meaning to you. At your lessons you will have to read aloud to me. But when you are reading to yourself, never pass over a bar that you don't understand. It has got to sound in your head, just as the words you read in a printed book really sound in your head if you read carefully and listen for them. You know exactly what they would be like if you said them aloud. Can you read, by the way? Have a try."

Falbe got down a volume of Bach and opened it at random.

"There," he said, "begin at the top of the page."

"But I can't," said Michael. "I shall have to spell it out."

"That's just what you mustn't do. Go ahead, and don't pause till you get to the bottom of the page. Count; start each bar when it comes to its turn, and play as many notes as you can in it."

This was a dismal experience. Michael hitherto had gone on the painstaking and thorough plan of spelling out his notes with laborious care. Now Falbe's inexorable voice counted for him, until it was lost in inextinguishable laughter.

"Go on, go on!" he shouted. "I thought it was Bach, and it is clearly Strauss's Don Quixote."

Michael, flushed and determined, with grave, set mouth, ploughed his way through amazing dissonances, and at the end joined Falbe's laughter.

"Oh dear," he said. "Very funny. But don't laugh so at me, Hermann."

Falbe dried his eyes.

"And what was it?" he said. "I declare it was the fourth fugue. An entirely different conception of it! A thoroughly original view! Now, what you've got to do, is to repeat that—not the same murder I mean, but other murders—for a couple of hours a day. . . . By degrees—you won't believe it—you will find you are not murdering any longer, but only mortally wounding. After six months I dare say you won't even be hurting your victims. All the same, you can begin with less muscular ones."

In this way Michael's musical horizons were infinitely extended. Not only did this system of Falbe's of flying at new music, and going recklessly and regardlessly on, give quickness to his brain and finger, make his wits alert to pick up the new language he was learning, but it gloriously extended his vision and his range of country. He ran joyfully, though with a thousand falls and tumbles, through these new and wonderful vistas; he worshipped at the grave, Gothic sanctuaries of Beethoven, he roamed through the enchanted garden of Chopin, he felt the icy and eternal frosts of Russia, and saw in the northern sky the great auroras spread themselves in spear and sword of fire; he listened to the wisdom of Brahms, and passed through the noble and smiling country of Bach. All this, so to speak, was holiday travel, and between his journeys he applied himself with the same eager industry to the learning of his art, so that he might reproduce for himself and others true pictures of the scenes through which he scampered. Here Falbe was not so easily moved to laughter; he was as severe with Michael as he was with himself, when it was the question of learning some piece with a view to really playing it. There was no light-hearted hurrying on through blurred runs and false notes, slurred phrases and incomplete chords. Among these pieces which had to be properly learned was the 17th Prelude of Chopin, on hearing which at Baireuth on the tuneless and catarrhed piano Falbe had agreed to take Michael as a pupil. But when it was played again on Falbe's great Steinway, as a professed performance, a very different standard was required.

Falbe stopped him at the end of the first two lines.

"This won't do, Michael," he said. "You played it before for me to see whether you could play. You can. But it won't do to sketch it. Every note has got to be there; Chopin didn't write them by accident. He knew quite well what he was about. Begin again, please."

This time Michael got not quite so far, when he was stopped again. He was playing without notes, and Falbe got up from his chair where he had the book open, and put it on the piano.

"Do you find difficulty in memorising?" he asked.

This was discouraging; Michael believed that he remembered easily; he also believed that he had long known this by heart.

"No; I thought I knew it," he said.

"Try again."

This time Falbe stood by him, and suddenly put his finger down into the middle of Michael's hands, striking a note.

"You left out that F sharp," he said. "Go on. . . . Now you are leaving out that E natural. Try to get it better by Thursday, and remember this, that playing, and all that differentiates playing from strumming, only begins when you can play all the notes that are put down for you to play without fail. You're beginning at the wrong end; you have admirable feeling about that prelude, but you needn't think about feeling till you've got all the notes at your fingers' ends. Then and not till then, you may begin to remember that you want to be a pianist. Now, what's the next thing?"

Michael felt somewhat squashed and discouraged. He had thought he had really worked successfully at the thing he knew so well by sight. His heavy eyebrows drew together.

"You told me to harmonise that Christmas carol," he remarked, rather shortly.

Falbe put his hand on his shoulder.

"Look here, Michael," he said, "you're vexed with me. Now, there's nothing to be vexed at. You know quite well you were leaving out lots of notes from those jolly fat chords, and that you weren't playing cleanly. Now I'm taking you seriously, and I won't have from you anything but the best you can do. You're not doing your best when you don't even play what is written. You can't begin to work at this till you do that."

Michael had a moment's severe tussle with his temper. He felt vexed and disappointed that Hermann should have sent him back like a schoolboy with his exercise torn over. Not immediately did he confess to himself that he was completely in the wrong.

"I'm doing the best I can," he said. "It's rather discouraging."

He moved his big shoulders slightly, as if to indicate that Hermann's hand was not wanted there. Hermann kept it there.

"It might be discouraging," he said, "if you were doing your best."

Michael's ill-temper oozed from him.

"I'm wrong," he said, turning round with the smile that made his ugly face so pleasant. "And I'm sorry both that I have been slack and that I've been sulky. Will that do?"

Falbe laughed.

"Very well indeed," he said. "Now for 'Good King Wenceslas.' Wasn't it—"

"Yes; I got awfully interested over it, Hermann. I thought I would try and work it up into a few variations."

"Let's hear," said Falbe.

This was a vastly different affair. Michael had shown both ingenuity and a great sense of harmonic beauty in the arrangement of the very simple little tune that Falbe had made him exercise his ear over, and the half-dozen variations that followed showed a wonderfully mature handling. The air which he dealt with haunted them as a sort of unseen presence. It moved in a tiny gavotte, or looked on at a minuet measure; it wailed, yet without being positively heard, in a little dirge of itself; it broadened into a march, it shouted in a bravura of rapid octaves, and finally asserted itself, heard once more, over a great scale base of bells.

Falbe, as was his habit when interested, sat absolutely still, but receptive and alert, instead of jerking and fidgeting as he had done over Michael's fiasco in the Chopin prelude, and at the end he jumped up with a certain excitement.

"Do you know what you've done?" he said. "You've done something that's really good. Faults? Yes, millions; but there's a first- rate imagination at the bottom of it. How did it happen?"

Michael flushed with pleasure.

"Oh, they sang themselves," he said, "and I learned them. But will it really do? Is there anything in it?"

"Yes, old boy, there's King Wenceslas in it, and you've dressed him up well. Play that last one again."

The last one was taxing to the fingers, but Michael's big hands banged out the octave scale in the bass with wonderful ease, and Falbe gave a great guffaw of pleasure at the rollicking conclusion.

"Write them all down," he said, "and try if you can hear it singing half a dozen more. If you can, write them down also, and give me leave to play the lot at my concert in January."

Michael gasped.

"You don't mean that?" he said.

"Certainly I do. It's a fine bit of stuff."

It was with these variations, now on the point of completion that Michael meant to spend his solitary and rapturous evening. The spirits of the air— whatever those melodious sprites may be—had for the last month made themselves very audible to him, and the half-dozen further variations that Hermann had demanded had rung all day in his head. Now, as they neared completion, he found that they ceased their singing; their work of dictation was done; he had to this extent expressed himself, and they haunted him no longer. At present he had but jotted down the skeleton of bars that could be filled in afterwards, and it gave him enormous pleasure to see the roles reversed and himself out of his own brain, setting Falbe his task.

But he felt much more than this. He had done something. Michael, the dumb, awkward Michael, was somehow revealed on those eight pages of music. All his twenty-five years he had stood wistfully inarticulate, unable, so it had seemed to him, to show himself, to let himself out. And not till now, when he had found this means of access, did he know how passionately he had desired it, nor how immensely, in the process of so doing, his desire had grown. He must find out more ways, other channels of projecting himself. The need for that, as of a diver throwing himself into the empty air and the laughing waters below him, suddenly took hold of him.

He took a clean sheet of music paper, into which he placed his pages, and with a pleasurable sense of pomp wrote in the centre of it:

VARIATIONS ON AN AIR.

By

Michael Comber.

He paused a moment, then took up his pen again.
"Dedicated to Sylvia Falbe," he wrote at the top.

CHAPTER VII

Michael had been so engrossingly employed since his return to London in the autumn that the existence of other ties and other people apart from those immediately connected with his work had worn a very shadow-like aspect. He had, it is true, written with some regularity to his mother, finding, somewhat to his dismay, how very slight the common ground between them was for purposes of correspondence. He could outline the facts that he had been to several concerts, that he had seen much of his music-master, that he had been diligent at his work, but he realised that there was nothing in detail about those things that could possibly interest her, and that nothing except them really interested him. She on her side had little to say except to record the welfare of Petsy, to remark on the beauty of October, and tell him how many shooting parties they had had.

His correspondence with his father had been less frequent, and absolutely one-sided, since Lord Ashbridge took no notice at all of his letters. Michael regretted this, as showing that he was still outcast, but it cannot be said to have come between him and the sunshine, for he had begun to manufacture the sunshine within, that internal happiness which his environment and way of life produced, which seemed to be independent of all that was not directly connected with it. But a letter which he received next morning from his mother stated, in addition to the fact that Petsy had another of her tiresome bilious attacks (poor lamb), that his father and she thought it right that he should come down to Ashbridge for Christmas. It conveyed the sense that at this joyful season a truce, probably limited in duration, and, even while it lasted, of the nature of a strongly-armed neutrality, was proclaimed, but the prospect was not wholly encouraging, for Lady Ashbridge added that she hoped Michael would not "go on" vexing his father. What precisely Michael was expected to do in order to fulfil that wish was not further stated, but he wrote dutifully enough to say that he would come down at Christmas.

But the letter rekindled his dormant sense of there being other people in the world beside his immediate circle; also, indefinably, it gave him the sense that his mother wanted him. That should be so then, and sequentially he remembered with a pang of self- reproach that he had not as much as indicated his presence in London to Aunt Barbara, or set eyes on her since their meeting in August. He knew she was in London, since he had seen her name in some paragraph in the papers not long before, and instantly wrote to ask her to dine with him at a near date. Her answer was characteristic.

"Of course I'll dine with you, my dear," she wrote; "it will be delightful. And what has happened to you? Your letter actually conveyed a sense of cordiality. You never used to be cordial. And I wish to meet some of your nice friends. Ask one or two, please— a prima donna of some kind and a pianist, I think. I want them weird and original—the prima donna with short hair, and the pianist with long. In Tony's new station in life I never see anybody except the sort of people whom your father likes. Are you forgiven yet, by the way?"

Michael found himself on the grin at the thought of Aunt Barbara suddenly encountering the two magnificent Falbes (prima donna and pianist exactly as she had desired) as representing the weird sort of people whom she pictured his living among, and the result quite came up to his expectations. As usual, Aunt Barbara was late, and came in talking rapidly about the various causes that had detained her, which her fruitful imagination had suggested to her as she dressed. In order, perhaps, to suit herself to the circle in which she would pass the evening, she had put on (or, rather, it looked as if her maid had thrown at her) a very awful sort of tea-gown, brown and prickly-looking, and adapted to Bohemian circles. She, with the same lively imagination, had pictured Michael in a velveteen coat and soft shirt, the pianist as very small, with spectacles and long hair, and the prima donna a full-blown kind of barmaid with Roman pearls. . . .

"Yes, my dear, I know I am late," she began before she was inside the door, "but Og had so much to say, and there was a block at Hyde Park Corner. My dear Michael, how smart you look!"

She came round the corner of the screen and the Falbes burst upon her, Hermann and Sylvia standing by the fire. For the short, spectacled pianist there was this very tall, English-looking young man, upright and soldierly, with his handsome, boyish face and well-fitting clothes. That was bad enough, but infinitely worse was she who was to have been the full-blown barmaid. Instead was this magnificent girl, nearly as tall as her brother, with her small oval face crowning the column of her neck, her eyes merry, her mouth laughing at some brotherly retort that Hermann had just made. Aunt Barbara took her in with one second's survey—her face, her neck, her beautiful dress, her whole air of ease and good- breeding, and gave a despairing glance at her own prickly tea-gown. For the moment, amiably accustomed as she was to laugh at herself, she did not find it humourous.

"Miss Sylvia Falbe, Aunt Barbara," said Michael with a little tremor in his voice; "and Mr. Hermann Falbe, Lady Barbara Jerome," he added, rather as if he expected nobody to believe it.

Aunt Barbara made the best of it: shook hands in her jolly manner, and burst into laughter.

"Michael, I could slay you," she said; "but before I do that I must tell your friends all about it. This horrible nephew of mine, Miss Falbe, promised me two weird musicians, and I expected—I really can't tell you what I expected—but there were to be spectacles and velveteen coats and the general air of an afternoon concert at Clapham Junction. But it is nice to be made such a fool of. I feel precisely like an elderly and sour governess who has been ordered to come down to dinner so that there shan't be thirteen. Give me your arm, Mr. Falbe, and take me in to dinner at once, where I may drown my embarrassment in soup. Or does Michael go in first? Go on, wretch!"

Presently they were seated at dinner, and Aunt Barbara could not help enlarging a little on her own discomfiture.

"It is all your fault, Michael," she said. "You have been in London all these weeks without letting me know anything about you or your friends, or what you were doing; so naturally I supposed you were leading some obscure kind of existence. Instead of which I find this sort of thing. My dear, what good soup! I shall see if I can't induce your cook to leave you. But bachelors always have the best of everything. Now tell me about your visit to Germany. Which was the point where we parted—Baireuth, wasn't it? I would not go to Baireuth with anybody!"

"I went with Mr. Falbe," said Michael.

"Ah, Mr. Falbe has not asked me yet. I may have to revise what I say," said Aunt Barbara daringly.

"I didn't ask Michael," said Hermann. "I got into his carriage as the train was moving; and my luggage was left behind."

"I was left behind," said Sylvia, "which was worse. But I sent Hermann's luggage."

"So expeditiously that it arrived the day before we left for Munich," remarked Hermann.

"And that's all the gratitude I get. But in the interval you lived upon Lord Comber."

"I do still in the money I earn by giving him music lessons. Mike, have you finished the Variations yet?"

"Variations—what are Variations?" asked Aunt Barbara.

"Yes, two days ago. Variations are all the things you think about on the piano, Aunt Barbara, when you are playing a tune made by somebody else."

"Should I like them? Will Mr. Falbe play them to me?" asked she.

"I daresay he will if he can. But I thought you loathed music."

"It certainly depends on who makes it," said Aunt Barbara. "I don't like ordinary music, because the person who made it doesn't matter to me. But if, so to speak, it sounds like somebody I know, it is a different matter."

Michael turned to Sylvia.

"I want to ask your leave for something I have already done," he said.

"And if I don't give it you?"

"Then I shan't tell you what it is."

Sylvia looked at him with her candid friendly eyes. Her brother always told her that she never looked at anybody except her friends; if she was engaged in conversation with a man she did not like, she looked at his shirt-stud or at a point slightly above his head.

"Then, of course, I give in," she said. "I must give you leave if otherwise I shan't know what you have done. But it's a mean trick. Tell me at once."

"I've dedicated the Variations to you," he said.

Sylvia flushed with pleasure.

"Oh, but that's absolutely darling of you," she said. "Have you, really? Do you mean it?"

"If you'll allow me."

"Allow you? Hermann, the Variations are mine. Isn't it too lovely?"

It was at this moment that Aunt Barbara happened to glance at Michael, and it suddenly struck her that it was a perfectly new Michael whom she looked at. She knew and was secretly amused at the fiasco that always attended the introduction of amiable young ladies to Ashbridge, and had warned her sister-in-law that Michael, when he chose the girl he wanted, would certainly do it on his own initiative. Now she felt sure that Michael, though he might not be aware of it himself, was, even if he had not chosen, beginning to choose. There was that in his eyes which none of the importations to Ashbridge had ever seen there, that eager deferential attention, which shows that a young man is interested because it is a girl he is talking to. That, she knew, had never been characteristic of Michael; indeed, it would not have been far from the truth to say that the fact that he was talking to a girl was sufficient to make his countenance wear an expression of polite boredom. Then for a while, as dinner progressed, she doubted the validity of her conclusion, for the Michael who was entertaining her to-night was wholly different from the Michael she had known and liked and pitied. She felt that she did not know this new one yet, but she was certain that she liked him, and equally sure that she did not pity him at all. He had found his place, he had found his work; he evidently fitted into his life, which, after all, is the surest ground of happiness, and it might be that it was only general joy, so to speak, that kindled that pleasant fire in his face. And then once more she went back to her first conclusion, for talking to Michael herself she saw, as a woman so infallibly sees, that he gave her but the most superficial attention—sufficient, indeed, to allow him to answer intelligently and laugh at the proper places, but his mind was not in the least occupied with her. If Sylvia moved his glance flickered across in her direction: it was she who gave him his alertness. Aunt Barbara felt that she could have told him truthfully that he was in love with her, and she rather thought that it would be news to him; probably he did not know it yet himself. And she wondered what his father would say when he knew it.

"And then Munich," she said, violently recalling Michael's attention towards her. "Munich I could have borne better than Baireuth, and when Mr. Falbe asks me there I shall probably go. Your Uncle Tony was in Germany then, by the way; he went over at the invitation of the Emperor to the manoeuvres."

"Did he? The Emperor came to Munich for a day during them. He was at the opera," said Michael.

"You didn't speak to him, I suppose?" she asked.

"Yes; he sent for me, and talked a lot. In fact, he talked too much, because I didn't hear a note of the second act."

Aunt Barbara became infinitely more interested.

"Tell me all about it, Michael," she said. "What did he talk about?"

"Everything, as far as I can remember, England, Ashbridge, armies, navies, music. Hermann says he cast pearls before swine—"

"And his tone, his attitude?" she asked.

"Towards us?—towards England? Immensely friendly, and most inquisitive. I was never asked so many questions in so short a time."

Aunt Barbara suddenly turned to Falbe.

"And you?" she asked. "Were you with Michael?"

"No, Lady Barbara. I had no pearls."

"And are you naturalised English?" she asked.

"No; I am German."

She slid swiftly off the topic.

"Do you wonder I ask, with your talking English so perfectly?" she said. "You should hear me talking French when we are entertaining Ambassadors and that sort of persons. I talk it so fast that nobody can understand a word I say. That is a defensive measure, you must observe, because even if I talked it quite slowly they would understand just as little. But they think it is the pace that stupefies them, and they leave me in a curious, dazed condition. And now Miss Falbe and I are going to leave you two. Be rather a long time, dear Michael, so that Mr. Falbe can tell you what he thinks of me, and his sister shall tell me what she thinks of you. Afterwards you and I will tell each other, if it is not too fearful."

This did not express quite accurately Lady Barbara's intentions, for she chiefly wanted to find out what she thought of Sylvia.

"And you are great friends, you three?" she said as they settled themselves for the prolonged absence of the two men.

Sylvia smiled; she smiled, Aunt Barbara noticed, almost entirely with her eyes, using her mouth only when it came to laughing; but her eyes smiled quite charmingly.

"That's always rather a rash thing to pronounce on," she said. "I can tell you for certain that Hermann and I are both very fond of him, but it is presumptuous for us to say that he is equally devoted to us."

"My dear, there is no call for modesty about it," said Barbara. "Between you—for I imagine it is you who have done it—between you you have made a perfectly different creature of the boy. You've made him flower."

Sylvia became quite grave.

"Oh, I do hope he likes us," she said. "He is so likable himself."

Barbara nodded

"And you've had the good sense to find that out," she said. "It's astonishing how few people knew it. But then, as I said, Michael hadn't flowered. No one understood him, or was interested. Then he suddenly made up his mind last summer what he wanted to do and be, and immediately did and was it."

"I think he told Hermann," said she. "His father didn't approve, did he?"

"Approve? My dear, if you knew my brother you would know that the only things he approves of are those which Michael isn't."

Sylvia spread her fine hands out to the blaze, warming them and shading her face.

"Michael always seems to us—" she began. "Ah, I called him Michael by mistake."

"Then do it on purpose next time," remarked Barbara. "What does Michael seem?"

"Ah, but don't let him know I called him Michael," said Sylvia in some horror. "There is nothing so awful as to speak of people formally to their faces, and intimately behind their backs. But Hermann is always talking of him as Michael."

"And Michael always seems—"

"Oh, yes; he always seems to me to have been part of us, of Hermann and me, for years. He's THERE, if you know what I mean, and so few people are there. They walk about your life, and go in and out, so to speak, but Michael stops. I suppose it's because he is so natural."

Aunt Barbara had been a diplomatist long before her husband, and fearful of appearing inquisitive about Sylvia's impression of Michael, which she really wanted to inquire into, instantly changed the subject.

"Ah, everybody who has got definite things to do is natural," she said. "It is only the idle people who have leisure to look at themselves in the glass and pose. And I feel sure that you have definite things to do and plenty of them, my dear. What are they?"

"Oh, I sing a little," said Sylvia.

"That is the first unnatural thing you have said. I somehow feel that you sing a great deal."

Aunt Barbara suddenly got up.

"My dear, you are not THE Miss Falbe, are you, who drove London crazy with delight last summer. Don't tell me you are THE Miss Falbe?"

Sylvia laughed.

"Do you know, I'm afraid I must be," she said. "Isn't it dreadful to have to say that after your description?"

Aunt Barbara sat down again, in a sort of calm despair.

"If there are any more shocks coming for me to-night," she said, "I think I had better go home. I have encountered a perfectly new nephew Michael. I have dressed myself like a suburban housekeeper to meet a Poiret, so don't deny it, and having humourously told Michael I wished to see a prima donna and a pianist, he takes me at my word and produces THE Miss Falbe. I'm glad I knew that in time; I should infallibly have asked you to sing, and if you had done so— you are probably good-natured enough to have done even that—I should have given the drawing-room gasp at the end, and told your brother that I thought you sang very prettily."

Sylvia laughed.

"But really it wasn't my fault, Lady Barbara," she said. "When we met I couldn't have said, 'Beware! I am THE Miss Falbe.'"

"No, my dear; but I think you ought, somehow, to have conveyed the impression that you were a tremendous swell. You didn't. I have been thinking of you as a charming girl, and nothing more."

"But that's quite good enough for me," said Sylvia.

The two young men joined them after this, and Hermann speedily became engrossed in reading the finished Variations. Some of these pleased him mightily; one he altogether demurred to.

"It's just a crib, Mike," he said. "The critics would say I had forgotten it, and put in instead what I could remember of a variation out of the Handel theme. That next one's, oh, great fun. But I wish you would remember that we all haven't got great orang- outang paws like you."

Aunt Barbara stopped in the middle of her sentence; she knew Michael's old sensitiveness about these physical disabilities, and she had a moment's cold horror at the thought of Falbe having said so miserably tactless a thing to him. But the horror was of infinitesimal duration, for she heard Michael's laugh as they leaned over the top of the piano together.

"I wish you had, Hermann," he said. "I know you'll bungle those tenths."

Falbe moved to the piano-seat.

"Oh, let's have a shot at it," he said. "If Lady Barbara won't mind, play that one through to me first, Mike."

"Oh, presently, Hermann," he said. "It makes such an infernal row that you can't hear anything else afterwards. Do sing, Miss Sylvia; my aunt won't really mind—will you, Aunt Barbara?"

"Michael, I have just learned that this is THE Miss Falbe," she said. "I am suffering from shock. Do let me suffer from coals of fire, too."

Michael gently edged Hermann away from the music-stool. Much as he enjoyed his master's accompaniment he was perfectly sure that he preferred, if possible, to play for Sylvia himself than have the pleasure of listening to anybody else.

"And may I play for you, Miss Sylvia?" he asked.

"Yes, will you? Thanks, Lord Comber."

Hermann moved away.

"And so Mr. Hermann sits down by Lady Barbara while Lord Comber plays for Miss Sylvia," he observed, with emphasis on the titles.

A sudden amazing boldness seized Michael.

"Sylvia, then," he said.

"All right, Michael," answered the girl, laughing.

She came and stood on the left of the piano, slightly behind him.

"And what are we going to have?" asked Michael.

"It must be something we both know, for I've brought no music," said she.

Michael began playing the introduction to the Hugo Wolff song which he had accompanied for her one Sunday night at their house. He knew it perfectly by heart, but stumbled a little over the difficult syncopated time. This was not done without purpose, for the next moment he felt her hand on his shoulder marking it for him.

"Yes, that's right," she said. "Now you've got it." And Michael smiled sweetly at his own amazing ingenuity.

Hermann put down the Variations, which he still had in his hand, when Sylvia's voice began. Unaccustomed as she was to her accompanist, his trained ear told him that she was singing perfectly at ease, and was completely at home with her player. Occasionally she gave Michael some little indication, as she had done before, but for the most part her fingers rested immobile on his shoulder, and he seemed to understand her perfectly. Somehow this was a surprise to him; he had not known that Michael possessed that sort of second-sight that unerringly feels and translates into the keys the singer's mood. For himself he always had to attend most closely when he was playing for his sister, but familiar as he was with her singing, he felt that Michael divined her certainly as well as himself, and he listened to the piano more than to the voice.

"You extraordinary creature," he said when the song was over. "Where did you learn to accompany?"

Suddenly Michael felt an access of shyness, as if he had been surprised when he thought himself private.

"Oh, I've played it before for Miss—I mean for Sylvia," he said.

Then he turned to the girl.

"Thanks, awfully," he said. "And I'm greedy. May we have one more?"

He slid into the opening bars of "Who is Sylvia?" That song, since he had heard her sing it at her recital in the summer, had grown in significance to him, even as she had. It had seemed part of her then, but then she was a stranger. To-night it was even more intimately part of her, and she was a friend.

Hermann strolled across to the fireplace at the end of this, and lit a cigarette.

"My sister's a blatant egoist, Lady Barbara," he said. "She loves singing about herself. And she lays it on pretty thick, too, doesn't she? Now, Sylvia, if you've finished—quite finished, I mean—do come and sit down and let me try these Variations—"

"Shall we surrender, Michael?" asked the girl. "Or shall we stick to the piano, now we've got it? If Hermann once sits down, you know, we shan't get him away for the rest of the evening. I can't sing any more, but we might play a duet to keep him out."

Hermann rushed to the piano, took his sister by the shoulders, and pushed her into a chair.

"You sit there," he said, "and listen to something not about yourself. Michael, if you don't come away from that piano, I shall take Sylvia home at once. Now you may all talk as much as you like; you won't interrupt me one atom—but you'll have to talk loud in certain parts."

Then a feat of marvellous execution began. Michael had taken an evil pleasure in giving his master, for whom he slaved with so unwearied a diligence, something that should tax his powers, and he gave a great crash of laughter when for a moment Hermann was brought to a complete standstill in an octave passage of triplets against quavers, and the performer exultantly joined in it, as he pushed his hair back from his forehead, and made a second attempt.

"It isn't decent to ask a fellow to read that," he shouted. "It's a crime; it's a scandal."

"My dear, nobody asked you to read it," said Sylvia.

"Silence, you chit! Mike, come here a minute. Sit down one second and play that. Promise to get up again, though, immediately. Just these three bars—yes, I see. An orang-outang apparently can do it, so why not I? Am I not much better than they? Go away, please; or, rather, stop there and turn over. Why couldn't you have finished the page with the last act, and started this one fresh, instead of making this Godforsaken arrangement? Now!"

A very simple little minuet measure followed this outrageous passage, and Hermann's exquisite lightness of touch made it sound strangely remote, as if from a mile away, or a hundred years ago, some graceful echo was evoked again. Then the little dirge wept for the memories of something that had never happened, and leaving out the number he disapproved of, as reminiscent of the Handel theme, Hermann gathered himself up again for the assertion of the original tune, with its bars of scale octaves. The contagious jollity of it all seized the others, and Sylvia, with full voice, and Aunt Barbara, in a strange hooting, sang to it.

Then Hermann banged out the last chord, and jumped up from his seat, rolling up the music.

"I go straight home," he said, "and have a peaceful hour with it. Michael, old boy, how did you do it? You've been studying seriously for a few months only, and so this must all have been in you before. And you've come to the age you are without letting any of it out. I suppose that's why it has come with a rush. You knew it all along, while you were wasting your time over drilling your toy soldiers. Come on, Sylvia, or I shall go without you. Good night, Lady Barbara. Half-past ten to-morrow, Michael."

Protest was clearly useless; and, having seen the two off, Michael came upstairs again to Aunt Barbara, who had no intention of going away just yet.

"And so these are the people you have been living with," she said. "No wonder you had not time to come and see me. Do they always go that sort of pace—it is quicker than when I talk French."

Michael sank into a chair.

"Oh, yes, that's Hermann all over," he said. "But—but just think what it means to me! He's going to play my tunes at his concert. Michael Comber, Op. 1. O Lord! O Lord!"

"And you just met him in the train?" said Aunt Barbara.

"Yes; second class, Victoria Station, with Sylvia on the platform. I didn't much notice Sylvia then."

This and the inference that naturally followed was as much as could be expected, and Aunt Barbara did not appear to wait for anything more on the subject of Sylvia. She had seen sufficient of the situation to know where Michael was most certainly bound for. Yet the very fact of Sylvia's outspoken friendliness with him made her wonder a little as to what his reception would be. She would hardly have said so plainly that she and her brother were devoted to him if she had been devoted to him with that secret tenderness which, in its essentials, is reticent about itself. Her half- hour's conversation with the girl had given her a certain insight into her; still more had her attitude when she stood by Michael as he played for her, and put her hand on his shoulder precisely as she would have done if it had been another girl who was seated at the piano. Without doubt Michael had a real existence for her, but there was no sign whatever that she hailed it, as a girl so unmistakably does, when she sees it as part of herself.

"More about them," she said. "What are they? Who are they?"

He outlined for her, giving the half-English, half-German parentage, the shadow-like mother, the Bavarian father, Sylvia's sudden and comet-like rising in the musical heaven, while her brother, seven years her senior, had spent his time in earning in order to give her the chance which she had so brilliantly taken. Now it was to be his turn, the shackles of his drudgery no longer impeded him, and he, so Michael radiantly prophesied, was to have his rocket-like leap to the zenith, also.

"And he's German?" she asked.

"Yes. Wasn't he rude about my being a toy soldier? But that's the natural German point of view, I suppose."

Michael strolled to the fireplace.

"Hermann's so funny," he said. "For days and weeks together you would think he was entirely English, and then a word slips from him like that, which shows he is entirely German. He was like that in Munich, when the Emperor appeared and sent for me."

Aunt Barbara drew her chair a little nearer the fire, and sat up.

"I want to hear about that," she said.

"But I've told you; he was tremendously friendly in a national manner."

"And that seemed to you real?" she asked.

Michael considered.

"I don't know that it did," he said. "It all seemed to me rather feverish, I think."

"And he asked quantities of questions, I think you said."

"Hundreds. He was just like what he was when he came to Ashbridge. He reviewed the Yeomanry, and shot pheasants, and spent the afternoon in a steam launch, apparently studying the deep-water channel of the river, where it goes underneath my father's place; and then in the evening there was a concert."

Aunt Barbara did not heed the concert.

"Do you mean the channel up from Harwich," she asked, "of which the Admiralty have the secret chart?"

"I fancy they have," said Michael. "And then after the concert there was the torchlight procession, with the bonfire on the top of the hill."

"I wasn't there. What else?"

"I think that's all," said Michael. "But what are you driving at, Aunt Barbara?"

She was silent a moment.

"I'm driving at this," she said. "The Germans are accumulating a vast quantity of knowledge about England. Tony, for instance, has a German valet, and when he went down to Portsmouth the other day to see the American ship that was there, he took him with him. And the man took a camera and was found photographing where no photography is allowed. Did you see anything of a camera when the Emperor came to Ashbridge?"

Michael thought.

"Yes; one of his staff was clicking away all day," he said. "He sent a lot of them to my mother."

"And, we may presume, kept some copies himself," remarked Aunt Barbara drily. "Really, for childish simplicity the English are the biggest fools in creation."

"But do you mean—"

"I mean that the Germans are a very knowledge-seeking people, and that we gratify their desires in a very simple fashion. Do you think they are so friendly, Michael? Do you know, for instance, what is a very common toast in German regimental messes? They do not drink it when there are foreigners there, but one night during the manoeuvres an officer in a mess where Tony was dining got slightly 'on,' as you may say, and suddenly drank to 'Der Tag.'"

"That means 'The Day,'" said Michael confidently.

"It does; and what day? The day when Germany thinks that all is ripe for a war with us. 'Der Tag' will dawn suddenly from a quiet, peaceful night, when they think we are all asleep, and when they have got all the information they think is accessible. War, my dear."

Michael had never in his life seen his aunt so serious, and he was amazed at her gravity.

"There are hundreds and hundreds of their spies all over England," she said, "and hundreds of their agents all over America. Deep, patient Germany, as Carlyle said. She's as patient as God and as deep as the sea. They are working, working, while our toy soldiers play golf. I agree with that adorable pianist; and, what's more, I believe they think that 'Der Tag' is near to dawn. Tony says that their manoeuvres this year were like nothing that has ever been seen before. Germany is a fighting machine without parallel in the history of the world."

She got up and stood with Michael near the fireplace.

"And they think their opportunity is at hand," she said, "though not for a moment do they relax their preparations. We are their real enemy, don't you see? They can fight France with one hand and Russia with the other; and in a few months' time now they expect we shall be in the throes of an internal revolution over this Irish business. They may be right, but there is just the possibility that they may be astoundingly wrong. The fact of the great foreign peril—this nightmare, this Armageddon of European war—may be exactly that which will pull us together. But their diplomatists, anyhow, are studying the Irish question very closely, and German gold, without any doubt at all, is helping the Home Rule party. As a nation we are fast asleep. I wonder what we shall be like when we wake. Shall we find ourselves already fettered when we wake, or will there be one moment, just one moment, in which we can spring up? At any rate, hitherto, the English have always been at their best, not their worst, in desperate positions. They hate exciting themselves, and refuse to do it until the crisis is actually on them. But then they become disconcertingly serious and cool- headed."

"And you think the Emperor—" began Michael.

"I think the Emperor is the hardest worker in all Germany," said Barbara. "I believe he is trying (and admirably succeeding) to make us trust his professions of friendship. He has a great eye for detail, too; it seemed to him worth while to assure you even, my dear Michael, of his regard and affection for England. He was always impressing on Tony the same thing, though to him, of course, he said that if there was any country nearer to his heart than England it was America. Stuff and nonsense, my dear!"

All this, though struck in a more serious key than was usual with Aunt Barbara, was quite characteristic of her. She had the quality of mind which when occupied with one idea is occupied with it to the exclusion of all others; she worked at full power over anything she took up. But now she dismissed it altogether.

"You see what a diplomatist I have become," she said. "It is a fascinating business: one lives in an atmosphere that is charged with secret affairs, and it infects one like the influenza. You catch it somehow, and have a feverish cold of your own. And I am quite useful to him. You see, I am such a chatterbox that people think I let out things by accident, which I never do. I let out what I want to let out on purpose, and they think they are pumping me. I had a long conversation the other day with one of the German Embassy, all about Irish affairs. They are hugely interested about Irish affairs, and I just make a note of that; but they can make as many notes as they please about what I say, and no one will be any the wiser. In fact, they will be the foolisher. And now I suppose I had better take myself away."

"Don't do anything of the kind," said Michael.

"But I must. And if when you are down at Ashbridge at Christmas you find strangers hanging about the deep-water reach, you might just let me know. It's no use telling your father, because he will certainly think they have come to get a glimpse of him as he plays golf. But I expect you'll be too busy thinking about that new friend of yours, and perhaps his sister. What did she tell me we had got to do? 'To her garlands let us bring,' was it not? You and I will both send wreaths, Michael, though not for her funeral. Now don't be a hermit any more, but come and see me. You shall take your garland girl into dinner, if she will come, too; and her brother shall certainly sit next me. I am so glad you have become yourself at last. Go on being yourself more and more, my dear: it suits you."

CHAPTER VIII

Some fortnight later, and not long before Michael was leaving town for his Christmas visit to Ashbridge, Sylvia and her brother were lingering in the big studio from which the last of their Sunday evening guests had just departed. The usual joyous chaos consequent on those entertainments reigned: the top of the piano was covered with the plates and glasses of those who had made an alfresco supper (or breakfast) of fried bacon and beer before leaving; a circle of cushions were ranged on the floor round the fire, for it was a bitterly cold night, and since, for some reason, a series of charades had been spontaneously generated, there was lying about an astonishing collection of pillow-cases, rugs, and table-cloths, and such articles of domestic and household use as could be converted into clothes for this purpose. But the event of the evening had undoubtedly been Hermann's performance of the "Wenceslas Variations"; these he had now learned, and, as he had promised Michael, was going to play them at his concert in the Steinway Hall in January. To-night a good many musician friends had attended the Sunday evening gathering, and there had been no two opinions about the success of them.

"I was talking to Arthur Lagden about them," said Falbe, naming a prominent critic of the day, "and he would hardly believe that they were an Opus I., or that Michael had not been studying music technically for years instead of six months. But that's the odd thing about Mike; he's so mature."

It was not unusual for the brother and sister to sit up like this, till any hour, after their guests had gone; and Sylvia collected a bundle of cushions and lay full length on the floor, with her feet towards the fire. For both of them the week was too busy on six days for them to indulge that companionship, sometimes full of talk, sometimes consisting of those dropped words and long silences, on which intimacy lives; and they both enjoyed, above all hours in the week, this time that lay between the friendly riot of Sunday evening and the starting of work again on Monday. There was between them that bond which can scarcely exist between husband and wife, since it almost necessarily implies the close consanguinity of brother and sister, and postulates a certain sort of essential community of nature, founded not on tastes, nor even on affection, but on the fact that the same blood beats in the two. Here an intense affection, too strong to be ever demonstrative, fortified it, and both brother and sister talked to each other, as if they were speaking to some physically independent piece of themselves.

Sylvia had nothing apparently to add on the subject of Michael's maturity. Instead she just raised her head, which was not quite high enough.

"Stuff another cushion under my head, Hermann," she said. "Thanks; now I'm completely comfortable, you will be relieved to hear."

Hermann gazed at the fire in silence.

"That's a weight off my mind," he said. "About Michael now. He's been suppressed all his life, you know, and instead of being dwarfed he has just gone on growing inside. Good Lord! I wish somebody would suppress me for a year or two. What a lot there would be when I took the cork out again. We dissipate too much, Sylvia, both you and I."

She gave a little grunt, which, from his knowledge of her inarticulate expressions, he took to mean dissent.

"I suppose you mean we don't," he remarked.

"Yes. How much one dissipates is determined for one just as is the shape of your nose or the colour of your eyes. By the way, I fell madly in love with that cousin of Michael's who came with him to- night. He's the most attractive creature I ever saw in my life. Of course, he's too beautiful: no boy ought to be as beautiful as that."

"You flirted with him," remarked Hermann. "Mike will probably murder him on the way home."

Sylvia moved her feet a little farther from the blaze.

"Funny?" she asked.

Instantly Falbe knew that her mind was occupied with exactly the same question as his.

"No, not funny at all," he said. "Quite serious. Do you want to talk about it or not?"

She gave a little groan.

"No, I don't want to, but I've got to," she said. "Aunt Barbara— we became Sylvia and Aunt Barbara an hour or two ago, and she's a dear—Aunt Barbara has been talking to me about it already."

"And what did Aunt Barbara say?"

"Just what you are going to," said Sylvia; "namely, that I had better make up my mind what I mean to say when Michael says what he means to say."

She shifted round so as to face her brother as he stood in front of the fire, and pulled his trouser-leg more neatly over the top of his shoe.

"But what's to happen if I can't make up my mind?" she said. "I needn't tell you how much I like Michael; I believe I like him as much as I possibly can. But I don't know if that is enough. Hermann, is it enough? You ought to know. There's no use in you unless you know about me."

She put out her arm, and clasped his two legs in the crook of her elbow. That expressed their attitude, what they were to each other, as absolutely as any physical demonstration allowed. Had there not been the difference of sex which severed them she could never have got the sense of support that this physical contact gave her; had there not been her sisterhood to chaperon her, so to speak, she could never have been so at ease with a man. The two were lover-like, without the physical apexes and limitations that physical love must always bring with it. The complement of sex that brought them so close annihilated the very existence of sex. They loved as only brother and sister can love, without trouble.

The closer contact of his fire-warmed trousers to the calf of his leg made Hermann step out of her encircling arm without any question of hurting her feelings.

"I won't be burned," he said. "Sorry, but I won't be burned. It seems to me, Sylvia, that you ought to like Michael a little more and a little less."

"It's no use saying what I ought to do," she said. "The idea of what I 'ought' doesn't come in. I like him just as much as I like him, neither more nor less."

He clawed some more cushions together, and sat down on the floor by her. She raised herself a little and rested her body against his folded knees.

"What's the trouble, Sylvia?" he said.

"Just what I've been trying to tell you."

"Be more concrete, then. You're definite enough when you sing."

She sighed and gave a little melancholy laugh.

"That's just it," she said. "People like you and me, and Michael, too, for that matter, are most entirely ourselves when we are at our music. When Michael plays for me I can sing my soul at him. While he and I are in music, if you understand—and of course you do—we belong to each other. Do you know, Hermann, he finds me when I'm singing, without the slightest effort, and even you, as you have so often told me, have to search and be on the lookout. And then the song is over, and, as somebody says, 'When the feast is finished and the lamps expire,' then—well, the lamps expire, and he isn't me any longer, but Michael, with the—the ugly face, and—oh, isn't it horrible of me—the long arms and the little stumpy legs—if only he was rather different in things that don't matter, that CAN'T matter! But—but, Hermann, if only Michael was rather like you, and you like Michael, I should love you exactly as much as ever, and I should love Michael, too."

She was leaning forward, and with both hands was very carefully tying and untying one of Hermann's shoelaces.

"Oh, thank goodness there is somebody in the world to whom I can say just whatever I feel, and know he understands," she said. "And I know this, too—and follow me here, Hermann—I know that all that doesn't really matter; I am sure it doesn't. I like Michael far too well to let it matter. But there are other things which I don't see my way through, and they are much more real—"

She was silent again, so long that Hermann reached out for a cigarette, lit it, and threw away the match before she spoke.

"There is Michael's position," she said. "When Michael asks me if I will have him, as we both know he is going to do, I shall have to make conditions. I won't give up my career. I must go on working— in other words, singing—whether I marry him or not. I don't call it singing, in my sense of the word, to sing 'The Banks of Allan Water' to Michael and his father and mother at Ashbridge, any more than it is being a politician to read the morning papers and argue about the Irish question with you. To have a career in politics means that you must be a member of Parliament—I daresay the House of Lords would do—and make speeches and stand the racket. In the same way, to be a singer doesn't mean to sing after dinner or to go squawking anyhow in a workhouse, but it means to get up on a platform before critical people, and if you don't do your very best be damned by them. If I marry Michael I must go on singing as a professional singer, and not become an amateur—the Viscountess Comber, who sings so charmingly. I refuse to sing charmingly; I will either sing properly or not at all. And I couldn't not sing. I shall have to continue being Miss Falbe, so to speak."

"You say you insist on it," said Hermann; "but whether you did or not, there is nothing more certain than that Michael would."

"I am sure he would. But by so doing he would certainly quarrel irrevocably with his people. Even Aunt Barbara, who, after all, is very liberally minded, sees that. They can none of them, not even she, who are born to a certain tradition imagine that there are other traditions quite as stiff-necked. Michael, it is true, was born to one tradition, but he has got the other, as he has shown very clearly by refusing to disobey it. He will certainly, as you say, insist on my endorsing the resolution he has made for himself. What it comes to is this, that I can't marry him without his father's complete consent to all that I have told you. I can't have my career disregarded, covered up with awkward silences, alluded to as a painful subject; and, as I say, even Aunt Barbara seemed to take it for granted that if I became Lady Comber I should cease to be Miss Falbe. Well, there she's wrong, my dear; I shall continue to be Miss Falbe whether I'm Lady Comber, or Lady Ashbridge, or the Duchess of anything you please. And—here the difficulty really comes in—they must all see how right I am. Difficulty, did I say? It's more like an impossibility."

Hermann threw the end of his cigarette into the ashes of the dying fire.

"It's clear, then," he said, "you have made up your mind not to marry him."

She shook her head.

"Oh, Hermann, you fail me," she said. "If I had made up my mind not to I shouldn't have kept you up an hour talking about it."

He stretched his hands out towards the embers already coated with grey ash.

"Then it's like that with you," he said, pointing. "If there is the fire in you, it is covered up with ashes."

She did not reply for a moment.

"I think you've hit it there," she said. "I believe there is the fire; when, as I said, he plays for me I know there is. But the ashes? What are they? And who shall disperse them for me?"

She stood up swiftly, drawing herself to her full height and stretching her arms out.

"There's something bigger than we know coming," she said. "Whether it's storm or sunshine I have no idea. But there will be something that shall utterly sever Michael and me or utterly unite us."

"Do you care which it is?" he asked.

"Yes, I care," said she.

He held out his hands to her, and she pulled him up to his feet.

"What are you going to say, then, when he asks you?" he said.

"Tell him he must wait."

He went round the room putting out the electric lamps and opening the big skylight in the roof. There was a curtain in front of this, which he pulled aside, and from the frosty cloudless heavens the starshine of a thousand constellations filtered down.

"That's a lot to ask of any man," he said. "If you care, you care."

"And if you were a girl you would know exactly what I mean," she said. "They may know they care, but, unless they are marrying for perfectly different reasons, they have to feel to the end of their fingers that they care before they can say 'Yes.'"

He opened the door for her to pass out, and they walked up the passage together arm-in-arm.

"Well, perhaps Michael won't ask you," he said, "in which case all bother will be saved, and we shall have sat up talking till— Sylvia, did you know it is nearly three—sat up talking for nothing!"

Sylvia considered this.

"Fiddlesticks!" she said.

And Hermann was inclined to agree with her.

This view of the case found confirmation next day, for Michael, after his music lesson, lingered so firmly and determinedly when the three chatted together over the fire that in the end Hermann found nothing to do but to leave them together. Sylvia had given him no sign as to whether she wished him to absent himself or not, and he concluded, since she did not put an end to things by going away herself, that she intended Michael to have his say.

The latter rose as the door closed behind Hermann, and came and stood in front of her. And at the moment Sylvia could notice nothing of him except his heaviness, his plainness, all the things that she had told herself before did not really matter. Now her sensation contradicted that; she was conscious that the ash somehow had vastly accumulated over her fire, that all her affection and regard for him were suddenly eclipsed. This was a complete surprise to her; for the moment she found Michael's presence and his proximity to her simply distasteful.

"I thought Hermann was never going," he said.

For a second or two she did not reply; it was clearly no use to continue the ordinary banter of conversation, to suggest that as the room was Hermann's he might conceivably be conceded the right to stop there if he chose. There was no transition possible between the affairs of every day and the affair for which Michael had stopped to speak. She gave up all attempt to make one; instead, she just helped him.

"What is it, Michael?" she asked.

Then to her, at any rate, Michael's face completely changed. There burned in it all of a sudden the full glow of that of which she had only seen glimpses.

"You know," he said.

His shyness, his awkwardness, had all vanished; the time had come for him to offer to her all that he had to offer, and he did it with the charm of perfect manliness and simplicity.

"Whether you can accept me or not," he said, "I have just to tell you that I am entirely yours. Is there any chance for me, Sylvia?"

He stood quite still, making no movement towards her. She, on her side, found all her distaste of him suddenly vanished in the mere solemnity of the occasion. His very quietness told her better than any protestations could have done of the quality of what he offered, and that quality vastly transcended all that she had known or guessed of him.

"I don't know, Michael," she said at length.

She came a step forward, and without any sense of embarrassment found that she, without conscious intention, had put her hands on his shoulders. The moment that was done she was conscious of the impulse that made her do it. It expressed what she felt.

"Yes, I feel like that to you," she said. "You're a dear. I expect you know how fond I am of you, and if you don't I assure you of it now. But I have got to give you more than that."

Michael looked up at her.

"Yes, Sylvia," he said, "much more than that."

A few minutes ago only she had not liked him at all; now she liked him immensely.

"But how, Michael?" she asked. "How can I find it?"

"Oh, it's I who have got to find it for you," he said. "That is to say, if you want it to be found. Do you?"

She looked at him gravely, without the tremor of a smile in her eyes.

"What does that mean exactly?" she said.

"It is very simple. Do you want to love me?"

She did not move her hands; they still rested on his shoulders like things at ease, like things at home.

"Yes, I suppose I want to," she said.

"And is that the most you can do for me at present?" he asked.

That reached her again; all the time the plain words, the plain face, the quiet of him stabbed her with daggers of which he had no idea. She was dismayed at the recollection of her talk with her brother the evening before, of the ease and certitude with which she had laid down her conditions, of not giving up her career, of remaining the famous Miss Falbe, of refusing to take a dishonoured place in the sacred circle of the Combers. Now, when she was face to face with his love, so ineloquently expressed, so radically a part of him, she knew that there was nothing in the world, external to him and her, that could enter into their reckonings; but into their reckonings there had not entered the one thing essential. She gave him sympathy, liking, friendliness, but she did not want him with her blood. And though it was not humanly possible that she could want him with more than that, it was not possible that she could take him with less.

"Yes, that is the most I can do for you at present," she said.

Still quite quietly he moved away from her, so that he stood free of her hands.

"I have been constantly here all these last months," he said. "Now that you know what I have told you, do you want not to see me?"

That stabbed her again.

"Have I implied that?" she asked.

"Not directly. But I can easily understand its being a bore to you. I don't want to bore you. That would be a very stupid way of trying to make you care for me. As I said, that is my job. I haven't accomplished it as yet. But I mean to. I only ask you for a hint."

She understood her own feeling better than he. She understood at least that she was dealing with things that were necessarily incalculable.

"I can't give you a hint," she said. "I can't make any plans about it. If you were a woman perhaps you would understand. Love is, or it isn't. That is all I know about it."

But Michael persisted.

"I only know what you have taught me," he said. "But you must know that."

In a flash she became aware that it would be impossible for her to behave to Michael as she had behaved to him for several months past. She could not any longer put a hand on his shoulder, beat time with her fingers on his arm, knowing that the physical contact meant nothing to her, and all—all to him. The rejection of him as a lover rendered the sisterly attitude impossible. And not only must she revise her conduct, but she must revise the mental attitude of which it was the physical counterpart. Up till this moment she had looked at the situation from her own side only, had felt that no plans could be made, that the natural thing was to go on as before, with the intimacy that she liked and the familiarity that was the obvious expression of it. But now she began to see the question from his side; she could not go on doing that which meant nothing particular to her, if that insouciance meant something so very particular to him. She realised that if she had loved him the touch of his hand, the proximity of his face would have had significance for her, a significance that would have been intolerable unless there was something mutual and secret between them. It had seemed so easy, in anticipation, to tell him that he must wait, so simple for him just—well, just to wait until she could make up her mind. She believed, as she had told her brother, that she cared for Michael, or as she had told him that she wanted to—the two were to the girl's mind identical, though expressed to each in the only terms that were possible—but until she came face to face with the picture of the future, that to her wore the same outline and colour as the past, she had not known the impossibility of such a presentment. The desire of the lover on Michael's part rendered unthinkable the sisterly attitude on hers. That her instinct told her, but her reason revolted against it.

"Can't we go on as we were, Michael?" she said.

He looked at her incredulously.

"Oh, no, of course not that," he said.

She moved a step towards him.

"I can't think of you in any other way," she said, as if making an appeal.

He stood absolutely unresponsive. Something within him longed that she should advance a step more, that he should again have the touch of her hands on his shoulders, but another instinct stronger than that made him revoke his desire, and if she had moved again he would certainly have fallen back before her.

"It may seem ridiculous to you," he said, "since you do not care. But I can't do that. Does that seem absurd to you I? I am afraid it does; but that is because you don't understand. By all means let us be what they call excellent friends. But there are certain little things which seem nothing to you, and they mean so much to me. I can't explain; it's just the brotherly relation which I can't stand. It's no use suggesting that we should be as we were before—"

She understood well enough for his purposes.

"I see," she said.

Michael paused for a moment.

"I think I'll be going now," he said. "I am off to Ashbridge in two days. Give Hermann my love, and a jolly Christmas to you both. I'll let you know when I am back in town."

She had no reply to this; she saw its justice, and acquiesced.

"Good-bye, then," said Michael.

He walked home from Chelsea in that utterly blank and unfeeling consciousness which almost invariably is the sequel of any event that brings with it a change of attitude towards life generally. Not for a moment did he tell himself that he had been awakened from a dream, or abandon his conviction that his dream was to be made real. The rare, quiet determination that had made him give up his stereotyped mode of life in the summer and take to music was still completely his, and, if anything, it had been reinforced by Sylvia's emphatic statement that "she wanted to care." Only her imagining that their old relations could go on showed him how far she was from knowing what "to care" meant. At first without knowing it, but with a gradually increasing keenness of consciousness, he had become aware that this sisterly attitude of hers towards him had meant so infinitely much, because he had taken it to be the prelude to something more. Now he saw that it was, so to speak, a piece complete in itself. It bore no relation to what he had imagined it would lead into. No curtain went up when the prelude was over; the curtain remained inexorably hanging there, not acknowledging the prelude at all. Not for a moment did he accuse her of encouraging him to have thought so; she had but given him a frankness of comradeship that meant to her exactly what it expressed. But he had thought otherwise; he had imagined that it would grow towards a culmination. All that (and here was the change that made his mind blank and unfeeling) had to be cut away, and with it all the budding branches that his imagination had pictured as springing from it. He could not be comrade to her as he was to her brother—the inexorable demands of sex forbade it.

He went briskly enough through the clean, dry streets. The frost of last night had held throughout the morning, and the sunlight sparkled with a rare and seasonable brightness of a traditional Christmas weather. Hecatombs of turkeys hung in the poulterers' windows, among sprigs of holly, and shops were bright with children's toys. The briskness of the day had flushed the colour into the faces of the passengers in the street, and the festive air of the imminent holiday was abroad. All this Michael noticed with a sense of detachment; what had happened had caused a veil to fall between himself and external things; it was as if he was sealed into some glass cage, and had no contact with what passed round him. This lasted throughout his walk, and when he let himself into his flat it was with the same sense of alienation that he found his cousin Francis gracefully reclining on the sofa that he had pulled up in front of the fire.

Francis was inclined to be querulous.

"I was just wondering whether I should give you up," he said. "The hour that you named for lunch was half-past one. And I have almost forgotten what your clock sounded like when it struck two."

This also seemed to matter very little.

"Did I ask you to lunch?" he said. "I really quite forgot; I can't even remember doing it now."

"But there will be lunch?" asked Francis rather anxiously.

"Of course. It'll be ready in ten minutes."

Michael came and stood in front of the fire, and looked with a sudden spasm of envy on the handsome boy who lay there. If he himself had been anything like that—

"I was distinctly chippy this morning," remarked Francis, "and so I didn't so much mind waiting for lunch. I attribute it to too much beer and bacon last night at your friend's house. I enjoyed it—I mean the evening, and for that matter the bacon—at the time. It really was extremely pleasant."

He yawned largely and openly.

"I had no idea you could frolic like that, Mike," he said. "It was quite a new light on your character. How did you learn to do it? It's quite a new accomplishment."

Here again the veil was drawn. Was it last night only that Falbe had played the Variations, and that they had acted charades? Francis proceeded in bland unconsciousness.

"I didn't know Germans could be so jolly," he continued. "As a rule I don't like Germans. When they try to be jolly they generally only succeed in being top-heavy. But, of course, your friend is half-English. Can't he play, too? And to think of your having written those ripping tunes. His sister, too—no wonder we haven't seen much of you, Mike, if that's where you've been spending your time. She's rather like the new girl at the Gaiety, but handsomer. I like big girls, don't you? Oh, I forgot, you don't like girls much, anyhow. But are you learning your mistake, Mike? You looked last night as if you were getting more sensible."

Michael moved away impatiently.

"Oh, shut it, Francis," he observed.

Francis raised himself on his elbow.

"Why, what's up?" he asked. "Won't she turn a favourable eye?"

Michael wheeled round savagely.

"Please remember you are talking about a lady, and not a Gaiety lady," he remarked.

This brought Francis to his feet.

"Sorry," he said. "I was only indulging in badinage until lunch was ready."

Michael could not make up his mind to tell his cousin what had happened; but he was aware of having spoken more strongly than the situation, as Francis knew of it, justified.

"Let's have lunch, then," he said. "We shall be better after lunch, as one's nurse used to say. And are you coming to Ashbridge, Francis?"

"Yes; I've been talking to Aunt Bar about it this morning. We're both coming; the family is going to rally round you, Mike, and defend you from Uncle Robert. There's sure to be some duck shooting, too, isn't there?"

This was a considerable relief to Michael.

"Oh, that's ripping," he said. "You and Aunt Barbara always make me feel that there's a good deal of amusement to be extracted from the world."

"To be sure there is. Isn't that what the world is for? Lunch and amusement, and dinner and amusement. Aunt Bar told me she dined with you the other night, and had a quantity of amusement as well as an excellent dinner. She hinted—"

"Oh, Aunt Barbara's always hinting," said Michael.

"I know. After all, everything that isn't hints is obvious, and so there's nothing to say about it. Tell me more about the Falbes, Mike. Will they let me go there again, do you think? Was I popular? Don't tell me if I wasn't."

Michael smiled at this egoism that could not help being charming.

"Would you care if you weren't?" he asked.

"Very much. One naturally wants to please delightful people. And I think they are both delightful. Especially the girl; but then she starts with the tremendous advantage of being—of being a girl. I believe you are in love with her, Mike, just as I am. It's that which makes you so grumpy. But then you never do fall in love. It's a pity; you miss a lot of jolly trouble."

Michael felt a sudden overwhelming desire to make Francis stop this maddening twaddle; also the events of the morning were beginning to take on an air of reality, and as this grew he felt the need of sympathy of some kind. Francis might not be able to give him anything that was of any use, but it would do no harm to see if his cousin's buoyant unconscious philosophy, which made life so exciting and pleasant a thing to him, would in any way help. Besides, he must stop this light banter, which was like drawing plaster off a sore and unhealed wound.

"You're quite right," he said. "I am in love with her. Furthermore, I asked her to marry me this morning."

This certainly had an effect.

"Good Lord!" said Francis. "And do you mean to say she refused you?"

"She didn't accept me," said Michael. "We—we adjourned."

"But why on earth didn't she take you?" asked Francis.

All Michael's old sensitiveness, his self-consciousness of his plainness, his awkwardness, his big hands, his short legs, came back to him.

"I should think you could see well enough if you look at me," he said, "without my telling you."

"Oh, that silly old rot," said Francis cheerfully. "I thought you had forgotten all about it."

"I almost had—in fact I quite had until this morning," said Michael. "If I had remembered it I shouldn't have asked her."

He corrected himself.

"No, I don't think that's true," he said. "I should have asked her, anyhow; but I should have been prepared for her not to take me. As a matter of fact, I wasn't."

Francis turned sideways to the table, throwing one leg over the other.

"That's nonsense," he said. "It doesn't matter whether a man's ugly or not."

"It doesn't as long as he is not," remarked Michael grimly.

"It doesn't matter much in any case. We're all ugly compared to girls; and why ever they should consent to marry any of us awful hairy things, smelling of smoke and drink, is more than I can make out; but, as a matter of fact, they do. They don't mind what we look like; what they care about is whether we want them. Of course, there are exceptions—"

"You see one," said Michael.

"No, I don't. Good Lord, you've only asked her once. You've got to make yourself felt. You're not intending to give up, are you?"

"I couldn't give up."

"Well then, just hold on. She likes you, doesn't she?"

"Certainly," said Michael, without hesitation. "But that's a long way from the other thing."

"It's on the same road."

Michael got up.

"It may be," he said, "but it strikes me it's round the corner. You can't even see one from the other."

"Possibly not. But you never know how near the corner really is. Go for her, Mike, full speed ahead."

"But how?"

"Oh, there are hundreds of ways. I'm not sure that one of the best isn't to keep away for a bit. Even if she doesn't want you just now, when you are there, she may get to want you when you aren't. I don't think I should go on the mournful Byronic plan if I were you; I don't think it would suit your style; you're too heavily built to stand leaning against the chimney-piece, gazing at her and dishevelling your hair."

Michael could not help laughing.

"Oh, for God's sake, don't make a joke of it," he said.

"Why not? It isn't a tragedy yet. It won't be a tragedy till she marries somebody else, or definitely says no. And until a thing is proved to be tragic, the best way to deal with it is to treat it like a comedy which is going to end well. It's only the second act now, you see, when everything gets into a mess. By the merciful decrees of Providence, you see, girls on the whole want us as much as we want them. That's what makes it all so jolly."

Michael went down next day to Ashbridge, where Aunt Barbara and Francis were to follow the day after, and found, after the freedom and interests of the last six months, that the pompous formal life was more intolerable than ever. He was clearly in disgrace still, as was made quite clear to him by his father's icy and awful politeness when it was necessary to speak to him, and by his utter unconsciousness of his presence when it was not. This he had expected. Christmas had ushered in a truce in which no guns were discharged, but remained sighted and pointed, ready to fire.

But though there was no change in his father, his mother seemed to Michael to be curiously altered; her mind, which, as has been already noticed, was usually in a stunned condition, seemed to have awakened like a child from its sleep, and to have begun vaguely crying in an inarticulate discomfort. It was true that Petsy was no more, having succumbed to a bilious attack of unusual severity, but a second Petsy had already taken her place, and Lady Ashbridge sat with him—it was a gentleman Petsy this time—in her lap as before, and occasionally shed a tear or two over Petsy II. in memory of Petsy I. But this did not seem to account for the wakening up of her mind and emotions into this state of depression and anxiety. It was as if all her life she had been quietly dozing in the sun, and that the place where she sat had passed into the shade, and she had awoke cold and shivering from a bitter wind. She had become far more talkative, and though she had by no means abandoned her habit of upsetting any conversation by the extreme obviousness of her remarks, she asked many more questions, and, as Michael noticed, often repeated a question to which she had received an answer only a few minutes before. During dinner Michael constantly found her looking at him in a shy and eager manner, removing her gaze when she found it was observed, and when, later, after a silent cigarette with his father in the smoking-room, during which Lord Ashbridge, with some ostentation, studied an Army List, Michael went to his bedroom, he was utterly astonished, when he gave a "Come in" to a tapping at his door, to see his mother enter. Her maid was standing behind her holding the inevitable Petsy, and she herself hovered hesitatingly in the doorway.

"I heard you come up, Michael," she said, "and I wondered if it would annoy you if I came in to have a little talk with you. But I won't come in if it would annoy you. I only thought I should like a little chat with you, quietly, secure from interruptions."

Michael instantly got up from the chair in front of his fire, in which he had already begun to see images of Sylvia. This intrusion of his mother's was a thing utterly unprecedented, and somehow he at once connected its innovation with the strange manner he had remarked already. But there was complete cordiality in his welcome, and he wheeled up a chair for her.

"But by all means come in, mother," he said. "I was not going to bed yet."

Lady Ashbridge looked round for her maid.

"And will Petsy not annoy you if he sits quietly on my knee?" she asked.

"Of course not."

Lady Ashbridge took the dog.

"There, that is nice," she said. "I told them to see you had a good fire on this cold night. Has it been very cold in London?"

This question had already been asked and answered twice, now for the third time Michael admitted the severity of the weather.

"I hope you wrap up well," she said. "I should be sorry if you caught cold, and so, I am sure, your father would be. I wish you could make up your mind not to vex him any more, but go back into the Guards."

"I'm afraid that's impossible, mother," he said.

"Well, if it's impossible there is no use in saying anything more about it. But it vexed him very much. He is still vexed with you. I wish he was not vexed. It is a sad thing when father and son fall out. But you do wrap up, I hope, in the cold weather?"

Michael felt a sudden pang of anxiety and alarm. Each separate thing that his mother said was sensible enough, but in the sum they were nonsense.

"You have been in London since September," she went on. "That is a long time to be in London. Tell me about your life there. Do you work hard? Not too hard, I hope?"

"No! hard enough to keep me busy," he said.

"Tell me about it all. I am afraid I have not been a very good mother to you; I have not entered into your life enough. I want to do so now. But I don't think you ever wanted to confide in me. It is sad when sons don't confide in their mothers. But I daresay it was my fault, and now I know so little about you."

She paused a moment, stroking her dog's ears, which twitched under her touch.

"I hope you are happy, Michael," she said. "I don't think I am so happy as I used to be. But don't tell your father; I feel sure he does not notice it, and it would vex him. But I want you to be happy; you used not to be when you were little; you were always sensitive and queer. But you do seem happier now, and that's a good thing."

Here again this was all sensible, when taken in bits, but its aspect was different when considered together. She looked at Michael anxiously a moment, and then drew her chair closer to him, laying her thin, veined hand, sparkling with many rings, on his knee.

"But it wasn't I who made you happier," she said, "and that's so dreadful. I never made anybody happy. Your father always made himself happy, and he liked being himself, but I suspect you haven't liked being yourself, poor Michael. But now that you're living the life you chose, which vexes your father, is it better with you?"

The shyness had gone from the gaze that he had seen her direct at him at dinner, which fugitively fluttered away when she saw that it was observed, and now that it was bent so unwaveringly on him he saw shining through it what he had never seen before, namely, the mother-love which he had missed all his life. Now, for the first time, he saw it; recognising it, as by divination, when, with ray serene and untroubled, it burst through the mists that seemed to hang about his mother's mind. Before, noticing her change of manner, her restless questions, he had been vaguely alarmed, and as they went on the alarm had become more pronounced; but at this moment, when there shone forth the mother-instinct which had never come out or blossomed in her life, but had been overlaid completely with routine and conventionality, rendering it too indolent to put forth petals, Michael had no thought but for that which she had never given him yet, and which, now it began to expand before him, he knew he had missed all his life.

She took up his big hand that lay on his knee and began timidly stroking it.

"Since you have been away," she said, "and since your father has been vexed with you, I have begun to see how lonely you must have been. What taught me that, I am afraid, was only that I have begun to feel lonely, too. Nobody wants me; even Petsy, when she died, didn't want me to be near her, and then it began to strike me that perhaps you might want me. There was no one else, and who should want me if my son did not? I never gave you the chance before, God forgive me, and now perhaps it is too late. You have learned to do without me."

That was bitterly true; the truth of it stabbed Michael. On his side, as he knew, he had made no effort either, or if he had they had been but childish efforts, easily repulsed. He had not troubled about it, and if she was to blame, the blame was his also. She had been slow to show the mother-instinct, but he had been just as wanting in the tenderness of the son.

He was profoundly touched by this humble timidity, by the sincerity, vague but unquestionable, that lay behind it.

"It's never too late, is it?" he said, bending down and kissing the thin white hands that held his. "We are in time, after all, aren't we?"

She gave a little shiver.

"Oh, don't kiss my hands, Michael," she said. "It hurts me that you should do that. But it is sweet of you to say that I am not too late, after all. Michael, may I just take you in my arms—may I?"

He half rose.

"Oh, mother, how can you ask?" he said.

"Then let me do it. No, my darling, don't move. Just sit still as you are, and let me just get my arms about you, and put my head on your shoulder, and hold me close like that for a moment, so that I can realise that I am not too late."

She got up, and, leaning over him, held him so for a moment, pressing her cheek close to his, and kissing him on the eyes and on the mouth.

"Ah, that is nice," she said. "It makes my loneliness fall away from me. I am not quite alone any more. And now, if you are not tired will you let me talk to you a little more, and learn a little more about you?"

She pulled her chair again nearer him, so that sitting there she could clasp his arm.

"I want your happiness, dear," she said, "but there is so little now that I can do to secure it. I must put that into other hands. You are twenty-five, Michael; you are old enough to get married. All Combers marry when they are twenty-five, don't they? Isn't there some girl you would like to be yours? But you must love her, you know, you must want her, you mustn't be able to do without her. It won't do to marry just because you are twenty-five."

It would no more have entered into Michael's head this morning to tell to his mother about Sylvia than to have discussed counterpoint with her. But then this morning he had not been really aware that he had a mother. But to tell her now was not unthinkable, but inevitable.

"Yes, there is a girl whom I can't do without," he said.

Lady Ashbridge's face lit up.

"Ah, tell me about her—tell me about her," she said. "You want her, you can't do without her; that is the right wife for you."

Michael caught at his mother's hand as it stroked his sleeve.

"But she is not sure that she can do with me," he said.

Her face was not dimmed at this.

"Oh, you may be sure she doesn't know her own mind," she said. "Girls so often don't. You must not be down-hearted about it. Who is she? Tell me about her."

"She's the sister of my great friend, Hermann Falbe," he said, "who teaches me music."

This time the gladness faded from her.

"Oh, my dear, it will vex your father again," she said, "that you should want to marry the sister of a music-teacher. It will never do to vex him again. Is she not a lady?"

Michael laughed.

"But certainly she is," he said. "Her father was German, her mother was a Tracy, just as well-born as you or I."

"How odd, then, that her brother should have taken to giving music lessons. That does not sound good. Perhaps they are poor, and certainly there is no disgrace in being poor. And what is her name?"

"Sylvia," said Michael. "You have probably heard of her; she is the Miss Falbe who made such a sensation in London last season by her singing."

The old outlook, the old traditions were beginning to come to the surface again in poor Lady Ashbridge's mind.

"Oh, my dear!" she said. "A singer! That would vex your father terribly. Fancy the daughter of a Miss Tracy becoming a singer. And yet you want her—that seems to me to matter most of all."

Then came a step at the door; it opened an inch or two, and Michael heard his father's voice.

"Is your mother with you, Michael?" he asked.

At that Lady Ashbridge got up. For one second she clung to her son, and then, disengaging herself, froze up like the sudden congealment of a spring.

"Yes, Robert," she said. "I was having a little talk to Michael."

"May I come in?"

"It's our secret," she whispered to Michael.

"Yes, come in, father," he said.

Lord Ashbridge stood towering in the doorway.

"Come, my dear," he said, not unkindly, "it's time for you to go to bed."

She had become the mask of herself again.

"Yes, Robert," she said. "I suppose it must be late. I will come. Oh, there's Petsy. Will you ring, Michael? then Fedden will come and take him to bed. He sleeps with Fedden."

CHAPTER IX

Michael, in desperate conversational efforts next morning at breakfast, mentioned the fact that the German Emperor had engaged him in a substantial talk at Munich, and had recommended him to pass the winter at Berlin. It was immediately obvious that he rose in his father's estimation, for, though no doubt primarily the fact that Michael was his son was the cause of this interest, it gave Michael a sort of testimonial also to his respectability. If the Emperor had thought that his taking up a musical career was indelibly disgraceful—as Lord Ashbridge himself had done—he would certainly not have made himself so agreeable. On anyone of Lord Ashbridge's essential and deep-rooted snobbishness this could not fail to make a certain effect; his chilly politeness to Michael sensibly thawed; you might almost have detected a certain cordiality in his desire to learn as much as possible of this gratifying occurrence.

"And you mean to go to Berlin?" he asked.

"I'm afraid I shan't be able to," said Michael; "my master is in London."

"I should be inclined to reconsider that, Michael," said the father. "The Emperor knows what he is talking about on the subject of music."

Lady Ashbridge looked up from the breakfast she was giving Petsy II. His dietary was rather less rich than that of the defunct, and she was afraid sometimes that his food was not nourishing enough.

"I remember the concert we had here," she said. "We had the 'Song to Aegir' twice."

Lord Ashbridge gave her a quick glance. Michael felt he would not have noticed it the evening before.

"Your memory is very good, my dear," he said with encouragement.

"And then we had a torchlight procession," she remarked.

"Quite so. You remember it perfectly. And about his visit here, Michael. Did he talk about that?"

"Yes, very warmly; also about our international relations."

Lord Ashbridge gave a little giggle.

"I must tell Barbara that," he said. "She has become a sort of Cassandra, since she became a diplomatist, and sits on her tripod and prophesies woe."

"She asked me about it," said Michael. "I don't think she believes in his sincerity."

He giggled again.

"That's because I didn't ask her down for his visit," he said.

He rose.

"And what are you going to do, my dear?" he said to his wife.

She looked across to Michael.

"Perhaps Michael will come for a stroll with me," she said.

"No doubt he will. I shall have a round of golf, I think, on this fine morning. I should like to have a word with you, Michael, when you've finished your breakfast."

The moment he had gone her whole manner changed: it was suffused with the glow that had lit her last night.

"And we shall have another talk, dear?" she said. "It was tiresome being interrupted last night. But your father was better pleased with you this morning."

Michael's understanding of the situation grew clearer. Whatever was the change in his mother, whatever, perhaps, it portended, it was certainly accompanied by two symptoms, the one the late dawning of mother-love for himself, the other a certain fear of her husband; for all her married life she had been completely dominated by him, and had lived but in a twilight of her own; now into that twilight was beginning to steal a dread of him. His pleasure or his vexation had begun to affect her emotionally, instead of being as before, merely recorded in her mind, as she might have recorded an object quite exterior to herself, and seen out of the window. Now it was in the room with her. Even as Michael left her to speak with him, the consciousness of him rose again in her, making her face anxious.

"And you'll try not to vex him, won't you?" she said.

His father was in the smoking-room, standing enormously in front of the fire, and for the first time the sense of his colossal fatuity struck Michael.

"There are several things I want to tell you about," he said. "Your career, first of all. I take it that you have no intention of deferring to my wishes on the subject."

"No, father, I am afraid not," said Michael.

"I want you to understand, then, that, though I shall not speak to you again about it, my wishes are no less strong than they were. It is something to me to know that a man whom I respect so much as the Emperor doesn't feel as I do about it, but that doesn't alter my view."

"I understand," said Michael.

"The next is about your mother," he said. "Do you notice any change in her?"

"Yes," said Michael.

"Can you describe it at all?"

Michael hesitated.

"She shows quite a new affection for myself," he said. "She came and talked to me last night in a way she had never done before."

The irritation which Michael's mere presence produced on his father was beginning to make itself felt. The fact that Michael was squat and long-armed and ugly had always a side-blow to deal at Lord Ashbridge in the reminder that he was his father. He tried to disregard this—he tried to bring his mind into an impartial attitude, without seeing for a moment the bitter irony of considering impartiality the ideal quality when dealing with his son. He tried to be fair, and Michael was perfectly conscious of the effort it cost him.

"I had noticed something of the sort," he said. "Your mother was always asking after you. You have not been writing very regularly, Michael. We know little about your life."

"I have written to my mother every week," said Michael.

The magical effects of the Emperor's interest were dying out. Lord Ashbridge became more keenly aware of the disappointment that Michael was to him.

"I have not been so fortunate, then," he said.

Michael remembered his mother's anxious face, but he could not let this pass.

"No, sir," he said, "but you never answered any of my letters. I thought it quite probable that it displeased you to hear from me."

"I should have expressed my displeasure if I had felt it," said his father with all the pomposity that was natural to him.

"That had not occurred to me," said Michael. "I am afraid I took your silence to mean that my letters didn't interest you."

He paused a moment, and his rebellion against the whole of his father's attitude flared up.

"Besides, I had nothing particular to say," he said. "My life is passed in the pursuit of which you entirely disapprove."

He felt himself back in boyhood again with this stifling and leaden atmosphere of authority and disapproval to breathe. He knew that Francis in his place would have done somehow differently; he could almost hear Aunt Barbara laughing at the pomposity of the situation that had suddenly erected itself monstrously in front of him. The fact that he was Michael Comber vexed his father—there was no statement of the case so succinctly true.

Lord Ashbridge moved away towards the window, turning his back on Michael. Even his back, his homespun Norfolk jacket, his loose knickerbockers, his stalwart calves expressed disapproval; but when his father spoke again he realised that he had moved away like that, and obscured his face for a different reason.

"Have you noticed anything else about your mother?" he asked.

That made Michael understand.

"Yes, father," he said. "I daresay I am wrong about it—"

"Naturally I may not agree with you; but I should like to know what it is."

"She's afraid of you," said Michael.

Lord Ashbridge continued looking out of the window a little longer, letting his eyes dwell on his own garden and his own fields, where towered the leafless elms and the red roofs of the little town which had given him his own name, and continued to give him so satisfactory an income. There presented itself to his mind his own picture, painted and framed and glazed and hung up by himself, the beneficent nobleman, the conscientious landlord, the essential vertebra of England's backbone. It was really impossible to impute blame to such a fine fellow. He turned round into the room again, braced and refreshed, and saw Michael thus.

"It is quite true what you say," he said, with a certain pride in his own impartiality. "She has developed an extraordinary timidity towards me. I have continually noticed that she is nervous and agitated in my presence—I am quite unable to account for it. In fact, there is no accounting for it. But I am thinking of going up to London before long, and making her see some good doctor. A little tonic, I daresay; though I don't suppose she has taken a dozen doses of medicine in as many years. I expect she will be glad to go up, for she will be near you. The one delusion—for it is no less than that—is as strange as the other."

He drew himself up to his full magnificent height.

"I do not mean that it is not very natural she should be devoted to her son," he said with a tremendous air.

What he did mean was therefore uncertain, and again he changed the subject.

"There is a third thing," he said. "This concerns you. You are of the age when we Combers usually marry. I should wish you to marry, Michael. During this last year your mother has asked half a dozen girls down here, all of whom she and I consider perfectly suitable, and no doubt you have met more in London. I should like to know definitely if you have considered the question, and if you have not, I ask you to set about it at once."

Michael was suddenly aware that never for a moment had Sylvia been away from his mind. Even when his mother was talking to him last night Sylvia had sat at the back, in the inmost place, throned and secure. And now she stepped forward. Apart from the impossibility of not acknowledging her, he wished to do it. He wanted to wear her publicly, though she was not his; he wanted to take his allegiance oath, though his sovereign heeded not.

"I have considered the question," he said, "and I have quite made up my mind whom I want to marry. She is Miss Falbe, Miss Sylvia Falbe, of whom you may have heard as a singer. She is the sister of my music-master, and I can certainly marry nobody else."

It was not merely defiance of the dreadful old tradition, which Lord Ashbridge had announced in the manner of Moses stepping down from Sinai, that prompted this appalling statement of the case; it was the joy in the profession of his love. It had to be flung out like that. Lord Ashbridge looked at him a moment in dead silence.

"I have not the honour of knowing Miss—Miss Falbe, is it?" he said; "nor shall I have that honour."

Michael got up; there was that in his father's tone that stung him to fury.

"It is very likely that you will not," he said, "since when I proposed to her yesterday she did not accept me."

Somehow Lord Ashbridge felt that as an insult to himself. Indeed, it was a double insult. Michael had proposed to this singer, and this singer had not instantly clutched him. He gave his dreadful little treble giggle.

"And I am to bind up your broken heart?" he asked.

Michael drew himself up to his full height. This was an indiscretion, for it but made his father recognise how short he was. It brought farce into the tragic situation.

"Oh, by no means," he said. "My heart is not going to break yet. I don't give up hope."

Then, in a flash, he thought of his mother's pale, anxious face, her desire that he should not vex his father.

"I am sorry," he said, "but that is the case. I wish—I wish you would try to understand me."

"I find you incomprehensible," said Lord Ashbridge, and left the room with his high walk and his swinging elbows.

Well, it was done now, and Michael felt that there were no new vexations to be sprung on his father. It was bound to happen, he supposed, sooner or later, and he was not sorry that it had happened sooner than he expected or intended. Sylvia so held sway in him that he could not help acknowledging her. His announcement had broken from him irresistibly, in spite of his mother's whispered word to him last night, "This is our secret." It could not be secret when his father spoke like that. . . . And then, with a flare of illumination he perceived how intensely his father disliked him. Nothing but sheer basic antipathy could have been responsible for that miserable retort, "Am I to bind up your broken heart?" Anger, no doubt, was the immediate cause, but so utterly ungenerous a rejoinder to Michael's announcement could not have been conceived, except in a heart that thoroughly and rootedly disliked him. That he was a continual monument of disappointment to his father he knew well, but never before had it been quite plainly shown him how essential an object of dislike he was. And the grounds of the dislike were now equally plain—his father disliked him exactly because he was his father. On the other hand, the last twenty-four hours had shown him that his mother loved him exactly because he was her son. When these two new and undeniable facts were put side by side, Michael felt that he was an infinite gainer.

He went rather drearily to the window. Far off across the field below the garden he could see Lord Ashbridge walking airily along on his way to the links, with his head held high, his stick swinging in his hand, his two retrievers at his heels. No doubt already the soothing influences of Nature were at work—Nature, of course, standing for the portion of trees and earth and houses that belonged to him—and were expunging the depressing reflection that his wife and only son inspired in him. And, indeed, such was actually the case: Lord Ashbridge, in his amazing fatuity, could not long continue being himself without being cheered and invigorated by that fact, and though when he set out his big white hands were positively trembling with passion, he carried his balsam always with him. But he had registered to himself, even as Michael had registered, the fact that he found his son a most intolerable person. And what vexed him most of all, what made him clang the gate at the end of the field so violently that it hit one of his retrievers shrewdly on the nose, was the sense of his own impotence. He knew perfectly well that in point of view of determination (that quality which in himself was firmness, and in those who opposed him obstinacy) Michael was his match. And the annoying thing was that, as his wife had once told him, Michael undoubtedly inherited that quality from him. It was as inalienable as the estates of which he had threatened to deprive his son, and which, as he knew quite well, were absolutely entailed. Michael, in this regard, seemed no better than a common but successful thief. He had annexed his father's firmness, and at his death would certainly annex all his pictures and trees and acres and the red roofs of Ashbridge.

Michael saw the gate so imperially slammed, he heard the despairing howl of Robin, and though he was sorry for Robin, he could not help laughing. He remembered also a ludicrous sight he had seen at the Zoological Gardens a few days ago: two seals, sitting bolt upright, quarrelling with each other, and making the most absurd grimaces and noises. They neither of them quite dared to attack the other, and so sat with their faces close together, saying the rudest things. Aunt Barbara would certainly have seen how inimitably his father and he had, in their interview just now, resembled the two seals.

And then he became aware that all the time, au fond, he had thought about nothing but Sylvia, and of Sylvia, not as the subject of quarrel, but as just Sylvia, the singing Sylvia, with a hand on his shoulder.

The winter sun was warm on the south terrace of the house, when, an hour later, he strolled out, according to arrangement, with his mother. It had melted the rime of the night before that lay now on the grass in threads of minute diamonds, though below the terrace wall, and on the sunk rims of the empty garden beds it still persisted in outline of white heraldry. A few monthly roses, weak, pink blossoms, weary with the toil of keeping hope alive till the coming of spring, hung dejected heads in the sunk garden, where the hornbeam hedge that carried its russet leaves unfallen, shaded them from the wind. Here, too, a few bulbs had pricked their way above ground, and stood with stout, erect horns daintily capped with rime. All these things, which for years had been presented to Lady Ashbridge's notice without attracting her attention; now filled her with minute childlike pleasure; they were discoveries as entrancing and as magical as the first finding of the oval pieces of blue sky that a child sees one morning in a hedge-sparrow's nest. Now that she was alone with her son, all her secret restlessness and anxiety had vanished, and she remarked almost with glee that her husband had telephoned from the golf links to say that he would not be back for lunch; then, remembering that Michael had gone to talk to his father after breakfast, she asked him about the interview.

Michael had already made up his mind as to what to say here. Knowing that his father was anxious about her, he felt it highly unlikely that he would tell her anything to distress her, and so he represented the interview as having gone off in perfect amity. Later in the day, on his father's return, he had made up his mind to propose a truce between them, as far as his mother was concerned. Whether that would be accepted or not he could not certainly tell, but in the interval there was nothing to be gained by grieving her.

A great weight was lifted off her mind.

"Ah, my dear, that is good," she said. "I was anxious. So now perhaps we shall have a peaceful Christmas. I am glad your Aunt Barbara and Francis are coming, for though your aunt always laughs at your father, she does it kindly, does she not? And as for Francis—my dear, if God had given me two sons, I should have liked the other to be like Francis. And shall we walk a little farther this way, and see poor Petsy's grave?"

Petsy's grave proved rather agitating. There were doleful little stories of the last days to be related, and Petsy II. was tiresome, and insisted on defying the world generally with shrill barkings from the top of the small mound, conscious perhaps that his helpless predecessor slept below. Then their walk brought them to the band of trees that separated the links from the house, from which Lady Ashbridge retreated, fearful, as she vaguely phrased it, "of being seen," and by whom there was no need for her to explain. Then across the field came a group of children scampering home from school. They ceased their shouting and their games as the others came near, and demurely curtsied and took off their caps to Lady Ashbridge.

"Nice, well-behaved children," said she. "A merry Christmas to you all. I hope you are all good children to your mothers, as my son is to me."

She pressed his arm, nodded and smiled at the children, and walked on with him. And Michael felt the lump in his throat.

The arrival of Aunt Barbara and Francis that afternoon did something, by the mere addition of numbers to the party, to relieve the tension of the situation. Lord Ashbridge said little but ate largely, and during the intervals of empty plates directed an impartial gaze at the portraits of his ancestors, while wholly ignoring his descendant. But Michael was too wise to put himself into places where he could be pointedly ignored, and the resplendent dinner, with its six footmen and its silver service, was not really more joyless than usual. But his father's majestic displeasure was more apparent when the three men sat alone afterwards, and it was in dead silence that port was pushed round and cigarettes handed. Francis, it is true, made a couple of efforts to enliven things, but his remarks produced no response whatever from his uncle, and he subsided into himself, thinking with regret of what an amusing evening he would have had if he had only stopped in town. But when they rose Michael signed to his cousin to go on, and planted himself firmly in the path to the door. It was evident that his father did not mean to speak to him, but he could not push by him or walk over him.

"There is one thing I want to say to you, father," said he. "I have told my mother that our interview this morning was quite amicable. I do not see why she should be distressed by knowing that it was not."

His father's face softened a moment.

"Yes, I agree to that," he said.

As far as that went, the compact was observed, and whenever Lady Ashbridge was present her husband made a point of addressing a few remarks to Michael, but there their intercourse ended. Michael found opportunity to explain to Aunt Barbara what had happened, suggesting as a consolatory simile the domestic difficulties of the seals at the Zoological Gardens, and was pleased to find her recognise the aptness of this description. But heaviest of all on the spirits of the whole party sat the anxiety about Lady Ashbridge. There could be no doubt that some cerebral degeneration was occurring, and Lady Barbara's urgent representation to her brother had the effect of making him promise to take her up to London without delay after Christmas, and let a specialist see her. For the present the pious fraud practised on her that Michael and his father had had "a good talk" together, and were excellent friends, sufficed to render her happy and cheerful. She had long, dim talks, full of repetition, with Michael, whose presence appeared to make her completely content, and when he was out or away from her she would sit eagerly waiting for his return. Petsy, to the great benefit of his health, got somewhat neglected by her; her whole nature and instincts were alight with the mother-love that had burnt so late into flame, with this tragic accompaniment of derangement. She seemed to be groping her way back to the days when Michael was a little boy, and she was a young woman; often she would seat herself at her piano, if Michael was not there to play to her, and in a thin, quavering voice sing the songs of twenty years ago. She would listen to his playing, beating time to his music, and most of all she loved the hour when the day was drawing in, and the first shadow and flame of dusk and firelight; then, with her hand in his, sitting in her room, where they would not be interrupted, she would whisper fresh inquiries about Sylvia, offering to go herself to the girl and tell her how lovable her suitor was. She lived in a dim, subaqueous sort of consciousness, physically quite well, and mentally serene in the knowledge that Michael was in the house, and would presently come and talk to her.

For the others it was dismal enough; this shadow, that was to her a watery sunlight, lay over them all—this, and the further quarrel, unknown to her, between Michael and his father. When they all met, as at meal times, there was the miserable pretence of friendliness and comfortable ease kept up, for fear of distressing Lady Ashbridge. It was dreary work for all concerned, but, luckily, not difficult of accomplishment. A little chatter about the weather, the merest small change of conversation, especially if that conversation was held between Michael and his father, was sufficient to wreathe her in smiles, and she would, according to habit, break in with some wrecking remark, that entailed starting this talk all afresh. But when she left the room a glowering silence would fall; Lord Ashbridge would pick up a book or leave the room with his high-stepping walk and erect head, the picture of insulted dignity.

Of the three he was far most to be pitied, although the situation was the direct result of his own arrogance and self-importance; but arrogance and self-importance were as essential ingredients of his character as was humour of Aunt Barbara's. They were very awkward and tiresome qualities, but this particular Lord Ashbridge would have no existence without them. He was deeply and mortally offended with Michael; that alone was sufficient to make a sultry and stifling atmosphere, and in addition to that he had the burden of his anxiety about his wife. Here came an extra sting, for in common humanity he had, by appearing to be friends with Michael, to secure her serenity, and this could only be done by the continued profanation of his own highly proper and necessary attitude towards his son. He had to address friendly words to Michael that really almost choked him; he had to practise cordiality with this wretch who wanted to marry the sister of a music-master. Michael had pulled up all the old traditions, that carefully-tended and pompous flower-garden, as if they had been weeds, and thrown them in his father's face. It was indeed no wonder that, in his wife's absence, he almost burst with indignation over the desecrated beds. More than that, his own self-esteem was hurt by his wife's fear of him, just as if he had been a hard and unkind husband to her, which he had not been, but merely a very self-absorbed and dominant one, while the one person who could make her quite happy was his despised son. Michael's person, Michael's tastes, Michael's whole presence and character were repugnant to him, and yet Michael had the power which, to do Lord Ashbridge justice, he would have given much to be possessed of himself, of bringing comfort and serenity to his wife.

On the afternoon of the day following Christmas the two cousins had been across the estuary to Ashbridge together. Francis, who, in spite of his habitual easiness of disposition and general good temper, had found the conditions of anger and anxiety quite intolerable, had settled to leave next day, instead of stopping till the end of the week, and Michael acquiesced in this without any sense of desertion; he had really only wondered why Francis had stopped three nights, instead of finding urgent private business in town after one. He realised also, somewhat with surprise, that Francis was "no good" when there was trouble about; there was no one so delightful when there was, so to speak, a contest of who should enjoy himself the most, and Francis invariably won. But if the subject of the contest was changed, and the prize given for the individual who, under depressing circumstances, should contrive to show the greatest serenity of aspect, Francis would have lost with an even greater margin. Michael, in fact, was rather relieved than otherwise at his cousin's immediate departure, for it helped nobody to see the martyred St. Sebastian, and it was merely odious for St. Sebastian himself. In fact, at this moment, when Michael was rowing them back across the full-flooded estuary, Francis was explaining this with his customary lucidity.

"I don't do any good here, Mike," he said. "Uncle Robert doesn't speak to me any more than he does to you, except when Aunt Marion is there. And there's nothing going on, is there? I practically asked if I might go duck-shooting to-day, and Uncle Robert merely looked out of the window. But if anybody, specially you, wanted me to stop, why, of course I would."

"But I don't," said Michael.

"Thanks awfully. Gosh, look at those ducks! They're just wanting to be shot. But there it is, then. Certainly Uncle Robert doesn't want me, nor Aunt Marion. I say, what do they think is the matter with her?"

Michael looked round, then took, rather too late, another pull on his oars, and the boat gently grated on the pebbly mud at the side of the landing-place. Francis's question, the good-humoured insouciance of it grated on his mind in rather similar fashion.

"We don't know yet," he said. "I expect we shall all go back to town in a couple of days, so that she may see somebody."

Francis jumped out briskly and gracefully, and stood with his hands in his pockets while Michael pushed off again, and brought the boat into its shed.

"I do hope it's nothing serious," he said. "She looks quite well, doesn't she? I daresay it's nothing; but she's been alone, hasn't she, with Uncle Robert all these weeks. That would give her the hump, too."

Michael felt a sudden spasm of impatience at these elegant and consoling reflections. But now, in the light of his own increasing maturity, he saw how hopeless it was to feel Francis's deficiencies, his entire lack of deep feeling. He was made like that; and if you were fond of anybody the only possible way of living up to your affection was to attach yourself to their qualities.

They strolled a little way in silence.

"And why did you tell Uncle Robert about Sylvia Falbe?" asked Francis. "I can't understand that. For the present, anyhow, she had refused you. There was nothing to tell him about. If I was fond of a girl like that I should say nothing about it, if I knew my people would disapprove, until I had got her."

Michael laughed.

"Oh, yes you would," he said, "if you were to use your own words, fond of her 'like that.' You couldn't help it. At least, I couldn't. It's—it's such a glory to be fond like that."

He stopped.

"We won't talk about it," he said—"or, rather, I can't talk about it, if you don't understand."

"But she had refused you," said the sensible Francis.

"That makes no difference. She shines through everything, through the infernal awfulness of these days, through my father's anger, and my mother's illness, whatever it proves to be—I think about them really with all my might, and at the end I find I've been thinking about Sylvia. Everything is she—the woods, the tide—oh, I can't explain."

They had walked across the marshy land at the edge of the estuary, and now in front of them was the steep and direct path up to the house, and the longer way through the woods. At this point the estuary made a sudden turn to the left, sweeping directly seawards, and round the corner, immediately in front of them was the long reach of deep water up which, even when the tide was at its lowest, an ocean-going steamer could penetrate if it knew the windings of the channel. To-day, in the windless, cold calm of mid-winter, though the sun was brilliant in a blue sky overhead, an opaque mist, thick as cotton-wool, lay over the surface of the water, and, taking the winding road through the woods, which, following the estuary, turned the point, they presently found themselves, as they mounted, quite clear of the mist that lay below them on the river. Their steps were noiseless on the mossy path, and almost immediately after they had turned the corner, as Francis paused to light a cigarette, they heard from just below them the creaking of oars in their rowlocks. It caught the ears of them both, and without conscious curiosity they listened. On the moment the sound of rowing ceased, and from the dense mist just below them there came a sound which was quite unmistakable, namely, the "plop" of something heavy dropped into the water. That sound, by some remote form of association, suddenly recalled to Michael's mind certain questions Aunt Barbara had asked him about the Emperor's stay at Ashbridge, and his own recollection of his having gone up and down the river in a launch. There was something further, which he did not immediately recollect. Yes, it was the request that if when he was here at Christmas he found strangers hanging about the deep- water reach, of which the chart was known only to the Admiralty, he should let her know. Here at this moment they were overlooking the mist-swathed water, and here at this moment, unseen, was a boat rowing stealthily, stopping, and, perhaps, making soundings.

He laid his hand on Francis's arm with a gesture for silence, then, invisible below, someone said, "Fifteen fathoms," and again the oars creaked audibly in the rowlocks.

Michael took a step towards his cousin, so that he could whisper to him.

"Come back to the boat," he said. "I want to row round and see who that is. Wait a moment, though."

The oars below made some half-dozen strokes, and then were still again. Once more there came the sound of something heavy dropped into the water.

"Someone is making soundings in the channel there," he said. "Come."

They went very quietly till they were round the point, then quickened their steps, and Michael spoke.

"That's the uncharted channel," he said; "at least, only the Admiralty have the soundings. The water's deep enough right across for a ship of moderate draught to come up, but there is a channel up which any man-of-war can pass. Of course, it may be an Admiralty boat making fresh soundings, but not likely on Boxing Day."

"What are you going to do?" asked Francis, striding easily along by Michael's short steps.

"Just see if we can find out who it is. Aunt Barbara asked me about it. I'll tell you afterwards. Now the tide's going out we can drop down with it, and we shan't be heard. I'll row just enough to keep her head straight. Sit in the bow, Francis, and keep a sharp look-out."

Foot by foot they dropped down the river, and soon came into the thick mist that lay beyond the point. It was impossible to see more than a yard or two ahead, but the same dense obscurity would prevent any further range of vision from the other boat, and, if it was still at its work, the sound of its oars or of voices, Michael reflected, might guide him to it. From the lisp of little wavelets lapping on the shore below the woods, he knew he was quite close in to the bank, and close also to the place where the invisible boat had been ten minutes before. Then, in the bewildering, unlocalised manner in which sound without the corrective guidance of sight comes to the ears, he heard as before the creaking of invisible oars, somewhere quite close at hand. Next moment the dark prow of a rowing-boat suddenly loomed into sight on their starboard, and he took a rapid stroke with his right-hand scull to bring them up to it. But at the same moment, while yet the occupants of the other boat were but shadows in the mist, they saw him, and a quick word of command rang out.

"Row—row hard!" it cried, and with a frenzied churning of oars in the water, the other boat shot by them, making down the estuary. Next moment it had quite vanished in the mist, leaving behind it knots of swirling water from its oar-blades.

Michael started in vain pursuit; his craft was heavy and clumsy, and from the retreating and faint-growing sound of the other, it was clear that he could get no pace to match, still less to overtake them. Soon he pantingly desisted.

"But an Admiralty boat wouldn't have run away," he said. "They'd have asked us who the devil we were."

"But who else was it?" asked Francis.

Michael mopped his forehead.

"Aunt Barbara would tell you," he said. "She would tell you that they were German spies."

Francis laughed.

"Or Timbuctoo niggers," he remarked.

"And that would be an odd thing, too," said Michael.

But at that moment he felt the first chill of the shadow that menaced, if by chance Aunt Barbara was right, and if already the clear tranquillity of the sky was growing dim as with the mist that lay that afternoon on the waters of the deep reach, and covered mysterious movements which were going on below it. England and Germany—there was so much of his life and his heart there. Music and song, and Sylvia.

CHAPTER X

Michael had heard the verdict of the brain specialist, who yesterday had seen his mother, and was sitting in his room beside his unopened piano quietly assimilating it, and, without making plans of his own initiative, contemplating the forms into which the future was beginning to fall, mapping itself out below him, outlining itself as when objects in a room, as the light of morning steals in, take shape again. And even as they take the familiar shapes, so already he felt that he had guessed all this in that week down at Ashbridge, from which he had returned with his father and mother a couple of days before.

She was suffering, without doubt, from some softening of the brain; nothing of remedial nature could possibly be done to arrest or cure the progress of the disease, and all that lay in human power was to secure for her as much content and serenity as possible. In her present condition there was no question of putting her under restraint, nor, indeed, could she be certified by any doctor as insane. She would have to have a trained attendant, she would live a secluded life, from which must be kept as far as possible anything that could agitate or distress her, and after that there was nothing more that could be done except to wait for the inevitable development of her malady. This might come quickly or slowly; there was no means of forecasting that, though the rapid deterioration of her brain, which had taken place during those last two months, made it, on the whole, likely that the progress of the disease would be swift. It was quite possible, on the other hand, that it might remain stationary for months. . . . And in answer to a question of Michael's, Sir James had looked at him a moment in silence. Then he answered.

"Both for her sake and for the sake of all of you," he had said, "one hopes that it will be swift."

Lord Ashbridge had just telephoned that he was coming round to see Michael, a message that considerably astonished him, since it would have been more in his manner, in the unlikely event of his wishing to see his son, to have summoned him to the house in Curzon Street. However, he had announced his advent, and thus, waiting for him, and not much concerning himself about that, Michael let the future map itself. Already it was sharply defined, its boundaries and limits were clear, and though it was yet untravelled it presented to him a familiar aspect, and he felt that he could find his allotted road without fail, though he had never yet traversed it. It was strongly marked; there could be no difficulty or question about it. Indeed, a week ago, when first the recognition of his mother's condition, with the symptoms attached to it, was known to him, he had seen the signpost that directed him into the future.

Lord Ashbridge made his usual flamboyant entry, prancing and swinging his elbows. Whatever happened he would still be Lord Ashbridge, with his grey top-hat and his large carnation and his enviable position.

"You will have heard what Sir James's opinion is about your poor mother," he said. "It was in consequence of what he recommended when he talked over the future with me that I came to see you."

Michael guessed very well what this recommendation was, but with a certain stubbornness and sense of what was due to himself, he let his father proceed with the not very welcome task of telling him.

"In fact, Michael," he said, "I have a favour to ask of you."

The fact of his being Lord Ashbridge, and the fact of Michael being his unsatisfactory son, stiffened him, and he had to qualify the favour.

"Perhaps I should not say I am about to ask you a favour," he corrected himself, "but rather to point out to you what is your obvious duty."

Suddenly it struck Michael that his father was not thinking about Lady Ashbridge at all, nor about him, but in the main about himself. All had to be done from the dominant standpoint; he owed it to himself to alleviate the conditions under which his wife must live; he owed it to himself that his son should do his part as a Comber. There was no longer any possible doubt as to what this favour, or this direction of duty, must be, but still Michael chose that his father should state it. He pushed a chair forward for him.

"Won't you sit down?" he said.

"Thank you, I would rather stand. Yes; it is not so much a favour as the indication of your duty. I do not know if you will see it in the same light as I; you have shown me before now that we do not take the same view."

Michael felt himself bristling. His father certainly had the effect of drawing out in him all the feelings that were better suppressed.

"I think we need not talk of that now, sir," he remarked.

"Certainly it is not the subject of my interview with you now. The fact is this. In some way your presence gives a certain serenity and content to your mother. I noticed that at Ashbridge, and, indeed, there has been some trouble with her this morning because I could not take her to come to see you with me. I ask you, therefore, for her sake, to be with us as much as you can, in short, to come and live with us."

Michael nodded, saluting, so to speak, the signpost into the future as he passed it.

"I had already determined to do that," he said. "I had determined, at any rate, to ask your permission to do so. It is clear that my mother wants me, and no other consideration can weigh with that."

Lord Ashbridge still remained completely self-sufficient.

"I am glad you take that view of it," he said. "I think that is all I have to say."

Now Michael was an adept at giving; as indicated before, when he gave, he gave nobly, and he could not only outwardly disregard, but he inwardly cancelled the wonderful ungenerosity with which his father received. That did not concern him.

"I will make arrangements to come at once," he said, "if you can receive me to-day."

"That will hardly be worth while, will it? I am taking your mother back to Ashbridge tomorrow."

Michael got up in silence. After all, this gift of himself, of his time, of his liberty, of all that constituted life to him, was made not to his father, but to his mother. It was made, as his heart knew, not ungrudgingly only, but eagerly, and if it had been recommended by the doctor that she should go to Ashbridge, he would have entirely disregarded the large additional sacrifice on himself which it entailed. Thus it was not owing to any retraction of his gift, or reconsideration of it, that he demurred.

"I hope you will—will meet me half-way about this, sir," he said. "You must remember that all my work lies in London. I want, naturally, to continue that as far as I can. If you go to Ashbridge it is completely interrupted. My friends are here too; everything I have is here."

His father seemed to swell a little; he appeared to fill the room.

"And all my duties lie at Ashbridge," he said. "As you know, I am not of the type of absentee landlords. It is quite impossible that I should spend these months in idleness in town. I have never done such a thing yet, nor, I may say, would our class hold the position they do if we did. We shall come up to town after Easter, should your mother's health permit it, but till then I could not dream of neglecting my duties in the country."

Now Michael knew perfectly well what his father's duties on that excellently managed estate were. They consisted of a bi-weekly interview in the "business-room" (an abode of files and stags' heads, in which Lord Ashbridge received various reports of building schemes and repairs), of a round of golf every afternoon, and of reading the lessons and handing the offertory-box on Sunday. That, at least, was the sum-total as it presented itself to him, and on which he framed his conclusions. But he left out altogether the moral effect of the big landlord living on his own land, and being surrounded by his own dependents, which his father, on the other hand, so vastly over-estimated. It was clear that there was not likely to be much accord between them on this subject.

"But could you not go down there perhaps once or twice a week, and get Bailey to come and consult you here?" he asked.

Lord Ashbridge held his head very high.

"That would be completely out of the question," he said.

All this, Michael felt, had nothing to do with the problem of his mother and himself. It was outside it altogether, and concerned only his father's convenience. He was willing to press this point as far as possible.

"I had imagined you would stop in London," he said. "Supposing under these circumstances I refuse to live with you?"

"I should draw my own conclusion as to the sincerity of your profession of duty towards your mother."

"And practically what would you do?" asked Michael.

"Your mother and I would go to Ashbridge tomorrow all the same."

Another alternative suddenly suggested itself to Michael which he was almost ashamed of proposing, for it implied that his father put his own convenience as outweighing any other consideration. But he saw that if only Lord Ashbridge was selfish enough to consent to it, it had manifest merits. His mother would be alone with him, free of the presence that so disconcerted her.

"I propose, then," he said, "that she and I should remain in town, as you want to be at Ashbridge."

He had been almost ashamed of suggesting it, but no such shame was reflected in his father's mind. This would relieve him of the perpetual embarrassment of his wife's presence, and the perpetual irritation of Michael's. He had persuaded himself that he was making a tremendous personal sacrifice in proposing that Michael should live with them, and this relieved him of the necessity.

"Upon my word, Michael," he said, with the first hint of cordiality that he had displayed, "that is very well thought of. Let us consider; it is certainly the case that this derangement in your poor mother's mind has caused her to take what I might almost call a dislike to me. I mentioned that to Sir James, though it was very painful for me to do so, and he said that it was a common and most distressing symptom of brain disease, that the sufferer often turned against those he loved best. Your plan would have the effect of removing that."

He paused a moment, and became even more sublimely fatuous.

"You, too," he said, "it would obviate the interruption of your work, about which you feel so keenly. You would be able to go on with it. Of myself, I don't think at all. I shall be lonely, no doubt, at Ashbridge, but my own personal feelings must not be taken into account. Yes; it seems to me a very sensible notion. We shall have to see what your mother says to it. She might not like me to be away from her, in spite of her apparent—er—dislike of me. It must all depend on her attitude. But for my part I think very well of your scheme. Thank you, Michael, for suggesting it."

He left immediately after this to ascertain Lady Ashbridge's feelings about it, and walked home with a complete resumption of his usual exuberance. It indeed seemed an admirable plan. It relieved him from the nightmare of his wife's continual presence, and this he expressed to himself by thinking that it relieved her from his. It was not that he was deficient in sympathy for her, for in his self-centred way he was fond of her, but he could sympathise with her just as well at Ashbridge. He could do no good to her, and he had not for her that instinct of love which would make it impossible for him to leave her. He would also be spared the constant irritation of having Michael in the house, and this he expressed to himself by saying that Michael disliked him, and would be far more at his ease without him. Furthermore, Michael would be able to continue his studies . . . of this too, in spite of the fact that he had always done his best to discourage them, he made a self-laudatory translation, by telling himself that he was very glad not to have to cause Michael to discontinue them. In fine, he persuaded himself, without any difficulty, that he was a very fine fellow in consenting to a plan that suited him so admirably, and only wondered that he had not thought of it himself. There was nothing, after his wife had expressed her joyful acceptance of it, to detain him in town, and he left for Ashbridge that afternoon, while Michael moved into the house in Curzon Street.

Michael entered upon his new life without the smallest sense of having done anything exceptional or even creditable. It was so perfectly obvious to him that he had to be with his mother that he had no inclination to regard himself at all in the matter; the thing was as simple as it had been to him to help Francis out of financial difficulties with a gift of money. There was no effort of will, no sense of sacrifice about it, it was merely the assertion of a paramount instinct. The life limited his freedom, for, for a great part of the day he was with his mother, and between his music and his attendance on her, he had but little leisure. Occasionally he went out to see his friends, but any prolonged absence on his part always made her uneasy, and he would often find her, on his return, sitting in the hall, waiting for him, so as to enjoy his presence from the first moment that he re- entered the house. But though he found no food for reflection in himself, Aunt Barbara, who came to see them some few days after Michael had been installed here, found a good deal.

They had all had tea together, and afterwards Lady Ashbridge's nurse had come down to fetch her upstairs to rest. And then Aunt Barbara surprised Michael, for she came across the room to him, with her kind eyes full of tears, and kissed him.

"My dear, I must say it once," she said, "and then you will know that it is always in my mind. You have behaved nobly, Michael; it's a big word, but I know no other. As for your father—"

Michael interrupted her.

"Oh, I don't understand him," he said. "At least, that's the best way to look at it. Let's leave him out."

He paused a moment.

"After all, it is a much better plan than our living all three of us at Ashbridge. It's better for my mother, and for me, and for him."

"I know, but how he could consent to the better plan," she said. "Well, let us leave him out. Poor Robert! He and his golf. My dear, your father is a very ludicrous person, you know. But about you, Michael, do you think you can stand it?"

He smiled at her.

"Why, of course I can," he said. "Indeed, I don't think I'll accept that statement of it. It's—it's such a score to be able to be of use, you know. I can make my mother happy. Nobody else can. I think I'm getting rather conceited about it."

"Yes, dear; I find you insufferable," remarked Aunt Barbara parenthetically.

"Then you must just bear it. The thing is"—Michael took a moment to find the words he searched for—"the thing is I want to be wanted. Well, it's no light thing to be wanted by your mother, even if—"

He sat down on the sofa by his aunt.

"Aunt Barbara, how ironically gifts come," he said. "This was rather a sinister way of giving, that my mother should want me like this just as her brain was failing. And yet that failure doesn't affect the quality of her love. Is it something that shines through the poor tattered fabric? Anyhow, it has nothing to do with her brain. It is she herself, somehow, not anything of hers, that wants me. And you ask if I can stand it?"

Michael with his ugly face and his kind eyes and his simple heart seemed extraordinarily charming just then to Aunt Barbara. She wished that Sylvia could have seen him then in all the unconsciousness of what he was doing so unquestioningly, or that she could have seen him as she had with his mother during the last hour. Lady Ashbridge had insisted on sitting close to him, and holding his hand whenever she could possess herself of it, of plying him with a hundred repeated questions, and never once had she made Michael either ridiculous or self-conscious. And this, she reflected, went on most of the day, and for how many days it would go on, none knew. Yet Michael could not consider even whether he could stand it; he rejected the expression as meaningless.

"And your friends?" she said. "Do you manage to see them?"

"Oh, yes, occasionally," said Michael. "They don't come here, for the presence of strangers makes my mother agitated. She thinks they have some design of taking her or me away. But she wants to see Sylvia. She knows about—about her and me, and I can't make up my mind what to do about it. She is always asking if I can't take her to see Sylvia, or get her to come here."

"And why not? Sylvia knows about your mother, I suppose."

"I expect so. I told Hermann. But I am afraid my mother will— well, you can't call it arguing—but will try to persuade her to have me. I can't let Sylvia in for that. Nor, if it comes to that, can I let myself in for that."

"Can't you impress on your mother that she mustn't?"

Michael leaned forward to the fire, pondering this, and stretching out his big hands to the blaze.

"Yes, I might," he said. "I should love to see Sylvia again, just see her, you know. We settled that the old terms we were on couldn't continue. At least, I settled that, and she understood."

"Sylvia is a gaby," remarked Aunt Barbara.

"I'm rather glad you think so."

"Oh, get her to come," said she. "I'm sure your mother will do as you tell her. I'll be here too, if you like, if that will do any good. By the way, I see your Hermann's piano recital comes off to- morrow."

"I know. My mother wants to go to that, and I think I shall take her. Will you come too, Aunt Barbara, and sit on the other side of her? My 'Variations' are going to be played. If they are a success, Hermann tells me I shall be dragged screaming on to the platform, and have to bow. Lord! And if they're not, well, 'Lord' also."

"Yes, my dear, of course I'll come. Let me see, I shall have to lie, as I have another engagement, but a little thing like that doesn't bother me."

Suddenly she clapped her hands together.

"My dear, I quite forgot," she said. "Michael, such excitement. You remember the boat you heard taking soundings on the deep-water reach? Of course you do! Well, I sent that information to the proper quarter, and since then watch has been kept in the woods just above it. Last night only the coastguard police caught four men at it—all Germans. They tried to escape as they did before, by rowing down the river, but there was a steam launch below which intercepted them. They had on them a chart of the reach, with soundings, nearly complete; and when they searched their houses— they are all tenants of your astute father, who merely laughed at us—they found a very decent map of certain private areas at Harwich. Oh, I'm not such a fool as I look. They thanked me, my dear, for my information, and I very gracefully said that my information was chiefly got by you."

"But did those men live in Ashbridge?" asked Michael.

"Yes; and your father will have four decorous houses on his hands. I am glad: he should not have laughed at us. It will teach him, I hope. And now, my dear, I must go."

She stood up, and put her hand on Michael's arm.

"And you know what I think of you," she said. "To-morrow evening, then. I hate music usually; but then I adore Mr. Hermann. I only wish he wasn't a German. Can't you get him to naturalise himself and his sister?"

"You wouldn't ask that if you had seen him in Munich," said Michael.

"I suppose not. Patriotism is such a degrading emotion when it is not English."

Michael's "Variations" came some half-way down the programme next evening, and as the moment for them approached, Lady Ashbridge got more and more excited.

"I hope he knows them by heart properly, dear," she whispered to Michael. "I shall be so nervous for fear he'll forget them in the middle, which is so liable to happen if you play without your notes."

Michael laid his hand on his mother's.

"Hush, mother," he said, "you mustn't talk while he's playing."

"Well, I was only whispering. But if you tell me I mustn't—"

The hall was crammed from end to end, for not only was Hermann a person of innumerable friends, but he had already a considerable reputation, and, being a

German, all musical England went to hear him. And to-night he was playing superbly, after a couple of days of miserable nervousness over his debut as a pianist; but his temperament was one of those that are strung up to their highest pitch by such nervous agonies; he required just that to make him do full justice to his own personality, and long before he came to the "Variations," Michael felt quite at ease about his success. There was no question about it any more: the whole audience knew that they were listening to a master. In the row immediately behind Michael's party were sitting Sylvia and her mother, who had not quite been torn away from her novels, since she had sought "The Love of Hermione Hogarth" underneath her cloak, and read it furtively in pauses. They had come in after Michael, and until the interval between the classical and the modern section of the concert he was unaware of their presence; then idly turning round to look at the crowded hall, he found himself face to face with the girl.

"I had no idea you were there," he said. "Hermann will do, won't he? I think—"

And then suddenly the words of commonplace failed him, and he looked at her in silence.

"I knew you were back," she said. "Hermann told me about— everything."

Michael glanced sideways, indicating his mother, who sat next him, and was talking to Barbara.

"I wondered whether perhaps you would come and see my mother and me," he said. "May I write?"

She looked at him with the friendliness of her smiling eyes and her grave mouth.

"Is it necessary to ask?" she said.

Michael turned back to his seat, for his mother had had quite enough of her sister-in-law, and wanted him again. She looked over her shoulder for a moment to see whom Michael was talking to.

"I'm enjoying my concert, dear," she said. "And who is that nice young lady? Is she a friend of yours?"

The interval was over, and Hermann returned to the platform, and waiting for a moment for the buzz of conversation to die down, gave out, without any preliminary excursion on the keys, the text of Michael's "Variations." Then he began to tell them, with light and flying fingers, what that simple tune had suggested to Michael, how he imagined himself looking on at an old-fashioned dance, and while the dancers moved to the graceful measure of a minuet, or daintily in a gavotte, the tune of "Good King Wenceslas" still rang in his head, or, how in the joy of the sunlight of a spring morning it still haunted him. It lay behind a cascade of foaming waters that, leaping, roared into a ravine; it marched with flying banners on some day of victorious entry, it watched a funeral procession wind by, with tapers and the smell of incense; it heard, as it got nearer back to itself again, the peals of Christmas bells, and stood forth again in its own person, decorated and emblazoned.

Hermann had already captured his audience; now he held them tame in the hollow of his hand. Twice he bowed, and then, in answer to the demand, just beckoned with his finger to Michael, who rose. For a moment his mother wished to detain him.

"You're not going to leave me, my dear, are you?" she asked anxiously.

He waited to explain to her quietly, left her, and, feeling rather dazed, made his way round to the back and saw the open door on to the platform confronting him. He felt that no power on earth could make him step into the naked publicity there, but at the moment Hermann appeared in the doorway.

"Come on, Mike," he said, laughing. "Thank the pretty ladies and gentlemen! Lord, isn't it all a lark!"

Michael advanced with him, stared and hoped he smiled properly, though he felt that he was nailing some hideous grimace to his face; and then just below him he saw his mother eagerly pointing him out to a total stranger, with gesticulation, and just behind her Sylvia looking at her, and not at him, with such tenderness, such kindly pity. There were the two most intimately bound into his life, the mother who wanted him, the girl whom he wanted; and by his side was Hermann, who, as Michael always knew, had thrown open the gates of life to him. All the rest, even including Aunt Barbara, seemed of no significance in that moment. Afterwards, no doubt, he would be glad they were pleased, be proud of having pleased them; but just now, even when, for the first time in his life, that intoxicating wine of appreciation was given him, he stood with it bubbling and yellow in his hand, not drinking of it.

Michael had prepared the way of Sylvia's coming by telling his mother the identity of the "nice young lady" at the concert; he had also impressed on her the paramount importance of not saying anything with regard to him that could possibly embarrass the nice young lady, and when Sylvia came to tea a few days later, he was quite without any uneasiness, while for himself he was only conscious of that thirst for her physical presence, the desire, as he had said to Aunt Barbara, "just to see her." Nor was there the slightest embarrassment in their meeting! it was clear that there was not the least difficulty either for him or her in being natural, which, as usually happens, was the complete solution.

"That is good of you to come," he said, meeting her almost at the door. "My mother has been looking forward to your visit. Mother dear, here is Miss Falbe."

Lady Ashbridge was pathetically eager to be what she called "good." Michael had made it clear to her that it was his wish that Miss Falbe should not be embarrassed, and any wish just now expressed by Michael was of the nature of a divine command to her.

"Well, this is a pleasure," she said, looking across to Michael with the eyes of a dog on a beloved master. "And we are not strangers quite, are we, Miss Falbe? We sat so near each other to listen to your brother, who I am sure plays beautifully, and the music which Michael made. Haven't I got a clever son, and such a good one?"

Sylvia was unerring. Michael had known she would be.

"Indeed, you have," she said, sitting down by her. "And Michael mustn't hear what we say about him, must he, or he'll be getting conceited."

Lady Ashbridge laughed.

"And that would never do, would it?" she said, still retaining Sylvia's hand. Then a little dim ripple of compunction broke in her mind. "Michael," she said, "we are only joking about your getting conceited. Miss Falbe and I are only joking. And—and won't you take off your hat, Miss Falbe, for you are not going to hurry away, are you? You are going to pay us a long visit."

Michael had not time to remind his mother that ladies who come to tea do not usually take their hats off, for on the word Sylvia's hands were busy with her hatpins.

"I'm so glad you suggested that," she said. "I always want to take my hat off. I don't know who invented hats, but I wish he hadn't."

Lady Ashbridge looked at her masses of bright hair, and could not help telegraphing a note of admiration, as it were, to Michael.

"Now, that's more comfortable," she said. "You look as if you weren't going away next minute. When I like to see people, I hate their going away. I'm afraid sometimes that Michael will go away, but he tells me he won't. And you liked Michael's music, Miss Falbe? Was it not clever of him to think of all that out of one simple little tune? And he tells me you sing so nicely. Perhaps you would sing to us when we've had tea. Oh, and here is my sister-in-law. Do you know her— Lady Barbara? My dear, what is your husband's name?"

Seeing Sylvia uncovered, Lady Barbara, with a tact that was creditable to her, but strangely unsuccessful, also began taking off her hat. Her sister-in-law was too polite to interfere, but, as a matter of fact, she did not take much pleasure in the notion that Barbara was going to stay a very long time, too. She was fond of her, but it was not Barbara whom Michael wanted. She turned her attention to the girl again.

"My husband's away," she said, confidentially; "he is very busy down at Ashbridge, and I daresay he won't find time to come up to town for many weeks yet. But, you know, Michael and I do very well without him, very well, indeed, and it would never do to take him away from his duties—would it, Michael?"

Here was a shoal to be avoided.

"No, you mustn't think of tempting him to come up to town," said Michael. "Give me some tea for Aunt Barbara."

This answer entranced Lady Ashbridge; she had to nudge Michael several times to show that she understood the brilliance of it, and put lump after lump of sugar into Barbara's cup in her rapt appreciation of it. But very soon she turned to Sylvia again.

"And your brother is a friend of Michael's, too, isn't he?" she said. "Some day perhaps he will come to see me. We don't see many people, Michael and I, for we find ourselves very well content alone. But perhaps some day he will come and play his concert over again to us; and then, perhaps, if you ask me, I will sing to you. I used to sing a great deal when I was younger. Michael—where has Michael gone?"

Michael had just left the room to bring some cigarettes in from next door, and Lady Ashbridge ran after him, calling him. She found him in the hall, and brought him back triumphantly.

"Now we will all sit and talk for a long time," she said. "You one side of me, Miss Falbe, and Michael the other. Or would you be so kind as to sing for us? Michael will play for you, and would it annoy you if I came and turned over the pages? It would give me a great deal of pleasure to turn over for you, if you will just nod each time when you are ready."

Sylvia got up.

"Why, of course," she said. "What have you got, Michael? I haven't anything with me."

Michael found a volume of Schubert, and once again, as on the first time he had seen her, she sang "Who is Sylvia?" while he played, and Lady Ashbridge had her eyes fixed now on one and now on the other of them, waiting for their nod to do her part; and then she wanted to sing herself, and with some far-off remembrance of the airs and graces of twenty-five years ago, she put her handkerchief and her rings on the top of the piano, and, playing for herself, emitted faint treble sounds which they knew to be "The Soldier's Farewell."

Then presently her nurse came for her to lie down before dinner, and she was inclined to be tearful and refuse to go till Michael made it clear that it was his express and sovereign will that she should do so. Then very audibly she whispered to him. "May I ask her to give me a kiss?" she said. "She looks so kind, Michael, I don't think she would mind."

Sylvia went back home with a little heartache for Michael, wondering, if she was in his place, if her mother, instead of being absorbed in her novels, demanded such incessant attentions, whether she had sufficient love in her heart to render them with the exquisite simplicity, the tender patience that Michael showed. Well as she knew him, greatly as she liked him, she had not imagined that he, or indeed any man could have behaved quite like that. There seemed no effort at all about it; he was not trying to be patient; he had the sense of "patience's perfect work" natural to him; he did not seem to have to remind himself that his mother was ill, and thus he must be gentle with her. He was gentle with her because he was in himself gentle. And yet, though his behaviour was no effort to him, she guessed how wearying must be the continual strain of the situation itself. She felt that she would get cross from mere fatigue, however excellent her intentions might be, however willing the spirit. And no one, so she had understood from Barbara, could take Michael's place. In his occasional absences his mother was fretful and miserable, and day by day Michael left her less. She would sit close to him when he was practising—a thing that to her or to Hermann would have rendered practice impossible—and if he wrestled with one hand over a difficult bar, she would take the other into hers, would ask him if he was not getting tired, would recommend him to rest for a little; and yet Michael, who last summer had so stubbornly insisted on leading his own life, and had put his determination into effect in the teeth of all domestic opposition, now with more than cheerfulness laid his own life aside in order to look after his mother. Sylvia felt that the real heroisms of life were not so much the fine heady deeds which are so obviously admirable, as such serene steadfastness, such unvarying patience as that which she had just seen.

Her whole soul applauded Michael, and yet below her applause was this heartache for him, the desire to be able to help him to bear the burden which must be so heavy, though he bore it so blithely. But in the very nature of things there was but one way in which she could help him, and in that she was powerless. She could not give him what he wanted. But she longed to be able to.

CHAPTER XI

It was a morning of early March, and Michael, looking out from the dining-room window at the house in Curzon Street, where he had just breakfasted alone, was smitten with wonder and a secret ecstasy, for he suddenly saw and felt that it was winter no longer, but that spring had come. For the last week the skies had screamed with outrageous winds and had been populous with flocks of sullen clouds that discharged themselves in sleet and snowy rain, and half last night, for he had slept very badly, he had heard the dashing of showers, as of wind-driven spray, against the window-panes, and had listened to the fierce rattling of the frames. Towards morning he had slept, and during those hours it seemed that a new heaven and a new earth had come into being; vitally and essentially the world was a different affair altogether.

At the back of the house on to which these windows looked was a garden of some half acre, a square of somewhat sooty grass, bounded by high walls, with a few trees at the further end. Into it, too, had the message that thrilled through his bones penetrated, and this little oasis of doubtful grass and blackened shrubs had a totally different aspect to-day from that which it had worn all those weeks. The sparrows that had sat with fluffed-up feathers in corners sheltered from the gales, were suddenly busy and shrilly vocal, chirruping and dragging about straws, and flying from limb to limb of the trees with twigs in their beaks. For the first time he noticed that little verdant cabochons of folded leaf had globed themselves on the lilac bushes below the window, crocuses had budded, and in the garden beds had shot up the pushing spikes of bulbs, while in the sooty grass he could see specks and patches of vivid green, the first growth of the year.

He opened the window and strolled out. The whole taste and savour of the air was changed, and borne on the primrose-coloured sunshine came the smell of damp earth, no longer dead and reeking of the decay of autumn, but redolent with some new element, something fertile and fecund, something daintily, indefinably laden with the secret of life and restoration. The grey, lumpy clouds were gone, and instead chariots of dazzling white bowled along the infinite blue expanse, harnessed to the southwest wind. But, above all, the sparrows dragged straws to and fro, loudly chirruping. All spring was indexed there.

For a moment Michael was entranced with the exquisite moment, and stood sunning his soul in spring. But then he felt the fetters of his own individual winter heavy on him again, and he could only see what was happening without feeling it. For that moment he had felt the leap in his blood, but the next he was conscious again of the immense fatigue that for weeks had been growing on him. The task which he had voluntarily taken on himself had become no lighter with habit, the incessant attendance on his mother and the strain of it got heavier day by day. For some time now her childlike content in his presence had been clouded and, instead, she was constantly depressed and constantly querulous with him, finding fault with his words and his silences, and in her confused and muffled manner blaming him and affixing sinister motives to his most innocent actions. But she was still entirely dependent on him, and if he left her for an hour or two, she would wait in an agony of anxiety for his return, and when he came back overwhelmed him with tearful caresses and the exaction of promises not to go away again. Then, feeling certain of him once more, she would start again on complaints and reproaches. Her doctor had warned him that it looked as if some new phase of her illness was approaching, which might necessitate the complete curtailment of her liberty; but day had succeeded to day and she still remained in the same condition, neither better nor worse, but making every moment a burden to Michael.

It had been necessary that Sylvia should discontinue her visits, for some weeks ago Lady Ashbridge had suddenly taken a dislike to her, and, when she came, would sit in silent and lofty displeasure, speaking to her as little as possible, and treating her with a chilling and awful politeness. Michael had enough influence with his mother to prevent her telling the girl what her crime had been, which was her refusal to marry him; but, when he was alone with his mother, he had to listen to torrents of these complaints. Lady Ashbridge, with a wealth of language that had lain dormant in her all her life, sarcastically supposed that Miss Falbe was a princess in disguise ("very impenetrable disguise, for I'm sure she reminds me of a barmaid more than a princess"), and thought that such a marriage would be beneath her. Or, another time, she hinted that Miss Falbe might be already married; indeed, this seemed a very plausible explanation of her attitude. She desired, in fact, that Sylvia should not come to see her any more, and now, when she did not, there was scarcely a day in which Lady Ashbridge would not talk in a pointed manner about pretended friends who leave you alone, and won't even take the trouble to take a two-penny 'bus (if they are so poor as all that) to come from Chelsea to Curzon Street.

Michael knew that his mother's steps were getting nearer and nearer to that border line which separates the sane from the insane, and with all the wearing strain of the days as they passed, had but the one desire in his heart, namely, to keep her on the right side for as long as was humanly possible. But something might happen, some new symptom develop which would make it impossible for her to go on living with him as she did now, and the dread of that moment haunted his waking hours and his dreams. Two months ago her doctor had told him that, for the sake of everyone concerned, it was to be hoped that the progress of her disease would be swift; but, for his part, Michael passionately disclaimed such a wish. In spite of her constant complaints and strictures, she was still possessed of her love for him, and, wearing though every day was, he grudged the passing of the hours that brought her nearer to the awful boundary line. Had a deed been presented to him for his signature, which bound him indefinitely to his mother's service, on the condition that she got no worse, his pen would have spluttered with his eagerness to sign.

In consequence of his mother's dislike to Sylvia, Michael had hardly seen her during this last month. Once, when owing to some small physical disturbance, Lady Ashbridge had gone to bed early on a Sunday evening, he had gone to one of the Falbes' weekly parties, and had tried to fling himself with enjoyment into the friendly welcoming atmosphere. But for the present, he felt himself detached from it all, for this life with his mother was close round him with a sort of nightmare obsession, through which outside influence and desire could only faintly trickle. He knew that the other life was there, he knew that in his heart he longed for Sylvia as much as ever; but, in his present detachment, his desire for her was a drowsy ache, a remote emptiness, and the veil that lay over his mother seemed to lie over him also. Once, indeed, during the evening, when he had played for her, the veil had lifted and for the drowsy ache he had the sunlit, stabbing pang; but, as he left, the veil dropped again, and he let himself into the big, mute house, sorry that he had left it. In the same way, too, his music was in abeyance: he could not concentrate himself or find it worth while to make the effort to absorb himself in it, and he knew that short of that, there was neither profit nor pleasure for him in his piano. Everything seemed remote compared with the immediate foreground: there was a gap, a gulf between it and all the rest of the world.

His father wrote to him from time to time, laying stress on the extreme importance of all he was doing in the country, and giving no hint of his coming up to town at present. But he faintly adumbrated the time when in the natural course of events he would have to attend to his national duties in the House of Lords, and wondered whether it would not (about then) be good for his wife to have a change, and enjoy the country when the weather became more propitious. Michael, with an excusable unfilialness, did not answer these amazing epistles; but, having basked in their unconscious humour, sent them on to Aunt Barbara. Weekly reports were sent by Lady Ashbridge's nurse to his father, and Michael had nothing whatever to add to these. His fear of him had given place to a quiet contempt, which he did not care to think about, and certainly did not care to express.

Every now and then Lady Ashbridge had what Michael thought of as a good hour or two, when she went back to her content and childlike joy in his presence, and it was clear, when presently she came downstairs as he still lingered in the garden, reading the daily paper in the sun, that one of these better intervals had visited her. She, too, it appeared, felt the waving of the magic wand of spring, and she noted the signs of it with a joy that was infinitely pathetic.

"My dear," she said, "what a beautiful morning! Is it wise to sit out of doors without your hat, Michael? Shall not I go and fetch it for you? No? Then let us sit here and talk. It is spring, is it not? Look how the birds are collecting twigs for their nests! I wonder how they know that the time has come round again. Sweet little birds! How bold and merry they are."

She edged her way a little nearer him, so that her shoulder leaned on his arm.

"My dear, I wish you were going to nest, too," she said. "I wonder—do you think I have been ill-natured and unkind to your Sylvia, and that makes her not come to see me now? I do remember being vexed at her for not wanting to marry you, and perhaps I talked unkindly about her. I am sorry, for my being cross to her will do no good; it will only make her more unwilling than ever to marry a man who has such an unpleasant mamma. Will she come to see me again, do you think, if I ask her?"

These good hours were too rare in their appearances and swift in their vanishings to warrant the certainty that she would feel the same this afternoon, and Michael tried to turn the subject.

"Ah, we shall have to think about that, mother," he said. "Look, there is a quarrel going on between those two sparrows. They both want the same straw."

She followed his pointing finger, easily diverted.

"Oh, I wish they would not quarrel," she said. "It is so sad and stupid to quarrel, instead of being agreeable and pleasant. I do not like them to do that. There, one has flown away! And see, the crocuses are coming up. Indeed it is spring. I should like to see the country to-day. If you are not busy, Michael, would you take me out into the country? We might go to Richmond Park perhaps, for that is in the opposite direction from Ashbridge, and look at the deer and the budding trees. Oh, Michael, might we take lunch with us, and eat it out of doors? I want to enjoy as much as I can of this spring day."

She clung closer to Michael.

"Everything seems so fragile, dear," she whispered. "Everything may break. . . . Sometimes I am frightened."

The little expedition was soon moving, after a slight altercation between Lady Ashbridge and her nurse, whom she wished to leave behind in order to enjoy Michael's undiluted society. But Miss Baker, who had already spoken to Michael, telling him she was not quite happy in her mind about her patient, was firm about accompanying them, though she obligingly effaced herself as far as possible by taking the box-seat by the chauffeur as they drove down, and when they arrived, and Michael and his mother strolled about in the warm sunshine before lunch, keeping carefully in the background, just ready to come if she was wanted. But indeed it seemed as if no such precautions were necessary, for never had Lady Ashbridge been more amenable, more blissfully content in her son's companionship. The vernal hour, that first smell of the rejuvenated earth, as it stirred and awoke from its winter sleep had reached her no less than it had reached the springing grass and the heart of buried bulbs, and never perhaps in all her life had she been happier than on that balmy morning of early March. Here the stir of spring that had crept across miles of smoky houses to the gardens behind Curzon Street, was more actively effervescent, and the "bare, leafless choirs" of the trees, which had been empty of song all winter, were once more resonant with feathered worshippers. Through the tussocks of the grey grass of last year were pricking the vivid shoots of green, and over the grove of young birches and hazel the dim, purple veil of spring hung mistlike. Down by the water-edge of the Penn ponds they strayed, where moor-hens scuttled out of rhododendron bushes that overhung the lake, and hurried across the surface of the water, half swimming, half flying, for the shelter of some securer retreat. There, too, they found a plantation of willows, already in bud with soft moleskin buttons, and a tortoiseshell butterfly, evoked by the sun from its hibernation, settled on one of the twigs, opening and shutting its diapered wings, and spreading them to the warmth to thaw out the stiffness and inaction of winter. Blackbirds fluted in the busy thickets, a lark shot up near them soaring and singing till it became invisible in the luminous air, a suspended carol in the blue, and bold male chaffinches, seeking their mates with twittered songs, fluttered with burr of throbbing wings. All the promise of spring was there—dim, fragile, but sure, on this day of days, this pearl that emerged from the darkness and the stress of winter, iridescent with the tender colours of the dawning year.

They lunched in the open motor, Miss Baker again obligingly removing herself to the box seat, and spreading rugs on the grass sat in the sunshine, while Lady Ashbridge talked or silently watched Michael as he smoked, but always with a smile. The one little note of sadness which she had sounded when she said she was frightened lest everything should break, had not rung again, and yet all day Michael heard it echoing somewhere dimly behind the song of the wind and the birds, and the shoots of growing trees. It lurked in the thickets, just eluding him, and not presenting itself to his direct gaze; but he felt that he saw it out of the corner of his eye, only to lose it when he looked at it. And yet for weeks his mother had never seemed so well: the cloud had lifted off her this morning, and, but for some vague presage of trouble that somehow haunted his mind, refusing to be disentangled, he could have believed that, after all, medical opinion might be at fault, and that, instead of her passing more deeply into the shadows as he had been warned was inevitable, she might at least maintain the level to which she had returned to-day. All day she had been as she was before the darkness and discontent of those last weeks had come upon her: he who knew her now so well could certainly have affirmed that she had recovered the serenity of a month ago. It was so much, so tremendously much that she should do this, and if only she could remain as she had been all day, she would at any rate be happy, happier, perhaps, than she had consciously been in all the stifled years which had preceded this. Nothing else at the moment seemed to matter except the preservation to her of such content, and how eagerly would he have given all the service that his young manhood had to offer, if by that he could keep her from going further into the bewildering darkness that he had been told awaited her.

There was some little trouble, though no more than the shadow of a passing cloud, when at last he said that they must be getting back to town, for the afternoon was beginning to wane. She besought him for five minutes more of sitting here in the sunshine that was still warm, and when those minutes were over, she begged for yet another postponement. But then the quiet imposition of his will suddenly conquered her, and she got up.

"My dear, you shall do what you like with me," she said, "for you have given me such a happy day. Will you remember that, Michael? It has been a nice day.

And might we, do you think, ask Miss Falbe to come to tea with us when we get back? She can but say 'no,' and if she comes, I will be very good and not vex her."

As she got back into the motor she stood up for a moment, her vague blue eyes scanning the sky, the trees, the stretch of sunlit park.

"Good-bye, lake, happy lake and moor-hens," she said. "Good-bye, trees and grass that are growing green again. Good-bye, all pretty, peaceful things."

Michael had no hesitation in telephoning to Sylvia when they got back to town, asking her if she could come and have tea with his mother, for the gentle, affectionate mood of the morning still lasted, and her eagerness to see Sylvia was only equalled by her eagerness to be agreeable to her. He was greedy, whenever it could be done, to secure a pleasure for his mother, and this one seemed in her present mood a perfectly safe one. Added to that impulse, in itself sufficient, there was his own longing to see her again, that thirst that never left him, and soon after they had got back to Curzon Street Sylvia was with them, and, as before, in preparation for a long visit, she had taken off her hat. To-day she divested herself of it without any suggestion on Lady Ashbridge's part, and this immensely pleased her.

"Look, Michael," she said. "Miss Falbe means to stop a long time. That is sweet of her, is it not? She is not in such a hurry to get away today. Sugar, Miss Falbe? Yes, I remember you take sugar and milk, but no cream. Well, I do think this is nice!"

Sylvia had seen neither mother nor son for a couple of weeks, and her eyes coming fresh to them noticed much change in them both. In Lady Ashbridge this change, though marked, was indefinable enough: she seemed to the girl to have somehow gone much further off than she had been before; she had faded, become indistinct. It was evident that she found, except when she was talking to Michael, a far greater difficulty in expressing herself, the channels of communication, as it were, were getting choked. . . . With Michael, the change was easily stated, he looked terribly tired, and it was evident that the strain of these weeks was telling heavily on him. And yet, as Sylvia noticed with a sudden sense of personal pride in him, not one jot of his patient tenderness for his mother was abated. Tired as he was, nervous, on edge, whenever he dealt with her, either talking to her, or watching for any little attention she might need, his face was alert with love. But she noticed that when the footman brought in tea, and in arranging the cups let a spoon slip jangling from its saucer, Michael jumped as if a bomb had gone off, and under his breath said to the man, "You clumsy fool!" Little as the incident was, she, knowing Michael's courtesy and politeness, found it significant, as bearing on the evidence of his tired face. Then, next moment his mother said something to him, and instantly his love transformed and irradiated it.

To-day, more than ever before, Lady Ashbridge seemed to exist only through him. As Sylvia knew, she had been for the last few weeks constantly disagreeable to him; but she wondered whether this exacting, meticulous affection was not harder to bear. Yet Michael, in spite of the nervous strain which now showed itself so clearly, seemed to find no difficulty at all in responding to it. It might have worn his nerves to tatters, but the tenderness and love of him passed unhampered through the frayed communications, for it was he himself who was brought into play. It was of that Michael, now more and more triumphantly revealed, that Sylvia felt so proud, as if he had been a possession, an achievement wholly personal to her. He was her Michael—it was just that which was becoming evident, since nothing else would account for her claim of him, unconsciously whispered by herself to herself.

It was not long before Lady Ashbridge's nurse appeared, to take her upstairs to rest. At that her patient became suddenly and unaccountably agitated: all the happy content of the day was wiped off her mind. She clung to Michael.

"No, no, Michael," she said, "they mustn't take me away. I know they are going to take me away from you altogether. You mustn't leave me."

Nurse Baker came towards her.

"Now, my lady, you mustn't behave like that," she said. "You know you are only going upstairs to rest as usual before dinner. You will see Lord Comber again then."

She shrank from her, shielding herself behind Michael's shoulder.

"No, Michael, no!" she repeated. "I'm going to be taken away from you. And look, Miss—ah, my dear, I have forgotten your name— look, she has got no hat on. She was going to stop with me a long time. Michael, must I go?"

Michael saw the nurse looking at her, watching her with that quiet eye of the trained attendant.

Then she spoke to Michael.

"Well, if Lord Comber will just step outside with me," she said, "we'll see if we can arrange for you to stop a little longer."

"And you'll come back, Michael," said she.

Michael saw that the nurse wanted to say something to him, and with infinite gentleness disentangled the clinging of Lady Ashbridge's hand.

"Why, of course I will," he said. "And won't you give Miss Falbe another cup of tea?"

Lady Ashbridge hesitated a moment.

"Yes, I'll do that," she said. "And by the time I've done that you will be back again, won't you?"

Michael followed the nurse from the room, who closed the door without shutting it.

"There's something I don't like about her this evening," she said. "All day I have been rather anxious. She must be watched very carefully. Now I want you to get her to come upstairs, and I'll try to make her go to bed."

Michael felt his mouth go suddenly dry.

"What do you expect?" he said.

"I don't expect anything, but we must be prepared. A change comes very quickly."

Michael nodded, and they went back together.

"Now, mother darling," he said, "up you go with Nurse Baker. You've been out all day, and you must have a good rest before dinner. Shall I come up and see you soon?"

A curious, sly look came into Lady Ashbridge's face.

"Yes, but where am I going to?" she said. "How do I know Nurse Baker will take me to my own room?"

"Because I promise you she will," said Michael.

That instantly reassured her. Mood after mood, as Michael saw, were passing like shadows over her mind.

"Ah, that's enough!" she said. "Good-bye, Miss—there! the name's gone again! But won't you sit here and have a talk to Michael, and let him show you over the house to see if you like it against the time— Oh, Michael said I mustn't worry you about that. And won't you stop and have dinner with us, and afterwards we can sing."

Michael put his arm around her.

"We'll talk about that while you're resting," he said. "Don't keep Nurse Baker waiting any longer, mother."

She nodded and smiled.

"No, no; mustn't keep anybody waiting," she said. "Your father taught me to be punctual."

When they had left the room together, Sylvia turned to Michael.

"Michael, my dear," she said, "I think you are—well, I think you are Michael."

She saw that at the moment he was not thinking of her at all, and her heart honoured him for that.

"I'm anxious about my mother to-night," he said. "She has been so— I suppose you must call it—well all day, but the nurse isn't easy about her."

Suddenly all his fears and his fatigue and his trouble looked out of his eyes.

"I'm frightened," he said, "and it's so unutterably feeble of me. And I'm tired: you don't know how tired, and try as I may I feel that all the time it is no use. My mother is slipping, slipping away."

"But, my dear, no wonder you are tired," she said. "Michael, can't anybody help? It isn't right you should do everything."

He shook his head, smiling.

"They can't help," he said. "I'm the only person who can help her. And I—"

He stood up, bracing mind and body.

"And I'm so brutally proud of it," he said. "She wants me. Well, that's a lot for a son to be able to say. Sylvia, I would give anything to keep her."

Still he was not thinking of her, and knowing that, she came close to him and put her arm in his. She longed to give him some feeling of comradeship. She could be sisterly to him over this without suggesting to him what she could not be to him. Her instinct had divined right, and she felt the answering pressure of his elbow that acknowledged her sympathy, welcomed it, and thought no more about it.

"You are giving everything to keep her," she said. "You are giving yourself. What further gift is there, Michael?"

He kept her arm close pressed by him, and she knew by the frankness of that holding caress he was thinking of her still either not at all, or, she hoped, as a comrade who could perhaps be of assistance to courage and clear-sightedness in difficult hours. She wanted to be no more than that to him just now; it was the most she could do for him, but with a desire, the most acute she had ever felt for him, she wanted him to accept that—to take her comradeship as he would have surely taken her brother's. Once, in the last intimate moments they had had together, he had refused to accept that attitude from her—had felt it a relationship altogether impossible. She had seen his point of view, and recognised the justice of the embarrassment. Now, very simply but very eagerly, she hoped, as with some tugging strain, that he would not reject it. She knew she had missed this brother, who had refused to be brother to her. But he had been about his own business, and he had been doing his own business, with a quiet splendour that drew her eyes to him, and as they stood there, thus linked, she wondered if her heart was following. . . . She had seen, last December, how reasonable it was of him to refuse this domestic sort of intimacy with her; now, she found herself intensely longing that he would not persist in his refusal.

Suddenly Michael awoke to the fact of her presence, and abruptly he moved away from her.

"Thanks, Sylvia," he said. "I know I have your—your good wishes. But—well, I am sure you understand."

She understood perfectly well. And the understanding of it cut her to the quick.

"Have you got any right to behave like that to me, Michael?" she asked. "What have I done that you should treat me quite like that?"

He looked at her, completely recalled in mind to her alone. All the hopes and desires of the autumn smote him with encompassing blows.

"Yes, every right," he said. "I wasn't heeding you. I only thought of my mother, and the fact that there was a very dear friend by me. And then I came to myself: I remembered who the friend was."

They stood there in silence, apart, for a moment. Then Michael came closer. The desire for human sympathy, and that the sympathy he most longed for, gripped him again.

"I'm a brute," he said. "It was awfully nice of you to—to offer me that. I accept it so gladly. I'm wretchedly anxious."

He looked up at her.

"Take my arm again," he said.

She felt the crook of his elbow tighten again on her wrist. She had not known before how much she prized that.

"But are you sure you are right in being anxious, Mike?" she asked. "Isn't it perhaps your own tired nerves that make you anxious?"

"I don't think so," he said. "I've been tired a long time, you see, and I never felt about my mother like this. She has been so bright and content all day, and yet there were little lapses, if you understand. It was as if she knew: she said good-bye to the lake and the jolly moor-hens and the grass. And her nurse thinks so, too.

She called me out of the room just now to tell me that. . . . I don't know why I should tell you these depressing things."

"Don't you?" she asked. "But I do. It's because you know I care. Otherwise you wouldn't tell me: you couldn't."

For a moment the balance quavered in his mind between Sylvia the beloved and Sylvia the friend. It inclined to the friend.

"Yes, that's why," he said. "And I reproach myself, you know. All these years I might, if I had tried harder, have been something to my mother. I might have managed it. I thought—at least I felt— that she didn't encourage me. But I was a beast to have been discouraged. And now her wanting me has come just when it isn't her unclouded self that wants me. It's as if—as if it had been raining all day, and just on sunset there comes a gleam in the west. And so soon after it's night."

"You made the gleam," said Sylvia.

"But so late; so awfully late."

Suddenly he stood stiff, listening to some sound which at present she did not hear. It sounded a little louder, and her ears caught the running of footsteps on the stairs outside. Next moment the door opened, and Lady Ashbridge's maid put in a pale face.

"Will you go to her ladyship, my lord?" she said. "Her nurse wants you. She told me to telephone to Sir James."

Sylvia moved with him, not disengaging her arm, towards the door.

"Michael, may I wait?" she said. "You might want me, you know. Please let me wait."

Lady Ashbridge's room was on the floor above, and Michael ran up the intervening stairs three at a time. He knocked and entered and wondered why he had been sent for, for she was sitting quietly on her sofa near the window. But he noticed that Nurse Baker stood very close to her. Otherwise there was nothing that was in any way out of the ordinary.

"And here he is," said the nurse reassuringly as he entered.

Lady Ashbridge turned towards the door as Michael came in, and when he met her eyes he knew why he had been sent for, why at this moment Sir James was being summoned. For she looked at him not with the clouded eyes of affection, not with the mother-spirit striving to break through the shrouding trouble of her brain, but with eyes of blank non-recognition. She saw him with the bodily organs of her vision, but the picture of him was conveyed no further: there was a blank wall behind her eyes.

Michael did not hesitate. It was possible that he still might be something to her, that he, his presence, might penetrate.

"But you are not resting, mother," he said. "Why are you sitting up? I came to talk to you, as I said I would, while you rested."

Suddenly into those blank, irresponsive eyes there leaped recognition. He saw the pupils contract as they focused themselves on him, and hand in hand with recognition there leaped into them hate. Instantly that was veiled again. But it had been there, and now it was not banished; it lurked behind in the shadows, crouching and waiting.

She answered him at once, but in a voice that was quite toneless. It seemed like that of a child repeating a lesson which it had learned by heart, and could be pronounced while it was thinking of something quite different.

"I was waiting till you came, my dear," she said. "Now I will lie down. Come and sit by me, Michael."

She watched him narrowly while she spoke, then gave a quick glance at her nurse, as if to see that they were not making signals to each other. There was an easy chair just behind her head, and as Michael wheeled it up near her sofa, he looked at the nurse. She moved her hand slightly towards the left, and interpreting this, he moved the chair a little to the left, so that he would not sit, as he had intended, quite close to the sofa.

"And you enjoyed your day in the country, mother?" asked Michael.

She looked at him sideways and slowly. Then again, as if recollecting a task she had committed to memory, she answered.

"Yes, so much," she said. "All the trees and the birds and the sunshine. I enjoyed them so much."

She paused a moment.

"Bring your chair a little closer, my darling," she said. "You are so far off. And why do you wait, nurse? I will call you if I want you."

Michael felt one moment of sickening spiritual terror. He understood quite plainly why Nurse Baker did not want him to go near to his mother, and the reason of it gave him this pang, not of nervousness but of black horror, that the sane and the sensitive must always feel when they are brought intimately in contact with some blind derangement of instinct in those most nearly allied to them. Physically, on the material plane, he had no fear at all.

He made a movement, grasping the arm of his chair, as if to wheel it closer, but he came actually no nearer her.

"Why don't you go away, nurse?" said Lady Ashbridge, "and leave my son and me to talk about our nice day in the country?"

Nurse Baker answered quite naturally.

"I want to talk, too, my lady," she said. "I went with you and Lord Comber. We all enjoyed it together."

It seemed to Michael that his mother made some violent effort towards self-control. He saw one of her hands that were lying on her knee clench itself, so that the knuckles stood out white.

"Yes, we will all talk together, then," she said. "Or—er—shall I have a little doze first? I am rather sleepy with so much pleasant air. And you are sleepy, too, are you not, Michael? Yes, I see you look sleepy. Shall we have a little nap, as I often do after tea? Then, when I am fresh again, you shall come back, nurse, and we will talk over our pleasant day."

When he entered the room, Michael had not quite closed the door, and now, as half an hour before, he heard steps on the stairs. A moment afterwards his mother heard them too.

"What is that?" she said. "Who is coming now to disturb me, just when I wanted to have a nap?"

There came a knock at the door. Nurse Baker did not move her head, but continued watching her patient, with hands ready to act.

"Come in," she said, not looking round.

Lady Ashbridge's face was towards the door. As Sir James entered, she suddenly sprang up, and in her right hand that lay beside her was a knife, which she had no doubt taken from the tea-table when she came upstairs. She turned swiftly towards Michael, and stabbed at him with it.

"It's a trap," she cried. "You've led me into a trap. They are going to take me away."

Michael had thrown up his arm to shield his head. The blow fell between shoulder and elbow, and he felt the edge of the knife grate on his bone.

And from deep in his heart sprang the leaping fountains of compassion and love and yearning pity.

CHAPTER XII

Michael was sitting in the big studio at the Falbes' house late one afternoon at the end of June, and the warmth and murmur of the full-blown summer filled the air. The day had so far declined that the rays of the sun, level in its setting, poured slantingly in through the big window to the north, and shining through the foliage of the plane-trees outside made a diaper of rosy illuminated spots and angled shadows on the whitewashed wall. As the leaves stirred in the evening breeze, this pattern shifted and twinkled; now, as the wind blew aside a bunch of foliage, a lake of rosy gold would spring up on the wall; then, as the breath of movement died, the green shadows grew thicker again faintly stirring. Through the window to the south, which Hermann had caused to be cut there, since the studio was not used for painting purposes, Michael could see into the patch of high-walled garden, where Mrs. Falbe was sitting in a low basket chair, completely absorbed in a book of high-born and ludicrous adventures. She had made a mild attempt when she found that Michael intended to wait for Sylvia's return to entertain him till she came; but, with a little oblique encouragement, remarking on the beauty and warmth of the evening, and the pleasure of sitting out of doors, Michael had induced her to go out again, and leave him alone in the studio, free to live over again that which, twenty-four hours ago, had changed life for him.

He reconstructed it as he sat on the sofa and dwelt on the pearl- moments of it. Just this time yesterday he had come in and found Sylvia alone. She had got up, he remembered, to give him greeting, and just opposite the fireplace they had come face to face. She held in her hand a small white rose which she had plucked in the tiny garden here in the middle of London. It was not a very fine specimen, but it was a rose, and she had said in answer to his depreciatory glance: "But you must see it when I have washed it. One has to wash London flowers."

Then . . . the miracle happened. Michael, with the hand that had just taken hers, stroked a petal of this prized vegetable, with no thought in his mind stronger than the thoughts that had been indigenous there since Christmas. As his finger first touched the rim of the town-bred petals, undersized yet not quite lacking in "rose-quality," he had intended nothing more than to salute the flower, as Sylvia made her apology for it. "One has to wash London flowers." But as he touched it he looked up at her, and the quiet, usual song of his thoughts towards her grew suddenly loud and stupefyingly sweet. It was as if from the vacant hive-door the bees swarmed. In her eyes, as they met his, he thought he saw an expectancy, a welcome, and his hand, instead of stroking the rose- petals, closed on the rose and on the hand that held it, and kept them close imprisoned and strongly gripped. He could not remember if he had spoken any word, but he had seen that in her face which rendered all speech unnecessary, and, knowing in the bones and the blood of him that he was right, he kissed her. And then she had said, "Yes, Michael."

His hand still was tight on hers that held the crumpled rose, and when he opened it, lover-like, to stroke and kiss it, there was a spot of blood in the palm of it, where a rose-thorn had pricked her, just one drop of Sylvia's blood. As he kissed it, he had wiped it away with the tip of his tongue between his lips, and she smiling had said, "Oh, Michael, how silly!"

They had sat together on the sofa where this afternoon he sat alone waiting for her. Every moment of that half hour was as distinct as the outline of trees and hills just before a storm, and yet it was still entirely dream-like. He knew it had happened, for nothing but the happening of it would account now for the fact of himself; but, though there was nothing in the world so true, there was nothing so incredible. Yet it was all as clean-cut in his mind as etched lines, and round each line sprang flowers and singing birds. For a long space there was silence after they had sat down, and then she said, "I think I always loved you, Michael, only I didn't know it. . . ." Thereafter, foolish love talk: he had claimed a superiority there, for he had always loved her and had always known it. Much time had been wasted owing to her ignorance . . . she ought to have known. But all the time that existed was theirs now. In all the world there was no more time than what they had. The crumpled rose had its petals rehabilitated, the thorn that had pricked her was peeled off. They wondered if Hermann had come in yet. Then, by some vague process of locomotion, they found themselves at the piano, and with her arm around his neck Sylvia has whispered half a verse of the song of herself. . . .

They became a little more definite over lover-confessions. Michael had, so to speak, nothing to confess: he had loved all along—he had wanted her all along; there never had been the least pretence or nonsense about it. Her path was a little more difficult to trace, but once it had been traversed it was clear enough. She had liked him always; she had felt sister-like from the moment when Hermann brought him to the house, and sister-like she had continued to feel, even when Michael had definitely declared there was "no thoroughfare" there. She had missed that relationship when it stopped: she did not mind telling him that now, since it was abandoned by them both; but not for the world would she have confessed before that she had missed it. She had loved being asked to come and see his mother, and it was during those visits that she had helped to pile the barricade across the "sister-thoroughfare" with her own hands. She began to share Michael's sense of the impossibility of that road. They could not walk down it together, for they had to be either more or less to each other than that. And, during these visits, she had begun to understand (and her face a little hid itself) what Michael's love meant. She saw it manifested towards his mother; she was taught by it; she learned it; and, she supposed, she loved it. Anyhow, having seen it, she could not want Michael as a brother any longer, and if he still wanted anything else, she supposed (so she supposed) that some time he would mention that fact. Yes: she began to hope that he would not be very long about it. . . .

Michael went over this very deliberately as he sat waiting for her twenty-four hours later. He rehearsed this moment and that over and over again: in mind he followed himself and Sylvia across to the piano, not hurrying their steps, and going through the verse of the song she sang at the pace at which she actually sang it. And, as he dreamed and recollected, he heard a little stir in the quiet house, and Sylvia came.

They met just as they met yesterday in front of the fireplace.

"Oh, Michael, have you been waiting long?" she said.

"Yes, hours, or perhaps a couple of minutes. I don't know."

"Ah, but which? If hours, I shall apologise, and then excuse myself by saying that you must have come earlier than you intended. If minutes I shall praise myself for being so exceedingly punctual."

"Minutes, then," said he. "I'll praise you instead. Praise is more convincing if somebody else does it."

"Yes, but you aren't somebody else. Now be sensible. Have you done all the things you told me you were going to do?"

"Yes."

Sylvia released her hands from his.

"Tell me, then," she said. "You've seen your father?"

There was no cloud on Michael's face. There was such sunlight where his soul sat that no shadow could fall across it.

"Oh, yes, I saw him," he said.

He captured Sylvia's hand again.

"And what is more he saw me, so to speak," he said. "He realised that I had an existence independent of him. I used to be a—a sort of clock to him; he could put its hands to point to any hour he chose. Well, he has realised—he has really— that I am ticking along on my own account. He was quite respectful, not only to me, which doesn't matter, but to you—which does." Michael laughed, as he plaited his fingers in with hers.

"My father is so comic," he said, "and unlike most great humourists his humour is absolutely unconscious. He was perfectly well aware that I meant to marry you, for I told him that last Christmas, adding that you did not mean to marry me. So since then I think he's got used to you. Used to you—fancy getting used to you!"

"Especially since he had never seen me," said the girl.

"That makes it less odd. Getting used to you after seeing you would be much more incredible. I was saying that in a way he had got used to you, just as he's got used to my being a person, and not a clock on his chimney-piece, and what seems to have made so much difference is what Aunt Barbara told him last night, namely, that your mother was a Tracy. Sylvia, don't let it be too much for you, but in a certain far-away manner he realises that you are 'one of us.' Isn't he a comic? He's going to make the best of you, it appears. To make the best of you! You can't beat that, you know. In fact, he told me to ask if he might come and pay his respects to your mother to-morrow.

"And what about my singing, my career?" she asked.

Michael laughed again.

"He was funny about that also," he said. "My father took it absolutely for granted that having made this tremendous social advance, you would bury your past, all but the Tracy part of it, as if it had been something disgraceful which the exalted Comber family agreed to overlook."

"And what did you say?"

"I? Oh, I told him that, of course, you would do as you pleased about that, but that for my part I should urge you most strongly to do nothing of the kind."

"And he?"

"He got four inches taller. What is so odd is that as long as I never opposed my father's wishes, as long as I was the clock on the chimney piece, I was terrified at him. The thought of opposing myself to him made my knees quake. But the moment I began doing so, I found there was nothing to be frightened at."

Sylvia got up and began walking up and down the long room.

"But what am I to do about it, Michael?" she asked. "Oh, I blush when I think of a conversation I had with Hermann about you, just before Christmas, when I knew you were going to propose to me. I said that I could never give up my singing. Can you picture the self-importance of that? Why, it doesn't seem to me to matter two straws whether I do or not. Naturally, I don't want to earn my living by it any more, but whether I sing or not doesn't matter. And even as the words are in my mouth I try to imagine myself not singing any more, and I can't. It's become part of me, and while I blush to think of what I said to Hermann, I wonder whether it's not true."

She came and sat down by him again.

"I believe you have got enough artistic instinct to understand that, Michael," she said, "and to know what a tremendous help it is to one's art to be a professional, and to be judged seriously. I suppose that, ideally, if one loves music as I do one ought to be able to do one's very best, whether one is singing professionally or not, but it is hardly possible. Why, the whole difference between amateurs and professionals is that amateurs sing charmingly and professionals just sing. Only they sing as well as they possibly can, not only because they love it, but because if they don't they will be dropped on to, and if they continue not singing their best, will lose their place which they have so hardly won. I can see myself, perhaps, not singing at all, literally never opening my lips in song again, but I can't see myself coming down to the Drill Hall at Brixton, extremely beautifully dressed, with rows of pearls, and arriving rather late, and just singing charmingly. It's such a spur to know that serious musicians judge one's performance by the highest possible standard. It's so relaxing to think that one can easily sing well enough, that one can delight ninety-nine hundredths of the audience without any real effort. I could sing 'The Lost Chord' and move the whole Drill Hall at Brixton to tears. But there might be one man there who knew, you or Hermann or some other, and at the end he would just shrug his shoulders ever so slightly, and I would wish I had never been born."

She paused a moment.

"I'll not sing any more at all, ever," she said, "or I must sing to those who will take me seriously and judge me ruthlessly. To sing just well enough to please isn't possible. I'll do either you like."

Mrs. Falbe strayed in at this moment with her finger in her book, but otherwise as purposeless as a wandering mist.

"I was afraid it might be going to get chilly," she remarked. "After a hot day there is often a cool evening. Will you stop and dine, Lord—I mean, Michael?"

"Please; certainly!" said Michael.

"Then I hope there will be something for you to eat. Sylvia, is there something to eat? No doubt you will see to that, darling. I shall just rest upstairs for a little before dinner, and perhaps finish my book. So pleased you are stopping."

She drifted towards the studio door, in thistledown fashion catching at corners a little, and then moving smoothly on again, talking gently half to herself, half to the others.

"And Hermann's not in yet, but if Lord—I mean, Michael, is going to stop here till dinnertime, it won't matter whether Hermann comes in in time to dress or not, as Michael is not dressed either. Oh, there is the postman's knock! What a noise! I am not expecting any letters."

The knock in question, however, proved to be Hermann, who, as was generally the case, had forgotten his latchkey. He ran into his mother at the studio door, and came and sat down, regardless of whether he was wanted or not, between the two on the sofa, and took an arm of each.

"I probably intrude," he said, "but such is my intention. I've just seen Lady Barbara, who says that the shock has not been too much for Mike's father. That is a good thing; she says he is taking nourishment much as usual. I suppose I oughtn't to jest on so serious a subject, but I took my cue from Lady Barbara. It appears that we have blue blood too, Sylvia, and we must behave more like aristocrats. A Tracy in the time of King John flirted, if no more, with a Comber. And what about your career, Sylvia? Are you going to continue to urge your wild career, or not? I ask with a purpose, as Blackiston proposes we should give a concert together in the third week in July. The Queen's Hall is vacant one afternoon, and he thinks we might sing and play to them. I'm on if you are. It will be about the last concert of the season, too, so we shall have to do our best. Otherwise we, or I, anyhow, will start again in the autumn with a black mark. By the way, are you going to start again in the autumn? It wouldn't surprise me one bit to hear that you and Mike had been talking about just that."

"Don't be too clever to live, Hermann," said Sylvia.

"I don't propose to die, if you mean that. Oh, Blackiston had another suggestion also. He wanted to know if we would consider making a short tour in Germany in the autumn. He says that the beloved Fatherland is rather disposed to be interested in us. He thinks we should have good audiences at Leipzig, and so on. There's a tendency, he says, to recognise poor England, a cordial intention, anyhow. I said that in your case there might be domestic considerations which— But I think I shall go in any case. Lord, fancy playing in Germany to Germans again. Fancy being listened to by a German audience; fancy if they approved."

Michael leaned forward, putting his elbow into Hermann's chest. Early December had already been mentioned as a date for their marriage, and as a pre-nuptial journey, this seemed to him a plan ecstatically ideal.

"Yes, Sylvia," he said. "The answer is yes. I shall come with you, you know. I can see it; a triumphal procession, you two making noises, and me listening. A month's tour, Hermann. Middle of October till middle of November. Yes, yes."

All his tremendous pride in her singing, dormant for the moment under the wonder of his love, rose to the surface. He knew what her singing meant to her, and, from their conversation together just now, how keen was her eagerness for the strict judgment of those who knew, how she loved that austere pinnacle of daylight. Here was an ideal opportunity; never yet, since she had won her place as a singer, had she sung in Germany, that Mecca of the musical artist, and in her case, the land from which she sprung. Had the scheme implied a postponement of their marriage, he would still have declared himself for it, for he unerringly felt for her in this; he knew intuitively what delicious beckoning this held for her.

"Yes, yes," he repeated, "I must have you do that, Sylvia. I don't care what Hermann wants or what you want. I want it."

"Yes, but who's to do the playing and the singing?" asked Hermann. "Isn't it a question, perhaps, for—"

Michael felt quite secure about the feelings of the other two, and rudely interrupted.

"No," he said. "It's a question for me. When the Fatherland hears that I am there it will no doubt ask me to play and sing instead of you two. Lord! Fancy marrying into such a distinguished family. I burst with pride!"

It required, then, little debate, since all three were agreed, before Hermann was empowered with authority to make arrangements, and they remained simultaneously talking till Mrs. Falbe, again drifting in, announced that the bell for dinner had sounded some minutes before. She had her finger in the last chapter of "Lady Ursula's Ordeal," and laid it face downwards on the table to resume again at the earliest possible moment. This opportunity was granted her when, at the close of dinner, coffee and the evening paper came in together. This Hermann opened at the middle page.

"Hallo!" he said. "That's horrible! The Heir Apparent of the Austrian Emperor has been murdered at Serajevo. Servian plot, apparently."

"Oh, what a dreadful thing," said Mrs. Falbe, opening her book. "Poor man, what had he done?"

Hermann took a cigarette, frowning.

"It may be a match—" he began.

Mrs. Falbe diverted her attention from "Lady Ursula" for a moment.

"They are on the chimney-piece, dear," she said, thinking he spoke of material matches.

Michael felt that Hermann saw something, or conjectured something ominous in this news, for he sat with knitted brow reading, and letting the match burn down.

"Yes; it seems that Servian officers are implicated," he said. "And there are materials enough already for a row between Austria and Servia without this."

"Those tiresome Balkan States," said Mrs. Falbe, slowly immersing herself like a diving submarine in her book. "They are always quarrelling. Why doesn't Austria conquer them all and have done with it?"

This simple and striking solution of the whole Balkan question was her final contribution to the topic, for at this moment she became completely submerged, and cut off, so to speak, from the outer world, in the lucent depths of Lady Ursula.

Hermann glanced through the other pages, and let the paper slide to the floor.

"What will Austria do?" he said. "Supposing she threatens Servia in some outrageous way and Russia says she won't stand it? What then?"

Michael looked across to Sylvia; he was much more interested in the way she dabbled the tips of her hands in the cool water of her finger bowl than in what Hermann was saying. Her fingers had an extraordinary life of their own; just now they were like a group of maidens by a fountain. . . . But Hermann repeated the question to him personally.

"Oh, I suppose there will be a lot of telegraphing," he said, "and perhaps a board of arbitration. After all, one expected a European conflagration over the war in the Balkan States, and again over their row with Turkey. I don't believe in European conflagrations. We are all too much afraid of each other. We walk round each other like collie dogs on the tips of their toes, gently growling, and then quietly get back to our own territories and lie down again."

Hermann laughed.

"Thank God, there's that wonderful fire-engine in Germany ready to turn the hose on conflagrations."

"What fire-engine?" asked Michael.

"The Emperor, of course. We should have been at war ten times over but for him."

Sylvia dried her finger-tips one by one.

"Lady Barbara doesn't quite take that view of him, does she, Mike?" she asked.

Michael suddenly remembered how one night in the flat Aunt Barbara had suddenly turned the conversation from the discussion of cognate topics, on hearing that the Falbes were Germans, only to resume it again when they had gone.

"I don't fancy she does," he said. "But then, as you know, Aunt Barbara has original views on every subject."

Hermann did not take the possible hint here conveyed to drop the matter.

"Well, then, what do you think about him?" he asked.

Michael laughed.

"My dear Hermann," he said, "how often have you told me that we English don't pay the smallest attention to international politics. I am aware that I don't; I know nothing whatever about them."

Hermann shook off the cloud of preoccupation that so unaccountably, to Michael's thinking, had descended on him, and walked across to the window.

"Well, long may ignorance be bliss," he said. "Lord, what a divine evening! 'Uber allen gipfeln ist Ruhe.' At least, there is peace on the only summits visible, which are house roofs. There's not a breath of wind in the trees and chimney-pots; and it's hot, it's really hot."

"I was afraid there was going to be a chill at sunset," remarked Mrs. Falbe subaqueously.

"Then you were afraid even where no fear was, mother darling," said he, "and if you would like to sit out in the garden I'll take a chair out for you, and a table and candles. Let's all sit out; it's a divine hour, this hour after sunset. There are but a score of days in the whole year when the hour after sunset is warm like this. It's such a pity to waste one indoors. The young people"— and he pointed to Sylvia and Michael—"will gaze into each other's hearts, and Mamma's will beat in unison with Lady Ursula's, and I will sit and look at the sky and become profoundly sentimental, like a good German."

Hermann and Michael bestirred themselves, and presently the whole little party had encamped on chairs placed in an oasis of rugs (this was done at the special request of Mrs. Falbe, since Lady Ursula had caught a chill that developed into consumption) in the small, high-walled garden. Beyond at the bottom lay the road along the embankment and the grey-blue Thames, and the dim woods of Battersea Park across the river. When they came out, sparrows were still chirping in the ivy on the studio wall and in the tall angle- leaved planes at the bottom of the little plot, discussing, no doubt, the domestic arrangements for their comfort during the night. But presently a sudden hush fell upon them, and their shrillness was sharp no more against the drowsy hum of the city. The sky overhead was of veiled blue, growing gradually more toneless as the light faded, and was unflecked by any cloud, except where, high in the zenith, a fleece of rosy vapour still caught the light of the sunken sun, and flamed with the soft radiance of some snow-summit. Near it there burned a molten planet, growing momentarily brighter as the night gathered and presently beginning to be dimmed again as a tawny moon three days past the full rose in the east above the low river horizon. Occasionally a steamer hooted from the Thames and the noise of churned waters sounded, or the crunch of a motor's wheels, or the tapping of the heels of a foot passenger on the pavement below the garden wall. But such evidence of outside seemed but to accentuate the perfect peace of this secluded little garden where the four sat: the hour and the place were cut off from all turmoil and activities: for a moment the stream of all their lives had flowed into a backwater, where it rested immobile before the travel that was yet to come. So it seemed to Michael then, and so years afterwards it seemed to him, as vividly as on this evening when the tawny moon grew golden as it climbed the empty heavens, dimming the stars around it.

What they talked of, even though it was Sylvia who spoke, seemed external to the spirit of the hour. They seemed to have reached a point, some momentary halting-place, where speech and thought even lay outside, and the need of the spirit was merely to exist and be conscious of its existence. Sometimes for a moment his past life with its self-repression, its mute yearnings, its chrysalis stirrings, formed a mist that dispersed again, sometimes for a moment in wonder at what the future held, what joys and troubles, what achings, perhaps, and anguishes, the unknown knocked stealthily at the door of his mind, but then stole away unanswered and unwelcome, and for that hour, while Mrs. Falbe finished with Lady Ursula, while Hermann smoked and sighed like a sentimental German, and while he and Sylvia sat, speaking occasionally, but more often silent, he was in some kind of Nirvana for which its own existence was everything. Movement had ceased: he held his breath while that divine pause lasted.

When it was broken, there was no shattering of it: it simply died away like a long-drawn chord as Mrs. Falbe closed her book.

"She died," she said, "I knew she would."

Hermann gave a great shout of laughter.

"Darling mother, I'm ever so much obliged," he said. "We had to return to earth somehow. Where has everybody else been?"

Michael stirred in his chair.

"I've been here," he said.

"How dull! Oh, I suppose that's not polite to Sylvia. I've been in Leipzig and in Frankfort and in Munich. You and Sylvia have been there, too, I may tell you. But I've also been here: it's jolly here."

His sentimentalism had apparently not quite passed from him.

"Ah, we've stolen this hour!" he said. "We've taken it out of the hurly-burly and had it to ourselves. It's been ripping. But I'm back from the rim of the world. Oh, I've been there, too, and looked out over the immortal sea. Lieber Gott, what a sea, where we all come from, and where we all go to! We're just playing on the sand where the waves have cast us up for one little hour. Oh, the pleasant warm sand and the play! How I love it."

He got out of his chair stretching himself, as Mrs. Falbe passed into the house, and gave a hand on each side to Michael and Sylvia.

"Ah, it was a good thing I just caught that train at Victoria nearly a year ago," he said. "If I had been five seconds later, I should have missed it, and so I should have missed my friend, and Sylvia would have missed hers, and Mike would have missed his. As it is, here we all are. Behold the last remnant of my German sentimentality evaporates, but I am filled with a German desire for beer. Let us come into the studio, liebe Kinder, and have beer and music and laughter. We cannot recapture this hour or prolong it. But it was good, oh, so good! I thank God for this hour."

Sylvia put her hand on her brother's arm, looking at him with just a shade of anxiety.

"Nothing wrong, Hermann?" she asked.

"Wrong? There is nothing wrong unless it is wrong to be happy. But we have to go forward: my only quarrel with life is that. I would stop it now if I could, so that time should not run on, and we should stay just as we are. Ah, what does the future hold? I am glad I do not know."

Sylvia laughed.

"The immediate future holds beer apparently," she said. "It also hold a great deal of work for you and me, if it is to hold Leipzig and Frankfort and Munich. Oh, Hermann, what glorious days!"

They walked together into the studio, and as they entered Hermann looked back over her into the dim garden. Then he pulled down the blind with a rattle.

"'Move on there!' said the policeman," he remarked. "And so they moved on."

The news about the murder of the Austrian Grand Duke, which, for that moment at dinner, had caused Hermann to peer with apprehension into the veil of the future, was taken quietly enough by the public in general in England. It was a nasty incident, no doubt, and the murder having been committed on Servian soil, the pundits of the Press gave themselves an opportunity for subsequently saying that they were right, by conjecturing that Austria might insist on a strict inquiry into the circumstances, and the due punishment of not only the actual culprits but of those also who perhaps were privy to the plot. But three days afterwards there was but little uneasiness; the Stock Exchanges of the European capitals—those highly sensitive barometers of coming storm—were but slightly affected for the moment, and within a week had steadied themselves again. From Austria there came no sign of any unreasonable demand which might lead to trouble with Servia, and so with Slavonic feeling generally, and by degrees that threatening of storm, that sudden lightning on the horizon passed out of the mind of the public. There had been that one flash, no more, and even that had not been answered by any growl of thunder; the storm did not at once move up and the heavens above were still clear and sunny by day, and starry-kirtled at night. But here and there were those who, like Hermann on the first announcement of the catastrophe, scented trouble, and Michael, going to see Aunt Barbara one afternoon early in the second week of July, found that she was one of them.

"I distrust it all, my dear," she said to him. "I am full of uneasiness. And what makes me more uneasy is that they are taking it so quietly at the Austrian Embassy and at the German. I dined at one Embassy last night and at the other only a few nights ago, and I can't get anybody—not even the most indiscreet of the Secretaries—to say a word about it."

"But perhaps there isn't a word to be said," suggested Michael.

"I can't believe that. Austria cannot possibly let an incident of that sort pass. There is mischief brewing. If she was merely intending to insist—as she has every right to do—on an inquiry being held that should satisfy reasonable demands for justice, she would have insisted on that long ago. But a fortnight has passed now, and still she makes no sign. I feel sure that something is being arranged. Dear me, I quite forgot, Tony asked me not to talk about it. But it doesn't matter with you."

"But what do you mean by something being arranged?" asked Michael.

She looked round as if to assure herself that she and Michael were alone.

"I mean this: that Austria is being persuaded to make some outrageous demand, some demand that no independent country could possibly grant."

"But who is persuading her?" asked Michael.

"My dear, you—like all the rest of England—are fast asleep. Who but Germany, and that dangerous monomaniac who rules Germany? She has long been wanting war, and she has only been delaying the dawning of Der Tag, till all her preparations were complete, and she was ready to hurl her armies, and her fleet too, east and west and north. Mark my words! She is about ready now, and I believe she is going to take advantage of her opportunity."

She leaned forward in her chair.

"It is such an opportunity as has never occurred before," she said, "and in a hundred years none so fit may occur again. Here are we— England—on the brink of civil war with Ireland and the Home Rulers; our hands are tied, or, rather, are occupied with our own troubles. Anyhow, Germany thinks so: that I know for a fact among so much that is only conjecture. And perhaps she is right. Who knows whether she may not be right, and that if she forces on war whether we shall range ourselves with our allies?"

Michael laughed.

"But aren't you piling up a European conflagration rather in a hurry, Aunt Barbara?" he asked.

"There will be hurry enough for us, for France and Russia and perhaps England, but not for Germany. She is never in a hurry: she waits till she is ready."

A servant brought in tea and Lady Barbara waited till he had left the room again.

"It is as simple as an addition sum," she said, "if you grant the first step, that Austria is going to make some outrageous demand of Servia. What follows? Servia refuses that demand, and Austria begins mobilisation in order to enforce it. Servia appeals to Russia, invokes the bond of blood, and Russia remonstrates with Austria. Her representations will be of no use: you may stake all you have on that; and eventually, since she will be unable to draw back she, too, will begin in her slow, cumbrous manner, hampered by those immense distances and her imperfect railway system, to mobilise also. Then will Germany, already quite prepared, show her hand. She will demand that Russia shall cease mobilisation, and again will Russia refuse. That will set the military machinery of France going. All the time the governments of Europe will be working for peace, all, that is, except one, which is situated at Berlin."

Michael felt inclined to laugh at this rapid and disastrous sequence of ominous forebodings; it was so completely characteristic of Aunt Barbara to take the most violent possible view of the situation, which no doubt had its dangers. And what Michael felt was felt by the enormous majority of English people.

"Dear Aunt Barbara, you do get on quick," he said.

"It will happen quickly," she said. "There is that little cloud in the east like a man's hand today, and rather like that mailed fist which our sweet peaceful friend in Germany is so fond of talking about. But it will spread over the sky, I tell you, like some tropical storm. France is unready, Russia is unready; only Germany and her marionette, Austria, the strings of which she pulls, is ready."

"Go on prophesying," said Michael.

"I wish I could. Ever since that Sarajevo murder I have thought of nothing else day and night. But how events will develop then I can't imagine. What will England do? Who knows? I only know what Germany thinks she will do, and that is, stand aside because she can't stir, with this Irish mill-stone round her neck. If Germany thought otherwise, she is perfectly capable of sending a dozen submarines over to our naval manoeuvres and torpedoing our battleships right and left."

Michael laughed outright at this.

"While a fleet of Zeppelins hovers over London, and drops bombs on the War Office and the Admiralty," he suggested.

But Aunt Barbara was not in the least diverted by this.

"And if England stands aside," she said, "Der Tag will only dawn a little later, when Germany has settled with France and Russia. We shall live to see Der Tag, Michael, unless we are run over by motor-buses, and pray God we shall see it soon, for the sooner the better. Your adorable Falbes, now, Sylvia and Hermann. What do they think of it?"

"Hermann was certainly rather—rather upset when he read of the Sarajevo murders," he said. "But he pins his faith on the German Emperor, whom he alluded to as a fire-engine which would put out any conflagration."

Aunt Barbara rose in violent incredulity.

"Pish and bosh!" she remarked. "If he had alluded to him as an incendiary bomb, there would have been more sense in his simile."

"Anyhow, he and Sylvia are planning a musical tour in Germany in the autumn," said Michael.

"'It's a long, long way to Tipperary,'" remarked Aunt Barbara enigmatically.

"Why Tipperary?" asked Michael.

"Oh, it's just a song I heard at a music-hall the other night. There's a jolly catchy tune to it, which has rung in my head ever since. That's the sort of music I like, something you can carry away with you. And your music, Michael?"

"Rather in abeyance. There are—other things to think about."

Aunt Barbara got up.

"Ah, tell me more about them," she said. "I want to get this nightmare out of my head. Sylvia, now. Sylvia is a good cure for the nightmare. Is she kind as she is fair, Michael?"

Michael was silent for a moment. Then he turned a quiet, radiant face to her.

"I can't talk about it," he said. "I can't get accustomed to the wonder of it."

"That will do. That's a completely satisfactory account. But go on."

Michael laughed.

"How can I?" he asked. "There's no end and no beginning. I can't 'go on' as you order me about a thing like that. There is Sylvia; there is me."

"I must be content with that, then," she said, smiling.

"We are," said Michael.

Lady Barbara waited a moment without speaking.

"And your mother?" she asked.

He shook his head.

"She still refuses to see me," he said. "She still thinks it was I who made the plot to take her away and shut her up. She is often angry with me, poor darling, but—but you see it isn't she who is angry: it's just her malady."

"Yes, my dear," said Lady Barbara. "I am so glad you see it like that."

"How else could I see it? It was my real mother whom I began to know last Christmas, and whom I was with in town for the three months that followed. That's how I think of her: I can't think of her as anything else."

"And how is she otherwise?"

Again he shook his head.

"She is wretched, though they say that all she feels is dim and veiled, that we mustn't think of her as actually unhappy. Sometimes there are good days, when she takes a certain pleasure in her walks and in looking after a little plot of ground where she gardens. And, thank God, that sudden outburst when she tried to kill me seems to have entirely passed from her mind. They don't think she remembers it at all. But then the good days are rare, and are growing rarer, and often now she sits doing nothing at all but crying."

Aunt Barbara laid her hand on him.

"Oh, my dear," she said.

Michael paused for a moment, his brown eyes shining.

"If only she could come back just for a little to what she was in January," he said. "She was happier then, I think, than she ever was before. I can't help wondering if anyhow I could have prolonged those days, by giving myself up to her more completely."

"My dear, you needn't wonder about that," said Aunt Barbara. "Sir James told me that it was your love and nothing else at all that gave her those days."

Michael's lips quivered.

"I can't tell you what they were to me," he said, "for she and I found each other then, and we both felt we had missed each other so much and so long. She was happy then, and I, too. And now everything has been taken from her, and still, in spite of that, my cup is full to overflowing."

"That's how she would have it, Michael," said Barbara.

"Yes, I know that. I remind myself of that."

Again he paused.

"They don't think she will live very long," he said. "She is getting physically much weaker. But during this last week or two she has been less unhappy, they think. They say some new change may come any time: it may be only the great change—I mean her death; but it is possible before that that her mind will clear again. Sir James told me that occasionally happened, like—like a ray of sunlight after a stormy day. It would be good if that happened. I would give almost anything to feel that she and I were together again, as we were."

Barbara, childless, felt something of motherhood. Michael's simplicity and his sincerity were already known to her, but she had never yet known the strength of him. You could lean on Michael. In his quiet, undemonstrative way he supported you completely, as a son should; there was no possibility of insecurity. . . .

"God bless you, my dear," she said.

CHAPTER XIII

One close thundery morning about a week later, Michael was sitting at his piano in his shirtsleeves, busy practising. He was aware that at the other end of the room the telephone was calling for him, but it seemed to be of far greater importance at the minute to finish the last page of one of the Bach fugues, than to attend to what anybody else might have to say to him. Then it suddenly flashed across him that it might be Sylvia who wanted to speak to him, or that there might be news about his mother, and his fingers leaped from the piano in the middle of a bar, and he ran and slid across the parquet floor.

But it was neither of these, and compared to them it was a case of "only" Hermann who wanted to see him. But Hermann, it appeared, wanted to see him urgently, and, if he was in (which he was) would be with him in ten minutes.

But the Bach thread was broken, and Michael, since it was not worth while trying to mend it for the sake of these few minutes, sat down by the open window, and idly took up the morning paper, which as yet he had not opened, since he had hurried over breakfast in order to get to his piano. The music announcements on the outside page first detained him, and seeing that the concert by the Falbes, which was to take place in five or six days, was advertised, he wondered vaguely whether it was about that that Hermann wanted to see him, and, if so, why he could not have said whatever he had to say on the telephone, instead of cutting things short with the curt statement that he wished to see him urgently, and would come round at once. Then remembering that Francis had been playing cricket for the Guards yesterday, he turned briskly over to the last page of sporting news, and found that his cousin had distinguished himself by making no runs at all, but by missing two expensive catches in the deep field. From there, after a slight inspection of a couple of advertisement columns, he worked back to the middle leaf, where were leaders and the news of nations and the movements of kings. All this last week he had scanned such items with a growing sense of amusement in the recollection of Hermann's disquiet over the Sarajevo murders, and Aunt Barbara's more detailed and vivid prognostications of coming danger, for nothing more had happened, and he supposed—vaguely only, since the affair had begun to fade from his mind—that Austria had made inquiries, and that since she was satisfied there was no public pronouncement to be made.

The hot breeze from the window made the paper a little unmanageable for a moment, but presently he got it satisfactorily folded, and a big black headline met his eye. A half-column below it contained the demands which Austria had made in the Note addressed to the Servian Government. A glance was sufficient to show that they were framed in the most truculent and threatening manner possible to imagine. They were not the reasonable proposals that one State had a perfect right to make of another on whose soil and with the connivance of whose subjects the murders had been committed; they were a piece of arbitrary dictation, a threat levelled against a dependent and an inferior.

Michael had read them through twice with a growing sense of uneasiness at the thought of how Lady Barbara's first anticipations had been fulfilled, when Hermann came in. He pointed to the paper Michael held.

"Ah, you have seen it," he said. "Perhaps you can guess what I wanted to see you about."

"Connected with the Austrian Note?" asked Michael.

"Yes."

"I have not the vaguest idea."

Hermann sat down on the arm of his chair.

"Mike, I'm going back to Germany to-day," he said. "Now do you understand? I'm German."

"You mean that Germany is at the back of this?"

"It is obvious, isn't it? Those demands couldn't have been made without the consent of Austria's ally. And they won't be granted. Servia will appeal to Russia. And . . . and then God knows what may happen. In the event of that happening, I must be in my Fatherland ready to serve, if necessary."

"You mean you think it possible you will go to war with Russia?" asked Michael.

"Yes, I think it possible, and, if I am right, if there is that possibility, I can't be away from my country."

"But the Emperor, the fire-engine whom you said would quench any conflagration?"

"He is away yachting. He went off after the visit of the British fleet to Kiel. Who knows whether before he gets back, things may have gone too far? Can't you see that I must go? Wouldn't you go if you were me? Suppose you were in Germany now, wouldn't you hurry home?"

Michael was silent, and Hermann spoke again.

"And if there is trouble with Russia, France, I take it, is bound to join her. And if France joins her, what will England do?"

The great shadow of the approaching storm fell over Michael, even as outside the sultry stillness of the morning grew darker.

"Ah, you think that?" asked Michael.

Hermann put his hand on Michael's shoulder.

"Mike, you're the best friend I have," he said, "and soon, please God, you are going to marry the girl who is everything else in the world to me. You two make up my world really—you two and my mother, anyhow. No other individual counts, or is in the same class. You know that, I expect. But there is one other thing, and that's my nationality. It counts first. Nothing, nobody, not even Sylvia or my mother or you can stand between me and that. I expect you know that also, for you saw, nearly a year ago, what Germany is to me. Perhaps I may be quite wrong about it all—about the gravity, I mean, of the situation, and perhaps in a few days I may come racing home again. Yes, I said 'home,' didn't I? Well, that shows you just how I am torn in two. But I can't help going."

Hermann's hand remained on his shoulder gently patting it. To Michael the world, life, the whole spirit of things had suddenly grown sinister, of the quality of nightmare. It was true that all the ground of this ominous depression which had darkened round him, was conjectural and speculative, that diplomacy, backed by the horror of war which surely all civilised nations and responsible govermnents must share, had, so far from saying its last, not yet said its first word; that the wits of all the Cabinets of Europe were at this moment only just beginning to stir themselves so as to secure a peaceful solution; but, in spite of this, the darkness and the nightmare grew in intensity. But as to Hermann's determination to go to Germany, which made this so terribly real, since it was beginning to enter into practical everyday life, he had neither means nor indeed desire to combat it. He saw perfectly clearly that Hermann must go.

"I don't want to dissuade you," he said, "not only because it would be useless, but because I am with you. You couldn't do otherwise, Hermann."

"I don't see that I could. Sylvia agrees too."

A terrible conjecture flashed through Michael's mind.

"And she?" he asked.

"She can't leave my mother, of course," said Hermann, "and, after all, I may be on a wild goose chase. But I can't risk being unable to get to Germany, if—if the worst happens."

The ghost of a smile played round his mouth for a moment.

"And I'm not sure that she could leave you, Mike," he added.

Somehow this, though it gave Michael a moment of intensest relief to know that Sylvia remained, made the shadow grow deeper, accentuated the lines of the storm which had begun to spread over the sky. He began to see as nightmare no longer, but as stern and possible realities, something of the unutterable woe, the divisions, the heart-breaks which menaced.

"Hermann, what do you think will happen?" he said. "It is incredible, unfaceable—"

The gentle patting on his shoulder, that suddenly and poignantly reminded him of when Sylvia's hand was there, ceased for a moment, and then was resumed.

"Mike, old boy," said Hermann, "we've got to face the unfaceable, and believe that the incredible is possible. I may be all wrong about it, and, as I say, in a few days' time I may come racing back. But, on the other hand, this may be our last talk together, for I go off this afternoon. So let's face it."

He paused a moment.

"It may be that before long I shall be fighting for my Fatherland," he said. "And if there is to be fighting, it may be that Germany will before long be fighting England. There I shall be on one side, and, since naturally you will go back into the Guards, you will be fighting on the other. I shall be doing my best to kill Englishmen, whom I love, and they will be doing their best to kill me and those of my blood. There's the horror of it, and it's that we must face. If we met in a bayonet charge, Mike, I should have to do my best to run you through, and yet I shouldn't love you one bit the less, and you must know that. Or, if you ran me through, I shall have to die loving you just the same as before, and hoping you would live happy, for ever and ever, as the story-books say, with Sylvia."

"Hermann, don't go," said Michael suddenly.

"Mike, you didn't mean that," he said.

Michael looked at him for a moment in silence.

"No, it is unsaid," he replied.

Hermann looked round as the clock on the chimney-piece chimed.

"I must be going," he said, "I needn't say anything to you about Sylvia, because all I could say is in your heart already. Well, we've met in this jolly world, Mike, and we've been great friends. Neither you nor I could find a greater friend than we've been to each other. I bless God for this last year. It's been the happiest in my life. Now what else is there? Your music: don't ever be lazy about your music. It's worth while taking all the pains you can about it. Lord! do you remember the evening when I first tried your Variations? . . . Let me play the last one now. I want something jubilant. Let's see, how does it go?"

He held his hands, those long, slim-fingered hands, poised for a moment above the keys, then plunged into the glorious riot of the full chords and scales, till the room rang with it. The last chord he held for a moment, and then sprang up.

"Ah, that's good," he said. "And now I'm going to say good-bye, and go without looking round."

"But might I see you off this afternoon?" asked Michael.

"No, please don't. Station partings are fussy and disagreeable. I want to say good-bye to you here in your quiet room, just as I shall say goodbye to Sylvia at home. Ah, Mike, yes, both hands and smiling. May God give us other meetings and talks and companionship and years of love, my best of friends. Good-bye."

Then, as he had said, he walked to the door without looking round, and next moment it had closed behind him.

Throughout the next week the tension of the situation grew ever greater, strained towards the snapping-point, while the little cloud, the man's hand, which had arisen above the eastern horizon grew and overspread the heavens in a pall that became ever more black and threatening. For a few days yet it seemed that perhaps even now the cataclysm might be averted, but gradually, in spite of all the efforts of diplomacy to loosen the knot, it became clear that the ends of the cord were held in hands that did not mean to release their hold till it was pulled tight. Servia yielded to such demands as it was possible for her to grant as an independent State; but the inflexible fingers never abated one jot of their strangling pressure. She appealed to Russia, and Russia's remonstrance fell on deaf ears, or, rather, on ears that had determined not to hear. From London and Paris came proposals for conference, for arbitration, with welcome for any suggestion from the other side which might lead to a peaceful solution of the disputed demands, already recognised by Europe as a firebrand wantonly flung into the midst of dangerous and inflammable material. Over that burning firebrand, preventing and warding off all the eager hands that were stretched to put it out, stood the figure of the nation at whose bidding it had been flung there.

Gradually, out of the thunder-clouds and gathering darkness, vaguely at first and then in definite and menacing outline, emerged the inexorable, flint-like face of Germany, whose figure was clad in the shining armour so well known in the flamboyant utterances of her War Lord, which had been treated hitherto as mere irresponsible utterances to be greeted with a laugh and a shrugged shoulder. Deep and patient she had always been, and now she believed that the time had come for her patience to do its perfect work. She had bided long for the time when she could best fling that lighted brand into the midst of civilisation, and she believed she had calculated well. She cared nothing for Servia nor for her ally. On both her frontiers she was ready, and now on the East she heeded not the remonstrance of Russia, nor her sincere and cordial invitation to friendly discussion. She but waited for the step that she had made inevitable, and on the first sign of Russian mobilisation she, with her mobilisation ready to be completed in a few days, peremptorily demanded that it should cease. On the Western frontier behind the Rhine she was ready also; her armies were prepared, cannon fodder in uncountable store of shells and cartridges was prepared, and in endless battalions of men, waiting to be discharged in one bull-like rush, to overrun France, and holding the French armies, shattered and dispersed, with a mere handful of her troops, to hurl the rest at Russia.

The whole campaign was mathematically thought out. In a few months at the outside France would be lying trampled down and bleeding; Russia would be overrun; already she would be mistress of Europe, and prepared to attack the only country that stood between her and world-wide dominion, whose allies she would already have reduced to impotence. Here she staked on an uncertainty: she could not absolutely tell what England's attitude would be, but she had the strongest reason for hoping that, distracted by the imminence of civil strife, she would be unable to come to the help of her allies until the allies were past helping.

For a moment only were seen those set stern features mad for war; then, with a snap, Germany shut down her visor and stood with sword unsheathed, waiting for the horror of the stupendous bloodshed which she had made inevitable. Her legions gathered on the Eastern front threatening war on Russia, and thus pulling France into the spreading conflagration and into the midst of the flame she stood ready to cast the torn-up fragments of the treaty that bound her to respect the neutrality of Belgium.

All this week, while the flames of the flung fire-brand began to spread, the English public waited, incredulous of the inevitable. Michael, among them, found himself unable to believe even then that the bugles were already sounding, and that the piles of shells in their wicker-baskets were being loaded on to the military ammunition trains. But all the ordinary interests in life, all the things that busily and contentedly occupied his day, one only excepted, had become without savour. A dozen times in the morning he would sit down to his piano, only to find that he could not think it worth while to make his hands produce these meaningless tinkling sounds, and he would jump up to read the paper over again, or watch for fresh headlines to appear on the boards of news- vendors in the street, and send out for any fresh edition. Or he would walk round to his club and spend an hour reading the tape news and waiting for fresh slips to be pinned up. But, through all the nightmare of suspense and slowly-dying hope, Sylvia remained real, and after he had received his daily report from the establishment where his mother was, with the invariable message that there was no marked change of any kind, and that it was useless for him to think of coming to see her, he would go off to Maidstone Crescent and spend the greater part of the day with the girl.

Once during this week he had received a note from Hermann, written at Munich, and on the same day she also had heard from him. He had gone back to his regiment, which was mobilised, as a private, and was very busy with drill and duties. Feeling in Germany, he said, was elated and triumphant: it was considered certain that England would stand aside, as the quarrel was none of hers, and the nation generally looked forward to a short and brilliant campaign, with the occupation of Paris to be made in September at the latest. But as a postscript in his note to Sylvia he had added:

"You don't think there is the faintest chance of England coming in, do you? Please write to me fully, and get Mike to write. I have heard from neither of you, and as I am sure you must have written, I conclude that letters are stopped. I went to the theatre last night: there was a tremendous scene of patriotism. The people are war-mad."

Since then nothing had been heard from him, and to-day, as Michael drove down to see Sylvia, he saw on the news-boards that Belgium had appealed to England against the violation of her territory by the German armies en route for France. Overtures had been made, asking for leave to pass through the neutral territory: these Belgium had rejected. This was given as official news. There came also the report that the Belgian remonstrances would be disregarded. Should she refuse passage to the German battalions, that could make no difference, since it was a matter of life and death to invade France by that route.

Sylvia was out in the garden, where, hardly a month ago, they had spent that evening of silent peace, and she got up quickly as Michael came out.

"Ah, my dear," she said, "I am glad you have come. I have got the horrors. You saw the latest news? Yes? And have you heard again from Hermann? No, I have not had a word."

He kissed her and sat down.

"No, I have not heard either," he said. "I expect he is right. Letters have been stopped."

"And what do you think will be the result of Belgium's appeal?" she asked.

"Who can tell? The Prime Minister is going to make a statement on Monday. There have been Cabinet meetings going on all day."

She looked at him in silence.

"And what do you think?" she asked.

Quite suddenly, at her question, Michael found himself facing it, even as, when the final catastrophe was more remote, he had faced it with Falbe. All this week he knew he had been looking away from it, telling himself that it was incredible. Now he discovered that the one thing he dreaded more than that England should go to war, was that she should not. The consciousness of national honour, the thing which, with religion, Englishmen are most shy of speaking about, suddenly asserted itself, and he found on the moment that it was bigger than anything else in the world.

"I think we shall go to war," he said. "I don't see personally how we can exist any more as a nation if we don't. We—we shall be damned if we don't, damned for ever and ever. It's moral extinction not to."

She kindled at that.

"Yes, I know," she said, "that's what I have been telling myself; but, oh, Mike, there's some dreadful cowardly part of me that won't listen when I think of Hermann, and . . ."

She broke off a moment.

"Michael," she said, "what will you do, if there is war?"

He took up her hand that lay on the arm of his chair.

"My darling, how can you ask?" he said. "Of course I shall go back to the army."

For one moment she gave way.

"No, no," she said. "You mustn't do that."

And then suddenly she stopped.

"My dear, I ask your pardon," she said. "Of course you will. I know that really. It's only this stupid cowardly part of me that— that interrupted. I am ashamed of it. I'm not as bad as that all through. I don't make excuses for myself, but, ah, Mike, when I think of what Germany is to me, and what Hermann is, and when I think what England is to me, and what you are! It shan't appear again, or if it does, you will make allowance, won't you? At least I can agree with you utterly, utterly. It's the flesh that's weak, or, rather, that is so strong. But I've got it under."

She sat there in silence a little, mopping her eyes.

"How I hate girls who cry!" she said. "It is so dreadfully feeble! Look, Mike, there are some roses on that tree from which I plucked the one you didn't think much of. Do you remember? You crushed it up in my hand and made it bleed."

He smiled.

"I have got some faint recollection of it," he said.

Sylvia had got hold of her courage again.

"Have you?" she asked. "What a wonderful memory. And that quiet evening out here next day. Perhaps you remember that too. That was real: that was a possession that we shan't ever part with."

She pointed with her finger.

"You and I sat there, and Hermann there," she said. "And mother sat—why, there she is. Mother darling, let's have tea out here, shall we? I will go and tell them."

Mrs. Falbe had drifted out in her usual thistledown style, and shook hands with Michael.

"What an upset it all is," she said, "with all these dreadful rumours going about that we shall be at war. I fell asleep, I think, a little after lunch, when I could not attend to my book for thinking about war."

"Isn't the book interesting?" asked Michael.

"No, not very. It is rather painful. I do not know why people write about painful things when there are so many pleasant and interesting things to write about. It seems to me very morbid."

Michael heard something cried in the streets, and at the same moment he heard Sylvia's step quickly crossing the studio to the side door that opened on to it. In a minute she returned with a fresh edition of an evening paper.

"They are preparing to cross the Rhine," she said.

Mrs. Falbe gave a little sigh.

"I don't know, I am sure," she said, "what you are in such a state about, Sylvia. Of course the Germans want to get into France the easiest and quickest way, at least I'm sure I should. It is very foolish of Belgium not to give them leave, as they are so much the strongest."

"Mother darling, you don't understand one syllable about it," said Sylvia.

"Very likely not, dear, but I am very glad we are an island, and that nobody can come marching here. But it is all a dreadful upset, Lord—I mean Michael, what with Hermann in Germany, and the concert tour abandoned. Still, if everything is quiet again by the middle of October, as I daresay it will be, it might come off after all. He will be on the spot, and you and Michael can join him, though I'm not quite sure if that would be proper. But we might arrange something: he might meet you at Ostend."

"I'm afraid it doesn't look very likely," remarked Michael mildly.

"Oh, and are you pessimistic too, like Sylvia? Pray don't be pessimistic. There is a dreadful pessimist in my book, who always thinks the worst is going to happen."

"And does it?" asked Michael.

"As far as I have got, it does, which makes it all the worse. Of course I am very anxious about Hermann, but I feel sure he will come back safe to us. I daresay France will give in when she sees Germany is in earnest."

Mrs. Falbe pulled the shattered remnants of her mind together. In her heart of hearts she knew she did not care one atom what might happen to armies and navies and nations, provided only that she had a quantity of novels to read, and meals at regular hours. The fact of being on an island was an immense consolation to her, since it was quite certain that, whatever happened, German armies (or French or Soudanese, for that matter) could not march here and enter her sitting-room and take her books away from her. For years past she had asked nothing more of the world than that she should be comfortable in it, and it really seemed not an unreasonable request, considering at how small an outlay of money all the comfort she wanted could be secured to her. The thought of war had upset her a good deal already: she had been unable to attend to her book when she awoke from her after-lunch nap; and now, when she hoped to have her tea in peace, and find her attention restored by it, she found the general atmosphere of her two companions vaguely disquieting. She became a little more loquacious than usual, with the idea of talking herself back into a tranquil frame of mind, and reassuring to herself the promise of a peaceful future.

"Such a blessing we have a good fleet," she said. "That will make us safe, won't it? I declare I almost hate the Germans, though my dear husband was one himself, for making such a disturbance. The papers all say it is Germany's fault, so I suppose it must be. The papers know better than anybody, don't they, because they have foreign correspondents. That must be a great expense!"

Sylvia felt she could not endure this any longer. It was like having a raw wound stroked. . . .

"Mother, you don't understand," she said. "You don't appreciate what is happening. In a day or two England will be at war with Germany."

Mrs. Falbe's book had slipped from her knee. She picked it up and flapped the cover once or twice to get rid of dust that might have settled there.

"But what then?" she said. "It is very dreadful, no doubt, to think of dear Hermann being with the German army, but we are getting used to that, are we not? Besides, he told me it was his duty to go. I do not think for a moment that France will be able to stand against Germany. Germany will be in Paris in no time, and I daresay Hermann's next letter will be to say that he has been walking down the boulevards. Of course war is very dreadful, I know that. And then Germany will be at war with Russia, too, but she will have Austria to help her. And as for Germany being at war with England, that does not make me nervous. Think of our fleet, and how safe we feel with that! I see that we have twice as many boats as the Germans. With two to one we must win, and they won't be able to send any of their armies here. I feel quite comfortable again now that I have talked it over."

Sylvia caught Michael's eye for a moment over the tea-urn. She felt he acquiesced in what she was intending to say.

"That is good, then," she said. "I am glad you feel comfortable about it, mother dear. Now, will you read your book out here? Why not, if I fetch you a shawl in case you feel cold?"

Mrs. Falbe turned a questioning eye to the motionless trees and the unclouded sky.

"I don't think I shall even want a shawl, dear," she said. "Listen, how the newsboys are calling! is it something fresh, do you think?"

A moment's listening attention was sufficient to make it known that the news shouted outside was concerned only with the result of a county cricket match, and Michael, as well as Sylvia, was conscious of a certain relief to know that at the immediate present there was no fresh clang of the bell that was beating out the seconds of peace that still remained. Just for now, for this hour on Saturday afternoon, there was a respite: no new link was forged in the intolerable sequence of events. But, even as he drew breath in that knowledge, there came the counter-stroke in the sense that those whose business it was to disseminate the news that would cause their papers to sell, had just a cricket match to advertise their wares. Now, when the country and when Europe were on the brink of a bloodier war than all the annals of history contained, they, who presumably knew what the public desired to be informed on, thought that the news which would sell best was that concerned with wooden bats and leather balls, and strong young men in flannels. Michael had heard with a sort of tender incredulity Mrs. Falbe's optimistic reflections, and had been more than content to let her rest secure in them; but was the country, the heart of England, like her? Did it care more for cricket matches, as she for her book, than for the maintenance of the nation's honour, whatever that championship might cost? . . . And the cry went on past the garden-walk. "Fine innings by Horsfield! Result of the Oval match!"

And yet he had just had his tea as usual, and eaten a slice of cake, and was now smoking a cigarette. It was natural to do that, not to make a fuss and refuse food and drink, and it was natural that people should still be interested in cricket. And at the moment his attitude towards Mrs. Falbe changed. Instead of pity and irritation at her normality, he was suddenly taken with a sense of gratitude to her. It was restful to suspense and jangled nerves to see someone who went on as usual. The sun shone, the leaves of the plane-trees did not wither, Mrs. Falbe read her book, the evening paper was full of cricket news. . . . And then the reaction from that seized him again. Supposing all the nation was like that. Supposing nobody cared. . . . And the tension of suspense strained more tightly than ever.

For the next forty-eight hours, while day and night the telegraph wires of Europe tingled with momentous questions and grave replies, while Ministers and Ambassadors met and parted and met again, rumours flew this way and that like flocks of wild-fowl driven backwards and forwards, settling for a moment with a stir and splash, and then with rush of wings speeding back and on again. A huge coal strike in the northern counties, fostered and financed by German gold, was supposed to be imminent, and this would put out of the country's power the ability to interfere. The Irish Home Rule party, under the same suasion, was said to have refused to call a truce. A letter had been received in high quarters from the German Emperor avowing his fixed determination to preserve peace, and this was honey to Lord Ashbridge. Then in turn each of these was contradicted. All thought of the coal strike in this crisis of national affairs was abandoned; the Irish party, as well as the Conservatives, were of one mind in backing up the Government, no matter what postponement of questions that were vital a month ago, their cohesion entailed; the Emperor had written no letter at all. But through the nebulous mists of hearsay, there fell solid the first drops of the imminent storm. Even before Michael had left Sylvia that afternoon, Germany had declared war on Russia, on Sunday Belgium received a Note from Berlin definitely stating that should their Government not grant the passage to the German battalions, a way should be forced for them. On Monday, finally, Germany declared war on France also.

The country held its breath in suspense at what the decision of the Government, which should be announced that afternoon, should be. One fact only was publicly known, and that was that the English fleet, only lately dismissed from its manoeuvres and naval review, had vanished. There were guard ships, old cruisers and what not, at certain ports, torpedo-boats roamed the horizons of

Deal and Portsmouth, but the great fleet, the swift forts of sea-power, had gone, disappearing no one knew where, into the fine weather haze that brooded over the midsummer sea. There perhaps was an indication of what the decision would be, yet there was no certainty. At home there was official silence, and from abroad, apart from the three vital facts, came but the quacking of rumour, report after report, each contradicting the other.

Then suddenly came certainty, a rainbow set in the intolerable cloud. On Monday afternoon, when the House of Commons met, all parties were known to have sunk their private differences and to be agreed on one point that should take precedence of all other questions. Germany should not, with England's consent, violate the neutrality of Belgium. As far as England was concerned, all negotiations were at an end, diplomacy had said its last word, and Germany was given twenty-four hours in which to reply. Should a satisfactory answer not be forthcoming, England would uphold the neutrality she with others had sworn to respect by force of arms. And at that one immense sigh of relief went up from the whole country. Whatever now might happen, in whatever horrors of long- drawn and bloody war the nation might be involved, the nightmare of possible neutrality, of England's repudiating the debt of honour, was removed. The one thing worse than war need no longer be dreaded, and for the moment the future, hideous and heart-rending though it would surely be, smiled like a land of promise.

Michael woke on the morning of Tuesday, the fourth of August, with the feeling of something having suddenly roused him, and in a few seconds he knew that this was so, for the telephone bell in the room next door sent out another summons. He got straight out of bed and went to it, with a hundred vague shadows of expectation crossing his mind. Then he learned that his mother was gravely ill, and that he was wanted at once. And in less than half an hour he was on his way, driving swiftly through the serene warmth of the early morning to the private asylum where she had been removed after her sudden homicidal outburst in March.

CHAPTER XIV

Michael was sitting that same afternoon by his mother's bedside. He had learned the little there was to be told him on his arrival in the morning; how that half an hour before he had been summoned, she had had an attack of heart failure, and since then, after recovering from the acute and immediate danger, she had lain there all day with closed eyes in a state of but semi-conscious exhaustion. Once or twice only, and that but for a moment she had shown signs of increasing vitality, and then sank back into this stupor again. But in those rare short intervals she had opened her eyes, and had seemed to see and recognise him, and Michael thought that once she had smiled at him. But at present she had spoken no word. All the morning Lord Ashbridge had waited there too, but since there was no change he had gone away, saying that he would return again later, and asking to be telephoned for if his wife regained consciousness. So, but for the nurse and the occasional visits of the doctor, Michael was alone with his mother.

In this long period of inactive waiting, when there was nothing to be done, Michael did not seem to himself to be feeling very vividly, and but for one desire, namely, that before the end his mother would come back to him, even if only for a moment, his mind felt drugged and stupefied. Sometimes for a little it would sluggishly turn over thoughts about his father, wondering with a sort of blunt, remote contempt how it was possible for him not to be here too; but, except for the one great longing that his mother should cleave to him once more in conscious mind, he observed rather than felt. The thought of Sylvia even was dim. He knew that she was somewhere in the world, but she had become for the present like some picture painted in his mind, without reality. Dim, too, was the tension of those last days. Somewhere in Europe was a country called Germany, where was his best friend, drilling in the ranks to which he had returned, or perhaps already on his way to bloodier battlefields than the world had ever dreamed of; and somewhere set in the seas was Germany's arch-foe, who already stood in her path with open cannon mouths pointing. But all this had no real connection with him. From the moment when he had come into this quiet, orderly room and saw his mother lying on the bed, nothing beyond those four walls really concerned him.

But though the emotional side of his mind lay drugged and insensitive to anything outside, he found himself observing the details of the room where he waited with a curious vividness. There was a big window opening down to the ground in the manner of a door on to the garden outside, where a smooth lawn, set with croquet hoops and edged with bright flower-beds, dozed in the haze of the August heat. Beyond was a row of tall elms, against which a copper beech glowed metallically, and somewhere out of sight a mowing-machine was being used, for Michael heard the click of its cropping journey, growing fainter as it receded, followed by the pause as it turned, and its gradual crescendo as it approached again. Otherwise everything outside was strangely silent; as the hot hours of midday and early afternoon went by there was no note of bird-music, nor any sound of wind in the elm-tops. Just a little breeze stirred from time to time, enough to make the slats of the half-drawn Venetian blind rattle faintly. Earlier in the day there had come in from the window the smell of dew-damp earth, but now that had been sucked up by the sun.

Close beside the window, with her back to the light and facing the bed, which projected from one of the side walls out into the room, sat Lady Ashbridge's nurse. She was reading, and the rustle of the turned page was regular; but regular and constant also were her glances towards the bed where her patient lay. At intervals she put down her book, marking the place with a slip of paper, and came to watch by the bed for a moment, looking at Lady Ashbridge's face and listening to her breathing. Her eye met Michael's always as she did this, and in answer to his mute question, each time she gave him a little head-shake, or perhaps a whispered word or two, that told him there was no change. Opposite the bed was the empty fireplace, and at the foot of it a table, on which stood a vase of roses.

Michael was conscious of the scent of these every now and then, and at intervals of the faint, rather sickly smell of ether. A Japan screen, ornamented with storks in gold thread, stood near the door and half-concealed the washing-stand. There was a chest of drawers on one side of the fireplace, a wardrobe with a looking-glass door on the other, a dressing-table to one side of the window, a few prints on the plain blue walls, and a dark blue drugget carpet on the floor; and all these ordinary appurtenances of a bedroom etched themselves into Michael's mind, biting their way into it by the acid of his own suspense.

Finally there was the bed where his mother lay. The coverlet of blue silk upon it he knew was somehow familiar to him, and after fitful gropings in his mind to establish the association, he remembered that it had been on the bed in her room in Curzon Street, and supposed that it had been brought here with others of her personal belongings. A little core of light, focused on one of the brass balls at the head of the bed, caught his eye, and he saw that the sun, beginning to decline, came in under the Venetian blind. The nurse, sitting in the window, noticed this also, and lowered it. The thought of Sylvia crossed his brain for a moment; then he thought of his father; but every train of reflection dissolved almost as soon as it was formed, and he came back again and again to his mother's face.

It was perfectly peaceful and strangely young-looking, as if the cool, soothing hand of death, which presently would quiet all trouble for her, had been already at work there erasing the marks that the years had graven upon it. And yet it was not so much young as ageless; it seemed to have passed beyond the register and limitations of time. Sometimes for a moment it was like the face of a stranger, and then suddenly it would become beloved and familiar again. It was just so she had looked when she came so timidly into his room one night at Ashbridge, asking him if it would be troublesome to him if she sat and talked with him for a little. The mouth was a little parted for her slow, even breathing; the corners of it smiled; and yet he was not sure if they smiled. It was hard to tell, for she lay there quite flat, without pillows, and he looked at her from an unusual angle. Sometimes he felt as if he had been sitting there watching for uncounted years; and then again the hours that he had been here appeared to have lasted but for a moment, as if he had but looked once at her.

As the day declined the breeze of evening awoke, rattling the blind. By now the sun had swung farther west, and the nurse pulled the blind up. Outside in the bushes in the garden the call of birds to each other had begun, and a thrush came close to the window and sang a liquid phrase, and then repeated it. Michael glanced there and saw the bird, speckle-breasted, with throat that throbbed with the notes; and then, looking back to the bed, he saw that his mother's eyes were open.

She looked vaguely about the room for a moment, as if she had awoke from some deep sleep and found herself in an unfamiliar place. Then, turning her head slightly, she saw him, and there was no longer any question as to whether her mouth smiled, for all her face was flooded with deep, serene joy.

He bent towards her and her lips parted.

"Michael, my dear," she said gently.

Michael heard the rustle of the nurse's dress as she got up and came to the bedside. He slipped from his chair on to his knees, so that his face was near his mother's. He felt in his heart that the moment he had so longed for was to be granted him, that she had come back to him, not only as he had known her during the weeks that they had lived alone together, when his presence made her so content, but in a manner infinitely more real and more embracing.

"Have you been sitting here all the time while I slept, dear?" she asked. "Have you been waiting for me to come back to you?"

"Yes, and you have come," he said.

She looked at him, and the mother-love, which before had been veiled and clouded, came out with all the tender radiance of evening sun, with the clear shining after rain.

"I knew you wouldn't fail me, my darling," she said. "You were so patient with me in the trouble I have been through. It was a nightmare, but it has gone."

Michael bent forward and kissed her.

"Yes, mother," he said, "it has all gone."

She was silent a moment.

"Is your father here?" she said.

"No; but he will come at once, if you would like to see him."

"Yes, send for him, dear, if it would not vex him to come," she said; "or get somebody else to send; I don't want you to leave me."

"I'm not going to," said he.

The nurse went to the door, gave some message, and presently returned to the other side of the bed. Then Lady Ashbridge spoke again.

"Is this death?" she asked.

Michael raised his eyes to the figure standing by the bed. She nodded to him.

He bent forward again.

"Yes, dear mother," he said.

For a moment her eyes dilated, then grew quiet again, and the smile returned to her mouth.

"I'm not frightened, Michael," she said, "with you there. It isn't lonely or terrible."

She raised her head.

"My son!" she said in a voice loud and triumphant. Then her head fell back again, and she lay with face close to his, and her eyelids quivered and shut. Her breath came slow and regular, as if she slept. Then he heard that she missed a breath, and soon after another. Then, without struggle at all, her breathing ceased. . . . And outside on the lawn close by the open window the thrush still sang.

It was an hour later when Michael left, having waited for his father's arrival, and drove to town through the clear, falling dusk. He was conscious of no feeling of grief at all, only of a complete pervading happiness. He could not have imagined so perfect a close, nor could he have desired anything different from that imperishable moment when his mother, all trouble past, had come back to him in the serene calm of love. . . .

As he entered London he saw the newsboards all placarded with one fact: England had declared war on Germany.

He went, not to his own flat, but straight to Maidstone Crescent. With those few minutes in which his mother had known him, the stupor that had beset his emotions all day passed off, and he felt himself longing, as he had never longed before, for Sylvia's presence. Long ago he had given her all that he knew of as himself; now there was a fresh gift. He had to give her all that those moments had taught him. Even as already they were knitted into him, made part of him, so must they be to her. . . . And when they had shared that, when, like water gushing from a spring she flooded him, there was that other news which he had seen on the newsboards that they had to share together.

Sylvia had been alone all day with her mother; but, before Michael arrived, Mrs. Falbe (after a few more encouraging remarks about war in general, to the effect that Germany would soon beat France, and what a blessing it was that England was an island) had taken her book up to her room, and Sylvia was sitting alone in the deep dusk of the evening. She did not even trouble to turn on the light, for she felt unable to apply herself to any practical task, and she could think and take hold of herself better in the dark. All day she had longed for Michael to come to her, though she had not cared to see anybody else, and several times she had rung him up, only to find that he was still out, supposedly with his mother, for he had been summoned to her early that morning, and since then no news had come of him. Just before dinner had arrived the announcement of the declaration of war, and Sylvia sat now trying to find some escape from the encompassing nightmare. She felt confused and distracted with it; she could not think consecutively, but only contemplate shudderingly the series of pictures that presented themselves to her mind. Somewhere now, in the hosts of the Fatherland, which was hers also, was Hermann, the brother who was part of herself. When she thought of him, she seemed to be with him, to see the glint of his rifle, to feel her heart on his heart, big with passionate patriotism. She had no doubt that patriotism formed the essence of his consciousness, and yet by now probably he knew that the land beloved by him, where he had made his home, was at war with his own. She could not but know how often his thoughts dwelled here in the dark quiet studio where she sat, and where so many days of happiness had been passed. She knew what she was to him, she and her mother and Michael, and the hosts of friends in this land which had become his foe. Would he have gone, she asked herself, if he had guessed that there would be war between the two? She thought he would, though she knew that for herself she would have made it as hard as possible for him to do so. She would have used every argument she could think of to dissuade him, and yet she felt that her entreaties would have beaten in vain against the granite of his and her nationality. Dimly she had foreseen this contingency when, a few days ago, she had asked Michael what he would do if England went to war, and now that contingency was realised, and Hermann was even now perhaps on his way to violate the neutrality of the country for the sake of which England had gone to war. On the other side was Michael, into whose keeping she had given herself and her love, and on which side was she? It was then that the nightmare came close to her; she could not tell, she was utterly unable to decide. Her heart was Michael's; her heart was her brother's also. The one personified Germany for her, the other England. It was as if she saw Hermann and Michael with bayonet and rifle stalking each other across some land of sand- dunes and hollows, creeping closer to each other, always closer. She felt as if she would have gladly given herself over to an eternity of torment, if only they could have had one hour more, all three of them, together here, as on that night of stars and peace when first there came the news which for the moment had disquieted Hermann.

She longed as with thirst for Michael to come, and as her solitude became more and more intolerable, a hundred hideous fancies obsessed her. What if some accident had happened to Michael, or what, if in this tremendous breaking of ties that the war entailed, he felt that he could not see her? She knew that was an impossibility; but the whole world had become impossible. And there was no escape. Somehow she had to adjust herself to the unthinkable; somehow her relations both with Hermann and Michael had to remain absolutely unshaken. Even that was not enough: they had to be strengthened, made impregnable.

Then came a knock on the side door of the studio that led into the street: Michael often came that way without passing through the house, and with a sense of relief she ran to it and unlocked it. And even as he stepped in, before any word of greeting had been exchanged, she flung herself on him, with fingers eager for the touch of his solidity. . . .

"Oh, my dear," she said. "I have longed for you, just longed for you. I never wanted you so much. I have been sitting in the dark desolate—desolate. And oh! my darling, what a beast I am to think of nothing but myself. I am ashamed. What of your mother, Michael?"

She turned on the light as they walked back across the studio, and Michael saw that her eyes, which were a little dazzled by the change from the dark into the light, were dim with unshed tears, and her hands clung to him as never before had they clung. She needed him now with that imperative need which in trouble can only turn to love for comfort. She wanted that only; the fact of him with her, in this land in which she had suddenly become an alien, an enemy, though all her friends except Hermann were here. And instantaneously, as a baby at the breast, she found that all his strength and serenity were hers.

They sat down on the sofa by the piano, side by side, with hands intertwined before Michael answered. He looked up at her as he spoke, and in his eyes was the quiet of love and death.

"My mother died an hour ago," he said. "I was with her, and as I had longed might happen, she came back to me before she died. For two or three minutes she was herself. And then she said to me, 'My son,' and soon she ceased breathing."

"Oh, Michael," she said, and for a little while there was silence, and in turn it was her presence that he clung to. Presently he spoke again.

"Sylvia, I'm so frightfully hungry," he said. "I don't think I've eaten anything since breakfast. May we go and forage?"

"Oh, you poor thing!" she cried. "Yes, let's go and see what there is."

Instantly she busied herself.

"Hermann left the cellar key on the chimney-piece, Michael," she said. "Get some wine out, dear. Mother and I don't drink any. And there's some ham, I know. While you are getting wine, I'll broil some. And there were some strawberries. I shall have some supper with you. What a good thought! And you must be famished."

As they ate they talked perfectly simply and naturally of the hundred associations which this studio meal at the end of the evening called up concerning the Sunday night parties. There was an occasion on which Hermann tried to recollect how to mull beer, with results that smelled like a brickfield; there was another when a poached egg had fallen, exploding softly as it fell into the piano. There was the occasion, the first on which Michael had been present, when two eminent actors imitated each other; another when Francis came and made himself so immensely agreeable. It was after that one that Sylvia and Hermann had sat and talked in front of the stove, discussing, as Sylvia laughed to remember, what she would say when Michael proposed to her. Then had come the break in Michael's attendances and, as Sylvia allowed, a certain falling-off in gaiety.

"But it was really Hermann and I who made you gay originally," she said. "We take a wonderful deal of credit for that."

All this was as completely natural for them as was the impromptu meal, and soon without effort Michael spoke of his mother again, and presently afterwards of the news of war. But with him by her side Sylvia found her courage come back to her; the news itself, all that it certainly implied, and all the horror that it held, no longer filled her with the sense that it was impossibly terrible. Michael did not diminish the awfulness of it, but he gave her the power of looking out bravely at it. Nor did he shrink from speaking of all that had been to her so grim a nightmare.

"You haven't heard from Hermann?" he asked.

"No. And I suppose we can't hear now. He is with his regiment, that's all; nor shall we hear of him till there is peace again."

She came a little closer to him.

"Michael, I have to face it, that I may never see Hermann again," she said. "Mother doesn't fear it, you know. She—the darling— she lives in a sort of dream. I don't want her to wake from it. But how can I get accustomed to the thought that perhaps I shan't see Hermann again? I must get accustomed to it: I've got to live with it, and not quarrel with it."

He took up her hand, enclosing it in his.

"But, one doesn't quarrel with the big things of life," he said. "Isn't it so? We haven't any quarrel with things like death and duty. Dear me, I'm afraid I'm preaching."

"Preach, then," she said.

"Well, it's just that. We don't quarrel with them: they manage themselves. Hermann's going managed itself. It had to be."

Her voice quivered as she spoke now.

"Are you going?" she asked. "Will that have to be?"

Michael looked at her a moment with infinite tenderness.

"Oh, my dear, of course it will," he said. "Of course, one doesn't know yet what the War Office will do about the Army. I suppose it's possible that they will send troops to France. All that concerns me is that I shall rejoin again if they call up the Reserves."

"And they will?"

"Yes, I should think that is inevitable. And you know there's something big about it. I'm not warlike, you know, but I could not fail to be a soldier under these new conditions, any more than I could continue being a soldier when all it meant was to be ornamental. Hermann in bursts of pride and patriotism used to call us toy-soldiers. But he's wrong now; we're not going to be toy- soldiers any more."

She did not answer him, but he felt her hand press close in the palm of his.

"I can't tell you how I dreaded we shouldn't go to war," he said. "That has been a nightmare, if you like. It would have been the end of us if we had stood aside and seen Germany violate a solemn treaty."

Even with Michael close to her, the call of her blood made itself audible to Sylvia. Instinctively she withdrew her hand from his.

"Ah, you don't understand Germany at all," she said. "Hermann always felt that too. He told me he felt he was talking gibberish to you when he spoke of it. It is clearly life and death to Germany to move against France as quickly as possible."

"But there's a direct frontier between the two," said he.

"No doubt, but an impossible one."

Michael frowned, drawing his big eyebrows together.

"But nothing can justify the violation of a national oath," he said. "That's the basis of civilisation, a thing like that."

"But if it's a necessity? If a nation's existence depends on it?" she asked. "Oh, Michael, I don't know! I don't know! For a little I am entirely English, and then something calls to me from beyond the Rhine! There's the hopelessness of it for me and such as me. You are English; there's no question about it for you. But for us! I love England: I needn't tell you that. But can one ever forget the land of one's birth? Can I help feeling the necessity Germany is under? I can't believe that she has wantonly provoked war with you."

"But consider—" said he.

She got up suddenly.

"I can't argue about it," she said. "I am English and I am German. You must make the best of me as I am. But do be sorry for me, and never, never forget that I love you entirely. That's the root fact between us. I can't go deeper than that, because that reaches to the very bottom of my soul. Shall we leave it so, Michael, and not ever talk of it again? Wouldn't that be best?"

There was no question of choice for Michael in accepting that appeal. He knew with the inmost fibre of his being that, Sylvia being Sylvia, nothing that she could say or do or feel could possibly part him from her. When he looked at it directly and simply like that, there was nothing that could blur the verity of it. But the truth of what she said, the reality of that call of the blood, seemed to cast a shadow over it. He knew beyond all other knowledge that it was there: only it looked out at him with a shadow, faint, but unmistakable, fallen across it. But the sense of that made him the more eagerly accept her suggestion.

"Yes, darling, we'll never speak of it again," he said. "That would be much wisest."

Lady Ashbridge's funeral took place three days afterwards, down in Suffolk, and those hours detached themselves in Michael's mind from all that had gone before, and all that might follow, like a little piece of blue sky in the midst of storm clouds. The limitations of man's consciousness, which forbid him to think poignantly about two things at once, hedged that day in with an impenetrable barrier, so that while it lasted, and afterwards for ever in memory, it was unflecked by trouble or anxiety, and hung between heaven and earth in a serenity of its own.

The coffin lay that night in his mother's bedroom, which was next to Michael's, and when he went up to bed he found himself listening for any sound that came from there. It seemed but yesterday when he had gone rather early upstairs, and after sitting a minute or two in front of his fire, had heard that timid knock on the door, which had meant the opening of a mother's heart to him. He felt it would scarcely be strange if that knock came again, and if she entered once more to be with him. From the moment he came upstairs, the rest of the world was shut down to him; he entered his bedroom as if he entered a sanctuary that was scented with the incense of her love. He knew exactly how her knock had sounded when she came in here that night when first it burned for him: his ears were alert for it to come again. Once his blind tapped against the frame of his open window, and, though knowing it was that, he heard himself whisper—for she could hear his whisper— "Come in, mother," and sat up in his deep chair, looking towards the door. But only the blind tapped again, and outside in the moonlit dusk an owl hooted.

He remembered she liked owls. Once, when they lived alone in Curzon Street, some noise outside reminded her of the owls that hooted at Ashbridge—she had imitated their note, saying it sounded like sleep. . . . She had sat in a chintz-covered chair close to him when at Christmas she paid him that visit, and now he again drew it close to his own, and laid his hand on its arm. Petsy II. had come in with her, and she had hoped that he would not annoy Michael.

There were steps in the passage outside his room, and he heard a little shrill bark. He opened his door and found his mother's maid there, trying to entice Petsy away from the room next to his. The little dog was curled up against it, and now and then he turned round scratching at it, asking to enter. "He won't come away, my lord," said the maid; "he's gone back a dozen times to the door."

Michael bent down.

"Come, Petsy," he said, "come to bed in my room."

The dog looked at him for a moment as if weighing his trustworthiness. Then he got up and, with grotesque Chinese high-stepping walk, came to him.

"He'll be all right with me," he said to the maid.

He took Petsy into his room next door, and laid him on the chair in which his mother had sat. The dog moved round in a circle once or twice, and then settled himself down to sleep. Michael went to bed also, and lay awake about a couple of minutes, not thinking, but only being, while the owls hooted outside.

He awoke into complete consciousness, knowing that something had aroused him, even as three days ago when the telephone rang to summon him to his mother's deathbed. Then he did not know what had awakened him, but now he was sure that there had been a tapping on his door. And after he had sat up in bed completely awake, he heard Petsy give a little welcoming bark. Then came the noise of his small, soft tail beating against the cushion in the chair.

Michael had no feeling of fright at all, only of longing for something that physically could not be. And longing, only longing, once more he said:

"Come in, mother."

He believed he heard the door whisper on the carpet, but he saw nothing. Only, the room was full of his mother's presence. It seemed to him that, in obedience to her, he lay down completely satisfied. . . . He felt no curiosity to see or hear more. She was there, and that was enough.

He woke again a little after dawn. Petsy between the window and the door had jumped on to his bed to get out of the draught of the morning wind. For the door was opened.

That morning the coffin was carried down the long winding path above the deep-water reach, where Michael and Francis at Christmas had heard the sound of stealthy rowing, and on to the boat that awaited it to ferry it across to the church. There was high tide, and, as they passed over the estuary, the stillness of supreme noon bore to them the tolling of the bell. The mourners from the house followed, just three of them, Lord Ashbridge, Michael, and Aunt Barbara, for the rest were to assemble at the church. But of all that, one moment stood out for Michael above all others, when, as they entered the graveyard, someone whom he could not see said: "I am the Resurrection and the Life," and he heard that his father, by whom he walked, suddenly caught his breath in a sob.

All that day there persisted that sense of complete detachment from all but her whose body they had laid to rest on the windy hill overlooking the broad water. His father, Aunt Barbara, the cousins and relations who thronged the church were no more than inanimate shadows compared with her whose presence had come last night into his room, and had not left him since. The affairs of the world, drums and the torch of war, had passed for those hours from his knowledge, as at the centre of a cyclone there was a windless calm. To-morrow he knew he would pass out into the tumult again, and the minutes slipped like pearls from a string, dropping into the dim gulf where the tempest raged. . . .

He went back to town next morning, after a short interview with his father, who was coming up later in the day, when he told him that he intended to go back to his regiment as soon as possible. But, knowing that he meant to go by the slow midday train, his father proposed to stop the express for him that went through a few minutes before. Michael could hardly believe his ears. . . .

CHAPTER XV

It was but a day or two after the outbreak of the war that it was believed that an expeditionary force was to be sent to France, to help in arresting the Teutonic tide that was now breaking over Belgium; but no public and authoritative news came till after the first draft of the force had actually set foot on French soil. From the regiment of the Guards which Michael had rejoined, Francis was among the first batch of officers to go, and that evening Michael took down the news to Sylvia. Already stories of German barbarity were rife, of women violated, of defenceless civilians being shot down for no object except to terrorise, and to bring home to the Belgians the unwisdom of presuming to cross the will of the sovereign people. To-night, in the evening papers, there had been a fresh batch of these revolting stories, and when Michael entered the studio where Sylvia and her mother were sitting, he saw the girl let drop behind the sofa the paper she had been reading. He guessed what she must have found there, for he had already seen the paper himself, and her silence, her distraction, and the misery of her face confirmed his conjecture.

"I've brought you a little news to-night," he said. "The first draft from the regiment went off to-day."

Mrs. Falbe put down her book, marking the place.

"Well, that does look like business, then," she said, "though I must say I should feel safer if they didn't send our soldiers away. Where have they gone to?"

"Destination unknown," said Michael. "But it's France. My cousin has gone."

"Francis?" asked Sylvia. "Oh, how wicked to send boys like that."

Michael saw that her nerves were sharply on edge. She had given him no greeting, and now as he sat down she moved a little away from him. She seemed utterly unlike herself.

"Mother has been told that every Englishman is as brave as two Germans," she said. "She likes that."

"Yes, dear," observed Mrs. Falbe placidly. "It makes one feel safer. I saw it in the paper, though; I read it."

Sylvia turned on Michael.

"Have you seen the evening paper?" she asked.

Michael knew what was in her mind.

"I just looked at it," he said. "There didn't seem to be much news."

"No, only reports, rumours, lies," said Sylvia.

Mrs. Falbe got up. It was her habit to leave the two alone together, since she was sure they preferred that; incidentally, also, she got on better with her book, for she found conversation rather distracting. But to-night Sylvia stopped her.

"Oh, don't go yet, mother," she said. "It is very early."

It was clear that for some reason she did not want to be left alone with Michael, for never had she done this before. Nor did it avail anything now, for Mrs. Falbe, who was quite determined to pursue her reading without delay, moved towards the door.

"But I am sure Michael wants to talk to you, dear," she said, "and you have not seen him all day. I think I shall go up to bed."

Sylvia made no further effort to detain her, but when she had gone, the silence in which they had so often sat together had taken on a perfectly different quality.

"And what have you been doing?" she said. "Tell me about your day. No, don't. I know it has all been concerned with war, and I don't want to hear about it."

"I dined with Aunt Barbara," said Michael. "She sent you her love. She also wondered why you hadn't been to see her for so long."

Sylvia gave a short laugh, which had no touch of merriment in it.

"Did she really?" she asked. "I should have thought she could have guessed. She set every nerve in my body jangling last time I saw her by the way she talked about Germans. And then suddenly she pulled herself up and apologised, saying she had forgotten. That made it worse! Michael, when you are unhappy, kindness is even more intolerable than unkindness. I would sooner have Lady Barbara abusing my people than saying how sorry she is for me. Don't let's talk about it! Let's do something. Will you play, or shall I sing? Let's employ ourselves."

Michael followed her lead.

"Ah, do sing," he said. "It's weeks since I have heard you sing."

She went quickly over to the bookcase of music by the piano.

"Come, then, let's sing and forget," she said. "Hermann always said the artist was of no nationality. Let's begin quick. These are all German songs: don't let's have those. Ah, and these, too! What's to be done? All our songs seem to be German."

Michael laughed.

"But we've just settled that artists have no nationality, so I suppose art hasn't either," he said.

Sylvia pulled herself together, conscious of a want of control, and laid her hand on Michael's shoulder.

"Oh, Michael, what should I do without you?" she said. "And yet— well, let me sing."

She had placed a volume of Schubert on the music-stand, and opening it at random he found "Du Bist die Ruhe." She sang the first verse, but in the middle of the second she stopped.

"I can't," she said. "It's no use."

He turned round to her.

"Oh, I'm so sorry," he said. "But you know that."

She moved away from him, and walked down to the empty fireplace.

"I can't keep silence," she said, "though I know we settled not to talk of those things when necessarily we cannot feel absolutely at one. But, just before you came in, I was reading the evening paper. Michael, how can the English be so wicked as to print, and I suppose to believe, those awful things I find there? You told me you had glanced at it. Well, did you glance at the lies they tell about German atrocities?"

"Yes, I saw them," said Michael. "But it's no use talking about them."

"But aren't you indignant?" she said. "Doesn't your blood boil to read of such infamous falsehoods? You don't know Germans, but I do, and it is impossible that such things can have happened."

Michael felt profoundly uncomfortable. Some of these stories which Sylvia called lies were vouched for, apparently, by respectable testimony.

"Why talk about them?" he said. "I'm sure we were wise when we settled not to."

She shook her head.

"Well, I can't live up to that wisdom," she said. "When I think of this war day and night and night and day, how can I prevent talking to you about it? And those lies! Germans couldn't do such things. It's a campaign of hate against us, set up by the English Press."

"I daresay the German Press is no better," said Michael.

"If that is so, I should be just as indignant about the German Press," said she. "But it is only your guess that it is so."

Suddenly she stopped, and came a couple of steps nearer him.

"Michael, it isn't possible that you believe those things of us?" she said.

He got up.

"Ah, do leave it alone, Sylvia," he said. "I know no more of the truth or falsity of it than you. I have seen just what you have seen in the papers."

"You don't feel the impossibility of it, then?" she asked.

"No, I don't. There seems to have been sworn testimony. War is a cruel thing; I hate it as much as you. When men are maddened with war, you can't tell what they would do. They are not the Germans you know, nor the Germans I know, who did such things—not the people I saw when I was with Hermann in Baireuth and Munich a year ago. They are no more the same than a drunken man is the same as that man when he is sober. They are two different people; drink has made them different. And war has done the same for Germany."

He held out his hand to her. She moved a step back from him.

"Then you think, I suppose, that Hermann may be concerned in those atrocities," she said.

Michael looked at her in amazement.

"You are talking sheer nonsense, Sylvia," he said.

"Not at all. It is a logical inference, just an application of the principle you have stated."

Michael's instinct was just to take her in his arms and make the final appeal, saying, "We love each other, that's all," but his reason prevented him. Sylvia had said a monstrous thing in cold blood, when she suggested that he thought Hermann might be concerned in these deeds, and in cold blood, not by appealing to her emotions, must she withdraw that.

"I'm not going to argue about it," he said. "I want you to tell me at once that I am right, that it was sheer nonsense, to put no other name to it, when you suggested that I thought that of Hermann."

"Oh, pray put another name to it," she said.

"Very well. It was a wanton falsehood," said Michael, "and you know it."

Truly this hellish nightmare of war and hate which had arisen brought with it a brood not less terrible. A day ago, an hour ago he would have merely laughed at the possibility of such a situation between Sylvia and himself. Yet here it was: they were in the middle of it now.

She looked up at him flashing with indignation, and a retort as stinging as his rose to her lips. And then quite suddenly, all her anger went from her, as her, heart told her, in a voice that would not be silenced, the complete justice of what he had said, and the appeal that Michael refrained from making was made by her to herself. Remorse held her on its spikes for her abominable suggestion, and with it came a sense of utter desolation and misery, of hatred for herself in having thus quietly and deliberately said what she had said. She could not account for it, nor excuse herself on the plea that she had spoken in passion, for she had spoken, as he felt, in cold blood. Hence came the misery in the knowledge that she must have wounded Michael intolerably.

Her lips so quivered that when she first tried to speak no words would come. That she was truly ashamed brought no relief, no ease to her surrender, for she knew that it was her real self who had spoken thus incredibly. But she could at least disown that part of her.

"I beg your pardon, Michael," she said. "I was atrocious. Will you forgive me? Because I am so miserable."

He had nothing but love for her, love and its kinsman pity.

"Oh, my dear, fancy you asking that!" he said.

Just for the moment of their reconciliation, it seemed to both that they came closer to each other than they had ever been before, and the chance of the need of any such another reconciliation was impossible to the verge of laughableness, so that before five minutes were past he could make the smile break through her tears at the absurdity of the moment that now seemed quite unreal. Yet that which was at the root of their temporary antagonism was not removed by the reconciliation; at most they had succeeded in cutting off the poisonous shoot that had suddenly sprouted from it. The truth of this in the days that followed was horribly demonstrated.

It was not that they ever again came to the spoken bitterness of words, for the sharpness of them, once experienced, was shunned by each of them, but times without number they had to sheer off, and not approach the ground where these poisoned tendrils trailed. And in that sense of having to take care, to be watchful lest a chance word should bring the peril close to them, the atmosphere of complete ease and confidence, in which alone love can flourish, was tainted. Love was there, but its flowers could not expand, it could not grow in the midst of this bitter air. And what made the situation more and increasingly difficult was the fact that, next to their love for each other, the emotion that most filled the mind of each was this sense of race-antagonism. It was impossible that the news of the war should not be mentioned, for that would have created an intolerable unreality, and all that was in their power was to avoid all discussion, to suppress from speech all the feelings with which the news filled them. Every day, too, there came fresh stories of German abominations committed on the Belgians, and each knew that the other had seen them, and yet neither could mention them. For while Sylvia could not believe them, Michael could not help doing so, and thus there was no common ground on which they could speak of them. Often Mrs. Falbe, in whose blood, it would seem, no sense of race beat at all, would add to the embarrassment by childlike comments, saying at one time in reference to such things that she made a point of not believing all she saw in the newspapers, or at another ejaculating, "Well, the Germans do seem to have behaved very cruelly again!" But no emotion appeared to colour these speeches, while all the emotion of the world surged and bubbled behind the silence of the other two.

Then followed the darkest days that England perhaps had ever known, when the German armies, having overcome the resistance of Belgium, suddenly swept forward again across France, pushing before them like the jetsam and flotsam on the rim of the advancing tide the allied armies. Often in these appalling weeks, Michael would hesitate as to whether he should go to see Sylvia or not, so unbearable seemed the fact that she did not and could not feel or understand what England was going through. So far from blaming her for it, he knew that it could not be otherwise, for her blood called to her, even as his to him, while somewhere in the onrush of those advancing and devouring waves was her brother, with whom, so it had often seemed to him, she was one soul. Thus, while in that his whole sympathy and whole comprehension of her love was with him, there was as well all that deep, silent English patriotism of which till now he had scarcely been conscious, praying with mute entreaty that disaster and destruction and defeat might overwhelm those advancing hordes. Once, when the anxiety and peril were at their height, he made up his mind not to see her that day, and spent the evening by himself. But later, when he was actually on his way to bed, he knew he could not keep away from her, and though it was already midnight, he drove down to Chelsea, and found her sitting up, waiting for the chance of his coming.

For a moment, as she greeted him and he kissed her silently, they escaped from the encompassing horror.

"Ah, you have come," she said. "I thought perhaps you might. I have wanted you dreadfully."

The roar of artillery, the internecine strife were still. Just for a few seconds there was nothing in the world for him but her, nor for her anything but him.

"I couldn't go to bed without just seeing you," he said. "I won't keep you up."

They stood with hands clasped.

"But if you hadn't come, Michael," she said, "I should have understood."

And then the roar and the horror began again. Her words were the simplest, the most directly spoken to him, yet could not but evoke the spectres that for the moment had vanished. She had meant to let her love for him speak; it had spoken, and instantly through the momentary sunlight of it, there loomed the fierce and enormous shadow. It could not be banished from their most secret hearts; even when the doors were shut and they were alone together thus, it made its entrance, ghost-like, terrible, and all love's bolts and bars could not keep it out.

Here was the tragedy of it, that they could not stand embraced with clasped hands and look at it together and so rob it of its terrors, for, at the sight of it, their hands were loosened from each other's, and in its presence they were forced to stand apart. In his heart, as surely as he knew her love, Michael knew that this great shadow under which England lay was shot with sunlight for Sylvia, that the anxiety, the awful suspense that made his fingers cold as he opened the daily papers, brought into it to her an echo of victorious music that beat to the tramp of advancing feet that marched ever forward leaving the glittering Rhine leagues upon leagues in their rear. The Bavarian corps in which Hermann served was known to be somewhere on the Western front, for the Emperor had addressed them ten days before on their departure from Munich, and Sylvia and Michael were both aware of that. But they who loved Hermann best could not speak of it to each other, and the knowledge of it had to be hidden in silence, as if it had been some guilty secret in which they were the terrified accomplices, instead of its being a bond of love which bound them both to Hermann.

In addition to the national anxiety, there was the suspense of those whose sons and husbands and fathers were in the fighting line. Columns of casualty lists were published, and each name appearing there was a sword that pierced a home. One such list, published early in September, was seen by Michael as he drove down on Sunday morning to spend the rest of the day with Sylvia, and the first name that he read there was that of Francis. For a moment, as he remembered afterwards, the print had danced before his eyes, as if seen through the quiver of hot air. Then it settled down and he saw it clearly.

He turned and drove back to his rooms in Half Moon Street, feeling that strange craving for loneliness that shuns any companionship. He must, for a little, sit alone with the fact, face it, adjust himself to it. Till that moment when the dancing print grew still again he had not, in all the anxiety and suspense of those days, thought of Francis's death as a possibility even. He had heard from him only two mornings before, in a letter thoroughly characteristic that saw, as Francis always saw, the pleasant and agreeable side of things. Washing, he had announced, was a delusion; after a week without it you began to wonder why you had ever made a habit of it. . . . They had had a lot of marching, always in the wrong direction, but everyone knew that would soon be over. . . . Wasn't London very beastly in August? . . . Would Michael see if he could get some proper cigarettes out to him? Here there was nothing but little black French affairs (and not many of them) which tied a knot in the throat of the smoker. . . . And now Francis, with all his gaiety and his affection, and his light pleasant dealings with life, lay dead somewhere on the sunny plains of France, killed in action by shell or bullet in the midst of his youth and strength and joy in life, to gratify the damned dreams of the man who had been the honoured guest at Ashbridge, and those who had advised and flattered and at the end perhaps just used him as their dupe. To their insensate greed and swollen- headed lust for world-power was this hecatomb of sweet and pleasant lives offered, and in their onward course through the vines and corn of France they waded through the blood of the slain whose only crime was that they had dared to oppose the will of Germany, as voiced by the War Lord. And as milestones along the way they had come were set the records of their infamy, in rapine and ruthless slaughter of the innocent. Just at first, as he sat alone in his room, Michael but contemplated images that seemed to form in his mind without his volition, and, emotion-numb from the shock, they seemed external to him. Sometimes he had a vision of Francis lying without mark or wound or violence on him in some vineyard on the hill-side, with face as quiet as in sleep turned towards a moonlit sky. Then came another picture, and Francis was walking across the terrace at Ashbridge with his gun over his shoulder, towards Lord Ashbridge and the Emperor, who stood together, just as Michael had seen the three of them when they came in from the shooting-party. As Francis came near, the Emperor put a cartridge into his gun and shot him. . . . Yes, that was it: that was what had happened. The marvellous peacemaker of Europe, the fire-engine who, as Hermann had said, was ready to put out all conflagrations, the fatuous mountebank who pretended to be a friend to England, who conducted his own balderdash which he called music, had changed his role and shown his black heart and was out to kill.

Wild panoramas like these streamed through Michael's head, as if projected there by some magic lantern, and while they lasted he was conscious of no grief at all, but only of a devouring hate for the mad, lawless butchers who had caused Francis's death, and willingly at that moment if he could have gone out into the night and killed a German, and met his death himself in the doing of it, he would have gone to his doom as to a bridal-bed. But by degrees, as the stress of these unsought imaginings abated, his thoughts turned to Francis himself again, who, through all his boyhood and early manhood, had been to him a sort of ideal and inspiration. How he had loved and admired him, yet never with a touch of jealousy! And Francis, whose letter lay open by him on the table, lay dead on the battlefields of France. There was the envelope, with the red square mark of the censor upon it, and the sheet with its gay scrawl in pencil, asking for proper cigarettes. And, with a pang of remorse, all the more vivid because it concerned so trivial a thing, Michael recollected that he had not sent them. He had meant to do so yesterday afternoon but something had put it out of his head. Never again would Francis ask him to send out cigarettes. Michael laid his head on his arms, so that his face was close to that pencilled note, and the relief of tears came to him.

Soon he raised himself again, not ashamed of his sorrow, but somehow ashamed of the black hate that before had filled him. That was gone for the present, anyhow, and Michael was glad to find it vanished. Instead there was an aching pity, not for Francis alone nor for himself, but for all those concerned in this hideous business. A hundred and a thousand homes, thrown suddenly to-day into mourning, were there: no doubt there were houses in that Bavarian village in the pine woods above which he and Hermann had spent the day when there was no opera at Baireuth where a son or a brother or a father were mourned, and in the kinship of sorrow he found himself at peace with all who had suffered loss, with all who were living through days of deadly suspense. There was nothing effeminate or sentimental about it; he had never been manlier than in this moment when he claimed his right to be one with them. It was right to pause like this, with his hand clasped in the hands of friends and foes alike. But without disowning that, he knew that Francis's death, which had brought that home to him, had made him eager also for his own turn to come, when he would go out to help in the grim work that lay in front of him. He was perfectly ready to die if necessary, and if not, to kill as many Germans as possible. And somehow the two aspects of it all, the pity and the desire to kill, existed side by side, neither overlapping nor contradicting one another.

His servant came into the room with a pencilled note, which he opened. It was from Sylvia.

"Oh, Michael, I have just called and am waiting to know if you will see me. I have seen the news, and I want to tell you how sorry I am. But if you don't care to see me I know you will say so, won't you?"

Though an hour before he had turned back on his way to go to Sylvia, he did not hesitate now.

"Yes, ask Miss Falbe to come up," he said.

She came up immediately, and once again as they met, the world and the war stood apart from them.

"I did not expect you to come, Michael," she said, "when I saw the news. I did not mean to come here myself. But—but I had to. I had just to find out whether you wouldn't see me, and let me tell you how sorry I am."

He smiled at her as they stood facing each other.

"Thank you for coming," he said; "I'm so glad you came. But I had to be alone just a little."

"I didn't do wrong?" she asked.

"Indeed you didn't. I did wrong not to come to you. I loved Francis, you see."

Already the shadow threatened again. It was just the fact that he loved Francis that had made it impossible for him to go to her, and he could not explain that. And as the shadow began to fall she gave a little shudder.

"Oh, Michael, I know you did," she said. "It's just that which concerns us, that and my sympathy for you. He was such a dear. I only saw him, I know, once or twice, but from that I can guess what he was to you. He was a brother to you—a—a—Hermann."

Michael felt, with Sylvia's hand in his, they were both running desperately away from the shadow that pursued them. Desperately he tried with her to evade it. But every word spoken between them seemed but to bring it nearer to them.

"I only came to say that," she said. "I had to tell you myself, to see you as I told you, so that you could know how sincere, how heartfelt—"

She stopped suddenly.

"That's all, my dearest," she added. "I will go away again now."

Across that shadow that had again fallen between them they looked and yearned for each other.

"No, don't go—don't go," he said. "I want you more than ever. We are here, here and now, you and I, and what else matters in comparison of that? I loved Francis, as you know, and I love Hermann, but there is our love, the greatest thing of all. We've got it—it's here. Oh, Sylvia, we must be wise and simple, we must separate things, sort them out, not let them get mixed with one another. We can do it; I know we can. There's nothing outside us; nothing matters—nothing matters."

There was just that ray of sun peering over the black cloud that illumined their faces to each other, while already the sharp peaked shadow of it had come between them. For that second, while he spoke, it seemed possible that, in the middle of welter and chaos and death and enmity, these two souls could stand apart, in the passionate serene of love, and the moment lasted for just as long as she flung herself into his arms. And then, even while her face was pressed to his, and while the riotous blood of their pressed lips sang to them, the shadow fell across them. Even as he asserted the inviolability of the sanctuary in which they stood, he knew it to be an impossible Utopia—that he should find with her the peace that should secure them from the raging storm, the cold shadow—and the loosening of her arms about his neck but endorsed the message of his own heart. For such heavenly security cannot come except to those who have been through the ultimate bitterness that the world can bring; it is not arrived at but through complete surrender to the trial of fire, and as yet, in spite of their opposed patriotism, in spite of her sincerest sympathy with Michael's loss, the assault on the most intimate lines of the fortress had not yet been delivered. Before they could reach the peace that passed understanding, a fiercer attack had to be repulsed, they had to stand and look at each other unembittered across waves and billows of a salter Marah than this.

But still they clung, while in their eyes there passed backwards and forwards the message that said, "It is not yet; it is not thus!" They had been like two children springing together at the report of some thunder-clap, not knowing in the presence of what elemental outpouring of force they hid their faces together. As yet it but boomed on the horizon, though messages of its havoc reached them, and the test would come when it roared and lightened overhead. Already the tension of the approaching tempest had so wrought on them that for a month past they had been unreal to each other, wanting ease, wanting confidence; and now, when the first real shock had come, though for a moment it threw them into each other's arms, this was not, as they knew, the real, the final reconciliation, the touchstone that proved the gold. Francis's death, the cousin whom Michael loved, at the hands of one of the nation to whom Sylvia belonged, had momentarily made them feel that all else but their love was but external circumstance; and, even in the moment of their feeling this, the shadow fell again, and left them chilly and shivering.

For a moment they still held each other round the neck and shoulder, then the hold slipped to the elbow, and soon their hands parted. As yet no word had been said since Michael asserted that nothing else mattered, and in the silence of their gradual estrangement the sanguine falsity of that grew and grew and grew.

"I know what you feel," she said at length, "and I feel it also."

Her voice broke, and her hands felt for his again.

"Michael, where are you?" she cried. "No, don't touch me; I didn't mean that. Let's face it. For all we know, Hermann might have killed Francis. . . . Whether he did or not, doesn't matter. it might have been. It's like that."

A minute before Michael, in soul and blood and mind and bones, had said that nothing but Sylvia and himself had any real existence. He had clung to her, even as she to him, hoping that this individual love would prove itself capable of overriding all else that existed. But it had not needed that she should speak to show him how pathetically he had erred. Before she had made a concrete instance he knew how hopeless his wish had been: the silence, the loosening of hands had told him that. And when she spoke there was a brutality in what she said, and worse than the brutality there was a plain, unvarnished truth.

There was no question now of her going away at once, as she had proposed, any more than a boat in the rapids, roared round by breakers, can propose to start again. They were in the middle of it, and so short a way ahead was the cataract that ran with blood. On each side at present were fine, green landing-places; he at the oar, she at the tiller, could, if they were of one mind, still put ashore, could run their boat in, declining the passage of the cataract with all its risks, its river of blood. There was but a stroke of the oar to be made, a pull on a rope of the rudder, and a step ashore. Here was a way out of the storm and the rapids.

A moment before, when, by their physical parting they had realised the strength of the bonds that held them apart this solution had not occurred to Sylvia. Now, critically and forlornly hopeful, it flashed on her. She felt, she almost felt—for the ultimate decision rested with him—that with him she would throw everything else aside, and escape, just escape, if so he willed it, into some haven of neutrality, where he and she would be together, leaving the rest of the world, her country and his, to fight over these irreconcilable quarrels. It did not seem to matter what happened to anybody else, provided only she and Michael were together, out of risk, out of harm. Other lives might be precious, other ideals and patriotisms might be at stake, but she wanted to be with him and nothing else at all. No tie counted compared to that; there was but one life given to man and woman, and now that her individual happiness, the individual joy of her love, was at stake, she felt, even as Michael had said, that nothing else mattered, that they would be right to realise themselves at any cost.

She took his hands again.

"Listen to me, Michael," she said. "I can't bear any longer that these horrors should keep rising up between us, and, while we are here in the middle of it all, it can't be otherwise. I ask you, then, to come away with me, to leave it all behind. It is not our quarrel. Already Hermann has gone; I can't lose you too."

She looked up at him for a moment, and then quickly away again, for she felt her case, which seemed to her just now so imperative, slipping away from her in that glance she got of his eyes, that, for all the love that burned there, were blank with astonishment. She must convince him; but her own convictions were weak when she looked at him.

"Don't answer me yet," she said. "Hear what I have to say. Don't you see that while we are like this we are lost to each other? And as you yourself said just now, nothing matters in comparison to our love. I want you to take me away, out of it all, so that we can find each other again. These horrors thwart and warp us; they spoil the best thing that the world holds for us. My patriotism is just as sound as yours, but I throw it away to get you. Do the same, then. You can get out of your service somehow. . . ."

And then her voice began to falter.

"If you loved me, you would do it," she said. "If—"

And then suddenly she found she could say no more at all. She had hoped that when she stated these things she would convince him, and, behold, all she had done was to shake her own convictions so that they fell clattering round her like an unstable card-house. Desperately she looked again at him, wondering if she had convinced him at all, and then again she looked, wondering if she should see contempt in his eyes. After that she stood still and silent, and her face flamed.

"Do you despise me, Michael?" she said.

He gave a little sigh of utter content.

"Oh, my dear, how I love you for suggesting such a sweet impossibility," he said. "But how you would despise me if I consented."

She did not answer.

"Wouldn't you?" he repeated.

She gave a sorrowful semblance of a laugh.

"I suppose I should," she said.

"And I know you would. You would contrast me in your mind, whether you wished to or not, with Hermann, with poor Francis, sorely to my disadvantage."

They sat silent a little, but there was another question Sylvia had to ask for which she had to collect her courage. At last it came.

"Have they told you yet when you are going?" she said.

"Not for certain. But—it will be before many days are passed. And the question arises—will you marry me before I go?"

She hid her face on his shoulder.

"I will do what you wish," she said.

"But I want to know your wish."

She clung closer to him.

"Michael, I don't think I could bear to part with you if we were married," she said. "It would be worse, I think, than it's going to be. But I intend to do exactly what you wish. You must tell me. I'm going to obey you before I am your wife as well as after."

Michael had long debated this in his mind. It seemed to him that if he came back, as might easily happen, hopelessly crippled, incurably invalid, it would be placing Sylvia in an unfairly difficult position, if she was already his wife. He might be hideously disfigured; she would be bound to but a wreck of a man; he might be utterly unfit to be her husband, and yet she would be tied to him. He had already talked the question over with his father, who, with that curious posthumous anxiety to have a further direct heir, had urged that the marriage should take place at once; but with his own feeling on the subject, as well as Sylvia's, he at once made up his mind.

"I agree with you," he said. "We will settle it so, then."

She smiled at him.

"How dreadfully business-like," she said, with an attempt at lightness.

"I know. It's rather a good thing one has got to be business-like, when—"

That failed also, and he drew her to him and kissed her.

CHAPTER XVI

Michael was sitting in the kitchen of a French farm-house just outside the village of Laires, some three miles behind the English front. The kitchen door was open, and on the flagged floor was cast an oblong of primrose-coloured November sunshine, warm and pleasant, so that the bluebottle flies buzzed hopefully about it, settling occasionally on the cracked green door, where they cleaned their wings, and generally furbished themselves up, as if the warmth was that of a spring day that promised summer to follow. They were there in considerable numbers, for just outside in the cobbled yard was a heap of manure, where they hungrily congregated. Against the white-washed wall of the house there lay a fat sow, basking contentedly, and snorting in her dreams. The yard, bounded on two sides by the house walls, was shut in on the third by a row of farm-sheds, and the fourth was open. Just outside it stood a small copse half flooded with the brimming water of a sluggish stream that meandered by the side of the farm-road leading out of the yard, which turned to the left, and soon joined the highway. This farm-road was partly under water, though not deeply, so that by skirting along its raised banks it was possible to go dry-shod to the highway underneath which the stream passed in a brick culvert.

Through the kitchen window, set opposite the door, could be seen a broad stretch of country of the fenland type, flat and bare, and intersected with dykes, where sedges stirred slightly in the southerly breeze. Here and there were pools of overflowed rivulets, and here and there were plantations of stunted hornbeam, the russet leaves of which still clung thickly to them. But in the main it was a bare and empty land, featureless and stolid.

Just below the kitchen window there was a plot of cultivated ground, thriftily and economically used for the growing of vegetables. Concession, however, was made to the sense of brightness and beauty, for on each side of the path leading up to the door ran a row of Michaelmas daisies, rather battered by the fortnight of rain which had preceded this day of still warm sun, but struggling bravely to shake off the effect of the adverse conditions under which they had laboured.

The kitchen itself was extremely clean and orderly. Its flagged floor was still damp and brown in patches from the washing it had received two hours before; but the draught between open window and open door was fast drying it. Down the centre of the room was a deal table without a cloth, on which were laid some half-dozen places, each marked with a knife and fork and spoon and a thick glass, ready for the serving of the midday meal. On the white- washed walls hung two photographs of family groups, in one of which appeared the father and mother and three little children, in the other the same personages some ten years later, and a lithograph of the Blessed Virgin. On each side of the table was a deal bench, at the head and foot two wooden armchairs. A dresser stood against the wall, on the floor by the oven was a frayed rug, and most important of all, to Michael's mind, was a big stewpot that stood on the top of the oven. From time to time a fat, comfortable Frenchwoman bustled in, and took off the lid of this to stir it, or placed on the dresser a plate of cheese, or a loaf of freshly cooked brown bread. Two or three of Michael's brother-officers were there, one sitting in the patch of sunlight with his back against the green door, another on the step outside. The post had come in not long before, and all of them, Michael included, were occupied with letters and papers.

To-day there happened to be no letters for Michael, and the paper which he glanced at seemed a very feeble effort in the way of entertainment. There was no news in it, except news about the war, which here, out at the front, did not interest him in the least. Perhaps in England people liked to know that a hundred yards of trenches had been taken at one place, and that three German attacks had failed at another; but when you were actually engaged (or had been or would soon again be) in taking part in those things, it seemed a waste of paper and compositor's time to record them. There was a column of letters also from indignant Britons, using violent language about the crimes and treachery of Germany. That also was uninteresting and far-fetched. Nothing that Germany had done mattered the least. There was no use in arguing and slinging wild expressions about; it was a stale subject altogether when you were within earshot of that incessant booming of guns. All the morning that had gone on without break, and no doubt they would get news of what had happened before they set out again that evening for another spell in the trenches. But in all probability nothing particular had happened. Probably the London papers would record it next day, a further tediousness on their part. It would be much more interesting to hear what was going on there, whether there were any new plays, whether there had been any fresh concerts, what the weather was like, or even who had been lunching at Prince's, or dining at the Carlton.

He put down his uninteresting paper, and strolled out into the farmyard, stepping over the legs of the junior officer who blocked the doorway, and did not attempt to move. On the doorstep was sitting a major of his regiment, who, more politely, shifted his place a little so that Michael should pass. Outside the smell of manure was acrid but not unpleasant, the old sow grunted in her sleep, and one of the green shutters outside the upper windows slowly blew to. There was someone inside the room apparently, for the moment after a hand and arm bare to the elbow were protruded, and fastened the latch of the shutter, so that it should not move again.

A little further on was a rail that separated the copse from the roadway, and here out of the wind Michael sat down, and lit a cigarette to stop his yearning for the bubbling stewpot, which would not be broached for half an hour yet. The day, he believed, was Wednesday, but the whole quiet of the place, apart from that drowsy booming on the eastern horizon, made it feel like Sunday. Nobody but the fat Frenchwoman who bustled about had anything to do; there was a

Sabbath leisure about everything, about the dozing sow, the buzzing flies, the lounging figures that read letters and papers. When last they were here, it is true, there were rather more of them. Eight officers had been billeted here last week, before they had been in the trenches and now there were but six. This evening they would set out again for another forty-eight hours in that hellish inferno, but to-morrow a fresh draft was arriving, so that when next they foregathered here, whatever had happened in the interval, there would probably be at least six of them.

It did not seem to matter much what six there would be, or whether there would be more than six or less. All that mattered at this moment, as he inhaled the first incense of his cigarette, was that the rain was over for the present, that the sun shone from a blue sky, that he felt extraordinarily well and tranquil, and that dinner would soon be ready. But of all these agreeable things what pleased him most was the tranquillity; to be alive here with the manure heap steaming in the sun, and the sow asleep by the house wall, and swallows settling on the eaves, was "Paradise enow." Somewhere deep down in him were streams of yearning and of horror, flowing like an underground river in the dark. He yearned for Sylvia, he thought with horror of the two days in the trenches that had preceded this rest in the white-washed farm-house, and with horror he thought of the days and nights that would succeed it. But both horror and yearnings were stupefied by the content that flooded the present moment. No doubt it was reaction from what had gone before, but the reaction was complete. Just now he asked for nothing but to sit in the sun and smoke his cigarette, and wait for dinner. As far as he knew he did not think of anything particular; he just existed in the sun.

The wind must have shifted a little, for before long it came round the corner of the house, and slightly spoiled the mellow warmth of the sunshine. This would never do. The Epicurean in him revolted at the idea of losing a moment of this complete well-being, and arguing that if the wind blew here, it must be dead calm below the kitchen window on the other side of the house, he got off his rail and walked along the slippery bank at the edge of the flooded road in order to go there. It was hard to keep his footing here, and his progress was slow, but he felt he would take any amount of trouble to avoid getting his feet wet in the flooded road. Then there was a patch of kitchen-garden to cross, where the mud clung rather annoyingly to his instep, and, having gained the garden path, he very carefully wiped his boots and with a fallen twig dug away the clots of soil that stuck to the instep.

He found that he had been quite right in supposing that the air would be windless here, and full of great content he sat down with his back to the house wall. A tortoise-shell butterfly, encouraged by the warmth, was flitting about among the Michaelmas daisies that bordered the path and settling on them, opening its wings to the genial sun. Two or three bees buzzed there also; the summer-like tranquillity inserted into the middle of November squalls and rain, deluded them as well as Michael into living completely in the present hour. Gnats hovered about. One settled on Michael's hand, where he instantly killed it, and was sorry he had done so. For the time the booming of guns which had sounded incessantly all the morning to the east, stopped altogether, and absolute quiet reigned. Had he not been so hungry, and so unable to get the idea of the stewpot out of his head, Michael would have been content to sit with his back to the sun-warmed wall for ever.

The high-road, raised and embanked above the low-lying fields, ran eastwards in an undeviating straight line. Just opposite the farm were the last outlying huts of the village, and from there onwards it lay untenanted. But before many minutes were passed, the quiet of the autumn noon began to be overscored by distant humming, faint at first, and then quickly growing louder, and he saw far away a little brown speck coming swiftly towards him. It turned out to be a dispatch-rider, mounted on a motor-bicycle, who with a hoot of his horn roared westward through the village. Immediately afterwards another humming, steadier and more sonorous, grew louder, and Michael, recognising it, looked up instinctively into the blue sky overhead, as an English aeroplane, flying low, came from somewhere behind, and passed directly over him, going eastwards. Before long it stopped its direct course, and began to mount in spirals, and when at a sufficient height, it resumed its onward journey towards the German lines. Then three or four privates, billeted in the village, and now resting after duty in the trenches, strolled along the road, laughing and talking. They sat down not a hundred yards from Michael and one began to whistle "Tipperary." Another and another took it up until all four were engaged on it. It was not precisely in tune nor were the performers in unison, but it produced a vaguely pleasant effect, and if not in tune with the notes as the composer wrote them, the sight and sound of those four whistling and idle soldiers was in tune with the air of security of Sunday morning.

Something far down the road caught Michael's eye, some moving line of brown wagons. As they came nearer he saw that they were the motor-ambulances of the Red Cross, moving slowly along the ruts and holes which the traffic had worn, so that the occupants should suffer as little jolting as was possible. They carried no doubt the wounded who had been taken from the trenches last night, and now, after calling for them at the first dressing station in the rear of the lines, were removing them to hospital. As they passed the four men sitting by the roadside, one of them shouted, "Cheer, oh, mates!" and then they fell to whistling "Tipperary" again. Then, oh, blessed moment! the fat Frenchwoman looked out of the kitchen window just above his head.

"Diner, m'sieu," she said, and Michael, without another thought of ambulance or aeroplane, scrambled to his feet. Somewhere in the middle distance of his mind he was sorry that this tranquil morning was over, just as below in the darkness of it there ran those streams of yearning and of horror, but all his ordinary work-a-day self was occupied with the immediate prospect of the stewpot. It was some sort of a ragout, he knew, and he lusted for it. Red wine of the country would be there, and cheese and new brown bread. . . . It surprised him to find how completely his bodily needs and the pleasure of their gratification had possession of him.

They were under orders to go back to the trenches shortly after sunset, and when their meal was over there remained but an hour or two before they had to start. The warmth and glory of the day was already gone, and streamers of cloud were beginning to form over the open sky. All afternoon these thickened till a dull layer of grey had thickly overspread the heavens and below that arch of vapour that cut off the sun the wind was blowing chilly. With that change in the weather, Michael's mood changed also, and the horror of the return to the trenches began to come to the surface. He was not as yet aware of any physical fear of death or of wound, rather, the feeling was one of some mental and spiritual shrinking from the whole of this vast business of murder, where hundreds and thousands of men along the battle front that stretched half-way across Europe, were employed, day and night, without having any quarrel with each other, in the unsleeping vigilant work of killing. Most of them in all probability, were quite decent fellows, like those four who had whistled "Tipperary" together, and yet they were spending months of young, sweet life up to the knees in water, in foul and ill-smelling trenches in order to kill others whom they had never seen except as specks on the sights of their rifles. Somewhere behind that gruesome business, as he knew, there stood the Cause, calm and serene, like some great statue, which made this insensate murdering necessary; but just for an hour to-day, as he waited till they had to be on the move again, he found himself unable to make real to his own mind the existence of that cause, and could not see beyond the bloody and hideous things that resulted from it.

Then, in this inaction of waiting, an attack of mere physical cowardice seized him, and he found himself imagining the mutilation and torture that perhaps awaited him personally in those deathly ditches. He tried to busy himself with the preparation of the few things that he would take with him, he tried to encourage himself by remembering that in his previous experiences there he had not been conscious of any fear, by telling himself that these were only the unreal anticipations that were always ready to pounce on one even before such mildly alarming affairs as a visit to the dentist; but in spite of his efforts, he found his hands growing clammy and cold at the thoughts which beset his brain. What if there happened to him what had happened to another junior officer who was close to him at the moment, when a fragment of shell turned him from a big gay boy into a writhing bundle at the bottom of the trench! He had lived for a couple of hours like that, moaning and crying out, "For God's sake kill me!" What if, more mercifully, he was killed outright, so that he would lie there in peace till next night they removed his body, or perhaps had to bury him in the trench itself, with a dozen handfuls of soil cast over him! At that he suddenly realised how passionately he wanted to live, to escape from this infernal butchery, to be safe again, gloriously or ingloriously, it mattered not which, to be with Sylvia once more. He told himself that he had been an utter fool ever to re-enter the army again like this. He could certainly have got some appointment as dispatch- carrier or had himself attached to the headquarters staff, or even have shuffled out of it altogether. . . . But, above all, he wanted Sylvia; he wanted to be allowed to lead the ordinary human life, safely and securely, with the girl he loved, and with the musical pursuits that were his passion. He had hated soldiering in times of peace; he found now that he was terrified of it in times of war. He felt physically sick, as with cold hands and trembling knees he stood and waited, lighting cigarettes and throwing them away, in front of the kitchen fire, where the stewpot was already bubbling again for those lucky devils who would return here to- night.

The Major of his company was sitting in the window watching him, though Michael was unaware of it. Suddenly he got up, and came across to the fire, and put his hand on his shoulder.

"Don't mind it, Comber," he said quietly. "We all get a touch of it sometimes. But you'll find it will pass all right. It's the waiting doing nothing that does it."

That touched Michael absolutely in the right place.

"Thanks awfully, sir," he said.

"Not a bit. But it's damned beastly while it lasts. You'll be all right when we move. Don't forget to take your fur coat up if you've got one. We shall have a cold night."

Just after sunset they set out, marching in the gathering dusk down the road eastwards, where in a mile or two they would strike the huge rabbit warren of trenches that joined the French line to the north and south. Once or twice they had to open out and go by the margin of the road to let ambulances or commissariat wagon go by, but there was but little traffic here, as the main lines of communication lay on other roads. High above them, scarcely visible in the dusk, an English aeroplane droned back from its reconnaissance, and once there was the order given to scatter over the fields as a German Taube passed across them. This caused much laughter and chaff among the men, and Michael heard one say, "Dove they call it, do they? I'd like to make a pigeon-pie of them doves." Soon they scrambled back on to the road again, and the interminable "Tipperary" was resumed, in whistle and song. Michael remembered how Aunt Barbara had heard it at a music-hall, and had spoken of it as a new and catchy tune which you could carry away with you. Nowadays, it carried you away. It had become the audible soul of the British army.

The trench which Michael's company were to occupy for the next forty-eight hours was in the first firing-line, and to reach it they had to pass in single file up a mile of communication trenches, from which on all sides, like a vast rabbit warren, there opened out other galleries and passages that led to different parts of this net-work of the lines. It ran not in a straight line but in short sections with angles intervening, so under no circumstances could any considerable length of it be enfiladed, and was lit here and there by little oil lamps placed in embrasures in one or other wall of it, or for some distance at a time it was dark except for the vague twilight of the cloudy sky overhead. Then again, as they approached the firing-line, it would suddenly become intensely bright, when from the English lines, or from those of the Germans which lay not more than two hundred yards in front of them, a fireball or star-shell was sent up, that caused everything it shone upon to leap into vivid illumination. Usually, when this happened, there came from one side or the other a volley of rifle shots, that sounded like the crack of stock-whips, and once or twice a bullet passed over their heads with the buzz as of some vicious stinging insect. Here and there, where the bottom lay in soft and clayey soil, they walked through mud that came half-way up to the knee, and each foot had to be lifted with an effort, and was set free with a smacking suck. Elsewhere, if the ground was gravelly, the rain which for two days previously had been incessant, had drained off, and the going was easy. But whether the path lay over dry or soft places the air was sick with some stale odour which the breeze that swept across the lines from the south-east could not carry away. There was a perpetual pervading reek that flowed along from the entrance of trenches to right and left, that reminded Michael of the smell of a football scrimmage on a wet day, laden with the odours of sweat and dripping clothes, and something deadlier and more acrid. Sometimes they passed under a section covered in with boards, over which the earth and clods of turf had been replaced, so that reconnoitring aeroplanes should not so easily spy it out, and here from dark excavations the smell hung overpoweringly. Now and then the ground over which they passed yielded uneasily to the foot, where lay, only lightly covered over, some corpse which it had been impossible to remove, and from time to time they passed a huddled bundle of khaki not yet taken away. But except for the artillery duel that day they had heard going on that morning, the last day or two had been quiet, and the wounded had all been got out, and for the most part the dead also.

After a long tramp in this communication trench they made a sharp turn to the right, and entered that which they were going to hold for the next forty-eight hours. Here they relieved the regiment that had occupied it till now, who filed out as they came in. Along it at intervals were excavations dug out in the side, some propped up with boards and posts, others, where the ground was of sufficiently holding character, just scooped out. In front, towards the German lines ran a parapet of excavated earth, with occasional peep-holes bored in it, so that the sentry going his rounds could look out and see if there was any sign of movement from opposite without showing his head above the entrenchment. But even this was a matter of some risk, since the enemy had located these peep-holes, and from time to time fired a shot from a fixed rifle that came straight through them and buried its bullet in the hinder wall of the trench. Other spy-holes were therefore being made, but these were not yet finished, and for the present till they were dug, it was necessary to use the old ones. The trench, like all the others, was excavated in short, zigzag lengths, so that no point, either to right or left, commanded more than a score of yards of it.

In front, from just outside the parapet to a depth of some twenty yards, stretched the spider-web of wire entanglements, and a little farther down on the right there had been a copse of horn-beam saplings. An attempt had been made by the enemy during the morning to capture and entrench this, thus advancing their lines, but the movement had been seen, and the artillery fire, which had been so incessant all the morning, denoted the searching of this and the rendering of it untenable. How thorough that searching had been was clear, for that which had been an acre of wood was now but a heap of timber fit only for faggots. Scarcely a tree was left standing, and Michael, looking out of one of the peep-holes by the light of a star-shell saw that the wire entanglements were thick with leaves that the wind and the firing had detached from the broken branches. In turn, the wire entanglements had come in for some shelling by the enemy, and a squad of men were out now under cover of the darkness repairing these. There was a slight dip in the ground here, and by crouching and lying they were out of sight of the trenches opposite; but there were some snipers in that which had been a wood, from whom there came occasional shots. Then, from lower down to the right, there came a fusillade from the English lines suddenly breaking out, and after a few minutes as suddenly stopping again. But the sniping from the wood had ceased.

Michael did not come on duty till six in the morning, and for the present he had nothing to do except eat his rations and sleep as well as he could in his dugout. He had plenty of room to stretch his legs if he sat half upright, and having taken his Major's advice in the matter of bringing his fur coat with him, he found himself warm enough, in spite of the rather bitter wind that, striking an angle in the trench wall, eddied sharply into his retreat, to sleep. But not less justified than the advice to bring his fur coat was his Major's assurance that the attack of the horrors which had seized him after dinner that day, would pass off when the waiting was over. Throughout the evening his nerves had been perfectly steady, and, when in their progress up the communication trench they had passed a man half disembowelled by a fragment of a shell, and screaming, or when, as he trod on one of the uneasy places an arm had stirred and jerked up suddenly through the handful of earth that covered it, he had no first-hand sense of horror: he felt rather as if those things were happening not to him but to someone else, and that, at the most, they were strange and odd, but no longer horrible. But now, when reinforced by food again and comfortable beneath his fur cloak he let his mind do what it would, not checking it, but allowing it its natural internal activity, he found that a mood transcending any he had known yet was his. So far from these experiences being terrifying, so far from their being strange and unreal, they suddenly became intensely real and shone with a splendour that he had never suspected. Originally he had been pitchforked by his father into the army, and had left it to seek music. Sense of duty had made it easy for him to return to it at a time of national peril; but during all the bitter anxiety of that he had never, as in the light of the perception that came to him now, as the wind whistled round him in the dim lit darkness, had a glimpse of the glory of service to his country. Here, out in this small, evil-smelling cavern, with the whole grim business of war going on round him, he for the first time fully realised the reality of it all. He had been in the trenches before, but until now that had seemed some vague, evil dream, of which he was incredulous. Now in the darkness the darkness cleared, and the knowledge that this was the very thing itself, that a couple of hundred yards away were the lines of the enemy, whose power, for the honour of England and for the freedom of Europe, had to be broken utterly, filled him with a sense of firm, indescribable joy. The minor problems which had worried him, the fact of millions of treasure that might have fed the poor and needy over all Britain for a score of years, being outpoured in fire and steel, the fact of thousands of useful and happy lives being sacrificed, of widows and orphans and childless mothers growing ever a greater company—all these things, terrible to look at, if you looked at them alone, sank quietly into their sad appointed places when you looked at the thing entire. His own case sank there, too; music and life and love for which he would so rapturously have lived, were covered up now, and at this moment he would as rapturously have died, if, by his death, he could have served in his own infinitesimal degree, the cause he fought for.

The hours went on, whether swiftly or slowly he did not consider. The wind fell, and for some minutes a heavy shower of rain plumped vertically into the trench. Once during it a sudden illumination blazed in the sky, and he saw the pebbles in the wall opposite shining with the fresh-falling drops. There were a dozen rifle- shots and he saw the sentry who had just passed brushing the edge of his coat against Michael's hand, pause, and look out through the spy-hole close by, and say something to himself. Occasionally he dozed for a little, and woke again from dreaming of Sylvia, into complete consciousness of where he was, and of that superb joy that pervaded him. By and by these dozings grew longer, and the intervals of wakefulness less, and for a couple of hours before he was roused he slept solidly and dreamlessly.

His spell of duty began before dawn, and he got up to go his rounds, rather stiff and numb, and his sleep seemed to have wearied rather than refreshed him. In that hour of early morning, when vitality burns lowest, and the dying part their hold on life, the thrill that had possessed him during the earlier hours of the night, had died down. He knew, having once felt it, that it was there, and believed that it would come when called upon; but it had drowsed as he slept, and was overlaid by the sense of the grim, inexorable side of the whole business. A disconcerting bullet was plugged through a spy-hole the second after he had passed it; it sounded not angry, but merely business-like, and Michael found himself thinking that shots "fired in anger," as the phrase went, were much more likely to go wide than shots fired calmly. . . . That, in his sleepy brain, did not sound nonsense: it seemed to contain some great truth, if he could bother to think it out.

But for that, all was quiet again, and he had returned to his dug- out, just noticing that the dawn was beginning to break, for the clouds overhead were becoming visible in outline with the light that filtered through them, and on their thinner margin turning rose-grey, when the alarm of an attack came down the line. Instantly the huddled, sleeping bodies that lay at the side of the trench started into being, and in the moment's pause that followed, Michael found himself fumbling at the butt of his revolver, which he had drawn out of its case. For that one moment he heard his heart thumping in his throat, and felt his mouth grow dry with some sudden panic fear that came from he knew not where, and invaded him. A qualm of sickness took him, something gurgled in his throat, and he spat on the floor of the trench. All this passed in one second, for at once he was master of himself again, though not master of a savage joy that thrilled him—the joy of this chance of killing those who fought against the peace and prosperity of the world. There was an attack coming out of the dark, and thank God, he was among those who had to meet it.

He gave the order that had been passed to him, and on the word, this section of the trench was lined with men ready to pour a volley over the low parapet. He was there, too, wildly excited, close to the spy-hole that now showed as a luminous disc against the blackness of the trench. He looked out of this, and in the breaking dawn he saw nothing but the dark ground of the dip in front, and the level lines of the German trenches opposite. Then suddenly the grey emptiness was peopled; there sprang from the earth the advance line of the surprise, who began hewing a way through the entanglements, while behind the silhouette of the trenches was broken into a huddled, heaving line of men. Then came the order to fire, and he saw men dropping and falling out of sight, and others coming on, and yet again others. These, again, fell, but others (and now he could see the gleam of bayonets) came nearer, bursting and cutting their way through the wires. Then, from opposite to right and left sounded the crack of rifles, and the man next to Michael gave one grunt, and fell back into the trench, moving no more.

Just immediately opposite were the few dozen men whose part it was to cut through the entanglements. They kept falling and passing out of sight, while others took their places. And then, for some reason, Michael found himself singling out just one of these, much in advance of the others, who was now close to the parapet. He was coming straight on him, and with a leap he cleared the last line of wire and towered above him. Michael shot him with his revolver as he stood but three yards from him, and he fell right across the parapet with head and shoulders inside the trench. And, as he dropped, Michael shouted, "Got him!" and then he looked. It was Hermann.

Next moment he had scaled the side of the trench and, exerting all his strength, was dragging him over into safety. The advance of this section, who were to rush the trench, had been stopped, and again from right and left the rifle-fire poured out on the heads that appeared above the parapet. That did not seem to concern him; all he had to do that moment was to get Hermann out of fire, and just as he dragged his legs over the parapet, so that his weight fell firm and solid on to him, he felt what seemed a sharp tap on his right arm, and could not understand why it had become suddenly powerless. It dangled loosely from somewhere above the elbow, and when he tried to move his hand he found he could not.

Then came a stab of hideous pain, which was over almost as soon as he had felt it, and he heard a man close to him say, "Are you hit, sir?"

It was evident that this surprise attack had failed, for five minutes afterwards all was quiet again. Out of the grey of dawn it had come, and before dawn was rosy it was over, and Michael with his right arm numb but for an occasional twinge of violent agony that seemed to him more like a scream or a colour than pain, was leaning over Hermann, who lay on his back quite still, while on his tunic a splash of blood slowly grew larger. Dawn was already rosy when he moved slightly and opened his eyes.

"Lieber Gott, Michael!" he whispered, his breath whistling in his throat. "Good morning, old boy!"

CHAPTER XVII

Three weeks later, Michael was sitting in his rooms in Half Moon Street, where he had arrived last night, expecting Sylvia. Since that attack at dawn in the trenches, he had been in hospital in France while his arm was mending. The bone had not been broken, but the muscles had been so badly torn that it was doubtful whether he would ever recover more than a very feeble power in it again. In any case, it would take many months before he recovered even the most elementary use of it.

Those weeks had been a long-drawn continuous nightmare, not from the effect of the injury he had undergone, nor from any nervous breakdown, but from the sense of that which inevitably hung over him. For he knew, by an inward compulsion of his mind that admitted of no argument, that he had to tell Sylvia all that had happened in those ten minutes while the grey morning grew rosy. This sense of compulsion was deaf to all reasoning, however plausible. He knew perfectly well that unless he told Sylvia who it was whom he had shot at point-blank range, as he leaped the last wire entanglement, no one else ever could. Hermann was buried now in the same grave as others who had fallen that morning: his name would be given out as missing from the Bavarian corps to which he belonged, and in time, after the war was over, she would grow to believe that she would never see him again.

But the sheer impossibility of letting this happen, though it entailed nothing on him except the mere abstention from speech, took away the slightest temptation that silence offered. He knew that again and again Sylvia would refer to Hermann, wondering where he was, praying for his safety, hoping perhaps even that, like Michael, he would be wounded and thus escape from the inferno at the front, and it was so absolutely out of the question that he should listen to this, try to offer little encouragements, wonder with her whether he was not safe, that even in his most depressed and shrinking hours he never for a moment contemplated silence. Certainly he had to tell her that Hermann was dead, and to account for the fact that he knew him to be dead. And in the long watches of the wakeful night, when his mind moved in the twilight of drowsiness and fever and pain, it was here that a certain temptation entered. For it was easy to say (and no one could ever contradict him) that some man near him, that one perhaps who had fallen back with a grunt, had killed Hermann on the edge of the trench. Humanly speaking, there was no chance at all of that innocent falsehood being disproved. In the scurry and wild confusion of the attack none but he would remember exactly what had happened, and as he thought of that tossing and turning, it seemed to one part of his mind that the innocence of that falsehood would even be laudable, be heroic. It would save Sylvia the horrible shock of knowing that her lover had killed her brother; it would save her all that piercing of the iron into her soul that must inevitably be suffered by her if she knew the truth. And who could tell what effect the knowledge of the truth would have on her? Michael felt that it was at the least possible that she could never bear to see him again, still less sleep in the arms of the one who had killed her brother. That knowledge, even if she could put it out of mind in pity and sorrow for Michael, would surely return and return again, and tear her from him sobbing and trembling. There was all to risk in telling her the truth; sorrow and bitterness for her and for him separation and a lifelong regret were piled up in the balance against the unknown weight of her love. Indeed, there was love on both sides of that balance. Who could tell how the gold weighed against the gold?

Yet, after those drowsy, pain-streaked nights, when the sober light of dawn crept in at the windows, then, morning after morning, Michael knew that the inward compulsion was in no way weakened by all the reasons that he had urged. It remained ruthless and tender, a still small voice that was heard after the whirlwind and the fire. For the very reason why he longed to spare Sylvia this knowledge, namely, that they loved each other, was precisely the reason why he could not spare her. Yet it seemed so wanton, so useless, so unreasonable to tell her, so laden with a risk both for him and her that no standard could measure. But he no more contemplated—except in vain imagination—making up some ingenious story of this kind which would account for his knowledge of Hermann's death than he contemplated keeping silence altogether. It was not possible for him not to tell her everything, though, when he pictured himself doing so, he found himself faced by what seemed an inevitable impossibility. Though he did not see how his lips could frame the words, he knew they had to. Yet he could not but remember how mere reports in the paper, stories of German cruelty and what not, had overclouded the serenity of their love. What would happen when this news, no report or hearsay, came to her?

He had not heard her foot on the stairs, nor did she wait for his servant to announce her; but, a little before her appointed time, she burst in upon him midway between smiles and tears, all tenderness.

"Michael, my dear, my dear," she cried, "what a morning for me! For the first time to-day when I woke, I forgot about the war. And your poor arm? How goes it? Oh, I will take care, but I must and will have you in my arms."

He had risen to greet her, and softly and gently she put her arms round his neck, drawing his head to her.

"Oh, my Michael!" she whispered. "You've come back to me. Lieber Gott, how I have longed for you!"

"Lieber Gott!" When last had he heard those words? He had to tell her. He would tell her in a minute or two. Perhaps she would never hold him like that again. He could not part with her at the very moment he had got her.

"You look ever so well, Michael," she said, "in spite of your wound. You're so brown and lean and strong. And oh, how I have wanted you! I never knew how much till you went away."

Looking at her, feeling her arms round him, Michael felt that what he had to say was beyond the power of his lips to utter. And yet, here in her presence, the absolute necessity of telling her climbed like some peak into the ample sunrise far above the darkness and the mists that hung low about it.

"And what lots you must have to tell me," she said. "I want to hear all—all."

Suddenly Michael put up his left hand and took away from his neck the arm that encircled it. But he did not let go of it. He held it in his hand.

"I have to tell you one thing at once," he said. She looked at him, and the smile that burned in her eyes was extinguished. From his gesture, from his tone, she knew that he spoke of something as serious as their love.

"What is it?" she said. "Tell me, then."

He did not falter, but looked her full in the face. There was no breaking it to her, or letting her go through the gathering suspense of guessing.

"It concerns Hermann," he said. "It concerns Hermann and me. The last morning that I was in the trenches, there was an attack at dawn from the German lines. They tried to rush our trench in the dark. Hermann led them. He got right up to the trench. And I shot him. I did not know, thank God!"

Suddenly Michael could not bear to look at her any more. He put his arm on the table by him and, leaning his head on it, covering his eyes he went on. But his voice, up till now quite steady, faltered and failed, as the sobs gathered in his throat.

"He fell across the parapet close to me, "he said. . . . "I lifted him somehow into our trench. . . . I was wounded, then. . . . He lay at the bottom of the trench, Sylvia. . . . And I would to God it had been I who lay there. . . . Because I loved him. . . . Just at the end he opened his eyes, and saw me, and knew me. And he said—oh, Sylvia, Sylvia!—he said 'Lieber Gott, Michael. Good morning, old boy.' And then he died. . . . I have told you."

And at that Michael broke down utterly and completely for the first time since the morning of which he spoke, and sobbed his heart out, while, unseen to him, Sylvia sat with hands clasped together and stretched towards him. Just for a little she let him weep his fill, but her yearning for him would not be withstood. She knew why he had told her, her whole heart spoke of the hugeness of it.

Then once more she laid her arm on his neck.

"Michael, my heart!" she said.

Printed in the United States
102883LV00005B/187/A